DEAD TO ME

DEAD TO ME

Cath Staincliffe

Minotaur Books
A Thomas Dunne Book
New York

A THOMAS DUNNE BOOK FOR MINOTAUR BOOKS.
An imprint of St. Martin's Publishing Group.

DEAD TO ME. Concept and text copyright © 2012 by Transworld Publishers; characters copyright © 2012 Red Production Company. All rights reserved. Printed in the United States of America. For information, address St. Martin's Press, 175 Fifth Avenue, New York, N.Y. 10010.

www.thomasdunnebooks.com
www.minotaurbooks.com

Library of Congress Cataloging-in-Publication Data

Staincliffe, Cath.
    Dead to me / Cath Staincliffe.—1st U.S. ed.
    p. cm.
    ISBN 978-1-250-03854-8 (hardcover)
    ISBN 978-1-250-03853-1 (e-book)
    1. Women detectives—Fiction. 2. Murder—Investigation—Fiction.
I. Title.
    PR6119.T345D43 2014
    823'.92—dc23

                                                        2013038926

Minotaur books may be purchased for educational, business, or promotional use. For information on bulk purchases, please contact Macmillan Corporate and Premium Sales Department at 1-800-221-7945, extension 5442, or write specialmarkets@macmillan.com.

First published in Great Britain by Corgi Books

First U.S. Edition: January 2014

10 9 8 7 6 5 4 3 2 1

For Tim – who made it possible

1

Rachel Bailey stood, freezing her tits off, on a crime-scene cordon in north Manchester. From her vantage point, at the edge of the recreation ground, she had a view across the rows of rooftops that rippled down the hillside, punctuated here and there by the bulk of a mill rising from the streets built in the same red brick as everything else. One she could see had its name picked out in white brick on the square mill tower: Heron. Rachel had been brought up in streets like this; well, dragged herself up, more like. A couple of miles to the west. Sunny Langley. Manchester didn't really stop, Rachel thought; there were boundaries of course, but you couldn't see the join. The city bled into the satellite towns that ringed the plain: Oldham, Rochdale, Ashton and on to even higher ground. The houses gradually changing from these brick mill terraces to stone-built weaver's cottages, getting smaller and sparser as the developments petered out on the foothills of the Pennines. The place looked tired and mucky this time of year, the brick dull, trees bare, the grass on the field yellow and scrubby.

Rachel shivered and stamped one foot then another. Sparrow's fart, November and she could see her breath, the same colour as the mist that hovered over the recreation ground, rising and floating a couple of feet above the grass. A special effect from a horror movie, but this was real life, her life. Nowhere else she'd rather be.

Manchester city centre lay on the far horizon, muffled in cloud, the Hilton tower breaking through, a tall, straight line. Nick's flat was near there. He would be down at the station now, Piccadilly to Euston. He was opening for the defence at the Old Bailey tomorrow. She couldn't help grinning as she remembered his excitement last night; his chambers were really backing him, a rising star. Impossible to know how long he'd be away for. But that was the score. My hotshot barrister, she thought, not bad for a kid from the wrong side of the tracks.

She narrowed her eyes as a car drew up and parked on the edge of the outer cordon. Her role, until uniform arrived and took over, was to make sure no one gained entry who didn't need to be there. *Protect and secure the scene, preserve and recover evidence.* One stray person could ruin everything. Today Rachel was an intelligent guard dog. She only knew the basics at this stage: dead body, white male.

Nowhere else she'd rather be. Not strictly true – she'd rather be inside the cordon than guarding the periphery.

She'd rather be in an MIT syndicate some day. Major Incidents: running a team, catching killers. But there was no shortcut. She had to work her way up, build her portfolio. And she was on track, she allowed herself a little pat on the back. Five years in uniform, nearly five in Sex Crimes. Stepping stones, foundations for the bigger stuff. Rachel did another shuffle, waved her arms to get the circulation going. Times like these she made the best use of, alert to what was required of her, but in the lulls when no one was entering or leaving the scene she practised her definitions. Knowing the law, criminal law, inside out, upside down; because anyone who had to enforce the law needed to understand it. She was practising homicide, murder or manslaughter now. That's where she wanted next. It was a big jump and they were queuing round the block for opportunities. She just needed a chance, an opening, and she needed to spot it before her competitors.

Rachel glanced behind her where the CSIs were still busying about, the tent now up, protecting the scene. She wanted to pee, but it could be hours. They never put that in the job description. *Candidates must be able to demonstrate significant bladder capacity.*

In the valley, a train sounded its hooter, taking people into work. Greater Manchester conurbation, home to 2.6 million people. In the police service over 8,000 cops, and Rachel was one of them, the only job she'd ever wanted. She could see the arterial roads filling up with commuters, too. The dual carriageways funnelling traffic to the M60 and the M62. *Manslaughter: voluntary*

and involuntary. Voluntary manslaughter – due to . . .
diminished responsibility, loss of control . . .

She watched the new arrival, suited, booted, carrying a face mask and gloves, cross the grass to meet her. 'Constable,' the woman said, barely glancing at Rachel, and made to pass through the cordon.

'Identification,' Rachel said bluntly, blocking her way.

The woman sighed, patted at her sides, then shoved a hand down the front of her disposable jumpsuit. 'Fuck,' she barked.

Rachel blinked, waited.

'DCI Gill Murray,' the woman rattled off, 'SIO.'

Shitshitshit. Gill Murray. And Rachel hadn't even recognized her. Blame the protective suit. Golden girl Gill. Though the gold had tarnished a bit since all the stuff with her husband. Rachel swallowed. 'I still need formal identification. "The preservation of the scene is a primary responsibility",' she quoted. ' "No exceptions".'

The DCI threw up her hands, bawled, 'No exceptions, *ma'am*!'

'Right, ma'am.' Rachel should have automatically added a term of respect, either boss or ma'am or chief inspector. Failing to do so gave an impression of insubordination. You never knew with bosses what they'd favour: some wanted rank and only rank, others were on first-name terms with everyone. Rachel had decided when she got to fling her weight around she'd want to be called boss. Not ma'am like some minor royalty, an old trout in a tiara.

Gill Murray flailed her hands again, turned round on the spot, first one way then the other, as if she was doing some weird robotic dance, then stalked off back across the grass.

Rachel had imagined she'd be taller, tall and slim like Rachel herself. But Murray was more petite. Looked good for her age; must have fifteen years on Rachel. Perhaps she'd had some 'work' done.

Inside her jacket, Rachel could feel a prickle of sweat under her arms. Stuff her, she told herself, if I'd let her through without ID, I'd have been in for a bollocking by the crime-scene manager. 'Procedure is there for a reason,' the instructor had drilled into them at training, 'because it works. Brains far mightier than yours have spent years identifying how we detect and prosecute crimes. You prat about, missing a step, trying to take a shortcut and nine times out of ten you're handing our offender a get-off-scot-free card. Do it. Do it how it should be done. Do it right.'

The DCI arrived back, her mouth screwed up tight, thrust a lanyard with her warrant card at Rachel. Painted nails, Rachel noticed, scarlet talons. There was something birdlike about the woman. Hawkish, attractive, cheekbones like scalpels, but hawkish all the same.

'DCI Gill Murray,' the woman said, her eyes flashing. Or reptilian, Rachel thought: lizard, velociraptor.

'Thank you,' Rachel said. She pulled off one of her thermal gloves and made a note in the log.

'And your name, Constable?' Gill Murray said

brusquely, pulling on her disposable gloves with a snap-snap.

Rachel took a breath. Oh God I am such a dick. She's gonna what . . . report me for doing my job? 'DC Rachel Bailey.'

'Working out of . . . ?' Nose wrinkled, as if Rachel was something she'd found on her shoe.

'Sex Crimes, boss.'

'Line manager?'

'John Sutton.' Sutton the Glutton.

'Right,' the DCI said, a sharp jerk of her head and she stepped through to the crime scene.

Rachel put her glove back on, her fingertips stung with cold. She wanted a fag now; a fag, a pee and a bacon-and-egg sandwich. And a hole in the ground to hide in while Gilly-knickers dreamt up her punishment.

They told us there were no superior officers, Rachel thought; senior, but not superior. Reflecting a more democratic force. You weren't supposed to say force any more either – too many connotations of police brutality and deaths in custody, riot gear. A service not a force, partnership with the people. Seemed they'd forgotten to tell Gill Murray she was no longer superior, treating Rachel like a kid who'd wet herself in assembly. I don't care, Rachel told herself, screw her. Godzilla. But she did care really. She really, really cared, because Gill Murray – well, she'd been the one Rachel wanted to be. The one Rachel followed in the news, the one everybody agreed was a superb detective, an inspired strategist, a charismatic leader. Clever and forward-thinking. The one who had broken through the glass ceiling without a scratch to show for it. And hadn't hauled the ladder up after her. Rachel had dreamed of meeting her, working with her someday. But now? She shook her head, annoyed, stamped her feet. The clouds were darkening, heavy and slate-coloured, blotting out the horizon. Sleet on the way. A kid on a bike circled at the edge of the outer cordon, stared over at her for a moment, then spat on the floor and swooped off.

Tosser, Rachel thought. *Infanticide . . . killing by any wilful act or omission of a child under twelve months old . . .*

The call came three weeks later. Rachel was processing papers for an indecency hearing. She'd got a head cold and it felt as though all the cavities in her skull were filled with heavy-duty glue and her throat with sand. She was still in work. Never took a sickie: she might miss something.

Her phone rang and she picked it up. 'DC Bailey.' Checked the time, pen poised over her daybook.

'Rachel – Gill Murray.' Clipped, bossy.

Rachel waited for the blow to land. Drew a noose in her notebook.

'I want you in my syndicate, week on Monday, Chadderton. Shift starts at eight.'

2

'Rachel Bailey.'

She said it like a threat, thought Janet, studying the woman who slammed her bag down on the desk facing hers and looked about as if disgruntled at what she found.

'DC,' Rachel Bailey added, and message delivered, gave a nod. Sat down.

'Janet Scott,' Janet said.

'Yeah, she said she wanted to put me with you.'

Oh, joy. Janet kept her expression open, pleasant, as she wondered what on earth Gill was playing at. They were already carrying Kevin, a knob who did knobby things, as a favour to Gill's mate on one of the other syndicates. And now she pitches up with a kid who has far too much attitude, a half-sneer on her face, and should have gone into modelling or lap-dancing, got the looks for it, and dumps her on Janet.

Janet went back to her screen, checking through her

emails, clearing her actions completed, getting up to speed on work in progress.

'So – you been here long?' Rachel Bailey asked.

Janet was reminded of playground interrogations – *what's your name, where d'you live?* All front and nerves shredding underneath.

'Thirteen years, twenty-five on the job.'

Rachel froze, looked at her. 'Straight up?'

Why would I lie? 'Yeah.'

'Never gone for promotion?' Rachel said.

'Yeah.' Shaking her head slightly, *tragic or what?* Janet wasn't bothered. She knew she was good at her job. She'd done a shedload of courses and got all the accreditations to prove it. She'd not the slightest interest in climbing the greasy pole. For what? Ulcers and politics and even more pressure? Promotion was a route away from the coalface, from the hands-on, face-to-face, stink-in-your-nose reality of catching killers. Gill Murray never got to so much as interview a suspect or a witness any more. She went to the scene and the post-mortem and she coordinated each investigation, managing her team, thinking about loopholes and implications, complications. Assessing evidence as they delivered it to her: was it robust enough for the CPS? Would it stand up in Crown Court? At appeal, in Europe? None of that pushed any buttons for Janet. She wanted to be eyeball-to-eyeball with the people who had done it, the people who had seen what was done. Making them sing.

'Not long till retirement,' Rachel observed, pegging

Janet for Mrs Average, time-server. The girl clicked her mouse, began to peer at her monitor. 'Kids?' Rachel asked.

'Two,' Janet said, a little echo of sadness inside. Happy for the newcomer to pigeonhole her: working mum, not fully committed either way, never gone for promotion, not had the drive, the vision, the brains. Mediocre. Just hanging on for her pension. Shoot me now.

The girl gave her a pitying look, then, losing interest, swivelled in her chair, scoping the room again. No one else in yet. Quarter to eight. The kid sighed, pulled her hair – glossy brown and waved (an effect that would take Janet's eldest, Elise, all morning to achieve) – up into a ponytail, let it drop.

'What about you?' Janet kept it civil.

'God no. Not the maternal type.'

She sounded almost like a teenager, that practised disdain, but she must be in her late twenties, Janet guessed. 'Where were you before?' Teeth not quite gritted.

'Sex Crimes, with Sutton,' Rachel said.

'John Sutton?'

Rachel nodded, glanced at her watch. 'I need a fag. Is there . . .' She whirled a finger in the air, asking for directions.

Janet toyed with the idea of sending her the wrong way, but only because the girl had got her back up. She'd never be that petty. 'Along the corridor, down the stairs, side door on the ground floor.'

Rachel snatched her bag and swung herself to her feet.

Janet watched her go. Took a breath, lowered her shoulders and returned to her inbox.

The office was open-plan, not a large space, desks crammed together in pairs, each with its computer terminal and phone. There was a bigger meeting room off it, which they used for briefings. Gill had a room to herself, roughly two and a half paces from Janet's desk. She was generally visible through the glass partition, unless she closed her blinds. It was a bad sign when the blinds went down. The team would wait, people trying to work more quietly, waiting to see who was in for a bollocking.

Gill was in before the others and Rachel was still off having her nicotine fix so Janet went straight into Gill's office.

The DCI had barely got her coat off when Janet jumped in: 'Why me?'

Gill froze, tilted her head to one side. 'It's an interesting philosophical question, kid, but you're going to have to give me a bit more . . .'

'Rachel Bailey.'

'She's here?' Gill beamed.

'I don't want her,' Janet said.

'Reason?'

'I've already got one teenager at home, and her sister's in a permanent state of revolution, I can do without it at work. Why put her with me? Put her with Mitch.'

'What's she done to you?' Gill was shifting through

paperwork on her desk now, easing into her chair. 'She's only been here five minutes.'

'Five minutes too long. Who sent her?'

'I picked her.'

'You picked her,' Janet said, appalled. 'Can't you unpick her?'

'She's a bit rough around the edges,' Gill allowed.

'Dog rough,' said Janet. A pit bull bitch, she thought but that seemed too harsh. Rude. 'Give her to Pete or Lee, or any of them.'

Gill took her glasses from her case, set them down and stared at Janet for a moment, then slapped her palms on her desk. 'She stays with you. That's how I want it.'

'Gill,' Janet groaned.

'End of.' Gill held up her hands, brooking no further discussion.

'Six weeks,' Janet tried. 'If I still feel the same . . .'

'We'll see.'

'We'll see!' Janet mocked, laughing. 'We'll see? That's what I say to the girls: "We'll see." It usually means, *No, but I haven't got the energy to argue with you now.*'

'You'll be good for her.' Gill slid her glasses on and began to open files on her computer.

'Sounds like a parasitic relationship,' Janet said.

'Symbiotic – she'll bring a bit of life into the place, shake the dust off.'

'What are you saying?' Was Gill implying she'd grown stale?

At that point, Rachel strode back into the outer

18

room, distracted but altering her demeanour, straightening her spine, as she caught sight of Gill through the glass.

'Welcome,' Gill shouted, waved a hand but didn't get to her feet. 'Team meeting in ten. Pack drill then.'

Rachel nodded. 'Great.' She sat back at her desk.

Janet waited for a second longer, but Gill, already devouring the information on the screen, pointed a finger towards the door. Dismissed.

As Janet sat down, Rachel leaned forward and whispered, 'What's she like? Bit of a dragon?' signalling with an upward flick of her eyes that she meant Gill in the office behind her.

'Gill?' Janet moved closer, eyes narrowing, sneaky and confidential. 'She's fucking brilliant!'

3

Gill drove over to Collyhurst, the furthest southern corner of their patch. The neighbourhood was spitting distance from Manchester city centre, nudging up to the Northern Quarter, where redevelopment had seen the decaying rag-trade warehouses converted into flats and most of the old porn shops transformed into bijou cafés and boutiques. Collyhurst was still a poor place, even with the splurge for the Commonwealth Games back in 2002 and the building of the new stadium near-by and the Velodrome. Whatever all the 'new jobs' were, it didn't seem as though many of the long-term unemployed in Collyhurst had got a look in. Pick a side road, any side road, and you'd soon spot the poverty. And Gill, like any copper with half a brain knew that poverty and crime were dancing partners. Plenty of families round here where thieving or domestic violence was passed on in the genes, imbibed with the baby formula and the rusks. Handy for prison visiting, though: if your nearest and dearest were doing time in

Strangeways you could see the prison from the rise on Rochdale Road across the railway lines.

By the time Gill was a beat bobby, drugs had arrived, and the mad mobsters had moved in. Hard men from Salford and Eccles who saw an opportunity to make a shitload of money. The burglary and brawling of the earlier years were replaced by turf wars and outbreaks of astonishing violence by the gangsters, accompanied by a spate of muggings and petty thefts by junkies needing a fix. When Gill moved into MIT in the 1990s everyone had come to the party: gangs in Cheetham, Longsight, Moss Side, links to Birmingham and Liverpool. The bloodbath peaked in 1999, over two hundred and forty shots fired, forty-three injured, seven dead and not a witness on the face of the earth. Gill had worked a few of those. Even got a conviction or two, against all the odds. Then they set up the special squad to tackle the scourge. Developed inter-agency strategies. Things had changed since then. Quieter now, a combination of prevention programmes and good detection, a rigorous support service for vulnerable and intimidated witnesses, weapons amnesties. As recently as 2008 they'd taken a whole load of drug scumbags off the streets, seriously weakening the gangs. The drugs were still out there, the dealers still busy and the related crimes went on, but it didn't feel quite the same lawless frontier country, Gunchester, of the 1990s.

Gill checked the address, Fairland Avenue, and took a left into the estate.

I've already got one teenager, Janet had complained.

She wasn't far wrong; there was something bratty about Rachel Bailey. Gill knew next to nothing about her background, but she could tell it wasn't silver spoon and skiing holidays. Local girl, she'd a wild edge to her, something simmering beneath the cover girl looks and the shrewd expression. And she was hungry for a chance. Gill could sense that. Drinking everything in at the morning's induction yet impatient to get on with the real work, the dirty work. Like me, Gill thought, the raw ambition.

Gill parked in the last remaining place on the pavement. The short street was cluttered with vans and cars. She got out and stood, took a moment first, considering the location. Only one route into the cul-de-sac, which forked off Gargrave Street, the main thoroughfare of the estate. Twenty houses in all, a turning circle at the far end. A gaggle of neighbours had gathered there, uniforms keeping them behind the tape. Victim's house, second on the right from the junction, number 3A. The houses opposite would have a clear view of anyone coming and going if they were peering out of their windows. It would be getting dark soon, the CSIs were making the most of the fading light, photographing and scouring the area immediately outside the house.

She put on her protective clothes and drew up her hood. Andy Pandy, ready to go and introduce herself to the CSM.

The houses were divided into flats, separate entrances, maisonettes really. 'It's the downstairs flat,' the uniform on the cordon told her as he logged her in.

Gill raised her hands, almost a surrender pose, though her palms faced her ears not forward. Looked daft. Some people chose to stuff their hands in their pockets, or laced their fingers together, got a bit sweaty in the gloves like that. All tricks to safeguard against mucking everything up by smearing fingerprints or other trace evidence: spittle, dandruff, cosmetics, snot, blood, that lurked waiting for detection and recovery. Door frames, handles – all would be examined. Gill's very first dead body on MIT, she'd leaned against a door-jamb and got a four-star bollocking from her boss. Since then she'd used the hands-up technique; she didn't want her hands in her pockets because she needed her hands to think, to analyse, to communicate.

'You're like a bloody windmill,' Janet once told her, 'or someone on the tote, at the races.'

One Christmas the team bought her a pair of white cotton gloves, the kind a magician wore. Gill had got very pissed at the works party and waxed lyrical about how what they did *was* magic of a sort. Dark magic, maybe, solving the sordid little details of the crime, turning a tragedy into an achievement.

'For who?' Andy had objected, winking at Janet. 'We've still got a dead body. Someone's still lost a family member.'

'But they know how, why. And that's all we can do for them,' she had said, taking another swig of vodka. 'Give them the story, the facts, the name, the face . . . At least we can do that.' She had sliced at one hand with

23

the other for emphasis, and Janet had laughed and shaken her head. 'Without that they are in bloody limbo for ever,' Gill said. They all knew that. Lee and Mitch had nodded, muttering in agreement.

She had drunk way too much that night; it wasn't long after Dave had gone walkabout, and she'd ended up curled over a bog in the Ladies, with Janet holding her hair out of the way and saying, 'Time for bed, Houdini. Got you a cab.'

Gill walked through the tiny porch on the stepping plates that had been laid down and turned ninety degrees into the narrow hallway, noting the bathroom immediately to the right. Straight ahead, a bedroom. The door ajar. Gill took in the mattress on the floor, the carpet littered with clothes and scraps of paper, cigarette papers, DVD cases, burn marks on the carpet. Someone had once attempted to redecorate the far wall either side of the window. It was painted a muddy ginger shade, reminding Gill of parkin, the cake they ate round Bonfire Night. But they'd obviously lost heart and the edge near the ceiling still showed the cream woodchip paper underneath. Gill could smell damp in the room mixing with the rank stench of stale fag ends and, peering carefully round the door, saw an area in the corner there mottled with mildew. She didn't go in, it had yet to be examined. The next ninety-degree turn took her past a storage cupboard on the right and into the living room at the end. The smell was different here, unpleasantly metallic.

24

'Hello,' Gill greeted them all.

The girl was under a duvet, face partly visible, wedged between a sofa and a squat, dark-coloured coffee table. The table was slightly askew and tilted, one leg broken. The technicians would already have filmed and photographed the room before anyone else was allowed in, creating a record of the scene as close as possible to how it had been found. Phil Sweet, the CSM, was logging details and supervising everyone. Gill had worked with him maybe half-a-dozen times. He raised a gloved hand in acknowledgement. 'Go round that way.'

Gill did as Phil said; using the stepping plates she skirted around the easy chair that stood near the kitchen door, close to where two markers indicated drops of blood, and past the coffee table to get closer to the victim.

She stared at the body, at the girl's head angled slightly back and to the right, touching the base of the sofa. There was a slick of blood on the carpet beneath her, some dark stains on the edge of the duvet. Gill didn't need a second opinion, this was a homicide. She straightened up and got out her phone to ring the coroner. The body legally belonged to the coroner and their authorization would be needed to order a post-mortem.

'Who called us?' she asked Phil as she selected the contact number.

'Boyfriend; came in and found her like this.'

Gill nodded. Because he had been at the scene, the

boyfriend would have to submit his clothes for examination as potential evidence and give a witness statement to assist the police.

'Hello, Mr Minchin, Gill Murray here from MIT,' she identified herself to the coroner. 'I'm out at a job in Collyhurst: young, white, adult female. I'm thinking we've got ID, not formal as yet, looking like a stab wound. I'm after doing a forensic post-mortem?'

'Be my guest. I'll take the details.'

Gill told him the rudiments: the address and the apparent name of the victim: Lisa Finn. Her next call was to the pathologist, Ranjeet Lateesh. No one would touch the body or disturb anything at the scene until he'd arrived and been able to examine the body in situ.

She watched one of the CSIs start work with his fingerprint kit on the doorway and door handles into the room. The silver sooty powder he was smothering over the surfaces would be a bugger to clean off again afterwards.

'Shoulder bag in the kitchen, bus ticket in there shows her on the bus at half-ten this morning. But we didn't find her phone,' Phil Sweet told them.

Gill groaned. The phone was a rich mine of information in any inquiry; traffic to and from helped them build not only a timeline but a network of contacts, and the content of texts would sometimes flag up animosity or threats. They'd have to approach the provider, who would be able to give them a log of incoming and outgoing calls and texts, but not the content of any texts, and not the pictures or music or videos or address book on the handset. With a little more time, the provider would also be able to give them the cell site location data and pinpoint where the phone was when calls were received and made. In effect, a tracking device.

'They covered her up,' Gill said. Wondering about that, whether it was a question of a perverted sense of respect or plain fear. It's an instinctive response to hide a body, hide and run. There hadn't been a duvet on the bed. Did the killer stop to fetch it? Wasting precious moments? No cover on the duvet. Gill could see patches of blood where it had soaked into the fabric along the top edge; there were older stains too, and the polycotton material was bobbled with use. Didn't look as though the thing had ever been washed. She could see the pieces of foil under the coffee table, the small plastic tube, the lighter. Knew laundry wasn't high on the priority list for a druggie.

When Ranjeet arrived he began by making an assessment of the scene as he found it. And agreed with Phil Sweet and Gill that the duvet should be tape-lifted for any potential forensic evidence before it was removed. Once that had been done and everybody was satisfied that they had thoroughly documented the scene as it was found, it was time to lift the bedding. A CSI took each end, aiming to remove the article as carefully as possible and cause minimum disruption. A CSI provided a large evidence sack for the duvet, sealed it and allocated a reference number.

Gill got her first good look at their victim. She wore an open, kimono-type housecoat, which was rucked up beneath her. A bloody incision marked her left breast close to her sternum and ribbons of blood had flowed from there down her side on to the floor. Blood on her right hand too, which lay on her belly. Nails bitten down. The housecoat was a floral design: white background with blowsy vivid pink-and-green flowers on. No knickers. She didn't have much pubic hair. Not shaved, Gill thought, just immature – a teenager. Her hair was two-tone, partly covering the left side of her face, a bad bleach job growing out. Her mouth and nose were peppered with pimples. A row of silver-coloured earrings edged each of her ears; they made Gill think of the clasps they put on paint tins to keep the lids on. Her left arm was twisted at a peculiar angle, the hand forced under the forearm and pressed up against the strut at the base of the coffee table. Gill thought she'd probably hit the table as she'd fallen.

Ranjeet made notes in his smart phone and the CSIs got busy with the cameras.

'Penetrating wound between the ribs,' Ranjeet said, 'massive blood loss. I suggest we tape-lift the body and swab in situ, then undress the body; rest post-mortem. We can move the table now.'

Gill stepped away, went to the window, looking out at the back, a tiny yard walled by broad, horizontal planks for fencing. Perfect climbing territory for a house burglar, but this girl had nothing worth taking. Unless somebody came to steal drugs. The telly in the corner by the window wasn't a flat screen but an old monster, impossible to move without transport.

As they moved the table, the victim's left arm slumped, gravity pulling it down, unfolding. 'No sign of rigor,' Gill said. If the body was still pliable and there were no obvious signs of decomposition, it meant the time of death was recent. Rigor came on a few hours after death and lasted for between one and three days, depending on the external conditions.

Ranjeet continued his examination. 'Wound to the left arm,' he pointed out, 'probably defensive.'

Gill squatted down, careful not to get her feet in the puddle of blood congealing around the girl's torso. The cut was a couple of inches below her wrist, along the edge of the bone. 'The weapon?' Gill asked.

'No sign,' said one of the CSI guys. Gill looked at the cut and at the tattoo that braceleted the girl's wrist in gothic script. 'Who's Sean?' she said.

'Boyfriend,' Phil supplied.

Ranjeet took the body temperature. He nodded at the result. 'Thirty-five point nine, still warm.' A CSI began the process of placing and removing tape on the girl's body and then taking swabs from the mouth, nose and vagina.

Gill and Phil discussed what further actions should be taken to retrieve crime-scene evidence, among them recovering the remaining bed linen from the bedroom.

'Undress her now.' A large plastic sheet was placed to the side of the dead girl and then the body was lifted as carefully as possible and laid on it. The CSIs removed the housecoat, the back of it drenched in blood, and put it in an evidence bag.

'We'll be ready to lift her soon,' Ranjeet said. The stretcher and the body bag were prepared. Any further examination of the body would be done at the mortuary as part of the post-mortem; they wouldn't turn her over here and risk destroying evidence.

So, Lisa Finn, thought Gill as she prepared to leave, what the hell happened to you?

4

There was always that buzz when they picked up a job. A spurt of something in the gut, a kick-start to the heart. 'You're a ghoul, Janet,' Ade had said to her one time.

'I'm a detective,' Janet said, 'this is what I do, this is what I'm good at. We find the bastards, we get them sent down.'

The DCI had asked Janet to do the death message and to take Rachel with her. The worst thing about delivering the bad news was the sheer unpredictability of the reaction you got. One woman laughed, another threw up. Some people simply refused to believe you, arguing the toss, insisting that so-and-so was fine, they had seen them last night, they'd spoken to them on the phone. You had to sit them down and spell it out in big fat letters: D.E.A.D. Repeat it until they stopped blethering on: *she was going on holiday, he's only twenty-two, she's got an operation next week, she's got children.* As if these facts – mundane, domestic, particular – could gainsay the truth. As if death could be reversed because *he'd got an interview for Morrisons tomorrow.*

Other people went numb, they listened and they nodded and didn't utter a peep. They were polite and cooperative, but when you looked in their eyes there was no one home. They were absent, hiding. Then there were the ones that shot the messenger, tried to shut the door on them, and if they couldn't do that in time, told them to fuck off, even lashed out, pinching, slapping, shoving.

Janet once had a cup of tea flung at her. A woman whose son had been killed in a homophobic attack. Five of them kicked him to death. When Janet broke the news, the woman had flinched, twisting her head to and fro as if trying to escape the facts she'd just heard, then reached for her mug and hurled the contents at Janet. The tea was hot but not boiling. Though she reared back, Janet had not cried out. She had simply wiped at her face and repeated her condolences, then assured the woman that they would find the people who had done it and put them in prison for life. And the woman had sat, shaking uncontrollably, the sound of her teeth chattering clear and loud in the stuffy room.

Where the victim was embroiled in violent crime already, the next of kin often knew before you said a word. *He's dead, isn't he? The stupid fucking bastard.* And behind the ruptured words all the years of effort and loving and arguing and fighting and the bitter knowledge that this was how it would end and now it had. *I told him. Never listened – silly sod wouldn't have it.*

32

Most were shocked, bewildered, sometimes tearful. It was important to keep things simple, straightforward, to give the minimum amount of information possible, because at that point in time *dead, murdered*, was all they needed to know. That in itself was overload. The torrent of whys and hows and whens and who and *why, why, why* came later.

'I'll do it, if you like,' Rachel said, in the car. 'I've done a couple.' It was pitch-dark now, the temperature dropping; there'd be freezing fog on the hills.

Janet glanced at her. 'No, you're fine,' she said, after a pause.

Rachel considered whether to argue for it. She wondered if Janet was going to be one of those greedy gits who kept all the good stuff for herself so it would take Rachel twice as long to get the experience she needed. Women were still a minority in the service, especially at higher ranks, and most of the ones Rachel had worked with were good teachers, making sure other women coming after them had the same bite of the cherry as their male colleagues, encouraging them to specialize, to set their sights on moving up. There was a lot of mentoring went on. But Janet Scott? Maybe Rachel was a threat? Rachel considered asking her to stop so she could have a fag, but what if she said no? She'd have one after they'd informed the family, Janet could hardly drive off and leave her there without proving herself to be a right cow.

Denise Finn lived in Harpurhey, a short bus ride from

Lisa's, a two-up, two-down. Garden terraces, the estate agents called them, flying in the face of all the evidence. They had no gardens, only titchy backyards that originally housed the outside bog.

The street was still, quiet when they got out of the car, people tucked in, keeping warm. Here and there, where the curtains hadn't been drawn at upper windows, the neon blue of televisions and computers flickered and swam. The windows at Denise's were dark, but the hall light was on and the diamond of glass in the front door glowed yellow.

There was no bell or knocker, so Janet rattled the letter box.

Rachel looked up; no stars in the sky, just the blanket of fog. They heard movement in the house. Then a shadow rippled behind the glass in the door.

'Denise Finn?' Janet said when the door opened. 'I'm DC Janet Scott, Manchester Metropolitan Police, and this is DC Rachel Bailey. May we come in?'

'Why?' the woman asked. She looked to be in her fifties, her face lined, nose and cheeks criss-crossed with broken veins, jawline softening, grey hair mixed with the brown. Her hair was frizzy, brittle. Her glasses magnified her eyes. She wore a black sweater that had seen better days and navy joggers. *10 Years Younger*, thought Rachel, prime candidate. Ten years older once she's heard what we've got to tell her.

'We'd like to come in,' Janet said, moving forward, giving the woman no choice but to back away and turn, taking them through the front room, past the open stairs and into the back where the television was showing *Emmerdale*. The house smelled of cigarettes and chip fat and some floral chemical, air freshener perhaps, that made Rachel want to gag.

Denise stood there. 'What's going on?' She picked up the remote, muted the television. 'Is it our Lisa? Is she in bother again?'

'Please, Mrs Finn, sit down,' Janet said.

The woman frowned, opened her mouth, then closed it. Sat on the sofa; Janet sat beside her. The woman still held the remote, gripped tight in both hands.

Rachel parked herself in the only armchair. Looked about. The television occupied one alcove at the far side of the chimney breast, in the other recess were shelves with knick-knacks and photos. Lisa as a toddler and older. One of her on a merry-go-round horse at the fair, another, an early teenager at some do, dressed up in skin-tight clothes: white skirt, silver boob tube and hoop earrings. There was a boy in other photos, and one of the two children together, a school photo, be about eleven or twelve, Rachel guessed. The boy looked older, but not by much. They shared the same snub nose and rosebud mouth. In every picture his hair was cropped close, his ears stuck out like jug handles.

'I am sorry, I've got some very sad news,' Janet spoke steadily, slowly.

Rachel waited, studying her own hands.

'Your daughter, Lisa, was found at her flat this afternoon with fatal injuries.'

Rachel glanced over. Denise froze, the room was

pin-drop quiet and Rachel could hear Denise's breath, a suck of sorts, a gulping sound, choking on the truth.

'Lisa is dead,' Janet added, lest there be any misunderstanding, in case *fatal* wasn't enough.

'Injuries?' Denise said dully, putting the remote on the arm of the sofa.

'Yes, we think she was attacked.'

Denise Finn gave a muffled shriek. And her feet shifted on the carpet as if they wanted to carry her away.

'I am very sorry, Mrs Finn. We will be trying to find out who did this to Lisa. A colleague of ours will be acting as your family liaison officer, they will support you and let you know how our inquiries are going. They're on their way now.'

Denise's hand clutched at the neck of her sweater. From outside, Rachel heard the thump of a car door and the cough of an engine, then the car horn, *toot-toot-toot*, a jolly farewell blast before the car moved off.

Denise Finn's eyes filled with tears. She took a cigarette from the packet on the side table and Rachel felt her own cravings kick in.

'Are you sure?' Denise said. The lunge for hope making her twist in her seat towards Janet.

Sure she's dead? Sure it's Lisa? Rachel could imagine all the chinks of light tempting the woman, a futile, last-ditch attempt to make the nightmare go away.

'We still need you to formally identify the body, but as she was found in Lisa's flat by Lisa's boyfriend Sean, who called the police, we are pretty certain that it is your daughter Lisa.'

Trembling, Denise lit her cigarette, the snick of the lighter, the first scent of burning tobacco, triggering saliva in Rachel's mouth. She breathed steadily in, happy to do a little passive smoking until she could get to the real thing.

'The post-mortem is being conducted this evening,' Janet said. 'We expect it will confirm the cause of death, and then we'd like you to come to the mortuary, probably tomorrow morning, to make the formal identification. The family liaison officer will come with you and they'll be able to answer any further questions you have.'

Denise nodded. She drew again on her cigarette, but her lips quivered as though she had lost control of them.

'You thought Lisa was in bother?' Rachel spoke, 'Why was that?'

Janet turned to Rachel, glaring daggers. *Pardon me for breathing.*

'She had . . .' Denise's words petered out, she closed her eyes, tilting her face upwards to the ceiling. 'Erm, she'd had a few run-ins with your lot. Shoplifting. Messing with drugs.'

Janet turned to Denise, turned more than was necessary, her back to Rachel, excluding her from the conversation. Tosser, Rachel thought to herself, acting as if Rachel had farted at the funeral. Well, she wasn't some newbie in uniform who would put up with being shut out. If Janet wouldn't give her the breaks, she would just have to grab them for herself. And she could do sympathy. Talk nice. She'd seen the videos.

'Is there anyone you'd like us to call, someone who can be with you?' asked Rachel. She looked at the photos. 'Your son, perhaps?'

Denise Finn stared at Rachel, her face collapsing, mouth drawn back in pain. 'Nathan's dead,' she stammered. 'He died in January.'

Oh, fuck. Just my piggin' luck.

And Denise began to cry.

'Nice one, Sherlock,' said Janet. The FLO had arrived and at last they could escape.

'How was I supposed to know?' Sarky cow.

'You weren't. Which is why you should have kept your mouth shut and let me handle it,' Janet spoke quietly. 'That woman is a victim, it was our job to inform her of the death and of the immediate procedure. You wade in asking questions. We were not there to take a witness statement. We were not there to ask questions. We were there to deliver a death message. Got it?'

'But she said it first—' Rachel began.

'Got it?' Janet repeated, unsmiling but still keeping her voice quiet like some frigid headmistress.

'I need a fag,' Rachel said.

'Well, I'm not standing out here, freezing to death.' Janet opened the car door. 'Those things will kill you.'

Save you the bother. Rachel lit up, took the first drag deep, held the smoke and waited to feel the drug work

38

its magic. Nick didn't like her smoking, they bickered about it, so when she was with him she had Nicorette – foul-tasting stuff, made her breath stink worse than cigarettes. She would give up probably, but not just yet. You needed to time it right, and at the start of a major new job was not the right time.

When Rachel climbed into the car Janet already had the radio on, some documentary about the law and assisted suicide. Rachel blanked it. Watched the streets, the gleam of ice on the roads and stone walls, the fog distorting shapes, shadows and distance, the ribbons of light marking the roads winding down the hills.

Janet dropped her outside the station, a curt, 'Night,' the only communication.

'Night,' Rachel said flatly, and as she pushed the car door shut muttered, 'Sour-faced bitch.'

5

Ade was in front of the telly, a pile of exercise books on the sofa beside him, red pen in hand.

''Lo,' Janet called from the doorway.

'Hi,' he grunted, not even bothering to look her way.

In the kitchen she opened the fridge, wondering if they had left her any tea. It was hit and miss. Time was Ade would have a hot meal for her whenever she was late home, would even sit with her while she ate, swapping tales from their days at work. She on the job, nothing strictly confidential of course, but the vagaries of policing, the cock-ups and triumphs, irritants among the team, the gossip, always someone shagging someone else. And Ade's stories of high school hell, the Machiavellian manoeuvring of the geography department, the dirty politics of management and the LEA and school governors. The trench warfare of the classroom. Thirty hormonal teenagers, most of them regarding geography as slightly less interesting than waiting for paint to dry. Flirting, fighting, giving cheek, the lads rife with BO and Lynx deodorant, the girls wearing enough product to blind a lab-full of rabbits.

That all seemed so long ago. Janet couldn't remember the last time they'd laughed together, the last time she'd saved up an anecdote to please him, relished the telling of it and his response. She opened the microwave, which was empty and looked a little like a crime scene. Blood spatter on the walls. She went back into the lounge. 'What did you have for tea?'

'Chilli,' he said.

'You save any for me?'

'Eh?' He scribbled something in the margin of an exercise book, slung it down, picked up the next. On the telly someone was explaining why drilling into the Arctic ice sheet was a good idea.

'Did you save me some?'

'There was a bit left. I think Taisie had it.'

'That girl must have a tapeworm,' Janet grumbled. Eleven years old and always hungry. Would eat twice her own body weight, given the chance. Never got podgy though. Taisie was out climbing. She got a lift there and back with one of the other parents. Next week Janet, or more likely Ade, would be the taxi.

Janet's thoughts flickered to Denise Finn, lost both her kids in a year. Tomorrow, Janet reminded herself. Work stayed at work. The separation was the only way to stay sane. She never brought her work home, just like she didn't lug her family stuff into the office.

She went up to see Elise, who was glued to Facebook. 'How was Drama?'

'What?'

'Drama?'

'Good. Yeah.'

'Put this lot in the wash.' The floor was thick with cast-off clothes. 'Or you'll have to borrow my knickers.'

'Rank!' said Elise.

Janet moved closer, taking the chance to peer over Elise's shoulder and scan the screen.

'This century would be good,' Janet said.

'Yeah.' Absently, same as Ade. I am the invisible woman, Janet thought.

'What's TFN then?' Janet asked, tripping over the acronym on the page. 'Ta-ta for now?'

'Total fucking nightmare,' Elise said.

'I knew that,' Janet said. And caught a quick grin from her daughter in the reflection on the screen.

Janet made herself an omelette and ate in the kitchen, the local evening paper propped on the ketchup bottle. One of their cases had gone to trial, a lad who had fallen out with his girlfriend, rung her up and persuaded her to meet him on her birthday. She thought they were getting back together again. He arranged to pick her up in the car park behind Tommyfield Market in Oldham. She had recognized his car, stepped out to wave, so he'd see her. He had accelerated. Ploughed into her at speed and tossed her thirty-five metres. She died at the scene. He claimed it was an accident, he hit the wrong pedal, swore every which way to Christmas that he was gutted. A broken man. The postings he put

42

online beforehand told a different tale. He was going down, unless the jury cocked it up big time; it was just a question of how long for. Janet had done the interviews with him. Let him drivel on for the first two days, nodding with understanding and encouragement as he had spun his fantasy, before she'd begun to pick his story apart, line by line, sentence by sentence. Finally finishing him with printouts from the Internet, the most damning being, *That cunt's getting a birthday present she never forget.* Thick as shit.

Janet had watched the light go out in his eyes, watched him squirm lower in his seat, knowing she had enough for the CPS, that she had dotted the i's and crossed the t's and gone through the whole alphabet with careful penmanship – win a flippin' calligraphy prize for it – and got it bang to rights.

She heard the clatter of Taisie arriving, the slam of the door that shook the floor beneath Janet's feet and rattled the double glazing.

'Shut it, don't slam it!' Janet yelled.

Taisie came through, glanced at Janet's plate, sucked her lip.

'Make some toast,' Janet said.

'Can't you do it? I'm tired.'

'I'm tired.'

'You want me to starve? I've just dragged myself thirty metres up a vertical rock face. My arms don't work.'

'And I've been sat on my arse all day making daisy chains out of paper clips.' Janet got to her feet anyway, opened the bread bin.

'Can I sleep over at Phoebe's on Saturday?' Taisie asked.

'Who else is?'

'I don't know.'

'More details,' Janet said.

'But . . .'

'And if it's a party, the answer is no. And I am going to ring her mother in advance to check.'

'I really like the way you trust me,' Taisie pouted.

Janet smiled.

'But can I?'

'We'll see,' Janet said, sticking the bread in the toaster. 'Jam or peanut butter?'

'Both.' She sat down heavily. 'Please, Mum?' she begged.

'We'll see.' Gill's words at work. Janet groaned inwardly, wondered if she could put up with Miss Bailey Cockypants for six whole weeks or if the MIT would end up investigating the murder of one of their own.

Rachel ordered pizza just for a change.

'Your usual?' the guy on the phone asked.

'Yeah, and extra garlic bread.'

'Ten minutes.'

The flat was on the first floor, a conversion in a big Victorian villa. High ceilings, huge windows, parking out front. Single, on a decent wage, she could afford a nice place to live. Not as swish as Nick's; he was in the middle of town, all mod cons, fridge the size of a walk-in wardrobe that made ice cubes by the chute-full, wet room, power shower, view over the city centre. Once she made sergeant, then she could get something like that, unless he invited her to move in. She wasn't rushing things, didn't want to frighten him off, sensing one thing he liked about her was her independence, the fact that she wasn't really into all the slushy side of relationships – the chocs and flowers left her cold. Leave that to people like Alison, her sister, who'd been swallowed up by marriage and motherhood and vomited back up like some loony 1950s bimbo, earth mother crossed with desperate housewife. Though she did actually have a job outside the home, she never stopped bleating on about how tough it was, how guilty she felt.

'I can help you plan your wedding!' Alison had squealed when Rachel had finally told her she was seeing someone, that it had been going on for several months.

'Be your funeral,' Rachel said.

'But there's a wedding fair . . .'

'Enough.' Rachel had held up her hands. 'It's not on the cards, it's not on the horizon, it's not even in the same solar system at the moment.'

Alison was always wittering on about Rachel needing a social life, trying to get her to do things: a night out with Alison's social-work pals, all dangly earrings and peculiar footwear, a trip to *Les Mis* in London on a coach, a book group. A book group, for fuck's sake!

'Do they read true crime?' Rachel asked her.

'No,' Alison tutted. 'Don't you get enough of that at

work? Fiction, Rachel. Booker prize, the Costa. Orange. We have some great discussions.'

'Spare me,' Rachel groaned, changing the subject by asking about one of the kids, guaranteed to get Alison warbling on for half an hour at least, like winding up a clockwork toy.

Rachel opened a bottle of red and poured herself a good measure. She got her daybook out of her bag and checked back through, all as it should be. She had a stack of reports from the National Police Improvement Agency – homework. The NPIA was where Gill Murray had worked before she headed up the syndicate. Called the Crime Faculty back then. Hard-to-solve cases from all over the country. That usually meant stranger murders. Interrupted by the take-away delivery, Rachel paid the guy and ate while she continued reading. She refilled her wine then texted Nick: *You busy? Gud day?*

He replied in seconds. *Cd take a break?*

Rachel smiled. She had an idea, would he be up for it? Won't know till you try, kid, she said to herself. *Dyin for a shag*, she texted.

!!! He came back.

Phone sex, she typed. *Call me if u want sum*. She set the work files aside and had a long swallow of wine. Settled herself down on the sofa. The mobile rang. She picked it up.

'So,' she heard the laughter in his voice, 'tell me what you're wearing, you slutty girl.'

6

Rachel was still working out who was who as the DCI
briefed them on the murder. She had already clocked
that Kevin was a bell-end. The sort of guy who wants to
be one of the gang but gets it wrong every time, his
humour off-colour, his instincts non-existent, social
skills strangled at birth. The sergeant, Andy Roper,
seemed OK, no pervy looks from him and he didn't pull
rank with any little jibes like some of them did. Dressed
well, too. Bit old for Rachel but he wasn't a bad looker.
The other DCs – the tall bloke Mitch, Pete the stocky
one and Lee, the only black guy on the team – she
hadn't got the measure of yet.

A collection of photographs from the crime scene
was doing the rounds along with a preliminary post-
mortem report. Rachel realized the DCI had gone
straight from the crime scene to the post-mortem and
she had probably worked all night collating this
while they had trotted off home. Now seven a.m.
and her ladyship was sparky, her face a bit pale maybe

but her eyes shining as she got into her stride.

'Lisa Finn,' the DCI said, 'seventeen years old, looked-after child until this April. Lisa is known to our Community colleagues for drug abuse and shoplifting. Cautions. Boyfriend Sean rang us at five past four to report the death, found Lisa on the living-room floor at the flat. Last saw her around ten the same morning, Monday thirteenth December. Cause of death is haemorrhage due to a stab wound to the chest. Defensive mark on the left wrist. Slight abrasions at the back of the neck. Not finger-prints, according to Ranjeet, something thin. The skin wasn't broken, so it may not have any significance.'

'A necklace?' Janet said, peering at the mark in the photographs.

'Possibly. Though it might simply be localized irritation – she was wearing something that rubbed at her neck, or she was slightly allergic.' Gill now looked to Lee. 'Was there a necklace at the scene?' Lee would be the exhibits officer, responsible for ensuring the chain of custody for the whole case.

'Some jewellery in the bedroom drawer, nothing in the living room,' he said.

'We also have a drop of blood here' – she indicated the ground plan of the flat – 'halfway to the kitchen, and another just inside the kitchen door.'

'The killer moved into the kitchen holding the knife – and what, washed it?' said Janet.

'No traces in the sink,' Gill replied. 'Post-mortem

shows signs of recent sexual activity, a forensic test found traces of lubricant from a condom.'

'Rape?' asked Janet.

'We don't know. Some bruising, could just be rough sex. No condom at the scene.'

So he flushed it or took it. Either way, it made things harder. Rachel knew that from Sex Crimes.

'DNA swabs from the body are with the lab.'

'In that case we can all go home till Christmas,' Pete said, and everyone laughed. The lab took a while to process stuff. Fingerprints could be done with fingerprint-recognition software by the officers themselves. And blood groups were pretty quick to get a label on, but all the other biological gubbins took a day or two at best.

'I know.' Gill pointed at Pete. 'Pain in the arse.'

Rachel watched as Kevin drew eyes, a little Hitler moustache, and breasts on his paper cup with a board marker. What a twat. Perhaps he had some relative in high command and Her Maj owed them a favour.

'Kevin – with Andy on house-to-house. Mitch – friends and acquaintances. See what her fellow druggies can tell us.'

'Was she on the game?' Rachel asked. It went with the territory, one of the few ways to get money to buy the drugs.

'Not to our knowledge. Janet and Rachel, get a full witness statement from Sean Broughton. Janet in the chair, Rachel – look and learn. He made an initial statement last night but we need to flesh it out.'

'Here or at his?' Rachel asked.

'Do it here, make him comfy.'

'I'll talk, you write,' Janet said to Rachel.

'I've got tier two,' Rachel said. Trained to know the definition of the offence and to prove each point in interviewing suspects.

Janet looked at her. 'You heard Gill.' The DCI had specifically asked Janet to run the witness statement from Sean Broughton. Did she really think Janet would just roll over and give her the task because she'd asked for it?

Rachel shrugged. 'Fine,' she said ungraciously.

The boy's eyes were dark brown, the whites bloodshot, and he had a slack look to him that made Janet suspect he was high, weed maybe, not twitchy enough for coke or crack. He wore an old Adidas trackie top and a Man City T-shirt that had seen better days, jeans, trainers, hi-tops. He had not shaved and there was a dusting of dark brown hair around his chin and upper lip. His hair was shortish and dyed the colour of hay, black roots showing. Perhaps he and Lisa had bleached their hair together? He had the coffee-coloured skin of a mixed race kid but Janet couldn't tell what the mix was. Could have been part Indian, or African-Caribbean or something else. No clue in his name either.

'Thank you for coming in, Sean. What we're going to do,' Janet explained once they settled into the easy chairs in the visitors' room slash soft interview space, 'is get a detailed witness statement from you. Now we have this camera in the corner running – nothing for you to worry about. It can feel a bit weird at first,' she smiled, 'but most people soon forget it's there. There are certain things I have to go through with you as a matter of procedure. I have to tell you that you are *not*,' she stressed the word, 'under arrest, and you are free to leave at any time. I must also tell you that you don't have to answer anything that you don't want to answer but if we go to court, anything you say here can be used. And you can ask to speak to a solicitor or to have a solicitor present. Do you understand?'

'Yes.'

They were sitting in easy chairs, a few feet apart, nothing between them, no desk, no barriers. 'If you need a break at any time, that's fine, we can stop. We might be here for quite a while – we don't want to rush things and it's important we take the time to get everything down as you remember. Is there anything you want to ask me before we start?'

'No,' Sean said.

'OK. I need you to confirm the details you gave yesterday.' Janet went through his name, DOB and address. No surprises. 'Thank you. Now, can you tell me how you know Lisa Finn?'

'She's my girlfriend.' He rubbed his palms on his jeans.

'And how long have you been together?'

'Couple of years.'

'Thank you. Now tell me in your own words what you remember from yesterday afternoon.' Janet sat back in her seat, giving him the floor, giving him space.

'I went round there about half three,' he said, 'went in and she were in the living room and she's on the floor, like . . .'

Janet nodded slowly. 'Yes, keep going.' She was barely aware of Rachel behind her making notes.

'She was . . .' Sean rocked forward in his chair and back again, shoved his hands between his knees, a comfort pose, a response to the distress, '. . . she was dead, like,' he said, his nose reddening. 'I could just tell. And I rang you.' He choked off the end of the sentence.

'Thank you,' Janet said. The atmosphere in the room had changed. Sean's grief thick in the air. She waited a moment, giving him time to regain his equilibrium. Janet remained composed, neutral, empathetic and professional. This is what all the weeks of interview training had taught her. 'Now I'm going to go through your statement and ask a little more about it. So we can get a complete picture from you. Is that OK?'

'Yes.' He cleared his throat. She saw his shoulders had relaxed slightly, a sign that he was feeling less threatened. Though she knew the process was fluid, his anxiety would advance and retreat as they went back and forth over the memories of him finding Lisa's body.

'How did you get to Lisa's?'

'Walked,' he said.

'Where had you been before that?'

'At my place, with my cousin Benny – he lives there too. I had to sign on in the morning and then I was at home.' He bit at his thumbnail.

'You told me you got to Lisa's at about half past three. Did you notice the time particularly, Sean?'

'That's when I said I'd be there.'

'Which way do you walk?'

'Down Garrigan Street,' he said.

'Do you remember seeing anyone on the way?'

'No, just . . . the school was coming out, on the brow, they finish at quarter past.'

Janet gave a nod. It was good to get some supporting information on the basic facts, something to corroborate what a witness said. So if they got to trial there would be no chance for the defence to play silly buggers, casting doubt on the timeline and jeopardizing a conviction.

Janet made eye contact. 'I'd like you to think about turning into the avenue: can you remember seeing anyone there?'

'I don't know,' he said.

'Any cars moving, anyone fetching kids from school?'

Sean licked his lips, shook his head. 'Don't remember.'

'You get to the front door, what then?'

'I went in.'

'You have a key?'

'Yeah, but – well, the latch is broken, so you can just push the door, if you know.'

Janet leaned forward. 'Lisa didn't get it fixed?'

'She was going to tell the landlord. Don't know if she did. Take them years to sort it anyway.'

'How long has it been broken?' Janet said.

'Few months.'

Good God.

'You couldn't tell, like,' he went on, "cos the door sticks so it looks shut.'

Janet felt a bit sick. Did this mean that Lisa could have been attacked by an intruder? Who what . . . ? Persuaded her to undress, then got her to put a kimono on before raping and stabbing her? Or had an intruder found her half-undressed and attacked her? The broken latch only seemed to muddy the waters. What it did mean was that Lisa hadn't necessarily invited her killer in, which is what they'd assumed until now.

He bent forward in his chair, hands on his knees, preparing for what was coming. Janet didn't want him to get too wound-up. Before walking him through the discovery again, the most traumatic part of his evidence, she reeled back a few hours. 'Had you and Lisa been in contact during the day?'

'I rang her just after one. She said she'd be back about half three. That's how I knew to go round, like.'

Janet gave a nod, reinforcing that what he was telling them was helpful, that he was doing well. 'Sean, do you still have that call on your phone?' she asked him.

'Yeah.'

'Good,' Janet said. Physical evidence, even though it wouldn't necessarily prove Lisa was alive at one o'clock, only that someone had used her phone then. The brighter sparks were catching on to how police used mobile phone data in investigations, and tried sending messages after the victim was dead to mislead the police. 'We might need to keep that for our records.'

'My phone?' he said, a little worried.

'Perhaps, I'll check with our telecoms people. Sometimes they can copy the information. In case it's needed in court.'

He signalled his agreement.

'When did you last see Lisa, before half past three?' Janet said.

'In the morning, before I went to sign on.'

'You had stayed at the flat together?'

He nodded, miserable. His eyes moist.

Janet kept going. 'Do you know what Lisa was planning to do?'

'She was heading into town.'

'For anything particular?'

'Just shopping,' he said. His voice rose on the last syllable and Janet wondered if that was to do with his sorrow or if the question itself unnerved him in some way.

'Does she go shopping a lot?' Janet asked.

'Not really.'

'What was she going to buy?'

'Dunno.' He was avoiding eye contact and Janet sensed that there was something about the shopping that Sean didn't want to discuss. Had they rowed about her going? Had she wanted him to go with her?

'Was she going on her own?' Janet said.

'Yeah.' He still wouldn't look at her. Janet didn't want to lose him now, digging down a diversion about the shopping, so judged it was time to return to the discovery of the body.

'You said in your initial statement that you went straight into the living room and saw Lisa there.' She softened her voice, kept it even.

'That's right.' He bit at his thumb again.

'I understand this will be hard for you, Sean, but please describe to me everything you saw.'

He swung his head down, bowing under the weight of her request. 'She was by the sofa,' he said, 'on the floor, on her back.' He shook his head, blinking rapidly, put a hand over his eyes. See no evil.

'By the sofa?' Janet echoed; she could hear Rachel writing. 'What else did you see?'

'Blood. I thought maybe she'd been shooting up – the blood all over her,' he added, by way of explanation. 'There was that much blood, I thought she'd messed up.'

'Where was the blood?' Janet asked him, hiding her puzzlement. She had in her mind the crime-scene photos from the book, the lumpy duvet covering the girl, part of Lisa's face visible at the top of it, half-covered with her hair. There was blood on the carpet, some on the duvet, but Sean had said it was *all over her*. How had Sean seen the blood?

He swallowed.

'Please can you tell me where you saw the blood?' Janet said.

'On her front and her dressing gown and the floor. All over.' He shuffled in his seat, wanting to move away from the pictures in his head.

Janet was still trying to work out how this fitted. 'Please can you describe the dressing gown?'

'A Chinese thing.'

'Was she wearing anything else?'

'No,' Sean said. He frowned hard, bit at his lip. 'That's why I covered her up. Made her decent.'

Oh, you dickhead, Janet's first thought. Sean had completely compromised their crime scene. Behind her she heard Rachel shift about, prayed she'd keep her lip buttoned. His misguided attempt to show Lisa some respect would make it that much harder to obtain solid forensic evidence for the case. Janet could have broken the interview there, to alert Gill to the new information, but judged it wise to keep going a few more minutes.

'Did Lisa usually shoot up?' Janet asked.

'No, she smoked. She didn't like needles.'

'OK. Where did you get the duvet from, Sean?'

'The bedroom.'

'When you covered Lisa up, did you touch her?'

'No,' he said, quickly, his face drawn, eyes troubled, frightened by the thought.

'Did you notice anything out of place?'

'The table was broke,' he said.

'Which table?'

'Coffee table,' he said.

'Where was the coffee table?'

'Next to Lisa.'

'Lisa was between the table and the sofa?'

'Yes,' he said.

'Did you touch anything else in the room?'

'No.' He looked away, staring at his hands.

Janet paused a moment to see if he'd renew eye

contact, but he didn't. 'Did you take anything from the flat?'

'No,' he answered, almost before she'd finished asking the question. Defensive. Something that made him uneasy.

'I'm going to have to ask you some very personal questions, Sean. I'm only asking them because they are crucial for our investigation, you understand?'

He dipped his head once.

'When did you and Lisa last have sex?'

'Last night,' he said. 'I mean, the night before,' correcting himself.

'Sunday night,' Janet clarified.

'Yeah.'

'OK, and did you use a condom on that occasion?'

He shook his head. 'She's got an implant.'

Janet smiled. Safe-sex messages had obviously gone right over this lad's head. 'After you covered Lisa with the duvet, what did you do?'

'I went outside and rang the police. I couldn't stay in there.' He pressed a fist to his mouth, scowling, eyes downcast.

'Sean, do you know how long you spent in the flat before you called the police?' He'd got there at half three, the call for help was five past four. What was he doing in that time?

'No.' Suddenly he was swiping his fingers at his eyes, no longer able to keep from weeping.

Janet waited a moment, then spoke: 'Sean, we'll have a break now,' she said. 'I'm sorry this is so distressing for you, but it helps us to do our job, it helps us find out who did this to Lisa. Is there anything else you want to tell me before we break?'

He shook his head.

'Would you like anything to eat or drink, or a cigarette break?'

'Yeah, a Coke,' he said, 'and a smoke.' He sniffed loudly and clenched his mouth tight. Janet pulled a face in sympathy. Poor bastard.

7

Gill was riled, summing up for the team: 'So, we've Mr Shit-for-brains to thank for coming over all prudish and ruining our crime scene.' She turned to Janet, 'Did he touch anything else?'

'Says not.'

'You believe him?'

'No,' Janet said.

'Mitch?' Gill invited him to chip in. The big lad was ex-army, a gentle giant. He was a good detective – they all were, bar Kevin, but Gill was determined to turn him round. His old boss had claimed Kevin was irredeemable, but Gill loved a challenge. Though she was beginning to wonder if Kevin was a lost cause. He didn't seem to learn from his mistakes, just repeated them bigger and better. Self-criticism of a woodlouse.

Mitch spoke: 'Sean Broughton in the system, fine for possession of Class B, cannabis. Oldham magistrates, five months ago.'

'Not a caution?' Gill asked, the usual policy for that offence.

'Already had two.'

'Naughty step not working for him,' Gill said. 'There were signs of Class As at the scene.'

'Paraphernalia,' Lee said. 'No drugs recovered, though.'

'Word is, both Sean and Lisa were using,' Mitch added.

'Supplying?' Gill said.

'No, not that I've heard.'

'Did have a couple of call-outs, domestics,' said Andy, 'knocking lumps out of each other.'

'Doncha just love 'em!' Gill shook her head. 'And where are we with—'

Rachel spoke up, interrupting her: 'The brother, Nathan Finn, he died in January, suicide – but he was a junkie too.'

'A family affair,' Gill said. 'Helps us how?' She stared, unsmiling, put Rachel on the spot. The girl was bright, did she think this contributed to the case?

'Dunno, background?' Rachel slumped in her seat, smarting perhaps. Gill didn't have time for it. 'Do we fancy Sean?' she asked the room.

'Kevin does,' Pete quipped. Laughter. Kevin gave him the finger.

'We need more,' Janet said. 'I think he's keeping something back but . . .' She shrugged. Lukewarm about Sean being a credible suspect.

Things could change, Gill knew; people cycle through the roles from victim to witness to suspect and back.

'There's another reason he delays calling us. Changes his clothes. Ranjeet reckons there would be some blood on the killer's clothes.' It was virtually impossible to knife someone and not come away with traces of blood. Especially when you retained the weapon. All they needed was a drop, a smear. Though with Sean, a defence lawyer would argue that he picked up blood traces in the process of covering Lisa up. It made the whole forensics side of it that much messier.

After talking it through with Phil Sweet, earlier in the day, Gill had put together her list for Gerry, the forensics submissions officer. She had wanted them to examine trace evidence from the body, from the duvet and from the sheet in the bedroom, but Gerry wasn't playing.

'I can't authorize all this premium rate, Gill,' he said. 'What are your priorities?'

'The body obviously, but given her state of dress and the indications that she had sex, I'd like to include the material from the bedroom.' She could try, couldn't she?

'Yeah, and I'd like a Lotus and early retirement on a six-figure pension. However . . . straitened times.'

'C'mon, Gerry.'

'The best I can do is put the body samples through premium rate as a first tranche and let you have the second lot as standard.'

At least he wasn't telling her to sit on part of her trace evidence, which might have happened. It would all get looked at, even if she had to wait longer for some of it. 'You're a hard man, Gerry.'

'I am God's gift, that's what I am. You're getting everything you want tested.'

'Not when I want.'

'Patience,' he had said.

'Go on,' she told him, 'bugger off and play with your budgets.'

'For now, Sean Broughton is our witness, but talk to him again. Lisa' – Gill moved the discussion on to focus on the victim – 'left care, Ryelands House, eight months ago. They no longer have a duty of care but we should still pay 'em a visit. Lisa's personal advisor is James Raleigh. Rachel, you talk to him: what was he dealing with, any recent trouble?' Gill glanced at her papers. 'Where's Mr Finn?' she said.

'Mickey?' Janet got there first.

'Droll,' said Gill. She saw a flicker of panic in Kevin's eyes as he joined in the laughter. Poor sod didn't know the term: Mickey Finn, a drink laced with drugs. Roofies the modern equivalent, rohypnol.

'Bernard Finn,' Pete said, 'Irish citizen. Whereabouts unknown. Left the area in ninety-three. HGV driver.'

'Right, now, we've only one FLO in place as yet and we are taking next-of-kin to do a formal ID.' She looked at Janet: 'OK, cock?'

'Fine,' Janet said.

'If she's fit, have a chat too.' Gill saw Rachel glance at Janet, body language between the two of them like a pair of alley cats bristling for a scrap. 'Take Rachel,' she added to Janet. Throw them together, force them to work it out.

'Thought I was doing the personal advisor?' said Rachel.

'Use your initiative,' Gill said briskly, 'time management. Kevin.' Gill fixed on him, watched his face: untroubled, a kid, eager.

'Boss?'

Gill waited.

Andy nudged him, gestured to Kevin's notes. Though whether he had anything there apart from the schoolboy doodles he specialized in, Gill had no idea.

'Yes, right.' Kevin scratched at his head. 'Erm.' Kevin was a tier one interviewer, talk and write at the same time; how he'd progressed to Major Incidents was a mystery to all who had the pleasure of commanding him.

'House-to-house,' Kevin finally got going, 'no sighting of Sean, though some more still to canvass. But old biddy at the end saw Lisa come home in a taxi.'

'Time?'

'*Heartbeat* was on, the first ad break.'

'Which is . . . ?' Gill saw Andy roll his eyes in despair. He'd probably already told Kevin to pinpoint the time.

'The one about the bobbies in the Dales.'

'Time!' yelled Gill.

'I'll check,' Kevin said, affronted.

'You do that,' she said, making a mental note to discuss this with Kevin, how one piece of information needed developing, verifying. Coming home with half the story was not good enough. He had to join the dots.

'Have we got the firm?' she said to him.

'I asked her that.' Kevin was obviously pleased with himself about this stunning piece of detective work. 'But she couldn't remember.'

'Get dialling, Kevin.'

His face fell.

'Are we done?' Gill surveyed them. Nods of assent. People made to move, gathering up papers, drinks, pens.

'Janet – a word.'

Gill went to her office. Once Janet was inside, Gill closed the door to give them some privacy as the lads filtered back to their desks. 'You've got your face on,' Gill said.

'I don't have a face,' Janet objected, baby blue eyes wide.

'Yes, you do. I know you, kid. You're sulking about Bailey. Not going to work, kiddo – drop it. Status quo.'

' "Whatever You Want"?' The tune popped into Janet's head.

'Things stay as they are.'

'I never did Greek,' Janet said. 'Look, we're at the mother's and she wades in, intrusive questions, clumsy assumptions. You know what she said? *Could we call the son round to be with her.*'

'Ouch!' Through the glass Gill could see Rachel at her desk.

'Right,' Janet said, with feeling.

'But you told her?' Gill asked.

'Yes,' Janet said, the tone in her voice: *Of course I did, what do you take me for?*

'Good, she's learning.'

'Seems to me it went in one ear and out the other,' Janet complained.

Gill had had enough. She needed to make it plain that Janet had to deal with this on her own, not come running to Gill with every gripe and squabble. 'Time will tell. I expect you to train her up. She wants this, she's got plenty between her ears, I've seen her files. She'll learn. You point out her mistakes and you encourage her to do better. Clear?'

'As glass.'

Gill gave the thumbs up and went to ring the CSM. They needed a sit-down, see where Sean Broughton's bed-making left them, forensically speaking.

8

'DC Rachel Bailey, Manchester Metropolitan Police. We sent you a request yesterday evening for call data on a missing phone.'

'Nothing for you, yet,' said the man on the other end.

'You do realize this is a murder I'm dealing with here?' Rachel complained. 'Can't you get your finger out?'

'You do realize that this is the police liaison department?' the man said frostily. 'All we deal with is murders. I've a stack of requests here. You wait your turn.' And he hung up. Rachel looked at the receiver for a moment, taken aback. Then she made a note in her daybook about the call.

Rachel was miffed at the way Godzilla had talked to her, making her look stupid in front of everyone. She had brought her into the syndicate and now she was being snotty to her. Making her tag along for the formal identification, for fuck's sake.

It had snowed in the early hours, not much, but

enough to mottle the landscape with patches of white, a piebald effect. Slush already on the main roads. On the drive over to the mortuary Janet had explained it was policy to have two FLOs in the initial stages of an inquiry, before they knew what flavour it was. You didn't know how many next-of-kin might come crawling out of the woodwork, you didn't know if there was bad blood. Things might kick off.

'One time,' Janet said, 'we had the father at the mortuary, he had been easy to trace. The mother had done a runner years before, leaving the kids . . .'

Rachel looked out of the window; she knew what that was like, aware of the old twist in her stomach, the anger just underneath. How could she, the bitch? Didn't want to think about her. Waste of space, waste of time. Dead. Good as.

'. . . but,' Janet went on, turning into the car park near the mortuary, 'mother pitches up, completely trollied, seen the death on the news, and attacks the father. Only one FLO there and yours truly, trying to pull them apart. I got a smack in the face for my trouble.'

Rachel still thought this was overkill, Denise Finn at the mortuary along with the FLO and two detectives. Three to one. Plus the mortuary staff. Janet obviously thought so, too. 'You can wait in the car?' she said when they arrived.

'You're all right,' Rachel replied.

'Frightened you'll miss something?' The woman thought she was a mind reader now.

So they waited, while Denise Finn stood in front of the viewing area where her daughter's body was laid out. The pale blue sheet pulled up to her neck. Blood washed away, her scuzzy hair combed – they'd have done that for the post-mortem, collecting trace material that might lead to her attacker. Denise Finn wore the same clothes as the previous evening, perhaps she had not slept. Perhaps she was a mucky one. She was huffing and puffing, a tissue balled in her hand. The FLO, Christopher Danes his name was, asked her the question: 'Can you tell me if this is your daughter, Lisa Anne Finn?'

'Yes,' Denise said in a sob, her shoulders heaving. The FLO put his hand on her shoulder, suggested she sit down for a minute. She stared at him, looking lost, he repeated the question and she nodded. He showed her into the visitors' room and came back out. The mortuary assistant closed the blinds. Rachel heard the squeal of the trolley as he wheeled it to the freezer.

Rachel's phone went. *Alison calling*. She let it go to voicemail. Her sister could talk for England; she went on about how overstretched she was at work, how big her caseload was, yet she still found time to make social calls in the day.

Janet spoke to the FLO: 'We'd like to talk to her again.'

He nodded. 'We're going back to the house now.'

'How's she been?' Janet said.

'Not said much,' he said. 'Dumbstruck.'

'She fit to talk?' Janet checked.

69

'Just about. She's on sedatives, as it is. GP's been, given her some sleeping tablets.'

'I get to listen again?' Rachel said on the way up, hoping she was wrong.

'I think that's wise,' Janet answered. 'You're not exactly going to be her favourite person, are you?'

'She'll have forgotten by now,' Rachel objected, 'with all she's got going on.'

'You think?' Janet gave her a knowing look. 'You don't give a toss, do you?'

'We're police officers, not agony aunts,' Rachel said. 'She can't be much of a mother, can she? If Lisa was taken into care.'

'Maybe Lisa was hard to handle. You can't go making assumptions. We don't know these people, we don't know what their lives are like.'

'Got a pretty good clue – trash.'

'An interview is a conversation,' Janet said, 'whether it's a witness or a suspect, it is a conversation – not a confrontation.' Repeating it as if it were some mantra she'd learnt. 'They need to trust us, we show respect, we listen, we don't judge.'

'I know.' Rachel flung her head back against the headrest.

'I don't think you do,' Janet said steadily. 'Your body language, your tone of voice . . . If you're sat there thinking, "What a slimebag, what a pitiful excuse for a human being", and you let it show, then you won't get that conversation.'

Rachel got her phone out, had enough of the lecture, listened to her voicemail from Alison. *Hi, it's me. We've got vouchers for BOGOFs for the new Vietnamese place in Moston, use by the end of the month. Thought maybe you and lover-boy would like to make a foursome. You can't keep him hidden for ever.* She gave a grating laugh. *Or are you ashamed of us?*

Yes. Truly, madly, deeply. It would be a horror show, Alison and Tony talking school admissions and tracker mortgages and offers on patio furniture from Wickes, and Nick strangling her with his eyes. Cottoning on that this was the Bailey family. With their tiny little lives. This was where Rachel had come from. The underclass, grotty estate on the wrong side of Middleton. She didn't want him to think of her that way. She was different from Alison, from Dom. Hadn't even told him of Dom's existence. And she was way different from her parents, who didn't even deserve the title. Langley was the past. She'd locked the door on it, she didn't need Alison blurting stuff out now. Amusing anecdotes of free school meals and scraping by in hand-me-downs, and knock-offs from the market. Rachel was making something of herself. Her dad was still knocking around Middleton. No fixed abode. Half a chance she'd get a call-out one day and find him. Sudden death. Wouldn't be that sudden really, been killing himself for years on the booze and the fags. Alison tried sorting him out every once in a while. Get him in a flat, take him to the hospital. Playing happy families. Same as Alison kept visiting Dom. Deluded.

If she ignored it, Alison would keep nudging: *Did you get the message? Have you decided?*

Rachel sent a text: *No can do, him away, me overtime.*

Best kept separate. Some things wouldn't mix, like putting lemon juice with milk: whole thing curdles.

The small room smelled sickly, stale, fruity of booze. There was a glass, sticky with fingerprints, and a bottle of sherry on the side table. The air was humid, condensation on the windows, a towel on the radiator.

The FLO left as they arrived, aiming to sort out some nebby neighbours whose offers of help were simply a way of having a good nosy.

'Can you tell me about Lisa?' said Janet, starting wide, letting Denise choose where to begin, what tack to take, which memories to share.

'What about her?' Denise asked.

'You told me yesterday that she had been in bother, messing with drugs.'

'That's right, and Sean, he put her up to it.'

'Did he? Why do you say that?'

'She wasn't doing so bad till she started going with him. It's his fault,' Denise said.

'What's his fault?' Janet said.

'That this . . . that she . . .' It wasn't unusual for those left behind to blame whoever was at hand. 'I told her to get shot of him. He's a junkie,' Denise said. 'He dragged her down in the muck with him. They was offering her rehab, but she wouldn't listen . . . If she can just . . .' She ground to a halt. Janet saw it almost like a truck hitting a wall. The impact striking the woman again, the reality. Lisa. Dead.

'How would you describe their relationship?'

'A bloody disaster,' Denise said. She cast about, found her cigarettes and lit one. Janet waited.

'Mrs Finn, do you have any reason to think Sean had some involvement in Lisa's death?'

'He hit her,' Denise said angrily, fanning the flames. 'I seen her black and blue. He's a right nasty piece of work.'

'Did you have a lot of contact with her?'

'She's my daughter,' Denise replied.

'How often did you see her?' Janet rephrased the question, aware that Denise had sidestepped it.

Denise gave a bitter laugh. 'More before he came on the scene. And then he sends her up here to scrounge. Expecting me to give them drug money.' She shook her head.

'Lisa was in Ryelands House until this April?'

'I couldn't manage. I tried . . .' Janet sensed the woman's shame at her inadequacy. 'My sister took Nathan, but she couldn't cope with the baby as well.'

'When did Lisa first go into care?' Janet said.

'Four months.'

An infant. 'Was she in care all her life?'

'No,' Denise tapped the ash off her cigarette. 'Only till I sorted myself out. I got her back when she was six, then . . . the end of primary and she just went wild. Running away, going missing, drinking.' Taisie's age,

73

thought Janet. At least we've not had any of that to deal with. 'I tried everything, but I couldn't handle her. I'd school attendance on my back and your lot every five minutes. I thought it was for the best, but Ryelands – there's more drugs in there than there is on the streets. Same as prison. Paedos hanging round an' all,' she said. 'Some of the kids in there'll do anything for twenty quid.'

Janet knew Rachel would follow up on this when she spoke to Lisa's personal advisor. Get details, help them sort out fact from fiction. But from what Denise said, it sounded as though Lisa had been experimenting with drugs before she hooked up with Sean. Janet brought the question round to recent contact again.

'Have you seen Lisa recently?'

Denise's eyes filled. She was in bits. 'No.'

'When did you last see her?'

'My birthday – in October.'

'Had you spoken to her on the phone?'

'Yes, well . . . I tried, but, because she knew I didn't want her with him, then she wouldn't always pick up. Talk to her personal advisor,' Denise said. 'He'll tell you, same as I have, Sean was bad news, every which way.' She played with the tissue, unfolding it then crushing it again.

'Can you remember when you last spoke to Lisa on the phone?'

'Yesterday.' Her voice cracking. 'She said she was busy. She hung up.'

Oh, God. Janet could imagine the 'what ifs' piling up

in Denise's head. *If only I had insisted, gone round there, got her to talk to me. Changed the future. Interrupted the sequence of events.* 'Do you remember what time that was, Denise?'

She pressed the tissue to her eyes. 'Why?' She turned on Janet, distraught, her face a mess of snot, lips cracked and swollen, the cigarette burned down to the filter now, an awful stench in the room. Janet saw she didn't want to think about the phone call, didn't want to be reminded of how things might have been different.

Because we want to get a time of death as close as we can, Janet thought. But said quietly, 'It'll help us with the investigation.'

'After dinner.'

Dinner being the midday meal in these parts, tea the food you had at the end of the working day. 'Could you tell where she was when you spoke to her?' Janet asked.

'She was out.'

'Did she say where?'

'No, but it was noisy.'

'What sort of noises?'

'I don't know!' she snapped, her patience thinning. The questions distracting her from her grief.

'People, traffic, music . . . ?' Janet suggested.

'Traffic.'

'It was after dinner, long after dinner? Could we check on your phone perhaps?'

'It's dead,' Denise said. A shocked silence in the room. And Janet saw the stumble, the echo that came back at Denise like a boot in the face. *Dead phone. Dead*

75

daughter. 'I'll put it on charge,' Denise whispered, 'get it for you then.'

'Thank you,' Janet said. 'You told me Lisa said she was busy. How did she sound otherwise?'

Denise took another cigarette and lit it. Janet thought she'd die from asphyxiation. If only they could open the window. But it was cold and bleak out there, sky the colour of grubby white sheets. Maybe more snow coming.

'Did she sound tired or anxious or frightened?'

'No,' Denise said.

'Did you get the sense that she was with anyone else?'

'Erm, no.'

'OK, is there anyone you know who might have wished her harm?'

Denise pressed her lips tight together, shaking her head slowly. 'I did my best,' she said, her voice quaking with emotion. 'I always . . .' She couldn't continue.

They heard the door go, the FLO returning. 'Denise . . .' He entered the room, heading for the scullery kitchen at the back of the house, took in the scene. The weeping woman. 'Denise, a cup of tea?'

She didn't respond, too far gone for politeness. Janet caught his eye. 'We'll be on our way.' Signalling with a tilt of her head that she wanted a word.

He stepped outside with them. A woman across the street with twins in a double buggy stopped to gawp.

'Take a picture,' Rachel muttered.

'Keep a close eye,' Janet said to the FLO. 'The woman's lost both her kids, she's already struggling, too fond of a drink, on tablets for her nerves, she's a wreck.'

'I know,' he said. 'I will. SIO tells me there was some problem at the scene.'

'Bit of rearranging of the furniture that shouldn't have happened. Can you get Denise's phone charged, check her calls.'

'Will do,' he said. 'What you after?'

'Call she made to Lisa early afternoon. We need the time.'

'Should have been sterilized,' Rachel said as they buckled up, 'not fit to raise a goldfish.'

Janet looked at her. Was the girl doing this to wind her up? Trying to shock? Negative attention better than being ignored? Like Taisie when she was being gobby.

'What?' Rachel demanded. 'I'm entitled to an opinion.'

Janet shook her head, started the engine and pulled out. She wouldn't waste her breath.

9

'How was it?' Gill rang Sammy.

'Not bad, I only just finished the last question, though.'

'Did you get Mussolini?' He was doing his AS practice papers and Gill thought it was touch and go whether he'd meet his target grades. It was hard weighing up how much to push and how much to trust him to get his course work and revision done under his own steam. Harder because she was dealing with it on her own. Thanks to Captain Arsehole.

'Yeah, that was good.'

'What you doing now?' Gill said.

'Going back to ours with Craig and Joe.'

'OK. Watch the china.'

'One thing!' His voice rose in mock indignation. 'We broke one thing. It wasn't even a nice lamp.'

Smiling to herself. 'And that's why skateboards are designed for outside use only.'

'I know, Mum.'

'Food in the fridge; don't eat the fish.'

'Minging. Laters.'

He was pretty self-sufficient. Had to be, given that both his parents worked all hours. Sammy had been three, nearly four, when Gill saw the job advertised with the National Crime Faculty. It was a fantastic opportunity, but she'd known it would mean a lot of travelling away from home. Could she make it work?

'What about Sammy?' Dave's first words when she told him she was thinking of applying. Not *Brilliant!* or *You go for it!* or even *When's the closing date?* but straight into obstacles, disincentives.

He was jealous. It hit her with a shock. He was actually jealous. There had always been a healthy competition between them. At least, she had imagined it to be healthy. Who could get the sergeant's exam first, who'd pass the tier three interview course quickest. But now she was confident enough to have a shot at working on a national level, knew she had a reasonable chance of getting selected, and he hadn't even considered applying. He begrudged her.

She'd tried to be diplomatic, no need to rub his nose in it, but she wasn't about to let Dave's resentment colour her decision. 'We'd have to get a nanny.'

'We're already struggling with the mortgage.'

The house had been bought off plan. One of a development of individually designed properties on the outskirts of Shaw near Oldham. It had been a rollercoaster of meetings and design discussions, site visits and fallings out with the builders, but now it was theirs.

And it was beautiful. Not overly ostentatious, but quality workmanship, everything from the York flags on the patio and the wooden-framed windows to the tiles in the bathrooms and the kitchen with its black marble and beech fittings had been chosen by them. Gill adored it. And it worked perfectly as a family home. Double garage. Enough space for Sammy to have a playroom that could be adapted to a den as he got older. There was a sun terrace outside their bedroom window at the back with an uninterrupted view over the farms and moorland up to the reservoir. Gill often brought work home and, unless it was freezing, it was a place she loved to sit while she did it.

'We're not struggling, Dave. That's not struggling. We're just having to be careful. Besides, I'd be on a bigger salary, from the start.'

'If you get it,' he pointed out. She bit her tongue. 'Sounds as if you've already made your mind up,' he complained.

'Your mum or mine can come over in emergencies. They'd love to help. We can make this work.' That was Gill's mindset: decide what you want, plan a strategy to get you there, and get on with it.

'He's only little,' Dave said. 'Maybe in a few years . . .'

Feeling a prickle of annoyance, Gill got up, walked to the French windows, looked out at the garden, the cherry blossom, Sammy's Jungle Gym. Turned to face him. 'I might not get the chance again,' she objected. 'You know how limited jobs at the faculty are. If I don't jump at—'

'All I'm saying,' Dave cut her off, putting on his reasonable voice, 'is that your priorities—'

'My priorities? *My* priorities.' She laughed, not in the slightest amused. 'Would we be having this conversation if it was you?'

'Of course,' he said, not even thinking about it.

'No,' she said, brusquely, 'we wouldn't. "He's only three, Dave, wait until he's at school, till he's bigger, he needs his father here", she mimicked. 'No way!' She felt close to losing her temper, her skin hot, harsh words, dangerous words crowding her throat. 'But *I'm* expected to put things on hold because *we* have a child. Takes two to tango,' she said. 'I need you to back me on this. So I'll think about my decision while you think about that.' She'd walked out then. Agitated, disappointed.

Janet had listened to her recounting the discussion with Dave over a bottle of wine in a bar in the town centre.

'You can't not apply,' Janet told her, 'you'd never forgive yourself. You're meant for this, you know you are. Supercop,' she added drily. 'You go, girl.'

'I'd be back in between jobs anyway,' Gill argued, 'have reasonable leave.'

Janet laughed. 'It's not as if you'd be going off to the Antarctic or something. This is the twentieth century, nearly the twenty-first. There's a girl in records, Indian, she's left two kids with her mum in Delhi while she makes some decent money over here for them all. We don't know we're born half the time.'

'I think he's miffed,' Gill said, raising her glass. 'Me doing it and not him.'

Janet raised her eyebrows. 'He's a big lad, he'll get over it. You know you could hack it. Maybe he couldn't.'

Gill looked at her for a moment. Janet always had this precise, understated way of telling the truth. No flag waving or drum rolls. Straight to the point, measured, sensible, incisive. 'Maybe that's gonna be a problem,' Gill said.

'He'll do all right for himself,' Janet said. 'He's ambitious enough.'

'What about you, though?' Gill held up the bottle and Janet accepted a top-up. 'You've never thought of moving into an MIT?'

'I'm fine as I am,' Janet said.

'So, you're going to stay on Division all your life. Not had enough of burglaries and assaults yet?' Gill asked.

'I get pulled on to the odd murder now and again when they need an extra detective. Not as if I never get a look-in. I'm not sure I'd want to do it all day every day.'

'Give it time.'

Gill was dragged back to the present by a knock on her office door, as Phil Sweet the CSM came in to discuss the implications of Sean Broughton moving the duvet.

'Snafu?' Gill asked.

'You could say that.'

10

James Raleigh, Lisa's personal advisor, was tall, maybe as tall as Mitch, six foot two or three with blond hair, blue eyes. Made Rachel think of a tennis player. He was her sort of age, she guessed, late twenties, early thirties. He worked out of the neighbourhood office in Newton Heath, an old stone building, modernized offices inside.

'It's a terrible thing,' he said, after offering her coffee, which she refused; if this place was anything like the nick, the coffee would be revolting. 'Can't believe it. I understand you want some background?'

'That's right,' said Rachel. 'As much as you've got.'

'Well, I've only been seeing Lisa since she left Ryelands in April. When she turned seventeen. Usually the social worker stays on the case for a while so there's some continuity, but Lisa's social worker was retiring at the time. A lot of the background I've picked up from the assessment reports.' He flipped open the file on his desk. Rachel wondered if Alison knew him, both being in social work, though Alison was doing geriatrics at the moment, dealing with old people at Oldham General.

'Lisa first came into care in August 1993, as a four-month-old. Mum on her own, not managing. Dad left during the pregnancy. Older sibling, two-year-old boy, went into the care of an aunt.'

'She just couldn't hack it?' Rachel asked. Thinking of her own mother, fleetingly.

'History of depression and alcohol dependency, no record of a problem with the first child, but two was obviously more than she could manage. Lisa remained in care, with periods in foster care, until she was six. Contact maintained with the mother and brother. Her brother Nathan returned home in 1996, when Lisa would have been three.'

'Must have been hard for her to understand, Nathan's at home and she's not.'

'Yes, it would,' he said. 'It's always difficult. In an ideal world the children are kept together, whether that's in foster care or the family home, but in reality . . .' He pulled a face. 'Age six to eleven, she was back in the family home. Then things deteriorated.' It all matched what Denise Finn had told them. He turned over the pages in the file. 'Pattern of risk-taking behaviour, absconding, solvent abuse, picked up for disorderly conduct, vandalism.' He looked up. 'Got into bad company, went off the rails. That's when the decision was made to put Lisa in Ryelands. The aim was to move her back home once Mrs Finn was deemed capable.'

'Which never happened?'

'No, Lisa stayed at Ryelands until April. You've heard about Nathan's death?' he said.

'Yeah.'

'Lisa took it very hard. Even though she and Nathan had been apart a lot, he was a significant person, only sibling. Her big brother.'

Dom, Rachel thought, my little brother. It was two years now, more, since she'd seen him. He'd written at first. She'd burnt the letters.

'Was Nathan living at home, then?'

'Yes. You can imagine, Lisa's gearing up to leave Ryelands, starting out on her own, and Nathan dies. Very difficult for her.'

'Lisa was using drugs?'

'Yes,' he said.

'Heroin?'

'Amongst others,' he said.

'Her mother thought she had been introduced to drugs while she was in care.'

'It happens,' he said. 'We're dealing with very vulnerable kids. Drugs can be a way of fitting in, buckling under peer pressure, or an escape, a way of checking out for a bit. Most teenagers experiment, ours even more so.' His phone rang.

'Do you need . . .' Rachel said.

'Voicemail's on.'

'What can you tell me about Sean?'

'He wasn't helping, that's for sure.' James Raleigh closed the file and sat back in his chair. 'They'd met before she began living independently. He was known as a small-time drug user. We got her the flat on the understanding that it was a sole tenancy, so he couldn't just move in there wholesale, but he had his feet under the table from the get-go.'

'And their relationship?' Rachel said.

'He was an enabler. Without Sean, Lisa might have kicked the drugs into touch. An outside chance. With Sean, forget it. Like trying to stop smoking when someone's waving a full pack of King Size in front of your face, lighter at the ready.'

Rachel instantly craved a cigarette. 'We've had reports of domestic violence,' she said.

He gave a nod. 'According to her records, Lisa had a reputation for violence when she was in Ryelands. Now and then she'd explode. A lot of anger.'

'Can't think why,' Rachel said.

He smiled. 'Sean, I don't know so much about, but he doesn't have any compunction about hitting a woman.'

'But it wasn't necessarily Lisa who was the punchbag?'

'No, though he'd be stronger than her.'

Rachel agreed. He wasn't a big lad, but he wasn't a weed either, and Lisa had been slightly built. 'Did Lisa ever use a knife?' She thought of the crime-scene album, the blood. Had Lisa gone for Sean and he'd wrested the weapon from her, used it?

'Not that I've come across. Anything to hand, I'd imagine. You think he might have done it?' Raleigh asked.

'Too early to say,' Rachel said. 'Would it surprise you?'

'No, not at all,' he said frankly.

'OK. Lisa was signing on?'

'That's right, we were looking at access courses and improving her literacy and numeracy skills. Getting Lisa into a job and getting shot of Sean would have been the way to turn it all around, but it's hopeless out there. That age especially. Dozens of kids after every minimum-wage vacancy.'

Rachel tried to imagine the girl on the mortuary trolley in a job interview. Failed.

'Things weren't great between Lisa and her mother. It was all or nothing. Denise veered from being a wreck unable to cope with anything to wanting to be best buddies. That inconsistency, it's very difficult for a child. Denise would get drunk and emotional and ring Lisa, and either Lisa would hang up or they'd end up in a shouting match. Our aim is to keep families together as much as is possible, but sometimes the family isn't a healthy unit. The relationships get stuck in a self-perpetuating cycle that doesn't help anybody.'

'Sounds hopeless,' Rachel said.

'Sometimes I think it is, but I'm not a complete pessimist.' He smiled. 'With the right sort of inter-vention, sustained and well resourced—'

'Throw money at it,' she said.

'Couldn't the same be said in crime prevention? Early intervention, working with the family as a whole? Tough love?' He was smiling, teasing her.

'How often did you see Lisa?'

'Every fortnight at first, then once a month. She could phone in between if there were problems.'

'Did she?'

'Couple of times. Cock-ups with the housing benefit, that sort of thing.'

'Was she involved in any other sexual relationships?' Rachel asked.

'No.' He looked curious.

'Prostitution?'

'No. Though she wouldn't necessarily tell me.'

'She didn't confide in you?'

'Not much. Conflicting view of social workers. She knew I was there to help, to give her support, but that can be read as bossing her about.' His phone rang again and he glanced at his watch. 'Timewise . . .'

'Nearly done,' Rachel said. She skimmed back over her notes. 'And when did you last see her?'

'The twenty-fifth of November.'

'And how was she then?'

'I had no particular concerns – nothing new, anyway,' he amended. 'I've tried talking to her about rehab, but it's got to come from them.'

'Was anyone threatening her? Did she have any enemies?'

'No.'

'Thanks. If anything else occurs, just give us a ring.' Rachel passed him a card, the MIT number. It didn't have her name on yet, something she'd have to ask Gill about – or Andy. As sergeant, he might be more approachable.

Raleigh got up to show her out. His phone was bleating and she signalled that she could make her own way
and left him to his work.

Rachel was still out when the mobile phone company
came back to say they had just emailed the data the
team were waiting on, so Janet printed off all
the details, waded through it and relayed the crucial bits
to Gill. Incoming text at half past twelve, from a
number not yet known to the inquiry. Outgoing text to
that number immediately after. No way of knowing the
content of the texts. Outgoing call at twelve fifty-five
p.m. to a local landline number. Two incoming calls, the
first at thirteen ten from Sean Broughton.

'As he told us, backed up by his phone log,' said
Gill.

'And the second, thirteen fourteen from Denise.
Which also fits,' Janet said. The FLO, true to his word,
had got Denise's mobile charged and then checked the
calls she'd made.

'Who's the landline?'

Janet shrugged. Gill picked up the office phone and
dialled.

'Taxi?' came the answer. Janet could hear from where
she was standing.

'Bingo,' Gill mouthed. She handed the receiver to
Janet so she could get details from the dispatcher and
locate the driver who had picked up Lisa.

When she came off the phone, Gill nodded: 'Put
Kevin out of his misery.'

Janet looked, *Do I have to?* Kevin still working his way through the directory – T for taxi.

'Be nice,' Gill warned. 'What about cell site location?'

'Later today, maybe first thing tomorrow,' Janet said. 'Right, I'm off to see a man about a cab.'

'Rachel still out?' Gill looked at her watch.

'Still with the personal advisor,' Janet guessed.

'If she's done, take her with you,' Gill said.

Oh, bloody marvellous. Gill was determined to force them together at every opportunity. Janet phoned Rachel: 'Where are you?' Hoping she'd be busy.

'On my way back,' Rachel said, an edge to her voice, as though she thought Janet didn't trust her.

'Meet me at Speedy Cabs.'

'We got the taxi!' Rachel suddenly alive and excited.

11

Speedy Cabs operated out of a railway arch close to the canal in Ardwick. Either side were a welding outfit and a pallets store. Janet wondered if the curved roof caused a headache for the pallets firm, space they paid for and couldn't use, not ideally suited to the square shape of the stock.

Rachel was there already having a fag by the railings. 'Kevin came through?' She sounded surprised.

Janet shook her head. ''Fraid not. Cell-phone provider.'

Rachel dropped her cig and ground it out. They crossed the cobbled street to the front of the archway, went in through a steel door that led in turn to the dispatcher's office and a small rest area where a couple of drivers were having lunch. The telly in the corner was showing a rerun of the latest Manchester derby.

'Ladies,' said the dispatcher.

Janet and Rachel showed their warrant cards.

'Kasim will be back any minute,' he said. Then 'Yes!'

to the screen as a shot bounced off the crossbar. 'Up the Blues,' he said, sniffing out their affiliation. A city of two teams. Sporting rivalry passed down from one generation to the next.

Rachel shrugged. 'Whatever.'

Disappointed, he looked at Janet. 'Me neither,' she said. Ade used to follow Oldham Athletic, a suicide mission if ever there was one; went to a few matches when he was younger. Janet never fancied it.

They heard a car trundle over the cobbles and a cab pulled up in front of the office.

'Kasim,' the man confirmed.

'Thanks, we'll talk outside,' Janet said. More privacy there.

Kasim was curious, bright-eyed and bushy-tailed. He had done that thing with his eyebrows, Janet noticed, lines cut through. Looked as though his hand slipped shaving. She didn't get it. I'm getting old, she thought. The taxi drivers look younger every day.

'She the girl that was murdered?' Kasim asked them when they told him what they were there for.

'That's right,' Janet said. 'You picked her up, when?'

'Just after one.'

'Where from?'

'Shudehill, near the Printworks,' he said.

'Where did you drop her?'

'Fairland Avenue.'

'She was on her own?' Janet said.

'Yeah.'

'Dispatch says she's a regular fare?'

He shrugged. 'We're reliable. People stick with you if they know you're gonna turn up.'

'Did she say anything?'

'No, just, maybe the weather?' Like he was guessing. Janet didn't want guesses.

'Can you remember what she was wearing?' Rachel said.

He exhaled noisily, indicating that was a really hard task. 'To be honest' – he shook his head – 'don't even notice what the girlfriend's wearing half the time.'

'Anything about the trip, about the girl? How was she?' said Janet.

'Quiet,' he ventured.

An unmemorable passenger had turned out to be front-page news, but Kasim had no juicy story to dine off. He could barely remember the fare.

'What time did you drop her?' Janet said.

He considered, rubbing his chin with one hand. 'Maybe quarter past one, no later.'

'She make or receive any calls?' Rachel said.

'A couple. I think her phone went.'

'And what was she saying?'

'Sorry. You zone out, you know? Eye on the road, the traffic. Nothing sticks.' He gave a shrug.

If Kasim's timing was accurate, and he wouldn't be far out, given the relatively short distance of the journey, then the calls between Sean and Lisa and Denise and Lisa would have taken place while she was on the way home.

There wasn't much more they could learn from

93

Kasim, but he had given them a last sighting.

'We know she was still alive at quarter past one and that she was dead by half three. That's a pretty tight window,' said Janet once they were back at the station, eating sandwiches from the deli. Janet was ravenous, had gone for a double-decker BLT and a flapjack.

Rachel didn't answer. Janet turned to look at her. She was staring into space, miles away. Dolly daydream now, thought Janet. Wonder what she has to daydream about?

Suddenly Rachel said, 'Why get a cab? Any number of buses go up that way, and she was opposite the bus station. She's on the dole. Why get a cab?'

Janet swallowed her mouthful. 'Lazy, feckless, spending her benefits on taxis. Only cost her four or five quid, anyway.'

'Buy twenty fags for that,' Rachel said, scowling, seemingly crushed that she couldn't make sense of it.

She remained preoccupied over lunch, the cab business obviously bugging her. But Janet didn't know that there was anything in it. Some folk had weird ways of budgeting. They saw it all the time: people with no carpets or curtains and a TV the size of a small car.

Gill had left instructions for Andy and Janet to co-ordinate reports for a case update and pull everyone in for early evening. Janet felt the familiar trip of her heart when she joined Andy in the meeting room.

'Made a start,' he said. 'Further forensics' – he pointed to a pile of printouts – 'witness statements, Sean

Broughton and' – he indicated another pile – 'Denise Finn.'

'Fine.' Janet nodded to the piles. 'Rachel's typing up the info from the personal advisor and I've adjusted the timeline. Cabbie set her down at quarter past one.'

'You want to start collating and I'll get Rachel?' He gave her a quick smile. The way he looked at her sometimes, she wondered if he could tell the old attraction hadn't gone away completely, could sense that she occasionally daydreamed about him. Like a lovesick teenager. Way back in training, that's when Janet first met Andy, had a fling – until she came to her senses and married Ade. The men were physically very different, Ade stouter, shorter; Andy leaner, taller. Andy had quick, bright eyes. These days there was an energy about Andy quite unlike Ade. It was as if Ade's batteries had worn down somewhere along the way and he couldn't be bothered to recharge them. Not that Andy was hyper or anything, but he was engaged, sharp, keen. It was a bonus, having him there in the syndicate – one she kept to herself – enjoying the chance to work with him, have the occasional flirtatious thought. Harmless, she told herself.

Janet sat at the desk, pulling reports from each pile into sets for the team. The arguments between her and Ade seemed to erupt with increasing frequency. Any exchange about the house or the cars or the girls suddenly exploding into a blame game over who was supposed to be sorting what out. Her overtime was unpredictable, her hours out of the house often longer than his, and Ade flung this back at her every chance he got. In the middle of their most recent row, he'd accused her of preferring being at work to being at home. 'I'm sick of living like a single parent,' he said. 'I do the lot and I get no thanks for it.' Trying to make her feel guilty – and succeeding, though she would not let it show, would not give him the satisfaction. And even after the rows were over, the atmosphere lingered. Ade could man the barricades for days, his bitter silence like a chemical weapon. Janet always crumbled first, said sorry. Which allowed him to do likewise . . . till next time.

She must have sighed out loud as Andy came back in because he said, 'Problem?'

'No, nothing.'

'If you need me to have a word with Rachel . . .' he volunteered. As sergeant, he had a different relationship to the DCs, could make use of his rank. Either to admonish or advise.

'No, that's fine, thanks.'

He was still watching her and Janet felt her skin glow warm, hated that she was blushing. He seemed to be thinking, hesitant. 'You really all right?' He sounded genuinely concerned.

She had a sudden urge to confide in him. Bad idea. Instead, she generalized: 'Oh, you know, kids, work – sometimes there's just not enough hours in the day.' She should be happy, counting her blessings: great job, kids safe, roof over her head, food on the table. Ade there to man the lifeboats, even if he wasn't a red-hot rocking

Romeo any more (was he ever?) But the shine had gone. Some days felt like a grind.

'And we pick one up right in time for Christmas.'

'Oh, we'll have cracked it by then,' Janet joked.

She had all that to do as well: Christmas presents. Most of it she'd do online, spend more than she intended because it was so easy to push a button. Taisie wanted money, but Janet baulked at that. Seemed so empty. Compromise maybe: half money, half gift. Inline skates? And what to get Ade? Nothing he needed. Some book? Janet groaned inwardly. She could suggest a weekend away – treat themselves. Mum'd watch the girls. A place with a spa and nice woodland walks, up in the Lakes maybe. It all sounded great, but the prospect of forty-eight hours alone together without demands and distractions, without work and domestic chores . . . She'd go mad.

How did it come to this? she thought sadly. What do I do? Let it drift on until . . . what? The kids leave home and we go our separate ways? Her stomach turned cold at the thought.

'Can't find Rachel,' Andy said.

'Did you try outside? She's probably having a fag. I'll see.' She set off. Elise, what did Elise want? Apart from an iPad, which was more than a few quid too far.

12

Gill was ready, the team were assembled round the table. All except one.

'Where's Rachel?' Gill demanded.

Janet shrugged.

'Anyone?' Gill said.

They sat there like a load of muppets. No one missed the briefing. Not without Gill's express permission. The team relied on everyone carrying their weight. Absent staff led to gaps in the shared knowledge that was crucial to a well-run investigation. 'We got her report?'

'No,' Andy said.

Gill shook her head, annoyed, considered sending someone to see if Rachel was having a fag, or in the canteen, but dismissed the idea. She wasn't running a nursery. If Rachel didn't exhibit the professionalism Gill required of her DCs then she'd be out on her ear. Gill thought the girl had more sense. Was Janet right? Was Rachel a bad fit?

'Lads,' Gill clapped her hands and began, 'good work. Timeline shaping up nicely. Look at the first page. Texts and calls made and received. Now this . . .' Gill pressed the remote and played part of the video recording of Sean Broughton's witness statements.

Janet asking, *When was the last time you heard from her?*

Sean's reply, *I rang her just after one. She said she'd be back about half three. That's how I knew to go round, like.*

Gill paused the tape. 'The phone records show us the call from Sean was made at ten past one when Lisa was practically home.'

'We haven't got cell-site location through yet,' Mitch pointed out.

'Accepted, but if they confirm that this call happened somewhere along the taxi route or even once she reached home, then we have an anomaly. Sean's telling us Lisa said she'll not be home for another hour and twenty minutes, so he bides his time and shows up at half three. Was Lisa lying to him because she wanted a bit of time to herself for some reason?'

'Or is he lying to us?' Janet said. 'Maybe he was at the flat earlier.'

'He found the body,' Lee said. Lee had been a psychiatric nurse in his previous life. He was well qualified, both in academic terms and in experience. Gill knew he had a keen interest in the way people's minds worked, in human behaviour.

'Which makes him of special interest,' Gill noted. A

significant proportion of killers actually 'discovered the body' and reported it to the police. Assumption being, in their tiny brains, that if they did this it put them above suspicion.

'We've got the domestic violence too,' Andy said.

'Agreed. Janet, your report flags up two areas—' Gill pointed the remote at her.

'Yes,' Janet said. 'Could be nothing, but at one point Sean hesitated more than I'd have expected and couldn't make eye contact. Then later he's anticipating a question and again he's tense, he won't look at me. I know we can't rely on body language, but . . .'

Gill nodded. It was notoriously difficult to spot lies from a person's gestures. The old saws of licking lips and eye movements (up and left for recall, up and right for invention), of sweaty brows and hands covering mouths had all been discredited in study after study. There was one rock-solid way to tell whether someone was lying: by proving what they said was untrue. Nevertheless, Gill trusted Janet's intuition.

Janet carried on speaking, 'First time was with the shopping, then when I asked if he'd taken anything—'

Rachel Bailey burst through the doors, a clutch of papers in her hands, breathless. 'Sorry, I'm late, it's just that I—'

'Sit.' Gill pointed to a chair.

'When I was going over the—'

'And shut it,' Gill said sharply.

Rachel sat down, placed the reports on the table. Gill

turned back to Janet: 'Go on.' She passed the remote to Janet.

'This bit – when he says she was going shopping – he was reluctant to talk about it.' Janet played them the sequence. 'And this is where I ask him about taking anything.' She skipped the tape forward to the next excerpt. When it had finished, Janet froze the image. 'Then we've the unaccounted for thirty-five minutes. It doesn't take that long to cover somebody with a duvet. Could've been his chance to clean up, get rid of the knife.'

'Boss,' Rachel interrupted again.

'Hey, madam!' Gill hated having her concentration broken. 'You swan in here late, you fail to provide a report on time – we've still not got cell-site location, which was on your slate. So stop bloody interrupting.'

'But the shopping . . .' Rachel ploughed on regardless. Gill was gobsmacked. Had she no sense of self-preservation? 'She's been in town all morning,' Rachel said urgently, 'but there was nothing in the exhibits. Where was the shopping?'

Gill froze. Valid point.

'Window shopping?' Mitch said. 'My missus does it all the time.'

'Only 'cos you're too tight to give her any spends,' Pete teased.

'Ask the taxi driver,' Gill said.

'I did,' Rachel said. 'He can't remember.'

'What about cards? Bank statements?' Gill asked.

101

'Debit card only, overdrawn. No activity yesterday,' Andy said.

'She could have used cash to buy stuff.'

'Or nicked it,' Rachel said. 'Her mother said she'd shoplifted stuff before.'

Janet chipped in: 'If Lisa was shoplifting, then maybe Sean took the "shopping".'

'And her phone,' said Lee.

And her life?

'For starters,' Gill replied, a tickle at the back of her neck, the case growing wings, the scent of a quarry, the excitement of identifying a potential suspect – caution, though; *softly, softly, catchee monkey* – 'I think we should get to know Sean a whole lot better.'

So, the girl done good, Gill thought. But she needs taming, follow the rules, cover the mundane stuff. No room on the team for a lone flyer. No prima donnas wanting to dance their own steps.

'The cab picked her up on Shudehill?' Gill tapped her forefinger on the papers. 'Had she got any shopping then or not? Where had she come from? Rachel, Kevin – CCTV. Trace her backwards.' She saw the clench of annoyance on Rachel's face. 'Crack on, then,' Gill said to them all. 'Keep it up.'

'Nice call,' Janet said to Rachel, chancing to be in the Ladies at the same time. Janet brushing her hair, Rachel washing her hands.

'Hard to tell,' Rachel said. 'Godzilla wasn't giving anything away.'

'You were late, you weren't prepped – two strikes.'

'Three and you're out?'

'Not quite, but some rules are best not broken. She's a stickler, she has to be. And she expects the same from us.' Janet pulled her hair back, fixing it with a barrette, and made to leave.

'There's something else,' Rachel said quickly, unsure whether to mention it, knowing it was iffy, tenuous.

'Go on.' Janet paused at the door.

'We picked up a rape, back in 2008: Rosie Vaughan. She'd been in Ryelands.' It was a brutal attack, which made it all the more frustrating that they'd never pinned it on anyone. 'There could be a connection,' Rachel said.

'Because they were both in Ryelands?' Janet said incredulously, giving a look: *You thick or what?* Eyebrows high, mouth turning up, half a sneer.

'They'd both been in Ryelands, but both were living independently when it happened.'

'Ours is a murder, not a rape,' Janet argued.

'It could be a rape, too – we don't know. He used a knife.'

'Vaughan – did he stab her?'

Rachel shook her head.

'That it?'

Rachel wished she'd never raised it now.

'There's thin and then there's non-existent,' Janet said.

'But two attacks within eighteen months, both girls from—'

'They're not the same,' Janet insisted. 'Besides, you run an analysis of crime stats and feed in that demographic and you know what you'll get. The very fact that they were in care increases the likelihood of becoming a victim of crime, including a victim of serious sexual assault, several times over. Dig enough and you could find more rapes, domestic violence, assaults – it doesn't mean we're looking for a serial offender.' Janet looked at her, face screwed up in disapproval. Snotty cow. 'Did you have anyone in the frame?'

'The neighbour, for a while. He'd done a stretch for previous and he'd been hassling her, but we had nothing. She refused to press charges, wouldn't tell us who'd done it. She knew him, I'm convinced of that. Sean Broughton picked Lisa up when she was still in Ryelands. Maybe he'd done the same with Rosie. You're going there anyway, to Ryelands, aren't you? It wouldn't do any harm to ask if Sean was known to them back then.'

'DNA?'

'The rapist used a condom. We had traces in the flat from the neighbour, but that could have been from a previous visit. He used to call round for a cup of tea, he said, watch porn together. We'd unidentified DNA too – hair and skin cells, no hits. Case is still on file. She was a fruitloop, anyway. The whole thing was a mess.'

Janet was shaking her head. 'Sean's in the system. If he was your rapist, there'd have been a match.' Rachel could see it in her eyes, on a hiding to nothing, mind made up. Maybe someone made a mistake, Rachel thought, it has been known. She gave it one last try. 'Look, I could at least find out if Rosie knew him.'

'You could,' Janet said flatly, 'or you could actually do what you're supposed to be doing.'

When Rachel got back to her desk, she'd an email through from Lisa's phone company, a document attached, with the cell-site locations. She pulled up the mapping software and entered the coordinates. The first call, to Speedy Cabs, was made close to the end of Cross Street, near the Arndale Centre and the big wheel. The other calls, the ones Lisa received from Sean and Denise, were both taken at points along Oldham Road on the way to Fairland Avenue. It dovetailed with their information so far. Rachel felt a glow of satisfaction.

Rachel went and knocked on her ladyship's door. Her Maj waved her in, impatient rather than welcoming. Rachel held up the printout. 'Cell-site locations, it's all good.'

Gill nodded, pointed to a tray on the table by the filing cabinet. Returned to her screen.

You're welcome and fuck you too, ma'am.

Kevin was waiting for her as she came out. 'We'd better get going. You and me, a dark room, popcorn . . .' He gave a sleazy grin.

'Zip it, pal,' Rachel said, 'or I'll zip it for you,' letting an edge of the streets through. And she was that close;

another inane bleat and she'd lamp him. 'I'm off for a fag, see you in the car park.'

Luckily for Kevin, luckily for Rachel's prospects in the Manchester Metropolitan Police, he took heed. Sidled off muttering something about lezzies under his breath.

13

Ryelands House was a converted Edwardian manse set in its own grounds near Phillips Park in Newton Heath. It would originally have been the mill owner's property, built away from the cluster of narrow streets on the other side of the park. Nice view over the trees to the gasworks.

Janet had had dealings with the institution back when she was on Division. Mainly petty burglaries that led to the kids there.

The place was well maintained, with landscaped gardens and a play area in the large front plot. Shiny red double doors between the pillars of the porch leading into the house. Double-glazed and carpeted.

Marlene was the manager, had been for years. She remembered Janet and they exchanged pleasantries before getting down to business.

'I liked her,' Marlene said, 'and she didn't make it easy. I think, with more support, if she had been able to stay off the drugs, she might have done all right, but . . .' she sighed. 'The boyfriend, Sean Broughton – worst thing that could have happened. Lisa didn't let anyone get close, trusted no one, and then rolled out the red carpet when he came along.'

'What about the family? She spent some time with her mum?' Janet had read through Rachel's report on the interview with James Raleigh, noting the key facts ahead of this visit.

'The mother tried, but, well, not exactly gifted with parenting skills. The acting out at the onset of puberty – Lisa wanted attention, she needed boundaries. The early disruption had left her quite damaged. Denise Finn didn't have the wherewithal. Problems of her own. Then the brother's suicide . . .'

'He hung himself,' Janet said.

'From a lamppost outside his mother's house.'

'Oh, God.' Janet tried to imagine it, opening the door or the curtains and seeing that, facing that, Taisie or Elise swinging. She squashed the thought. But how would you ever forget the image? The rope or the belt, the body suspended, still, the face distorted. How did you ever reach a place where the earlier, innocent photos of school and holidays came into your head, instead of the ghastly death mask?

Janet had sat with victims' relatives in the past, heard them say, *I just can't get it out of my head, seeing her that way. Every time I close my eyes . . .* One distraught young son had seen his mother beaten to death with a poker by her ex-husband: *It's stuck there*, he cried, *I can't remember what she really looked like, she's just gone.* At least with Joshua, he'd looked peaceful, as if he was sleeping. Janet swallowed, fixed on what Marlene was saying.

'Nathan had problems of his own, was off his head on everything going. He'd started shooting up, stealing off Denise, mugging people. We offered Lisa bereavement counselling. I think she went a couple of times.'

'Tell me about Lisa's drug use when she was here,' Janet said.

Marlene raised her hands, a gesture of frustration. 'It's impossible to police. We're a home, not a secure unit. Drugs are out there, they get in here. Lisa was caught with aerosols, glue, weed – well, most of them try weed,' she said as an aside.

'Any Class A?'

'That only started once Sean came on the scene. We could see the signs. But she was never found with any.'

'He supplied it?'

'That'd be my guess,' Marlene said.

'James Raleigh had been talking to her about rehab,' Janet said.

There was a scuffling sound at the door and it swung wide open. An Asian girl wearing an outsize tracksuit and a red baseball cap burst into the room. 'Marlene? Oh, soz.'

'I'll be a few more minutes, Punam.'

'Cool.' The girl flicked a peace sign in their direction and left. Janet smiled; the energy, the liveliness, reminded her of Taisie on a good day.

'She's a doll,' Marlene said. 'She'll make it.' She

stretched in her seat. 'Lisa's social worker, Martin Dalbeattie, retired this spring. We've still got his number – I'm sure he'd be happy to talk to you, if you needed to know any more details about her time here.'

Janet thanked her and would have left it at that, but Rachel's persistent questions meant she had to ask. Just to convince herself there was nothing to it. 'Sean Broughton – had he been around here before he latched on to Lisa?'

'Don't think so.' Marlene thought harder. 'No.' She leaned forward, her head tilted, as if she'd share a confidence. 'And I am the all-seeing-eye,' she laughed.

It was a miracle Denise Finn was still talking and walking, given the trauma she'd been through. Where did she summon the strength to carry on? Perhaps after Nathan had died, she kept going for Lisa. But now? I couldn't do it, Janet thought, I would just lay down and die, a bit of help maybe, from the car exhaust, stones in pockets, pills and booze. But it wasn't true. She'd weathered hard times, survived. Not only with the baby, but before then. When she got ill.

Thinking of it brought the old, familiar tremor of anxiety. Like a faint aftershock from an earthquake, travelling from the soles of her feet to the crown of her head. She allowed herself to revisit the memories as she made the journey back to the office, having discovered that, if she tried to deny the feelings and not think about the events that had first triggered them, it only seemed to feed her fears, making them stronger, more feral.

Fifteen, studying for GCSEs and worried about her exams, Janet was finding it hard to sleep at night. They all expected her to do well. Her mother was sorting through a box of old photographs, one of her clean-ups. Janet at the dining-room table, trying to learn chunks of *King Lear* to regurgitate for the English Paper. *Oh, let me not be mad, not mad, sweet heaven . . .*

'Look at you there, then' – her mother thrust an old school photograph under her nose – 'butter wouldn't melt.'

Janet glanced dutifully at the photo. Primary school, class picture. She was seated, cross-legged on the front row. She could remember the hall, which doubled as a gym, the parquet floor that stank of polish and feet. The way you could make squeaky noises as you walked, especially with your pumps on.

'And there's Veronica next to you.'

Janet grunted. Veronica had bad teeth, sort of greeny grey at the front, that reminded her of bread with mould on. She had a plastic coat that was meant to look like leather but didn't. The coat squeaked too.

'They never did find out who killed her,' Janet's mother mused.

Time stopped. Janet stared at the girl's face; Veronica was grinning. 'What?'

'She was murdered,' her mum said. 'Awful.'

'You said she'd gone away.' Janet looked at her mother.

'You were six,' her mother said. 'I wasn't going to tell you what had really happened. You'd have been petrified.'

'What did happen?' Janet felt confused, angry.

'She was abducted,' her mother said, 'on the way home from school one day. They found her in the woods, stuffed in a holdall.'

Her mum took back the photograph.

Janet tried to carry on with her revision, but it was impossible to concentrate. She brooded over it for the rest of the day: how could she not have known about a murder? But she realized that, aged six, she would not have watched the news, or read the papers. She used to walk home with Veronica sometimes. She remembered that. They weren't best mates or anything, not in the same group at playtime, just lived in the same direction. One day, Veronica had been offered a lift. Janet said no – it had been drummed into them: *Don't take sweets from strangers, don't go with a stranger, don't get into a stranger's car* – but Veronica had known the driver. At least, that's the impression Janet had got. But Janet knew that didn't count for her. If she didn't know the person herself, then she mustn't get into the car. She had to say no. Was that the day of the abduction?

Janet felt sick. She laid awake half the night, trying to remember more, frustrated that she couldn't. I should have stopped her, she thought, asked her who it was, if she really knew them. She might still be alive if I'd only done that.

Why hadn't the police solved the murder? Why hadn't they asked Janet about it? She could have described the car if it had been fresh in her memory.

The guilt grew like a fungus inside her. And the

anxiety, the sensation of the floor heaving, something crawling up her spine, twisting in her belly.

In an effort to find out more, she went to Oldham Central Library and scoured the microfiche, nervous in case one of the librarians saw what she was looking up and told her off. She read what she could quickly, almost not wanting to know, the details lodging in her mind, her back tense, her mouth dry. A navy-blue holdall, a shallow grave, someone walking the dog, a brutal murder. They didn't say exactly how Veronica died. What Janet didn't know, she made up. Her darkest fantasies filling the vacuum.

The murder played over and over in her head like a reel of film. Veronica's terror became her own. She felt the unease as the car drove away from town, the spittle of the killer on her face, his hand in her knickers, the soil in her nose and mouth.

She would open her biology textbook or *King Lear – How sharper than a serpent's tooth it is, To have a thankless child* – and the words swam. What was the point?

Abandoning any hope of sleep, she tried to study through the night. Her head ached and she felt sick all the time. Her dad, sensing something was going on, tried to jolly her along: 'Exams won't last for ever, and then you can burn your books.'

'She'll do no such thing,' her mother retorted. 'She's still got her A-levels to do.'

Janet pretended to be going to a friend's and went to the doctor's to ask if they could give her something to help her sleep. The doctor was very sympathetic, said she had a lot of people with exam nerves, but generally it was better to let nature take its course. A regular routine was good, no tea or coffee in the evening. At that point, Janet had burst into tears. The doctor calmed her down, asked if there was anything else. Janet considered telling her about Veronica, but decided it would sound crazy.

The doctor gave her a week's supply of sleeping pills. *Take one at bedtime. Get you back in the habit.* They worked, pulling her down into a black velvet tunnel. But after the week was up, it was the same as before, lying there with the light on, her limbs rigid, the pictures rolling through her. Then it was her first exam.

She couldn't go in the gate. She couldn't do it. If she had to go and sit in the silent hall with the sound of the clock ticking and other people's breathing and the pictures in her head – the disgusting thoughts in her head, Veronica with worms in her mouth – Janet knew all that stuff inside her head would escape. She would lose control, turn her desk over, shout obscenities, tell them all it was her fault.

And so Janet stood, humming with tension, while the pupils streamed into school. While the clock struck nine and the invigilator told them to turn over their papers. While her fellow pupils printed their names and began to read through the questions. She stood, cold and shaky. Where could she go?

'Janet?'

Ade from down the road. Lower sixth. 'You lost?' He smiled, his little joke.

She began to shiver.

'Shouldn't you be in there?'

'I can't, I can't . . .' she stammered. Words failing. Janet failing.

'OK.' He came closer, concern in his face. But not fear. Why wasn't he frightened? If he knew what she was thinking . . . She bit her knuckles, rocking forward.

He put his arm around her, it felt warm across her shoulders, safe.

'Would you like to go home?' he said.

She nodded.

'OK, then.' And he walked her back. He was so kind. Here she was, a total nutter, throwing a fit, and he didn't freak or anything, just walked her back. Went in with her, made a cup of tea.

'I'm scared,' she told him, her eyes stinging, her body trembling, nerves singing. 'I'm so scared, I don't know what to do. I don't know what to do.'

He put his hand on her arm. 'Do you want me to ring the doctor?'

She had seen *One Flew Over the Cuckoo's Nest*. Felt a fresh lurch of fear. 'What will they do?'

'Don't know,' he admitted. 'But they'll try and help, yeah? What about your mum?'

'No!' Janet didn't want her parents, didn't want to have to explain. See the look on their faces when they knew she had missed her exam.

Ade shrugged and phoned the surgery for her.

She was biting her hand again and she tasted blood.

He waited while they came and talked to her. Even when Janet let the panic free and began to hit at the table and talk too fast, he stayed.

And then he came to visit. Getting the bus three times a week. He made her smile, he brought her little treats, left her letters. He was solid. Unfazed. Their first kiss – on the psychiatric ward.

She got better, came home, re-did fifth form. Passed her exams the year Ade did his A-levels. He went to Leeds to do Geography. Janet had chosen Sociology, English and Biology at A-level. Courses that the careers service said would be useful for her ambition to join the police. She hadn't saved Veronica, but maybe one day she could find out what had happened to her. Get her some justice. And if not for Veronica, then maybe she could do the same for other families.

Ade, her knight in shining armour. Not just then but later. She'd said as much to Gill in the long dark days after Joshua's death: *He rescued me.*

14

Gill worked till half eight then called it a day. Drove home and found Sammy playing on the Xbox, his friends gone. She thought she could smell the faint trace of tobacco, but wasn't sure enough to challenge him.

'Revision?' she asked.

'Done a bit.'

'Enough?'

He nodded his head.

'OK.'

She put the fresh tuna on the griddle and dug out some salad, emptied leftover potatoes into a dish for the microwave. She had got into the habit of making extra food to use up the following day and save herself time.

The kitchen wasn't too messy, though the waste bin was overflowing with plastic pop bottles and pot noodle containers. Why was it beyond Sammy to make use of the recycling bins? She took the bottles outside. The temperature had plummeted and the cold nipped at her fingers and nose. She could see lights glowing from the windows of the farmhouse on the moor. Above, the cloud had cleared and she could make out some stars. Not many, not like on holidays. That was one of the things that was so memorable about trips away, so vivid. The wealth of stars under foreign skies. Sitting on a veranda with Dave while Sammy slept soundly, exhausted by the day's snorkelling or skiing. Gill relishing their time together. They had some brilliant holidays – not many, it had been a nightmare getting their diaries in synch for time off. Especially as they had to go in school breaks. So when they could pull it off, they went all out. Splurged on the Maldives, the Rockies, or a safari in Kenya. Scuba-diving. White-water rapids. They worked so hard the rest of the time. 'We deserve it,' Dave would say. And she agreed.

All that had changed. No fancy holidays now.

She dashed back in and put the food on her plate. Once she'd finished eating she dug out the chocolate from its hiding place in the top cupboard. As if by magic, Sammy wandered in.

'Oh, yes,' he said, seeing the slab.

'Mine.' Gill narrowed her eyes.

'One piece – go on.'

She gave him a black look, broke off a bit and handed it to him. 'Give you spots,' she warned.

'I've already got spots,' he said. 'Oh, it was well good . . .' his eyes lit up, 'in the Russian test, the one before ours, this girl said she felt ill and the teacher said she couldn't leave the room and she just barfed, like threw up everywhere. And the worst thing was' – his face animated, relishing the memory – 'the rest of them had to stay there and do the test after that!'

'They cleared it up?' Gill said.

'Yeah, but you could still smell it. We could even smell it in the afternoon. They should give us extra marks.'

'In your dreams, matey.'

'A bit more?' He nodded at the chocolate.

'No. You'll be sick.'

'Har har.'

'Want me to test you?'

'No,' he said. 'Gonna watch *Peep Show*.'

'You start.'

They shared a love of good comedy and there wasn't much else they watched together. Sammy liked extreme sports and adventure stuff. Gill's guilty pleasure was costume drama. Something a million miles away from work, that she could deride and poke fun at, but that felt cosy, comforting, the televisual equivalent of hot chocolate. She heard Sammy laughing from the other room. He was a good kid.

Three years since she and Dave split up. Sammy wasn't doing so bad, but Gill still couldn't tell whether he was putting a brave face on things for her sake. She had done her best not to slag Dave off in front of Sammy, always referring to him in a civilized tone, but the boy wasn't a fool, he knew Dave had wrecked the marriage, that it was Dave who had been shagging around and who now lived across town with the uniform from Pendlebury. Sammy had been hurt; he missed his dad, although recently they had got into the routine of weekend visits together.

It was Janet who Gill had turned to for help in the wake of walking in on Dave and said uniform. Her own house, her own bed, her own so-called husband, arse in the air, blonde bimbo with a fake tan, cooing, 'Ooh, Dave, ooh, Dave!' as Gill stood there, sick, seething.

There had been a vase of lilies on the dressing table: big, white, waxy flowers, a heavy, thick glass vase. Gill had grabbed it, hurled with all her might before escaping downstairs and out of the house. Beside herself with fury and the pain. To tell Janet. To get drunk.

'I can't sling him out,' Gill had said to Janet. 'I'm back in Grimsby on Monday on the dock job – nearly done but I can't blob now.' A double murder, body parts recovered from tea chests on the dockside. North Yorkshire force had got nowhere in nine long months so asked the crime faculty for input.

'The packing case?' Janet said.

'Hah!' Gill laughed at the pun. Thinking: How can I laugh? How is it possible to laugh? Why is something still functioning when I feel so broken? 'He'll have to look after Sammy. But I can't stay with him, not in the long run. I won't.'

'Have you talked to him?' Janet said.

'No.' Gill shook her head. 'I can't look at him, can't bear the sight of him.'

'You have to talk to him,' Janet said.

'I know. She can't be more than twenty-five, the whore.' Gill groaned: 'I feel such a fool.'

'You're not.'

Gill pressed her hands to her temples. Took a breath, exhaled slowly. 'I knew.'

'What?' Janet had peered at her, surprised.

'Maybe not name, rank and badge number, but . . . the flirting . . . the charm offensive. Easy to pretend that's all it was, but—' She thought of all the moments, little jarring moments, like missteps in a dream. Over the years, so many glances from Dave to . . . well, pick a woman, any woman. Then there were those occasional phone calls: *Is Dave there?* Her thinking, and who the fuck are you? Smelling deceit, but playing the game. Years of lies about where he'd been or who he'd seen. With Gill traipsing around the country, he had free rein. 'You remember when I started at the faculty? Ten years ago. I thought he was having an affair then. Sammy was four at the time. I came back for the weekend and Dave had changed the sheets?'

'You thought the nanny had done it,' Janet said.

'That's right, thanked her, not part of her job. She hadn't. I couldn't let it go. He swore there was nothing going on. Then he got the hump. Slung his phone at me, diary, the lot. 'Look at it,' he said, 'all of it.' And I didn't. I chose to believe him. I didn't want to know, Janet.'

Janet nodded, a wry smile on her face.

'Same way I've tuned out the gossip over the years. Little snippets. Bastard! In our bed! In our house!' She wanted to punch something. Rip up his clothes, batter his car with a sledgehammer, superglue his cock to his

121

arse, cut off his balls and post them to Pendlebury. She wanted to weep. 'Did you know?'

'That he was having an affair? No,' Janet said.

'Affairs plural,' Gill asked. 'You knew he was putting it about?'

Janet paused. Gill trusted her to be honest, they'd been through too much together not to be. 'Like you say, there were rumours,' Janet said.

'But you never came to me. You didn't think I should know?' Gill asked her, anxious now, fearful of losing Janet, too. Of feeling betrayed by everyone that mattered.

'They were rumours, Gill. If there had ever been something concrete staring me in the face, then I would have told you. Of course I would.'

Gill nodded, relieved. But the anger and the sense of humiliation flooded back through her. 'I can just imagine it when word gets out.' She dragged a hand through her hair. 'All the clichés. I'm a walking fucking cliché. Wifey the last to know. Cat's away and the mice – fuck!'

'You'll be all right. It doesn't feel that way now, but you will.'

'I hope she gives him herpes. I hope they get scabies too, and that everything they touch turns to shit. This is killing me. I can't do it. It'll kill me.' She caught the twinkle in Janet's eyes, saw Janet fighting not to laugh. Gill punched her in the arm. 'I'm allowed to be melo-dramatic,' she said. 'If ever there was a time for melodrama, this is it.'

'I'll give you that.'

'I am not going to be that woman who stands by her man, smile glued in place,' Gill said.

'Whatever happens, you'll be all right. You've got a fantastic job, you've got Sammy, you've got mates.'

'And a big fuck-off house,' Gill added. 'He's not getting his paws on that.'

'Can you afford to buy him out?'

'Probably not, but I'm not losing that house. I'll live on bread and dripping first. Take in lodgers, anything. But I'll keep that house.'

'Good,' Janet said.

And I have, Gill thought now. Still here, living and breathing. She opened the fridge and poured herself a glass of milk. Took it through and sat down on the sofa. Sammy moved over, raising his feet so she could massage them.

'You showered?'

'Not yet.'

'Forget it then.'

He laughed and slid his legs off her knees.

Gill smiled and turned her attention to the screen where one of the characters was going into meltdown. She should make a date with Janet. Hard with so much on, but you let things slide and when you finally look up your social life has curled up in a corner and died. Yes, she'd do that. Time they had a proper catch-up.

15

Rachel and Kevin walked the streets around Shudehill, identifying cameras before visiting the monitoring centre to download the relevant files. Lee, as exhibits officer, checked the downloads in and then Rachel and Kevin settled in for the duration. Sitting side by side, with a screen each, running film from different cameras, aiming to retrace Lisa's movements back through town. Rachel found her on the footage within ten minutes of starting, found Kasim's cab first, on Shudehill at 13.06, opposite the bus station. Played the tape backwards to see Lisa stepping out of the taxi, with a load of shopping bags in her hands. The taxi reversing away and Lisa setting the bags down on the pavement. Rachel's pulse gave a jump. Yes! 'Someone's had fun,' she said.

That was by far the easiest part of the task. It had taken another hour and a half, by which point Rachel's back was killing her and she was gagging for a smoke, to find Lisa coming out of the Arndale, down the big steps, on Cross Street. To trace the movements inside the complex, they needed to view the separate footage from the retailers' cameras. Kevin rang and put in a request via the security manager there.

Rachel could have gone home then, she knew she probably should have gone home then, but *should* was a word she refused to kowtow to. It's worth checking out, she told herself. All my own time. If it's a dead end who's to know?

She could still remember where Rosie Vaughan had lived, a block of flats in New Moston. She could still remember her first glimpse of the girl, the misshapen face, the bloodied eye, split lips, the bruises that marked her body. The smell of shit. Rosie had soiled herself in the course of the beating.

A neighbour had called them – not the pervy one but the tenant below who had heard shouts and screams above the noise from the television. Unable to get a response and with reason to believe there was a risk of harm, the police had broken in. The assailant had gone by then.

Now Rachel parked and made her way to the entrance, didn't have to wait long for someone to leave the building and let her into the foyer. Once inside she chose the stairwell over the lift. Stepped over the chip papers and lager cans that littered the half-landings. She could smell the concrete and piss and a trace of gunpowder. Kids messing with fireworks.

Rachel knocked on the door and listened. Heard only

vacant silence. And from somewhere down below a dog barking, rapid and gruff.

She knocked again, louder, and the door across the hall opened, the pervy bloke appeared. 'She's probably out,' he said, narrowing his eyes. Was he trying to place her? Rachel hadn't ever interviewed the man, she'd dealt with Rosie mainly.

'Rosie?' Rachel said, needed to check she still lived in the block, that they were talking about the same person.

'You can come in and wait,' he leered, scratching at his chest.

Jesus, she could smell him from here. The sweet stench of human grime. His fingernails were black with dirt. Food crumbs in his beard. Rachel tensed, ready to run, or knee the bloke if he lunged for her. 'Where would she be?'

He'd mad eyes, glittering like beads. 'The canal, or maybe the old chapel.'

Rachel walked off, not too quickly, not prepared to let him think he'd rattled her, but on her toes, ready. He didn't follow.

She reached the canal on foot, it ran behind the flats. The street lighting was brutal, an attempt to improve security. The water between the stone banks looked oily in the glare. Smelled pungent in the cold air. The canal was full of rubbish, plastic bags and bottles, chunks of polystyrene. There was no one about, but ahead on the left she saw the bridge and a glow of yellow flickering in the tunnel underneath. A fire.

She walked, as quietly as she could, along the

towpath and drawing closer made out a group of people huddled round the flames. Three lads, and at the far side of the semicircle, Rosie. Stick thin, ginger hair, glasses, a denim jacket. She didn't even have a hat on, though it was close to freezing.

Rachel considered the lads: older teenagers, their hoodies and tracksuits shabby, nothing new. Edging nearer, she could see a giant-sized bottle of cheap wine. A smoke was doing the rounds. Weed, maybe? Yes, she could detect the distinctive heady smell of cannabis. Sudden laughter. And Rosie kicked out at one of the lads.

'Rosie?'

The group stilled, one of the lads jumped up. 'What d'you want?' he said. Rachel stared at his face, noted the jut of his chin, the slack expression, mouth breather. 'A word with Rosie there, all right, pal?' Not frightened of him.

Rosie got up, she stumbled, and Rachel saw she was very drunk.

'You're police?' said one of them.

Rosie hesitated, Rachel was worried she'd topple in the canal if she didn't move away from the edge. But the lads shuffled back and the girl walked past, skirting the fire.

'Youse the cops?' the lad said again.

'Shut it, Dec,' said his mate.

Rosie came closer, her eyes bleary, the bones of her cheeks and her clavicle jutting out.

Rachel walked her along a few metres to where there

was a simple plank bench. 'You remember me?' she said. 'Here,' Rachel offered the girl a cigarette, took one herself. Lit them. 'How've you been?' Needing to start somewhere, though she could see the kid was half off her head.

''Kay.' Looking back to her mates, to the fire. She shook with cold.

'The assault, the rape . . .' Rachel said, seeing the girl stiffen immediately. 'It was someone you knew?'

'No,' the girl said quickly.

Rachel didn't believe her. 'I think it was,' Rachel said. 'That's why you refused to make a statement, why you wouldn't press charges. You were frightened of him. Frightened he would make you pay if you shopped him.'

The girl shook her head, then sucked hard on the cigarette.

A train rattled past somewhere close, making it difficult to hear anything else. As the racket faded away, Rachel said, 'I'm investigating another case. It might be the same bloke.' She studied the girl, who just sat shivering, staring across the canal, tapping nervously at the end of her cigarette with her thumbnail. 'Does the name Sean Broughton mean anything to you?'

Rosie shook her head slowly. No reaction, no increase in stress as far as Rachel could see.

'This other girl, she was in Ryelands, too.' Rachel caught the flinch that the name of the home provoked and felt her own heartbeat quicken. 'Was it someone you knew from Ryelands?' Rachel asked. 'Just tell me that. I don't need a name, I can find out.' Speaking fast, rushing to convince her.

Rosie turned. 'No, it wasn't. No, it wasn't,' she cried. 'Why have you come back?' Her face white with anxiety, eyes wide, the pupils huge from the drugs or the drink. She was shuddering, her breath catching and uneven. 'I didn't see his face. I just want to forget it, I told you before.'

'How? Look at the state of you,' Rachel said. 'You've not forgotten. You let them get away with it. And now they might have hurt someone else.' All things she should have kept to herself, unhelpful, unprofessional. 'We can protect you,' Rachel went on.

'I never seen him,' Rosie shouted. 'Just go, will you, fuck off.' She leapt to her feet and walked unsteadily back to her friends, and Rachel heard the hubbub of questions and remarks as she reached the tunnel.

Rachel lobbed her cigarette into the canal, retraced her steps. Rosie didn't know Sean, she trusted her on that, but Ryelands? There was something there, but she needed to find a way to introduce it to the inquiry without getting a total bollocking or being laughed out of court.

16

Janet was shattered at the start of the day. She'd arrived home the night before to find Elise and Taisie going at it like something off *Jerry Springer*. Ade out at a leaving do for someone at school. As Janet came through the door, she could hear thumping from upstairs and Taisie screaming, 'Give it me back, you slag. You bitch. Give it me now.'

'Oy!' Janet called out. 'What's going on?'

'Give it me!'

Janet got halfway upstairs in time to see Taisie land a kick on Elise's bedroom door. Taisie was incandescent, her face red with exertion, eyes wild.

'What's going on?' Janet said again.

Taisie, only now aware of her there, rounded on her mother, as though Janet was also to blame: 'She's got my phone and she won't give it back!'

'Elise?' Janet called. 'Open the door.'

'She tried to hit me,' Elise said, slightly muffled. 'Tell her off.'

'Why did you hit her?' Janet asked Taisie, who was unable to stand still, seething with outrage.

'I didn't, I missed,' snapped Taisie. 'And she took my phone, I told you, dumbo.'

'Hey!' Janet glared at Taisie. 'Open the door, Elise,' she said again.

She heard Elise fumbling with the lock. She had seen it so many times before. Taisie wronged by her bigger brighter sister, going off like a warehouse full of fire-crackers while Elise, sensible and clever and sometimes a little holier than thou, took the moral high ground.

Elise opened the door and Taisie lunged, but Janet caught her arm. 'Cool it, lady,' she said. Then turned to Elise, 'Give her the phone.'

Elise was flushed, a righteous look on her face. 'But she—'

'Give it,' Janet said firmly, 'and then you can explain.'

'I haven't done anything wrong,' Elise protested, all wounded innocence. 'Anyway, she's—'

'Elise,' Janet cautioned.

Elise thrust out the phone, which Taisie snatched, snarling, 'Loser.'

'Taisie.'

'Well, she is,' Taisie retorted. 'She's no life of her own, so she's spying on me.'

Janet looked to Elise for an explanation.

'Why don't you ask her what she's got on her phone?' Elise said. 'You've heard of cyber bullying?'

Janet turned to Taisie.

'It's not, it's just a joke,' the younger girl said.

'Unless you're on the receiving end,' Elise said sharply.

Janet held out her hand for the phone. Taisie coloured and Janet could see her gauging whether to refuse. 'Give it.'

'I hate you, you sad cow,' Taisie yelled at Elise, as she plonked the phone in Janet's outstretched hand.

'Hate you more,' Elise said.

Janet wasn't sure what she was looking for on the phone but needed to appear in control. 'I'll keep this for now,' she stalled. 'You both must have some homework to do.'

'It's in the picture files,' Elise said smugly.

Taisie stamped off to her room, banging the door hard.

Don't slam it, Janet thought, but let it go.

She ate the warmed-up remains of beef curry as she navigated the phone. Found the picture directory, spotted the file name: *Mr Fairy*. It was Taisie's form tutor, doctored to show the man with breasts and a tutu. It was crudely done, but effective if you wanted to lampoon the bloke. Janet could take him or leave him but had gathered he was unpopular with the kids. All the same, there was something cruel and distasteful in what they were doing. Eleven-year-olds!

Leaving Taisie to stew, Janet ran a bath. She thought about Lisa Finn's missing phone. What might be on there, what it might tell them? Someone had taken it, concealed it. Because of what it might reveal? Or something more basic? Phone equals dosh. Sean would have reason to take it if he needed money for drugs. Or the killer might have stolen it, knowing it betrayed clues as to his identity. Was Sean the killer? She couldn't tell. And that was OK; early days. You couldn't rush an investigation, you'd be likely to muck it up if you did.

After her bath, Janet went to Taisie, the phone in hand. Taisie was sitting on her bed, school books spread out around her, but Janet had no idea whether she had done any work or simply arranged them for effect. Parents' evenings, the ones she made it to, and the ones Ade had reported back on, brought less-than-glowing reports on Taisie's work. She was slapdash and careless. Her reading and numeracy levels were almost a year short of the average for her age, though the school couldn't find any specific problem to account for it, no dyslexia or other learning difficulty. Her attitude was found wanting too. They had hoped that the move to High School would be a fresh start, a turning point, but this didn't bode well.

Janet sometimes thought it was as if Taisie, realizing Elise was a high achiever, motivated and hard-working, the swot of the family, had decided to carve out a different niche for herself in reaction. Wayward, bolshie, bold. At the end of the day, Janet wanted both her girls to be happy. Unlike Ade, she didn't care over-much if Taisie shunned the academic route, but she passionately wanted her to do well in some field, to know the sense of achievement, the boost to self-esteem, the sheer engagement that came from a job well done, from having skills and being a success. Whenever Taisie showed any glimmer of interest in something: street dance, ice-skating, guitar, woodwork, Janet was 100 per cent behind her: encouraging, interested, shelling out for all the gear. And all too often Taisie's interest faded as quickly as it had blossomed. The roof space was half-full of discarded tennis racquets and jewellery-making kits, magic sets and martial arts outfits.

'How do you think he feels?' Janet held up the phone.

'It's only a joke,' Taisie said.

'I'm not laughing. Would you like it if it was you? Would it make you laugh?'

'I wouldn't care,' Taisie said dismissively, with a toss of her head.

'You think?' Janet said. 'And if it was me or your dad?'

She didn't say anything.

'This is a form of bullying.' Janet sat on the edge of the bed. 'I don't want you to be a bully. You're better than that.'

'It's not,' Taisie began, though Janet could see the alteration in her expression, a hint of embarrassment.

'It is,' Janet said, 'and it can start with a picture like this, and then another, and then something worse, something online. And everyone's having a laugh, but it gets nastier and people say awful things, mean and hurtful things.'

'We didn't mean anything bad,' Taisie said, her voice small, mouth turned down.

'The police get involved sometimes, you know. Intentional harassment – it's taken seriously.'

Taisie stared at her, her face a mix of anxiety and bravado.

'Exactly this sort of thing,' Janet went on. 'Bullying.'

'He's a teacher,' Taisie said.

'Doesn't matter. He's a person, he's a human being. You don't have to like him, but you treat him the same as you'd want for yourself.' Taisie had gone quiet. Janet knew she was getting through to her. 'So how are you going to make this right?'

Taisie shrugged, a jerk of the shoulders up and back, one fingernail scraping at the nail polish she'd tried last week.

At ten? Ade had said, *tarting herself up, rampant sexualization.*

It's hardly nipple tassels and a thong, Janet had replied. *You make a fuss and she'll push it further, you know what she's like.*

'Absolutely no idea?' Janet prompted Taisie.

'Delete it.'

'Be a start. And you could tell your friends to do the same, and tell them your mum's talking about opening an investigation if there's any more of it.'

'Mum!'

'It's not a joke,' Janet said. 'So you do that and then give me your phone.'

'What?' Taisie glared at her.

'No phone for a week. No MSN – the lot.'

'That is so not fair. That is tight!'

'Yep,' Janet said. 'So maybe you'll think twice next time.' She got up to leave. 'And tell whoever did the

135

photoshop that the tutu was too small,' she added on her way out.

'It was the only one—' Taisie stopped abruptly, but not soon enough.

Gotcha! Janet paused at the door. Taisie had the grace to blush. Perhaps art was the way to go? Or IT? Collage or photomontage her thing. Get her a camera for Christmas, given her recent surge of interest in photography. How much was a decent camera these days? Too much? Ade could do some research.

Elise was on the landing, pretending to come out of the bathroom. 'Heard enough?' Janet asked her.

'Is she grounded?' Elise said. 'Have you taken her phone?'

'No phone for a week. But you could have waited till I got back, let me deal with it.'

'She'd have wiped it by then,' Elise protested.

By the time Janet got downstairs Ade had arrived and she had to fill him in on it all, and when she finally did get to bed she remembered she still had to sort out her mum's birthday present. And she worried about Taisie. She did her best, but what if it wasn't enough? What then?

I did my best, Denise Finn had said. We all do. Until it goes wrong and all you can hear is that mocking voice inside, nagging away: *Could I have done more, done it differently?*

Ade snored all night. She kicked him every so often and he made huffing sounds and turned over and after a few minutes he was off snoring again. By the time she sat down to plan an interview strategy for Sean Broughton the next morning she felt dog rough. Damned if she'd let it show though.

17

As in the first interview, Janet reminded Sean that he was not under arrest and was free to leave; she made it clear he did not have to answer any of the questions and could ask for a solicitor if he wished. She thanked him for coming in.

Once again Rachel made notes.

Janet had taken Rachel through the strategy, showing her how she aimed to first recap with Sean his existing statement and then ask more probing questions about the details that concerned them: the missing shopping, the missing phone, the lapse of time between Sean's alleged discovery of the body and the 999 call. Rachel had listened carefully, stopped to clarify points, clearly fascinated. 'Anything else you suggest?' Janet had invited her to contribute.

Rachel thought for a moment. 'The knife, the weapon – could he tell if there was one missing? Did he remove it from the scene?'

'What do we know about the weapon?'

'Not much. According to the post-mortem, it's a medium-sized kitchen-type knife,' Rachel said.

'Was it in the flat or brought to the flat?'

Rachel shrugged. 'We don't know.'

'Are we sure a knife was used?'

'Well, a knife or similar implement.'

Janet studied Rachel; she hadn't picked up on the difference between discussing the weapon and the other items. 'We can't demonstrate any of those things,' Janet explained. 'No conflicting evidence, so we can't prove or disprove what he's telling us. Whether he's lying. But with the shopping, the phone, and timing of the emergency call we have distinct evidence, separately acquired, which we can use to test Sean's account.'

'Catch him out.' Rachel gave a nod of understanding, a glint in her eyes. 'I want to go for tier three.' Janet caught a glimpse of the girl's ambition, her hunger to learn. Now all she needed was to apply that willingness to all the areas of the job instead of just the bits she liked.

Sean appeared to be calmer than on the previous day. Numb around the edges. Eyes still bloodshot, though. Had he slept?

Janet had decided she would open with the phone call to Lisa. This wasn't one of the three key areas, but it remained an anomaly. Would his story have changed? 'Yesterday, you told me that you rang Lisa shortly after one o'clock. And we've been able to confirm that from phone records. Please can you tell me again what the phone call was about?'

'I wanted to know when she'd be back, like,' Sean replied, 'and she said about half three.' Although she was practically home by then.

'Was there anything unusual about the call?'

'No,' he said.

'You told me yesterday that Lisa had gone shopping, that's correct?'

'Yes,' he agreed, perhaps a tinge of uncertainty underlying the answer.

'What was Lisa going to get?'

'Don't know. Some clothes, I think.' He tried to sound casual, but Janet could feel the tension rising in the room. He rubbed at his chest, a soothing gesture. Was his heart racing? His breath becoming hard to catch?

'Did she buy anything?'

'I don't know,' he said. He looked at Janet, but his gaze soon slipped away.

'When you came back to the flat at half past three, was there any shopping there?'

He gave a little sigh, almost a moan, and laced his fingers together. 'No, I didn't see any.'

'We have been able to establish that Lisa got a taxi home from town and she was carrying five bags of shopping. The taxi took her home. Yet you say when you went to the flat there was no shopping. Can you explain that to me?'

'Dunno, maybe she put it away,' he said hesitantly.

'And the shopping bags? We didn't find those in the flat either. Can you account for that?' He didn't speak. Janet saw his jaw tighten. She waited a few seconds, then: 'Where did Lisa usually keep her phone when she was at home?'

Sean moved in his seat, reacting to the new topic. 'What d'you mean?' Buying time.

'Where would her phone be when she was in the flat?'

'In her pocket or . . . on the table.'

'The coffee table?'

'Yes.'

Janet remembered the photographs, the table topsy-turvy, Lisa's body wedged alongside it. 'Yesterday, you said you didn't see Lisa's phone when you went to the flat. Is that true?'

'Yes. I didn't see anything,' he said, 'just her, seeing her like that . . . That's all I remember.' His voice was shaky.

'I asked you yesterday if you had removed anything from the flat and you said you hadn't. I'm going to ask you that question again now: did you remove anything from the flat?'

'I didn't,' he said, 'I didn't take anything.' Blinking.

'Lisa came back from town with five bags of shopping and her mobile phone. When you called us to the flat, those items were missing. That makes me think that they are of significance to this inquiry.' Or you wanted to make some easy money robbing the dead. 'Can tell me anything about that?'

'No, I don't know,' he said.

'We need your help to find out who did this to Lisa.'

'I'd tell you if I could. Course I would.'

He was becoming alarmed, so Janet lowered her

voice, deliberately relaxing her posture before she went on: 'In your statement you said that you arrived at the flat at three thirty and found Lisa, and covered her with a duvet. Then rang the police. Is that right?'

'Yes.'

'Are you absolutely certain it was that time when you got there?'

'About then.'

'Can you think of anyone who saw you on your way there who could confirm that for us?'

'No. No one I knew, like. The school, you could ask them,' he said.

'How long does it take to walk to Lisa's from your house?'

'Five minutes.'

'You covered Lisa with the duvet then; please describe to me what you did next.'

'I called the police.' His face looked drawn, his hands clamped together.

'That call didn't come into us until five past four. That means there was a period of thirty-five minutes between you finding Lisa and summoning help.' Janet kept her eyes on his face. 'How do you account for that?'

He didn't say anything.

'Can you describe to me what you were doing during that time?'

'Can't remember,' he said. A weak response.

'Did you leave the flat between half past three and four o'clock?'

'No.'

'You live five minutes away. Did you go home and return to the flat and then ring us?' Change your clothes, Janet thought, get rid of the shopping and the phone, hide the knife.

'No.'

'Sean, is there anything in your statement you would like to change?'

'No.' He bit at his thumb again, an almost childish gesture.

'You see, I'm having a problem seeing how these things fit together. That makes me think that perhaps events weren't exactly how you describe them.'

He sat silently, though his face flickered with emotion.

'Let's go back to the phone call . . .' Janet began again.

After another hour of persistent questioning, examining Sean's account in minute detail, presenting him time and again with the inconsistencies, there was a knock at the door. Rachel went to answer it and returned with a piece of paper that she gave to Janet. Janet opened the paper: CCTV *from Arndale – Lisa shoplifting items and placing them in her own bags.* Oh, yes! Another piece of the puzzle. But why was Sean lying? In the light of murder, shoplifting was way down the priority list. So why bother trying to cover up that? Or were his lies designed to conceal his part in Lisa's death? Janet still had no idea. All she could do was continue to chip away.

'That was fresh evidence,' she told Sean. 'I am able to tell you that we now know Lisa was shoplifting in town, that she came home with stolen goods. I'll ask you again: can you tell me where those items are?'

Sean angled his face up to the ceiling, let his hands slump by his sides. Submission. 'I took them,' he said, then looked briefly at Janet. 'I got rid of them.'

Janet resisted the temptation to make eye contact with Pete or to turn round and see Rachel's reaction at the breakthrough this represented. It was important to maintain the connection with Sean. As long as he was still talking to her, she was in effect the only person in the room with him. 'Why?' Janet asked. To sell them on? Funding a drug habit was no easy thing. 'Why did you take them?'

'I just did.'

'What did you do with them?'

'I got rid of them, I told you,' he said.

'Why?'

'I don't know.'

'Where did you get rid of them?'

He sat for a few moments, his eyes downcast. Running through the possibilities? 'In the bins, the dumpsters behind the shops, on Garrigan Street.'

'When?'

'Straight after. After I saw her.'

'Before you rang the police?' Janet said.

'Yes.'

'So, you did leave the flat?'

'Yes.' He swallowed.

'And Lisa's phone?'

'I took that too.'

'What did you do with the phone?'

'Same,' he said.

'Why?'

'Dunno.'

'There must be a reason,' Janet said.

'No, I'm just . . . I wasn't thinking right.'

'Why didn't you tell us this in your original statement?' Janet said.

He shrugged, shook his head. He looked close to tears.

'Sean, is there anything else you'd like to tell us?'

'No.'

'Anything else you'd like to change from your original statement?'

'No,' he said.

'Sean, I need to ask you something now, and I want you to think very, very carefully about your answer. Can you tell me anything about how Lisa died?'

'No, no,' he shook his head, 'I just found her.' He was frightened. With good cause. He had waited to call the police for over half an hour. He had taken items away from the crime scene, he had disturbed the crime scene, he had a volatile relationship with the victim. Janet thought they might be moving close to an arrest. She concluded the interview, but told Sean he would be expected to return to the station when requested as they would definitely need to talk to him again.

* * *

Gill had been observing the interview and told Janet she had already contacted Phil Sweet to secure the bins behind the parade of shops on Garrigan Street. 'Not much of the parade left,' Gill said. 'There's only a pound shop, an offie and a hairdresser's still open.'

Pete had established that bin day was Thursday, which meant the rubbish would not have been collected since Sean left the things there on Monday. MIT were able to give Phil Sweet a list describing the carrier bags that Lisa was seen carrying on the various CCTV tapes.

In order to protect evidence and minimize the risk of cross-contamination the dumpsters would be removed wholesale to one of the forensic units where the search would be systematically documented.

18

Rachel hadn't said anything to Janet about visiting Rosie Vaughan. She'd only get her knuckles rapped, or maybe worse. Definitely worse if Janet snitched to Gill. They were pretty pally. Rachel got the impression they were mates outside of work.

Perhaps Sean wasn't the link; she'd thought some more about Sean's DNA not being a match and about Rosie's reactions. It was Ryelands that was important. She read the report that Janet had put in after her visit there, turned to the final page, which she hadn't bothered with before, just a list of extra bits of information. Among them the name of Lisa's social worker, now retired. *Martin Dalbeattie*. Rachel felt her scalp tighten. Martin Dalbeattie had been Rosie's social worker too. *Available for background*, Janet had noted, *contact via Ryelands House*. So he hadn't died or gone off round the world. He could still be in Manchester.

Rachel picked up the phone and rang Ryelands. Marlene Potter answered.

'DC Bailey, Manchester Metropolitan Police,' Rachel said briskly, one eye on the door into the corridor in case anyone came in. 'You spoke to my colleague yesterday.'

'Janet, yes.'

'She's . . . Janet's asked me to get contact details for Martin Dalbeattie. You thought he'd be happy to help if we needed him?'

'Sure, give me a second.'

Rachel waited, her pulse too loud in her ears, tapping her pen on the desk until Marlene came back on. 'It's a Stalybridge number . . .' and she reeled it off.

As Rachel repeated it, writing it down, Kevin walked in. He came over to her desk where she finished scribbling and ended the call. She turned the paper over.

'Doing something you shouldn't?' he asked. 'Personal call in work time?' He was smirking like some big schoolboy.

'Phone sex,' Rachel said. 'Helps pay the bills.' Enjoying the way he blanched. 'You ruined the moment.'

He began to laugh a little nervously.

She scooped up the note and her bag. 'You think I'm kidding?' she flung over her shoulder as she left. She went into the Ladies, where he wasn't able to follow. Now she had to decide how to tackle Martin Dalbeattie.

Gill called them into the meeting room. Rachel made sure to be on time. Was Gill quick to forgive misdemeanours? Or one of those bosses who never let it go? Rachel felt disgruntled. It was she who'd cottoned on to the shopping in the first place. Yes they'd have got there eventually – well, soon as they did the CCTV trail – but Rachel had been thinking one step ahead *and* it had turned out to be a significant issue. Because Sean had stolen the clothes and the phone, and denied doing so for long enough.

'CSM's been on,' Gill said, not looking very happy about it. 'No bags, no phone. Whatever Sean Broughton did with them, he didn't stick 'em in the bins as he claims.'

'Why tell us he had?' Rachel spoke out. 'He must know we'd find out.'

Janet said, 'He was winging it. He took the stuff but didn't want to tell us where he'd left it, so he makes up a story.'

'Arse over elbow. He cops for taking the stuff' – Gill flung out one hand – 'but tells porkies about disposal . . .' she waved the other. 'Isn't taking it the bigger deal? Once he's rolled over on that, why send us on a wild-goose chase?'

'Because he's hiding something else,' Andy said, 'at his place.'

'Maybe he's lying about the shopping because, wherever he dumped it, he dumped the knife, too,' Rachel said.

'Had crossed my mind,' Gill remarked drily.

'Can't give us one without the other,' said Janet.

'On that . . .' Kevin said.

'Kevin,' Gill said brightly, 'you're awake!'

Rachel smothered a laugh.

Kevin glowered. 'We've extended the house-to-house and we have a sighting of Sean outside the school, heading downhill at three twenty.'

'Reliable?'

'Lollipop lady.'

'I like it.' Gill beamed. 'So, perhaps he's not lying about his time of arrival. Only what he did after.'

'He'd have time to kill her, nip home and change, taking the shopping and the phone, and get back,' said Lee.

'Have we enough for an arrest?' Janet said.

'I'd say.' Gill nodded. 'I'll talk to command. What are you getting from friends and associates?'

Mitch took the floor. 'Pretty much tallies with what we've heard so far. Sean is regarded as the type of bloke who'll get into a scrap, rise to the occasion, if she's goading him – which is apparently how it went. Lisa was on the shorter fuse. But he's not known for carrying a knife, or using one. Unlike Lisa's mother, most people wouldn't have thought him capable.'

'We're all capable,' Gill said. 'Have we spoken to the cousin – Benny?'

'Says he and Sean were in the house that afternoon until three. At that time Benny left: he was helping another cousin lay carpets. His story checks out,' Mitch told them. 'Mind you, he might have been coached.'

Gill tilted her head, inviting him to elaborate. 'He's a bit slow,' Mitch said.

'OK, so Sean is alibied until three, seen outside the school at twenty past. He still had opportunity. And he's a liar. I think he's got a shock coming.' Gill raised her arms like a conductor, hands splayed in invitation: 'Carry on,' she dismissed them.

At her desk, the phone was ringing and Rachel grabbed it, rattling off her name, still a flush of pride as she added, 'MIT.'

What she heard at the other end of the line made the hairs on the back of her neck stand up. She went straight into Gill, who glared at her. 'Knock first.'

'Sorry, boss. Someone's using Lisa's phone.'

'What!'

'Telecoms just picked it up.'

'Where?'

'Piccadilly Gardens. Boss, can I—?'

Gill silenced her with a look.

'Please?'

'You've no idea what you'll find. Where's Janet?'

'Prepping for Sean.'

'Go on then, but not on your own.'

Rachel's heart jumped. She nodded eagerly, her mouth dry.

19

Mitch drove while Rachel kept an eye on the data from the telecoms officer who was monitoring the phone. 'Still in the vicinity of Piccadilly Gardens,' she relayed as they crossed the inner ring road. Traffic was busy in town, but Mitch was a good driver, just pushy enough to make his way through the throng of buses and cars without taking risks. Rachel continue to navigate until they reached the large square and Mitch pulled into a bus-stop bay to park. 'Still on the Piccadilly side.'

They got out and scanned the street. The wide pavement was busy with shoppers, hawkers flogging hats and brollies, tourists and paper-sellers, queues waiting for buses, a band of African drummers were working the gardens, the music carrying to where Rachel stood.

Rachel tried Lisa's number and she and Mitch watched the passers-by to see if anyone chose that moment to answer their phone. Nothing. Plenty of people had their handsets glued to the side of their heads, but neither of them saw anyone answer a call –

though someone did answer. ''Lo?' a female voice. Rachel didn't reply. Didn't want to spook whoever had the phone before they had them in their sights. Rachel surveyed the nearby properties. A newsagent's, a gaming parlour, a bank, a kebab shop.

'Let's start in there.' She signalled to the gaming parlour. Somewhere to chuck good money after bad, as far as Rachel was concerned. Losers spending their benefits the same day they got them. The place was murky inside, impossible to tell whether it was day or night, the carpeted floor sticky underfoot. The clatter of slot machines and the clamour of sound effects from the games made it impossible to hear much else. Rachel, Mitch at her elbow, scoped the aisles. There was a mish-mash of people, all ages, most down-at-heel. Some solos, others in couples or little groups. Rachel dialled the number again, heard the ringing sound in her ear and watched. She saw a girl respond. One of a trio at the end of the room round a fruit machine, tarted up as if for a night out: short skirts, low-cut tops, back-combed hair, thick glittery make-up. The slutty look. Never know it was winter. Two blondes, little and large, and a redhead. It was the big blonde that had moved.

'Back wall,' Rachel said to Mitch. 'Watch her.' Rachel saw the girl slide the phone open and glance at the display. Hesitate, scowling at the number, then answer. Her voice was guarded, 'Yeah?'

'Can I have a word?' Rachel said over the phone, closing the distance between them.

'Who is it?' the blonde said, frowning with uncertainty.

153

'DC Bailey,' Rachel said as she reached the trio, closing her phone, 'and DC Ian Mitchell, Manchester Metropolitan Police.' She showed her warrant card.

'I'm eighteen, for fuck's sake,' the girl said, thinking they were after her for playing the slots.

'I don't care,' Rachel said. 'Step this way.'

'What the—?' The girl was all bluster and outrage. Her friends, swapping sideways glances, uneasy.

'We'll talk outside,' Rachel said, 'in the car.'

'What about?' she said crossly. But she followed them.

Once in the car, Rachel noted her details and checked her record, which was clean. Watched an accordion player, an old woman with a face like leather, take a spot near the gaming parlour, set down a battered hat and begin to play.

'Where did you get the phone, Bethany?'

The girl's face fell. 'The lying bastard,' she said. 'Is it stolen?'

'Where did you get it?'

She paused a moment then sighed. 'The Blue Dog.'

'New Moston?' Mitch asked.

It was a scuzzy little pub that closed every few months but never seemed to stay under.

'This lad had them. He swore they weren't nicked.'

'When?'

'Last night.'

'How much did you pay?' Rachel said.

'Twenty.'

'Worth, what – maybe one-fifty? And no bells rang?

154

No big flashing warning signs?' Rachel said sarcastically.

'He said they were charity. You know, people up-grading, sending them in.'

'I'm going to have to take the phone,' Rachel said.

'Oh, brilliant, that is,' she said gloomily.

'And I need a complete description of him. We'll also be asking you to make a formal statement and you may be required to testify in court.'

'It's just a phone.' She cramped her lips together. 'Bastard.'

'And then I'm going to have to ask you not to attempt to contact the person who sold you this. That clear?'

The girl nodded.

'Have you deleted any information?' Rachel said.

'No, it was clear.'

'Have you created a password or a pin?'

'No. Just topped up the credit. Can I get that back?'

Rachel laughed, didn't answer. 'So, the bloke who sold you it – you know his name?'

She didn't, but she gave them a good enough description, and the landlord of the Blue Dog, anxious to help and quick to point out that he knew nothing about any black-marketeering on his premises, supplied a name: Desmond Rattigan. Des the Rat. Who could normally be found in the betting shop on Rochdale Road when it was open.

The bookies exuded that particular mix of hope and despair common to such places and reflected in the décor: the bullet-proof glass and the industrial carpeting with its dubious stains vying with the glossy showcards of airbrushed horses and their riders, or the perfect curve of a football above an emerald pitch and the judicious placement of quotes from happy winners.

Like betting shops Rachel had seen before, the aim was to promote itself as a source of leisure not a place of addiction, but a quick look at the body language of the punters, the pent-up anticipation, the bitten-down nails, the isolation as they waited for the dice to roll or the race to end, told a different story. Rachel flashed back to an image of her own father, stub of pencil in one hand, fag in the other, poring over the sports pages. Preparing to go and spend yet more money they hadn't got on some lively little filly in the 2.10 at Doncaster.

'Give it to me,' she'd said once. A week when he'd refused her money for a new sweater even when she thrust out her arms, showing how the sleeves wouldn't cover her wrists any more. Him saying things were too tight. 'I'll put it towards a new jumper.'

He'd halted over his paper and looked at her, set his fag in the ashtray and risen to his feet. 'What?'

She didn't back down. 'Your stake, give it me.'

He'd given her the back of his hand, sent her flying. Setting Dom off, only five and bawling the house down. Bringing Alison in from the kitchen to sort them out, placate their father, shoot Rachel a black look.

Mitch said, 'Rattigan's not here.'

No one fitting the description. 'We could wait a bit? Or ask if he's already been in?'

Right then the door swung open and in he walked,

pegged them for police as soon as he laid eyes on them. Rachel saw him think about legging it, but Mitch had moved behind him, blocking the exit. Handy having someone Mitch's size on your team. Ex-army and he had that confidence; no need for any macho stuff, from what Rachel had seen of him.

'Desmond Rattigan,' Rachel said, flipping her warrant card his way. 'DC Bailey.' The other punters put on a good show: pretended not to notice the exchange, though you could tell by the angling of heads, the cessation of movement, that they were all ear-wigging like mad. 'Could you step outside with us?'

Rattigan didn't ask why, just shrugged, affecting non-chalance, and did as she asked. They talked to him in the car. Rachel showed him Lisa's phone in a clear exhibits bag. 'You sold this phone last night in the Blue Dog. I want to know where you got it.'

'I never seen it before,' he said.

Like that, is it? 'Try again, pal,' Rachel said sharply, 'or we could just nick you, take you down the station, search your address, look at building a case against you for handling stolen goods. What's that these days, Mitch?'

'Anything up to fourteen years. More, with aggravating circumstances.'

'We got any aggravating circumstances?' Rachel said.

'Very aggravating.' Mitch didn't smile, not so much as a twinkle in his eye or the hint of humour in his voice. That, coupled with the sheer size of the bloke, sent a clear message: *Deep shit.*

'Where did you get the phone?'

Rattigan hesitated. Rachel felt her impatience growing until he spoke: 'Lad came round floggin' it. Didn't know him. Said it was clean.'

'You took him at his word? Bit risky, for a man in your line of work.'

'He said his mate put him on to me, someone I know, so I thought he was OK.'

'This mate have a name?'

'Benny Broughton,' he said.

Rachel felt her spine tingle. 'And what was the lad who sold it to you called?'

'He didn't say.'

'Describe him,' she said.

'Half-caste, twenties, bleached hair.' He described Sean Broughton. ''S all I remember.'

'He say why he was selling it?'

'He said he'd found it.'

'What time was this?'

'Half seven.'

'Yesterday,' Rachel checked.

He nodded.

The day after the murder. 'Did you check the phone out?'

'Yeah, it was fine.'

'Anything on it? Messages, contacts?'

'Bit of credit, that was it.'

'OK.'

'Can I go then?'

'No, sunshine, you come with us. We need a statement from you. Beats working, eh?'

He swore under his breath, but buckled up when she told him to and sat there letting out weary sighs at regular intervals as they returned to the nick.

20

The atmosphere in the room had changed up a gear with the developments and Rachel enjoyed being part of it. Mitch was recounting the scene in the gaming parlour when Gill returned, crackling with energy and barking instructions and questions. 'Statement the girl now. Janet, how much more time to prep? Hold back on Benny Broughton till we've arrested Sean. We have the DNA profile through from traces on the body, matching Sean Broughton as anticipated – after all, he had slept with Lisa the previous night, and covered her with the duvet at the very least. Toxicology just in: heroin present, modest level, non fatal – suggests that Lisa partook shortly before her death.'

'Must have been after she got home,' Rachel said. 'There's no point in the shopping trip when she had an opportunity to take drugs.'

'Is that why she put off Sean coming round sooner?' Janet said. 'Hogging it?'

'Or sharing it with someone else? Her dealer?' said Pete.

'She had sex with someone,' Kevin said.

'Or was raped,' said Rachel. Still wanting to factor in the Ryelands link, even if only in her own head as yet. That won her a look from Janet.

'We've not got Sean supplying, as such,' Pete said.

'So who was?' Janet said.

Gill's phone went and she took the call. Held up a hand to quieten the room. 'Andy?' she listened, eyes alert, raised an eyebrow. 'Well, that's one for the mix!' She ended the call, looked at them. 'Neighbour opposite swears blind that there were no shopping bags when Lisa got out of the cab. How does that work?'

'She made a detour en route, visited a fence,' said Janet.

'Then the cabbie's lying,' said Rachel.

'Was he a scrote?' Gill asked Janet.

'Not on first impressions – regular bloke. But if the neighbour's right,' Janet went on, 'Sean's telling us he left the flat with non-existent shopping.'

'OK,' Gill said quickly, 'when would someone admit to a crime they didn't commit?'

'Cover up something else,' Janet said.

Like murder, thought Rachel.

'Misdirect us,' said Pete.

'Protect someone else,' Lee said.

'Now I really need some more time,' Janet said.

'Too right,' Gill said. 'And our rodent friend has described Sean Broughton selling the phone, so you can chuck that into the mix. OK? I'll get busy on an arrest strategy.'

* * *

Gill sought Janet out. 'For all he's yanking us about, we've still no physical evidence tying Sean Broughton to the murder itself. We've found him present and correct all over the body, but he can still argue innocence. They were a couple. The lubricant, the condom . . .' Gill said, something she'd been musing over. 'Suppose Lisa did have someone else in the flat. She puts Sean off, shags mystery man, who leaves, then Sean rolls up, puts it together, kills her in a jealous rage . . .' She waited for Janet to raise objections.

'If she fenced the shopping, we can assume that's to buy drugs.'

'Likely,' said Gill.

'Lover boy may have been her dealer – or it was another way to make some dosh,' said Janet.

'She'd gone on the game?'

'Would he care?' Janet said. 'If they could buy gear as a result, he wouldn't really mind, would he?'

'Find out,' Gill said. Hard to know. A lot of lowlifes pimped out their girlfriends. Sex being the only currency they had. Those without a girl to hand would sell themselves if they got desperate enough. Sex'n'drugs'n'rock'n'roll – nothing glamorous about the scene in north Manchester. Gill checked her watch. 'If we do go for an arrest, then we go early doors tomorrow.'

Janet said, 'Dawn raid in December, eh?'

'Wear your thermals,' Gill said. 'Hey, when things are less frantic, we should get out, make a night of it.'

162

'I'd like that,' Janet said.

'Work round any plans you and Ade have.'

'No plans,' Janet said, sounding a bit flat. 'Can't remember when we last had plans – least not plans that weren't about school concerts and dental check-ups.'

'You do need to get out,' Gill said, surprised at the tone in Janet's voice. Janet and Ade had been together for ever, high school sweethearts. And though, in later years, Janet sometimes joked about how mundane her homelife was, it was done in good humour; disparaging, but with affection. Now, there was a bitter edge.

Gill remembered her first meeting with Janet. Janet was in shock. Full-blown shock. The sort that sent the body into physiological protection mode. Gill only had to look at Janet to see: face white as flour, lips tinged blue, the body channelling all available resources to preserve the most basic functions – the beating heart, the blood flow to the brain, the central nervous system. Janet's pupils were dark as pitch, so that there was only a ring of bright blue iris visible. Her skin, when Gill touched her hand, was clammy, fingers waxen.

When Gill had arrived she was still trying to revive the baby. Kneeling on the floor, the baby on the bed, blowing soft breaths into his mouth and nose. Massaging his chest with the tips of her fingers. Standard first aid.

The doctor was there and a paramedic, but it was finally Gill whose words seemed to reach her. 'The

163

doctor needs to check Joshua now, Janet, see if anything can be done.' They all knew it was too late; Janet herself probably did, but Gill saw that so long as she acted as if salvation was possible she did not have to admit the terrible, terrible truth.

Janet had paused in her efforts, turned her stark face, bottomless eyes, to Gill and given the fraction of a nod.

The doctor had calmly assessed the baby, ensuring there was no blockage in the airways, listening for the heartbeat, checking the pulse, conferred quietly with the paramedic for a moment, who then left the room.

'I am so sorry, Janet, Adrian,' the doctor said. Ade stood against the wall, his face a mask of pain. He didn't need telling. 'But Joshua is dead.'

Janet had closed her eyes, rocked back on her heels.

'We'll give you a little time together,' Gill said.

Janet had climbed up on to the bed and scooped the infant up, one hand behind the boy's head, the other under his bottom. His limbs were floppy, offering no resistance as she moulded him to herself.

Gill had insisted on medical help, understanding immediately that the needs of the police inquiry were secondary to the safety and the well-being of the young couple.

Gill had not had any children herself back then. It was another four years before Sammy had been born. But she understood Janet's visceral grief. She'd had no idea Janet was a fellow officer when they first met, Gill responding to the report of a sudden unexplained death,

164

twelve-month-old boy. The death was judged to be due to SIDS. A catch-all for deaths of infants where there was no discernible cause.

Gill was soon working on other jobs, but she kept in contact with Janet, dropping in on her way home from work, imagining the evenings must be hardest. All those hours without the demands of feeding and bedtime and the long, bleak nights when once you would have prayed not to be disturbed, prayed that the child would sleep through.

It was Gill who brought with her tales of police work that permeated the barrier of Janet's indifference. Only a year apart in age, the women shared the experience of being young female coppers in the 1980s when it was still very much a macho zone.

Ade always welcomed Gill warmly. 'It really helps,' he told her one time, 'you coming.'

As their friendship grew, Janet sometimes opened up to Gill about the impact of losing the baby. 'My greatest fear was always losing my mind,' she said once in that plain, quiet way of hers, 'but this has been worse. What puzzles me is why didn't it drive me mad? Why haven't I ended up in the loony bin?'

Gill hadn't had any slick answers to that. But as she learned about what Janet had been through as a teenager, she thought perhaps the breakdown had left her stronger. It was Gill who coaxed Janet back to work, arguing with her when she questioned whether she was still cut out to be a police officer. 'I'd say this will only make you better at the job,' Gill said.

'You know I never put it on my application form – that I'd been in a psychiatric hospital.'

Gill had paused. That sort of misrepresentation could lead to a charge of misconduct, a termination of employment. She wished Janet hadn't told her, but knew already that she'd honour the confidence.

'There was so much prejudice,' Janet said, 'still is. I wouldn't have got the job.'

'Maybe so. But think about coming back. We need you, people like you, women – women with brains.'

And Janet had returned. Their career paths diverged, Gill moved into CID before Sammy was born and then to the crime faculty when he was four. Janet still on Division. But in 2004, once Taisie started school, Janet joined an MIT.

Now Gill was her boss as well as her friend. Janet had been there for Gill in the wake of the Dave debacle. And Gill would do the same if Janet's marriage fell apart. But it was hard to imagine, after all that Janet and Ade had been through together, and Ade being such a good dad, happy to do all the parenting stuff when Janet had over-time or was working in the school holidays, that they wouldn't find a way to get things back on an even keel. Or maybe that's the problem, Gill thought, as she began checking through the mountain of paperwork that the case was generating. Maybe it's been on an even keel for too long. Maybe it's all got stale and boring. Whatever. Janet would tell her when she was good and ready.

21

Rachel grabbed her coat and checked the time.

'You off?' Janet was surrounded by reams of paper, still working out Sean's next interview, when he'd be under arrest.

'Speedy Cabs,' Rachel said.

'The case of the disappearing shopping,' Janet said drily. 'It'd be handy to have that sorted to include in this', she gestured to the papers. 'The more I've got pinned down, the less his wiggle room. I'm going round in circles now, though.'

'Come with us, if you like,' Rachel offered. She hadn't expected Janet to agree, but she did.

It was dark again and wet, heavy rain that drummed on the roof of the car and streamed down the windscreen.

Rachel parked by the arches and dashed across the cobbles. It was a different dispatcher, an old bloke with a beard you could knit Brillo pads from. He said Kasim had just done a run to Ashton and should be returning soon.

She ran back to sit with Janet in the car. 'If he took Lisa to flog the shopping on the way home, it'd have to be somewhere nearby,' Rachel said.

'Shifting all the time, though, isn't it? Stuff changing hands, one week it's so-and-so that's the man to see, next week it's the next-door neighbour, or the lad round the corner,' Janet said.

'Say she flogs the stuff, makes some money, scores – maybe that's what Sean took, along with the phone?' Rachel said. 'He wouldn't want to tell us that, would he; he'd be worried about being done for possession.' *Up to seven years imprisonment and an unlimited fine.*

'He should be worried about being done for murder,' Janet said.

Maybe, as Andy said, the gear was at Sean's gaff, along with the knife and bloodstained clothing, and Sean had been playing for time.

'I asked at Ryelands,' Janet said. 'They didn't know Sean.'

Rachel wondered whether to say anything about Martin Dalbeattie being responsible for both girls, but at that moment a cab, its sign illuminated, headlights capturing the rain, drove along the cobbles. As the car came to a halt beneath the street light, Rachel recognized Kasim. 'There he is.' She turned to open the door.

'Ask him to come over here,' Janet said, then groaned. 'This weather!'

Rachel stepped out of their car at the same time as Kasim got out of his. She saw him glance her way, then

168

his face altered, an expression of alarm as he realized who she was. He ducked back into the cab and gunned the engine.

Rachel leapt into the car and turned the ignition. Repeating his car reg out loud.

'What on earth's he . . . ?' Janet said.

Kasim reversed at speed up the narrow street, the beams of his lights jouncing over the wet stones and brick walls.

Rachel stamped on the accelerator and swept up the road after him. At the junction, Kasim backed out into the main road and sped off, his engine screeching.

Rachel's heart was thumping. Janet ferreted in her bag for the radio and began calling for backup, asking uniformed patrols and Traffic to stop the taxi.

Kasim raced along Hyde Road and Rachel kept pace, eyes alert to any hazards ahead. She had done the advanced driving course and was confident she could handle the vehicle. But the rain didn't help, a slew of water across the windscreen, wipers going full speed, moments of road blindness before the next sweep of the blades.

'He's taking a left,' Janet said, 'April Place,' having to raise her voice over the noise of the car.

Rachel swerved on the turn, felt the back wheels spin, the sideways slide. Corrected well. Pressed the accelerator to the floor.

'And right, into Moby Street,' Janet said over the airwaves. Then, staring at Rachel: 'You're enjoying this.'

'Beats Alton Towers, any day,' Rachel said. Eyes locked on the rear lights of the taxi, red coals in the dark.

The car jolted over a manhole cover and they both jumped in their seats.

'Christ! Slow down!' Janet yelled. 'Another right, Logan Street,' she read the road name. 'Where the hell's he taking us?'

Rachel kept her foot down, thanking God it was night-time and there were few pedestrians about. They were approaching a small industrial estate. Half a dozen or so units, roller-shutter doors and corrugated roofs. And beyond them Rachel knew was a road that led to the motorway.

'Slow down,' Janet screamed. 'Rachel, stop – let patrol take it.'

'We can't let him get to the slip road,' she shouted above the howl of the engine. 'Hold tight.'

'You'll fucking kill us!'

Rachel knew she could wring a bit more speed from the car and she was practically on his bumper. She kept the accelerator on the floor and roared closer. Gripping the wheel, she slung the car out and to the right to overtake, then nosed back in towards the cab. Almost level, she was dimly aware of Janet shouting next to her, 'You're too close, too close, stop!' and voices coming over the radio. A final spurt, but then he slammed on his brakes and there was no chance to avoid him. A scream of metal and the impact shunting them back in their seats, activating the airbags and forcing the cab into the wall of one of the units. The cars travelled together for several metres. Rachel saw sparks flying as the metal of the taxi's nearside scraped along the breeze blocks, then both cars ground to a halt. The cab parallel to the building, their car at an angle, its front end pressed against the offside rear door.

'Fuck!' said Janet, fighting from behind her airbag. 'You bloody idiot! What the hell are you playing at!'

'He's off!' Rachel yelled.

Kasim was out of the cab, and running. Rachel shoved her way past the airbag and hared after him.

He ran along the edge of the units. Triggering security lights. He was fast. But I'm faster, pal. Rachel ran, hard, powerful strikes, arms pumping. Breathing heavily. Not for nothing had she been top of her intake with the bleep test. Running back and forth to beat the bleep, the intervals growing shorter each time. She was fast and she was strong. She made a point of visiting the gym at least twice a week. And she'd run a marathon last year. So some scumbag cabbie tosspot was not going to get away from her.

Arms going like pistons, her windpipe aching, sweat breaking out on her back and her chest, she increased her pace, the rain soaking her hair, her face, blinking continuously to clear her vision. Closer now.

Kasim dived into an opening between two of the buildings and Rachel followed, she could see his speed slowing, his legs letting him down. She made out chain-link ahead. He went left along the rear of the building, stumbling once, allowing her to narrow the gap between them. She didn't yell, saved her breath. Her muscles were burning in her legs, clamouring for oxygen, her face on fire. Panting now, rapid and harsh.

Kasim veered left again, heading along the other side of the unit towards the central area where the cars were. Ahead, the flicker of blue lights, the wail of sirens. Patrols arriving. He'd be harder to corner there and she was so close. She willed herself on, her heart pounding in her chest, breath raw in her throat, lungs screaming, and as they rounded the corner into the open space, in view of her car and the cab, Rachel lunged. She caught his jacket, held on, he strained forward but she pulled on his shoulder, got purchase, then she was on him, knocking him over. Sat on his back, yanked his wrists behind him, fishing the cuffs from her pocket and snapping them on, gasping, 'You are nicked.'

Janet was at her side, hands on hips, a peculiar look on her face. 'You mad bitch!' she spat the words. Her face was wide with anger, or maybe fear. She was pissed off, whichever. 'You could have killed us both. You stupid cow.'

'You're all right, aren't you?' Rachel peered up at her. 'Nothing broken.'

Janet shook her head in disgust, walked a few steps away, then swung back. 'That was dangerous driving.'

'Nobody died.'

'Screw you. Next time I'll take the bus,' Janet said, still furious.

Rachel blew out, winded, got to her feet, dizzy now and her calf muscles cramping. 'How's the car?' she said.

'Buggered. They'll want a proper look at everything.' Janet gestured to the patrols. The collision would have to be investigated. The cars examined. They would both be breathalysed – standard practice in any collision involving an officer. Rachel was sure she'd be clear.

'I know. Need my bag, though,' Rachel said. 'Watch him, will you.'

'You really don't give a shit, do you?' Janet said. Rachel didn't reply. 'Where'd you learn to run like that, anyroad?'

Langley. Always running away from something, away from aggro, trouble, away from Dad, or running after Dom.

'Lads,' Janet called to the uniforms, told them to take Kasim to the station and get him settled.

Rachel got her bag and went to see what everyone was goggling at, all clustered round the front of the taxi. Torches out, Janet with them. Rachel was shivering, sweat chilling her skin, the rain finding its way down the back of her neck.

'Look at this,' someone said as Rachel reached them. They moved aside to allow her access to the driver's door. A uniform trained his torch on the open glove compartment. Rachel saw the pile of baggies, each containing light brown powder. Street heroin. Brilliant! 'A nice little earner,' she said to Janet. 'The dispatcher reckoned Lisa was a regular. Maybe it wasn't just the lift home she wanted.' She grinned.

Janet still had her sour face on. Christ! There was no pleasing some people.

22

Janet set the alarm for half five. Ade groaning as it woke him too. The bedroom was cold, the heating didn't come on for another hour. Once she was downstairs, she made porridge and a mug of tea. She wanted toast, but there were only a few slices of bread left. Barely enough for the girls' sandwiches. In fact, if they wanted toast, too, Ade would have go out to the corner shop for another loaf. Janet didn't want him accusing her of taking bread out of the mouths of their babes.

Still dark, and the rain of the night before had frozen leaving ice on her windscreen. Janet scraped it off, letting the car heater run to warm up the inside. In theory. Something dicky with the thermostat and never time to get it seen to, so it was like driving a fridge freezer to work. She drove slowly, wise to the patches of black ice on the road. Still smarting as she recalled Rachel's antics behind the wheel and her cavalier attitude.

*   *   *

Although everyone was busy preparing for the raid, she managed to grab Gill's attention for a few minutes, wanting her to do something about Rachel Bailey. 'She didn't need to act like bloody Jenson Button. I'd radioed control. There were half a dozen patrols could have done the job. I can't do six weeks of this, Gill.'

'Were you hurt?'

'I was petrified, and she ignored me when I told her to slow down. I could have been hurt. It was a miracle I wasn't. And you could have been visiting Ade with a death message.'

Gill raised an eyebrow. 'Not the teeniest bit exciting?'

Janet gave her a baleful look. 'Are you mad?'

Through the window Janet saw Rachel at her desk. Noticed her glance quickly away. Could she tell that Janet was still pissed off? You'd never have guessed Rachel had been up half the night in the aftermath of her *Top Gear* stunt. News of her escapade had spread through the nick like wildfire and her desk had been festooned with a large chequerboard flag and a mashed-up dinky model of a police car.

'Very fitting,' Gill had said when she spied it. 'Down by lunchtime.' She allowed the team their horseplay and practical jokes but expected the office to look like a place of work, to reflect their professionalism.

'It's pushed things forward,' Gill told Janet, 'the cabbie, the drugs.'

'We'd have got there anyway, but Bailey had to be centre stage, acting like a one-man SWAT team. She's doing my head in. You know what she said about the victim's mother? "Should have been sterilized at birth".'

'We all have our opinions.' Gill started moving towards the office door.

'Yeah, but we don't all say them out loud. Aren't you the slightest bit bothered that she trashed the car?'

'That is a black mark,' Gill agreed, 'but you know they palm us off with the old jalopies; it was never going to make it through the MOT.'

'They probably won't replace it,' Janet said.

'That's for me to worry about.'

'They'll be giving us scooters next,' Janet said.

'I can just see it, Rachel on pillion.'

'Funny.'

'You OK?' Andy said, meeting Janet in the corridor.

'No, I'm not,' she said. 'I think she was wrong to drive like that with me in the car. If she'd been on her own . . .'

'Her funeral,' he said.

'Exactly.'

He smiled and Janet smiled in return and felt that lurch again. 'And I'd happily send flowers but—' She shook her head.

'Impetuous,' he said of Rachel.

'And then some: headstrong, tactless.' Like Taisie, Janet thought. Though a wilder streak in Rachel, something dark there, something damaged even. No excuses, Janet told herself; she nearly killed me.

'And Gill?' Andy asked.

'Pleased with the upshot, given I've no visible scars.'

'But psychologically . . .' He grinned, taking the piss.

'Oh, already a lost cause,' she joked.

'Glad you're OK, though.'

'Me an' all. See you down there.' And she carried on to the stairs.

They'd got their body armour on, and personal safety equipment to hand. Rachel had picked up the keys to an old saloon before Janet could beat her to it. Janet hadn't bothered with any chummy greetings, too fed up with Rachel's blasé attitude and the fact that Gill hadn't given Janet the backing she wanted, apparently still set on forcing them to work together.

'How's the whiplash?' Rachel said.

Cheeky cow. 'Keys,' Janet held out her hand.

'Why can't I—'

'You are kidding! I'd rather walk there on my knees than get in that thing with you at the wheel.'

'I promise I'll—'

'Keys.' She was adamant.

'I've done the advanced driving course,' Rachel said.

'Bully for you. I'd never have guessed.' Janet stuck her hand out again.

'I get carsick in the passenger seat.'

'Bring a sick bag.'

Rachel tutted and rolled her eyes skywards, then chucked the keys. Janet caught them.

They went into the property at seven.

Sean was in bed, looking dazed and disorientated,

when Janet made the arrest. Shaking his head when she delivered the caution as though she'd got him all wrong. She told him they would be searching the premises too.

'Stupid bitch,' he muttered.

Janet had heard it all before, water off a duck's back.

The other occupant, Benny, who slept in the smaller room, stood on the landing in some leopard-print boxers, scratching his belly, stupefied by proceedings.

The place was a tip. There was a sickly looking kitten in the living room, which had obviously not been house trained; everywhere reeked of cat shit. The sofa had been clawed to shreds. If Sean was dealing in stolen goods, he certainly wasn't making any money to speak of.

Once Sean and his cousin had been driven to the station, and the kitten removed by the RSPCA, a CSI team began a search of the property. They were after the murder weapon, any bloodstained clothing or footwear and any property of Lisa's.

It never rains but it pours, Gill thought. They'd be doing back-to-back interviews all day, as well as processing the new forensics from the Broughton house. The cells were busy, Kasim was down there talking to the duty solicitor, and Sean awaiting the arrival of his solicitor while cousin Benny was in the soft interview room.

Was Rachel a loose cannon? Maybe so, but when Gill had rung Sutton to sound him out, he reckoned Bailey had leadership potential and said he'd be sorry to lose her. Perhaps the driving display had been a way to try and prove herself. Showing off for Gill? Or maybe the kid just had a hunter's instinct. Someone scarpers and you give chase; don't stop till you've felt his collar.

That tenacity – brave or foolish – was an admirable quality, but Rachel needed to temper it with consideration for her fellow officers. Without the ability to communicate, to engender respect and loyalty, leadership was a closed door. Gone were the days when a tinpot dictator could ride roughshod over the views and feelings of those under his command. A leader now had to demonstrate they had people skills, bring out the best in their junior officers, identify and encourage the brightest, support those who struggled, helping them to build on their strengths. Which made her think of Kevin. Which sent her in search of sustenance, a mug of coffee and a Danish, before she met with her detectives.

'What about Benny?' Janet asked her, once they were all assembled.

'Not the brightest bunny in the burrow,' Gill said. 'He's got mild learning disabilities, so we're waiting for an appropriate adult. I'd like Janet, with Mitch, to chat to him before we start on Sean. That also gives us time to see if we get anything through forensics on the Broughton house and to find out what the cabbie can give us. Save Sean for the main course.'

Janet nodded, amended her notes.

'Rachel and Pete – with Kasim. I'll have a word with his brief – maybe he'll play ball. You can start, Rachel, see how you do. Run through your strategy with Andy.'

Gill took Kasim's solicitor aside and explained that there was no way they could do anything about the drug charge; the evidence was so overwhelming, CPS would wave it through without drawing breath. 'We show them a picture of what we found in the cab and it's a done deal. But the fact that your client was the last person to see our victim alive means we have a very great interest in what he might be able to tell us. I can give you an undertaking that we will not prefer any charges of intent to supply our victim – that won't be pursued. In return, we're interested in information he may be able to furnish us with regarding the murder and not the drugs.'

'I'll put it to him,' the solicitor said.

It was a fairly simple matter to test for blood traces – Luminol glows blue when it comes into contact with blood – so Gill soon got word that none of Sean's clothing at his house gave a positive result. It was a disappointment. But the news wasn't all bad. Lee came to her, eager to talk about an item recovered from Sean's house: a small gold-plated chain with a chunky cross on. The chain was broken.

'Something else he nicked from Lisa?' Gill ventured. 'Remember the abrasions on her neck?'

'Could be.'

'We'll ask the mother if she recognizes it. I need to meet her, anyway,' Gill said. It was expected practice for the SIO in a murder inquiry to meet the next of kin in the early days of an investigation. The family needed to know who was ultimately in charge of their fate and the hunt for the truth, to see that someone with authority was dedicated to their case.

Gill phoned the FLO and asked him to set up a meeting with Denise Finn at a place of her choice. And told him to inform her about the arrest. He came back on and said that Denise wanted to see her at the police station. That was preferable from Gill's point of view; it meant she could talk to Denise first, then have one of her DCs ask her about the cross and chain.

A sense of anticlimax spread through the room as Gill passed on the news that the team at Sean's house had not found either bloodstained clothing or the murder weapon. She needed to get them thinking where this took them. 'Did Sean Broughton go somewhere else before he called us? Dispose of the murder weapon and his clothes?' she put it to them. 'Perhaps he had spare clothes at Lisa's that he could change into. Andy, have we got cameras in the area?'

'Traffic lights on Oldham Road are nearest; four hundred metres away from the junction with Garrigan Street, heading out of town. Next camera is at the petrol station on Oldham Road, about three hundred metres towards the city centre.'

Gill nodded. 'Can we do a trawl of those, between one and four p.m. on Monday, specifically for any sign of Sean on foot, or of Kasim's cab leaving.'

'If he went back to base after dropping Lisa,' Mitch said, 'he'd pass the petrol station.'

'Good – Kevin, see what you can find.'

'Can't Rachel do it?' he objected. 'Keep her off the streets – road safety,' he sniggered.

'I'm asking you,' Gill said brusquely.

She reminded them of the progress they had already made, aiming to keep them keen. 'I'm very pleased,' she announced. 'We've made substantial headway and Sean Broughton is giving us more each time we talk to him. We've still a lot of ground to cover, but we should have help from DNA before very long. So let's get on with it.'

23

Christopher Danes, the FLO, brought Denise in to the station. Gill greeted her and introduced herself, offered her tea or coffee, which she declined. Denise was dishevelled, looked unwashed, her glasses smeared. She reeked of booze.

'I'm leading the investigation and I wanted to tell you that we are doing everything we can to find out who did this to your daughter. I know Christopher has been keeping you up to date with developments, but if there's anything you want to ask me I'll do my best to answer it.'

'You've arrested him?'

'I can tell you that we have arrested a twenty-two-year-old man who is helping with our inquiries.'

'It's him though, isn't it?' she grimaced, a note of bitter triumph in her tone.

Gill paused, deliberately not denying it before saying, 'I'm not at liberty to say. As soon as we can tell you any more, I give you my assurance you will be the first to hear.'

'I've a right to know,' Denise said defiantly.

'Yes,' Gill agreed, 'and as soon as any steps are taken, any charges brought, anything like that, you will be told. You have my word.'

'And the funeral?' The muscles in her face twitched.

'We can't release Lisa yet, the defence have the right to have Lisa examined for themselves.'

'I can't afford to bury her.' Tears filled her eyes and the red blotches across her nose and cheeks darkened.

'There's help available,' Gill said. 'Christopher will put you in touch, help you with that.' What had she done for her son? Burial? Cremation? Gill thought it prudent not to go there. Add more weight to the woman's burden. 'The Press Office are planning to send out a release – an update on the inquiry so far. They would like to include a few words about Lisa, and wonder if you could suggest something.'

Denise drew back, appalled. 'On the telly?'

'No, no,' Gill rushed to reassure her. God, no! Seeing Denise in the state she was in would be unlikely to attract much sympathy or propel people to try and assist the police. The fact that Lisa had been in care and was living alone at seventeen already influenced some of the reporting. The tone would have been far different if she'd been from a cosy, middle-class home, a model pupil with a clutch of GCSEs and a bright future.

'It would be written down,' Gill said, 'and something I might quote from in interviews.'

Gill quite enjoyed press conferences; the performer in her, perhaps. She felt confident and articulate and

185

didn't ruffle easily. She had had plenty of practice, too, all those years in the crime faculty when the cases were invariably high profile. In one way or another, the regional media liked to make much of the 'invasion' of the national detectives into their local patch: *SUPER-SLEUTHS TAKE THE REINS, MURDER ELITE IN TOWN, TOP COPS FOR THE LONG SLOG* – some of the headlines she remembered. Their reception in the regional forces had varied. Many colleagues had been glad of the faculty's help, keen to solve the murders that were frustrating them and grateful for the extra staff and resources, the fresh viewpoint that they brought. But others were prats with a parochial, dog-in-the-manger attitude: *If we can't solve this then no bugger will.* That meant everything took twice as long, with obstruction bordering on sabotage in some cases, the faculty detectives working in an atmosphere of thinly veiled hostility. It had only served to make Gill even more determined to solve the case.

'What would I say?' Denise asked her.

'People often say something about the person's inter-ests and personality.' Best not mention the nasty temper or the hard drugs, though. 'Something to make people realize that Lisa was someone's daughter, somebody's family. Not just a photo in the paper but a real person.'

'She used to sing,' Denise said. 'She'd a lovely voice, hit all the top notes.'

'That's good.'

'And I, erm . . .' She broke off, pressed a hand to her mouth. Distressed.

'Perhaps we could say something about the family being devastated to lose her?'

'Yes,' her voice wobbled.

'Lively, perhaps?' Not bubbly. Gill hated bubbly. Pendlebury was bubbly.

'She was definitely that.' Denise half rose. 'Sorry, I can't—'

'That's all right. Please, sit down. Take your time. I know DC Bailey wants to talk to you, if you could stay a little bit longer. How about that cup of tea now?'

Denise gave a nod and took a tissue to wipe at her eyes.

Gill found Christopher and took him aside. 'She seems to be all alone in the world. Has she any support?'

'Couple of neighbours have been round with offers of help, left some food. She's not touched it.'

'What happened to the sister? The one who took Nathan in when Denise couldn't cope?'

'Moved to Wales back in 2005. Died in a motorway pile-up three weeks later.'

Christ, talk about broken families. At least Sammy had spent fourteen years in a stable home. Gill's turning a blind eye to Dave's philandering had contributed to that. And when the shit did hit the fan, Gill had made it clear to Sammy that Dave still loved him – that in betraying her, he was not betraying his son. But her guts told her differently: collateral damage was damage all the same. She remembered Sammy's face when she had sat him down to explain why Dave wouldn't be living with them any more. His expression close to tears, the way he bit at his lip. 'He's met someone else,' she said.

'How d'you know?' Sammy had asked.

She refrained from sharing the grisly facts. 'Your dad's told me. He's coming round tonight, he wants to take you out for a—'

'I'm not going!' Sammy jumped to his feet. 'He can eff off.'

'Sammy, he didn't want to hurt you. Come here, come here.' Her eyes burning, she'd opened her arms.

He had stomped towards her, hugged her, then she felt his shoulders shake as he began to cry. Gulping back her own emotion, she squeezed him tight. 'It's gonna be all right, kid. You and me, eh? You're my best boy' – her familiar phrase – 'always will be. My lovely boy. And it's all right to be sad and it's all right to be angry. But this is not your fault – don't you ever even think that. And it's not my fault,' she added. Which leaves . . .

Sammy was angry, furious for weeks, refusing to speak to his father. Gill wasn't sure she could ever forgive Dave for that. Screw forgiveness.

'I know you've arrested him,' Denise said to Rachel, mouth pinched tight.

'We've arrested a twenty-two-year-old male, that's all I can tell you at the moment,' Rachel said. The standard response. But Denise knew, course she did. Rachel could tell. They always did. How many other twenty-two-year-old men had been potential suspects in the murder?

188

Rachel watched Denise nod emphatically. 'I told you it was him. First time I set eyes on him, I knew he was the worst thing that could happen to her.'

Weren't so hot yourself, Rachel thought. James Raleigh's words came back: *a wreck unable to cope . . . depression and alcohol dependency.* Though Denise had at least tried a bit, she supposed, unlike Rosie's mother, who had closed her eyes, stuck two fingers in her ears and sung la-la-la at the top of her voice every time her new fella or any of his mates abused her daughter. Rosie had been removed to local authority care for her own safety. And then the rape on top of all that. No wonder the girl was struggling. What a life. Rachel wondered where Rosie's social worker was. She'd be someone's responsibility, surely, given the state of her. In 2008 the woman looking after her was run off her feet, struggling to keep up with her caseload. Assuming someone was still seeing her now, how much could they realistically do? They had offered rape crisis counselling for Rosie, back then, at St Mary's, the specialist unit, one of the best services in the country. She'd refused. It seemed she no longer had the resources to hope, to contemplate change, to consider herself worth saving.

'We've recovered something from a property today that we would like you to look at and tell us if you recognize it,' Rachel said.

Denise leaned forward. Up close, the smell of booze was sickening, sweet and chemical. The woman was probably sweating pure alcohol.

Rachel put the exhibits bag containing the cross and chain on the table.

Denise's hands went to her mouth; her hands were wrinkled and liver-spotted, though she was only in her thirties. Tears glimmered behind her glasses. 'It's Lisa's,' she said. 'Where was it?'

'You're sure it's Lisa's?'

'I gave her it her, for her seventeenth.' April. 'She never took it off.'

'You last saw Lisa in October, you said?'

'Yes, my birthday. She came round for a bit. She'd got me a present,' her voice faded to a whisper: 'a scarf.'

'Was Lisa wearing the cross and chain then?'

'Yes.'

'But you didn't see her after that?' Rachel tried not to imply anything untoward, but given that they only lived a bus ride apart, you'd have thought she'd have made more of an effort.

'It was his fault,' Denise said. 'He turned her against me.'

Not far to turn, maybe a couple of degrees, judging by what James Raleigh had said about the family set-up.

'But I kept trying. I rang her every week. Sometimes we'd have a chat, depending what mood she was in. Sometimes – when he was there, I reckon – she'd just hang up on me.'

She couldn't even bring herself to use Sean's name, Rachel noted. 'When you rang her on Monday, what happened?' she asked.

Denise slowly closed her eyes, defeat plain in her expression. 'She said she was busy.'

'Did you ring for any particular reason?'

'I wanted to ask her about the rehab, if she'd talked to Mr Raleigh about it, but I never got the chance.'

'I'm afraid we can't return Lisa's possessions to you yet,' Rachel said.

'Where did you find it?' Denise said.

'I can't tell you that at the moment. It may be of significance to the inquiry.'

'What's happening with him – Sean?' she said.

'Your FLO will have explained to you—' Rachel began.

'Don't you think I've a right to know?' She was getting angry.

'You will be the first to be informed if any charges are brought.'

Denise shook her head, chewing at her lip, deep grooves etched in her forehead. As though Rachel's answer really wasn't good enough.

What would she have left to remember her daughter? A broken necklace. The handful of pictures on the living-room shelves. The scarf Lisa gave her for her birthday. The few memories from all the years they had been apart or those together in an uneasy truce.

Christmas coming. And both her kids dead since this time last year. Had Lisa been round last Christmas? Had the three of them sat down as a family at Denise's, or had Lisa spent the day at Ryelands? Christmas had always been a minefield in the Bailey household. The kids desperate to enjoy it, Dad in danger of getting drunk and sentimental or drunk and short-tempered.

Alison playing Mother, determined that they would have a good time. Paying into the Christmas Club some years, getting enough to buy selection boxes and a turkey and a silver plastic tree with lights from Woolies. Rachel going along with it, more for Dom's sake than her own. But under the surface, acutely aware that each winter marked another year without so much as a card. Christmas, the time of the nativity, seemed to mock the hole at the heart of their family. The quality of presents veered wildly. Usually they got sweets and pocket-money toys: catapult, skipping rope, yo-yos, knock-off Tamagotchi. But some years there were more extravagant offerings, if he'd won on the horses or succumbed to stuff off the back of a lorry doing the rounds dirt cheap. One year's windfall netted them a table football set. Rachel and Dom spent most of Christmas morning fixing it together. It'd been a great toy. They had tournaments – all four of them, sometimes. One of the few Christmases that she could look back on with affection.

Until the end of March, when the final demand for the gas bill arrived and he flogged it to the next-door neighbours, shamefaced and sorry as he told the kids that he had no choice.

24

The mother had identified the cross and chain as belonging to her daughter. Gill asked Lee for the exhibit, she wanted to talk to Phil Sweet and Ranjeet Lateesh about it and the mark on Lisa's neck.

'It could have come off in the struggle,' Ranjeet agreed. 'Someone yanked it hard enough to snap the chain.'

'Test for DNA traces,' Gill said.

Phil picked up the exhibits bag. 'There's a reasonable chance of material being trapped within the links, or on the cross. In fact, if we dust we might get partial prints off the cross, too – it's quite broad here, and that's the part you'd pull at.' He made the gesture with his hand. 'It's a shame it was removed from the crime scene; that could have contaminated any traces.'

'Well, have a go,' Gill said. 'We've still nothing forensically on Sean Broughton. I don't want a case that's based on circumstance.'

'Will Gerry approve it?' Phil asked.

'He'd bloody better,' Gill said.

* * *

Benny Broughton's appropriate adult arrived. Her role was to ensure that Benny understood the questions being put to him and to be there to support him during the interview process.

'We want to talk to you about this phone, Benny.' Janet put Lisa's phone, in its exhibits bag, on the table. 'Have you seen it before?'

'Yes,' he said.

'When did you see it?'

'On Tuesday. Sean said he wanted to sell it. And sometimes I do that.'

'What do you do?'

'Sell phones. To Desmond,' he said.

'Right. This phone – Sean showed it to you?'

'Yes, and I said, "Desmond", and Sean wanted me to take it but it was freezing and I didn't want to go.'

'So what happened then?'

'He thumped me, said I was a mong, and I said, "Well, I'm not going now." And that's the truth. And I didn't.' He pursed his lips, still wounded by the treatment.

'And what did Sean do after that?'

'He went. I give him the address.'

'What can you tell me about Monday?'

He looked stumped.

'In the morning, did you go to the job centre?' Janet said.

'Oh yes,' he agreed. 'We signed on. And then we came back to the house.'

'And what did you do next?'

194

He pulled a face. 'Just hung out.'

'Did you do anything else, apart from hanging out?'

'I had to go to Dusty's to do the carpet.'

'Who's Dusty?'

'My cousin.'

'What time did you go?' Janet said.

'I had to be there for quarter past three and not be late, so I went at three o'clock and I wasn't late. I was early,' he said cheerily.

'Thank you, Benny. When you left to go to Dusty's, where was Sean?'

'In the living room.'

'At your house?'

'Yes,' he sniffed. 'He was in a bad mood. Because she was late and she should've been back and she wasn't.'

'Do you mean Lisa?' Janet said.

'Yes, she was late.'

'And he was in a bad mood, just because she was late?'

'He was, you know . . .' For the first time he became coy, hesitant.

'What?' Janet said.

Benny twitched his shoulders, sniffed again. 'He needed his stuff.'

'You mean drugs, Benny?'

'Yeah. She was bringing it.'

'What time did you get back from Dusty's?'

'Not till late, about half nine.'

'Did you know Lisa?' Janet said.

'Not really. She never came to ours much. Met her, you know.'

'Did Sean say anything to you about Lisa, on Monday night?'

'He said she was dead, someone had stabbed her.' He looked crestfallen.

'Anything else?' Janet said.

'No.'

'Was he upset?'

'Yeah, really upset, but then he had some stuff and nodded off.'

'He had some drugs?' From Lisa? Taken from her, from the flat?

'Yeah,' he yawned.

'Do you know if he got them from Lisa?'

'Dunno. Probably.'

'Since then,' Janet said, 'has Sean said anything else to you about Lisa?'

'No.'

'Did Sean do any washing?'

Benny looked blank, probably wasn't familiar with the concept. 'Did he wash any clothes that day?'

'I don't know.'

'When you came home, did you see any wet clothes anywhere, or any laundry bags?'

He thought. 'No,' he said finally.

'Did Sean make a fire? Burn anything?'

'No,' he laughed, the idea tickled him.

'Did you see any clothes in the rubbish bin?'

He shook his head.

Nothing there to suggest Sean had changed his clothes at the house, though he might have been wise enough to hide them well. If so, the team would find them. They'd not found anything yet, but they'd take the place apart. Still, there was increasing uncertainty about the clothes. From a call to the jobcentre, Andy had obtained CCTV of Sean and Benny attending their Jobseeker's appointments. That footage told them that Sean was wearing a dark Puffa jacket with a hood, jeans and black-and-white trainers. They couldn't tell what top he wore under the coat, but the rest of his outfit matched the clothes retained as exhibits when Sean had reported finding the body. That made it less likely that he had changed clothes that afternoon.

'Is there anything else you'd like to tell me?'

'Is there a reward?' Benny said.

'Sorry?'

'You know, like a reward for saying stuff.'

Christ! Had he been trying to tell her the things he thought she wanted to hear, get brownie points and land a reward? 'There isn't, no. But everything you've told me today, that's exactly what happened?' Janet checked.

'Yes.'

'You didn't make anything up?'

'No.' He smiled. 'It's all true.' Like taking candy from a babe.

Kevin had revisited the neighbour, Mrs Kenny, who had seen the taxi drop Lisa off and who confirmed her account. *It's down there in black and white with my signature on it. I know what I saw.* But although she had seen the taxi arrive and Lisa climb out without any shopping, Mrs Kenny had returned to her television, *Heartbeat* recommencing, and did not see the taxi leave. If it *did* leave then. Kevin passed all this on to Rachel in a bored monotone, adding, 'The old bag'll probably kick the bucket before we ever get to court anyway.'

'You found him on the cameras?'

'Not yet, no.'

'What you waiting for, then? Jog on.'

Rachel wondered if Kasim would go no comment. From the interviews she'd conducted in Sex Crimes, she knew that hardened criminals could keep this up till hell froze over. But Kasim wasn't known to them and was not involved in the gangs, according to their colleagues who specialized in gang-related crime. He was facing up to life and an unlimited fine for possession with intent to supply. He'd likely get something in the region of eight years. There was no way he'd get off. But they needed to establish whether his involvement with Lisa extended beyond driving her home and selling her drugs.

Then Gill gave her the news that they'd made a deal. No further drug charges would be preferred as a result of anything he said to them; in return, he would answer their questions.

He rolled his eyes when Rachel came in and went through the interview spiel. Not his favourite person, perhaps, the girl who'd outrun him, but she resisted the temptation to lord it over him. Gill had drummed into her how important it was to get every last bit of detail from the guy.

'On Monday, you picked Lisa up from Shudehill and drove her to Fairland Avenue. Did you accompany Lisa into the flat?'

'No, she got out and I left,' he said.

'How well did you know Lisa?'

'She was a customer, that's all.'

'How often did you pick her up?'

'Once a week, but it wasn't regular. Not the same day or anything.'

'Had a relationship developed between you?'

'No.' He didn't like that suggestion.

'We believe she swapped the shopping in exchange for drugs. Did she also pay you in kind, with sex?'

'No way.' He scowled.

'We are comparing your DNA to traces found at the scene of her murder. Is there anything you can tell me about that?'

'I never left the cab,' he said.

'You've already told us Lisa took two phone calls. In one of those, she allegedly told someone she wouldn't be home until half past three. Yet you say you dropped her at quarter past one. And we know you did arrive at that time as we have an eyewitness who verifies it. Perhaps Lisa wanted some time alone with you?'

'I just drive the cab,' he protested.

And push heroin. 'You were the last person to see her alive,' Rachel said.

'Yeah, she *was* alive, she got out, I drove away.' He was irate, showing his teeth.

'Can you remember anything else that afternoon? People in the area? Anything outside the flat?'

He shook his head.

The interview was interrupted with a request for Rachel to come to the office. It was Kevin. If he was wasting her time, she'd deck him. He said he'd captured Kasim's taxi, driving away down Oldham Road at one twenty, which fitted his story like a glove. And meant he'd had no time to screw Lisa or undress her or anything else. He was alibied. When Rachel went back in she focused on anything he might have noticed on the avenue. Precisely fuck all. And then carried on asking about the journey. 'We appreciate your help, is there anything else you can tell us about the ride?'

'I told you everything,' he said.

'The phone calls – tell us about them. There were two?'

'That's right.'

'What can you tell us about the content of those calls?'

He shrugged.

'Were they practical, businesslike? Did Lisa talk or just listen?'

'They were short, that's all.' He closed his eyes. 'One of them, she was upset, like.'

Now you tell us, numbnuts. 'You didn't think this was significant?'

He gave a quick shrug.

'Upset about what?'

'Just saying stuff like, "I'm sick of you interfering, my life's none of your business, I don't want to see you any more" – that sort of thing.'

'Thank you. Anything else?'

He shook his head.

'And did Lisa talk to you about the call afterwards?'

'No.'

It wasn't much, but it was all she could get from him. Rachel couldn't tell whether it was her fault, something lacking in her technique, maybe his resentment at her running him to ground, or whether Kasim was simply the unobservant prat he claimed to be.

25

Janet found Rachel in the canteen while she was waiting for Sean to finish instructing his solicitor. 'I should tell him we've been talking to Benny,' Janet said, 'and he might as well put his hands up and confess to everything. The guy leaks like a sieve.'

Sean Broughton had been badly shaken by the raid. For the first time he seemed to grasp that the police were seriously considering him as a suspect. He was agitated before they started. Janet wondered if there was any withdrawal going on, though she knew that Sean, once arrested and detained at the police station, would have been taken through the medical questionnaire and any drug dependency discussed. The custody sergeant would have determined that he was competent to answer questions.

'Sean, the last time we spoke, you told me that you had removed Lisa's phone from the flat and disposed of it, along with clothing she had brought from town, behind the shops on the parade on Garrigan Street. We now know that was not the case. How do you account for that?'

'Dunno,' he said uneasily.

'What did you do with the phone?'

He didn't say anything.

'Sean?'

'Wiped it clean, then sold it,' he said quietly.

'Who to?' Janet said.

'Bloke called Des Rattigan.'

'When?'

'Tuesday,' he said.

'What time?'

He opened his mouth as if to complain about the string of questions, then thought better of it. 'Seven-ish.' All his answers tallying with what they had established already.

'Can you tell me why you sold the phone?'

'For the money.'

'There may have been information on that phone of use to the investigation into Lisa's murder. Information you deleted,' she said.

'There wasn't,' he said.

'I don't know, do I, Sean? Because you destroyed it. And I have to ask myself whether that was because you had something to hide.'

'No, I don't, I didn't,' he said urgently, his dark eyes gleaming.

'You also told me that you removed several bags containing clothes from the flat, but we now have evidence to show those items were never in the flat.'

He swallowed.

'Can you explain to me why you made that up?'

'It's just – you kept going on about the shopping, I just said it.'

'Are you now admitting that there was no shopping?'

'Yes,' he said.

'We know Lisa had stolen some clothing in town. Do you have any idea what she intended to do with that clothing?'

'No,' he said thickly, but with little conviction.

'If I told you we have reason to believe Lisa traded those items for Class A drugs, namely heroin, what would you say?'

He was still for a moment, though his eyes were jittery, darting here and there. 'I don't know nothing about that,' he said. He was scared. Frightened of dobbing in Kasim, of any repercussions? Or of the prospect of a murder charge?

'You have told me on several occasions that you went to the flat on Fairland Avenue at half past three to meet Lisa and that when you got there she was dead?'

'Yes,' he said.

'You also told me that you covered Lisa with a duvet and rang the police – correct?'

'Yes.'

'But that call was not logged until five past four. Which would have given you time to take anything you wanted to from the flat and return home. It would have given you time to change your clothes and return to the flat and then to call the police.'

The import of what she was saying provoked a strong response. 'No way,' he said. 'Listen, I took the phone, that's all.'

And the cross and chain? Janet shook her head slowly, as though she didn't believe a word of it.

He ran on: 'All right, I took the gear an' all, the drugs. I couldn't leave it there. I needed it, yeah?' The desperation of an addict. 'I never hurt her, I never touched her.'

Janet went on, as if ignoring his admission: 'We are currently searching your premises. If you are concealing anything from us, we will find it.'

Sean sat back, arms folded tight.

'What would you say to me if I told you that Lisa got home at just after one o'clock on Monday?'

He frowned. 'You're lying,' he said uncertainly.

'We have an independent witness who saw her arrive home.'

'She said half three.'

'So you keep telling me,' Janet said. 'But that doesn't fit with what our eyewitness saw. And they would have no reason to make it up. Would Lisa have lied to you, Sean?'

'No,' he said, shuffling in his seat, but doubt rang clear beneath his rebuttal.

'Or are you lying to us?'

'I'm not,' he said.

'First you tell me that you did not take anything from the flat. Then you tell me you took a phone and some shopping and discarded it. When that proves to be untrue, you change your story again. Seems to me that you've been lying to us all along. Perhaps you're lying about finding Lisa dead as well.'

'I'm not, I swear,' he said quickly, his hands trembling.

'Why would Lisa not tell you the correct time of her arrival home? Was she sleeping with anyone else?'

'No way!' he retorted.

'You see, I can't understand why she would put you off. And we know she had sex not long before her death. And if that wasn't you . . .'

'It wasn't.' He was boxing himself into a corner. Whichever way he jumped caused problems.

'Did you find out she had slept with someone else?'

'No.'

'Did you argue? Things got violent?'

'No, I didn't. She was dead, just like I told you.'

When Janet showed Sean Broughton the photograph of the cross and chain he began to weep. Janet thought they had him then. The moment when the strain of maintaining all the lies, of repeating a story concocted to hide his guilt, became too much to bear.

There was usually a physical response before the words came. Not always tears; sometimes it was slumping in the chair, a letting go of posture, of muscle tension, other times head in hands or head flung back, throat exposed. Surrender.

'We found this item, this cross and chain, at your house, in your room. Can you tell me how it got there?'

His face had flushed, his mouth began to work, then he was crying. Janet let him cry. Waited until he quietened. Knew he would be forced to fill the silence.

'I took it.'

'Where from?'

'From the flat.'

'From Lisa?' Janet said.

'No, it was in the kitchen.' Still trying to distance himself from the body, the violence.

'Whereabouts?'

'Just on the floor, in the kitchen.' He sniffed, his nose blocked.

'Was it broken?'

'I don't know.'

'OK,' Janet said. 'I want you to tell me exactly what order you did things in from the moment you stepped into the flat.'

He wiped at his face, but more tears kept leaking from his eyes. Janet almost felt sorry for him. They'd pulled together a little of his background in the days since the murder. Father in and out of prison for theft and burglary until he contracted hepatitis B and died as a result of complications. Mother suffering from early onset dementia in a care home in Wigan. No known siblings. Sean had left Wigan for the bright lights of Manchester as a sixteen-year-old. Probably because his father's sister was here, Benny's mum. She didn't want anything to do with him – her new fella not interested in connections that pre-dated him, including Benny – so Sean ended up sharing Benny's place and ducking and

207

diving for a living. Watching his hopes for a fresh start disappear down the drain like so much dirty water. His universe contracting to Lisa and drugs. Heroin seducing him with that unbelievable high that made everything seem fabulous, beautiful. Then the comedown. And the longing. The grip of the drugs on him, savage.

'I came in and called out . . .' Distraught still, his words breaking up. 'There was no answer.'

'You were expecting Lisa to have something for you, after her trip?'

He closed his eyelids. 'Yes, some smack.'

'Heroin?'

He nodded. 'I went into the living room—'

'Not the bedroom?' Janet interrupted.

'I could see she wasn't in there, like. The door was open.'

'Go on.'

'She was just lying there, you know . . .' He'd said it before but obviously didn't like the word in his mouth.

'Describe her to me.'

He took a big breath and wiped at his nose. 'I told you.'

'I know, but we need to hear it all again, Sean, because a lot of what you've told us keeps changing.'

'Not this,' he said on a sob.

'What did you see?'

He huffed again and then spoke: 'She was lying there by the sofa and there was blood on her and her eyes were stuck, not moving.'

'Did you touch her?'

'No. I went and got the duvet.'

'Before that, what was Lisa wearing?'

'Her Chinese dressing gown,' he said.

'Any underwear?'

'No.' His voice cracked.

'Would she usually wear that by itself?'

'No.' His mouth stretched with emotion.

'Carry on,' Janet said.

'I brung the duvet and put it on her,' he said.

'How? Did you kneel?'

'No, I just dropped it down, like.'

'And you didn't touch her?'

'I told you,' he shouted, 'I never touched her! How many more t— For fuck's sake.'

'What then?' Janet remained calm.

'The smack was on the floor, under the table. I picked it up. And her phone.'

'What did you do after you picked up the phone?'

'I went in the kitchen.'

If this is true, Janet felt like shaking him, what were you thinking of? The person closest to you in the whole world, the girl that presumably you claim to love, lies dead in a slick of her own blood, and your second thought after covering her up is to nick everything that isn't nailed down. 'Why the kitchen?'

He hesitated. 'I don't know, really, to see . . . I don't know. The light was on . . . and I went in and saw her cross on the floor and picked it up and then went back home.'

'Did you see a knife?'

'No.'

'And the cross and chain, what were you going to do with them?'

'See if I could sell 'em.' Not even a keepsake. That was sad. 'Lisa said it was gold. They pay more for gold now, like,' he added. A man with his eye on the markets. There was shame in the way he said it and the cast of his eyes. Not your proudest moment. Janet felt he understood how low he had stooped, how low his addiction had brought him. But if all the other stuff was flannel and he *had* stabbed her before stealing from her, then those thefts paled into insignificance.

'What did you do at home?'

'I put everything in my room and I had a hit,' he said.

'You took heroin?' Janet said.

'Just a bit,' he said. 'I knew I had to ring the police, but I was freaking. Then I went back to the flat, like I said.'

'Did you go into the living room?'

'I couldn't see her again,' he shuddered.

'Who would want to do that to Lisa?' Janet said, thinking to herself that throughout the whole process he had never asked that question, or offered an opinion, unlike Denise.

'I don't know,' he said. 'It doesn't make no sense. They didn't take anything, not even the brown an' . . . look, I loved her, right, but she could be a right bitch when she got going. But she hadn't crossed anyone, nothing like that.'

Oh, what a eulogy. 'She'd crossed you,' Janet pointed out.

'I didn't know that, I swear.' He shook his head.

'Why didn't you tell us about stealing the heroin and the cross?'

'I didn't want to go to prison,' he said simply.

'You've just said you took some heroin when you got home – what about the rest?'

He bit his lip, swung his head from side to side. It was a test, the truth was all or nothing. He'd been giving it them it in instalments each time they pushed him into a corner, now she needed to see how open he really was being.

'Where's the rest?' If he lied about this . . .

'In the yard, at my house, behind some bricks,' he said. Janet gave a nod. Something else they could verify.

'Who was Lisa sleeping with?' Janet said, hoping the sudden change of topic might catch him out.

'She wasn't sleeping with anyone,' he flushed.

'She'd had sex.'

'Maybe they raped her, and then did it, like.'

'Killed her?'

He chewed at his thumb, a pained expression on his face. 'Yeah.'

'The phone call you made, did Lisa get upset with you?'

'No, she just said she'd not be home till half three. That was it,' he said.

'Maybe she'd had enough, Sean, wanted you out of her life, off her back.'

211

'No, no, that's not true, that's lies!' He raised his voice: 'That's fucking lies!'

Over the next few hours Sean Broughton was taken through his story time and again and nothing changed. He was by turns sullen, defensive, distressed and resigned, but he never gave an inch when pressed on the murder and his motive. Janet tried every technique she knew and failed to trip him up. No contradictions, no blind spots. He gave full details of where he'd hidden the last of the drugs and when Mitch made a trip there he found them exactly as described.

As things stood, they could charge him with theft and possession of illegal drugs.

Either he was a lot cleverer than he seemed, or some-one else killed Lisa Finn.

26

The boss had told them they'd leave Sean to have his eight hours and review the situation in the morning. If it'd been up to Rachel, she'd have kept going, wear the bastard down, but they had to keep to PACE rules, or anything he did say wouldn't be watertight. His defence would whinge about coercion or contravention of his human rights and a case could be chucked out of court: *Section 76 of the PACE Act 1984 any evidence obtained by oppression must not be admitted in court. Oppression includes torture, inhuman and degrading treatment and the use or threat of violence.*

The lack of anything tangible linking Sean to the stabbing was a disappointment. They'd found a partial fingerprint on the cross, but it hadn't been his. He'd not shown himself to be a particularly quick thinker (what with all the pratting about over the bins), so Rachel didn't think he'd had some brilliant plan to hide bloody clothes and the knife. That in turn made her question if he was their man. After all, if Sean had killed Lisa and wanted to cover his tracks, wouldn't he say he'd arrived at four p.m. and called them straight away? Not fess up to an awkward half-hour gap.

If it wasn't Sean, the only other whiff of where to look was in the link to Rosie Vaughan and Ryelands. Another bite of the cherry couldn't hurt.

At first Rosie wouldn't open the door. That brought knobby neighbour out, and Rachel had to hold her breath so she wouldn't breathe in his miasma.

'You back? Can't stay away, eh? I never forget a pretty face.'

Rachel ignored him and banged on the door again. Heard movement inside. The door began to open, but as soon as Rosie was able to see who was there, she tried to shut it in Rachel's face. Rachel had already edged her foot in the gap and kept pushing. The girl was pin thin, weak with neglect, it wasn't a fair contest.

'I just want to talk to you,' Rachel said.

'No! Leave me alone.' Rosie's eyes were sunken behind her glasses, her cheeks hollow. Was she starving herself, too? She wore a flimsy dress, cream and pink, handkerchief sleeves, with leggings and broken-down jewelled slippers. The flat was perishing.

Rachel wondered whether she'd get further if she tried a different tack. 'Let me get you something to eat,' she said, moving towards Rosie along the small hallway. 'Got some bread?'

'Get out.' Rosie was quaking. 'It's my flat, I don't want you here.'

Rachel passed the bedroom. The door was ajar so she could see into the room; light from the walkway outside bled through the windows. The room was bare, not a stick of furniture or any carpet. Nothing. It was there Rosie had suffered the rape, the worst of the beating. That's where they found her.

Rosie, still backing away, reached the door to the living room and Rachel could see the window at the far side, the tiny balcony.

'Get out.' Rosie lifted her arm: she held a knife, a large penknife. Rachel glimpsed the ladder of scars on the underside of her forearm. Deliberate self-harm. Still doing it. No wonder.

Rachel paused. She hadn't got her body armour on, hadn't got anything, gas or radio. She was meant to carry personal safety equipment at all times but didn't bother. And this wasn't strictly official business. Which meant nobody knew she was here.

Rosie's eyes glittered, she looked feverish.

Rachel ignored the knife, acted as though there was nothing to be worried about, kept moving forward. Rosie stepped over the threshold into the living room, the knife shaking in her hand. In the centre of the living room was a low couch with a sleeping bag and cushions on it, and around it on the floor a bizarre array of cans and bottles and foil food trays. Not litter – arranged in a wide circle, strung together with wool. 'What's this?' Rachel said, and then she understood: an early warning system, like the things people rigged up on their allotments to scare birds or cats. If anyone entered the room while the girl slept on the couch, they would trip over the wool and make a noise. Except they wouldn't. It was easy to see, simple to step across. Pathetic.

'You've told him, haven't you? You've told him,' Rosie repeated, the knife jerking as she spoke.

Told him what? She was off her trolley.

'He's going to come back now. I promised.'

'I can protect you,' Rachel said, trying to get on the same wavelength. 'I haven't told anybody anything. It was Martin Dalbeattie, Rosie, wasn't it?'

'Martin?' Bewildered, she gave an impatient shake of her head. 'I shouldn't have let you in,' she said, little gulps as she spoke. 'You shouldn't have come – he'll know, he'll come back.' She looked round the room, her eyes darting this way and that, seeing terrors at every turn. 'You get out! You've brought them in.' Them? Who's them? Rosie jabbed the knife towards Rachel, who edged away. The angry cuts on the girl's arm were slashes, but now she was making a stabbing motion. Her breath fast, and shallow, hyperventilating.

Rachel was pretty sure she could overpower her, but whether she could do it and avoid Rosie injuring herself, she was uncertain. She was empowered under the Mental Health Act to detain someone for their own safety when they were in immediate risk of serious harm to themselves or anyone else. This was that sort of call. Rachel was no psychiatrist, but Rosie was mad as a box of frogs. 'Will you come with me, Rosie?' Rachel said simply, as though she needed her hand holding. 'I can take you somewhere safe.'

Rosie gave a laugh or a sob, hard to tell. 'You lying bitch – you brought them here.'

'Brought who?'

'All the devils.'

Oh, fuck: loonytunes. 'You don't feel safe here, we don't have to stay. We can go together – my car's downstairs. You'll have to leave the knife, though. I'll take you to a doctor.'

'Get out!' Rosie yelled and leapt. Rachel jumped back, but not quick enough to prevent the knife catching the edge of her left hand. Bringing a stinging pain then a throb, nauseating as the blood welled up.

Rosie seized the chance to slam the living-room door.

Rachel was through it in a second, but already Rosie was at the balcony doors, pulling them open.

As she ran, Rachel called to the girl, 'Rosie wait, come in, wait.' The wind snatched at her cries, so she had no idea if Rosie heard them. The girl never hesitated; still clutching the knife, she scrambled up over the balcony wall and fell.

Rachel ran to the balcony, looked down, saw the bundle that was Rosie on the tarmac below. Felt her own heart clench and burn, tears start in her eyes. Oh, you daft, bloody bitch.

She ran down the stairs, jumping two and three at a time, feeling sick.

There was nothing she could do for the girl.

No sound, it was so quiet, just Rachel's breath coming fast. She wanted to run. To run as far as she could and hide herself away. She could feel the impulse in her legs, in the back of her skull. Quick! Now! Go! Panic rising through her, high and fierce. She clamped down on all those reactions. *In case of sudden death report to Division* . . .

She called an ambulance, then Janet – she didn't know who else to try. Janet answered, sounding wary: 'Rachel?'

'Janet . . .' Choking up, she couldn't speak, she bit her cheek hard, fought hard to keep from breaking down.

'Rachel? You OK? What's going on?'

'I fucked up,' Rachel cried.

'Where are you?'

27

Rachel was huddled under a blanket, trembling like a leaf. She looked up at Janet, an expression of bitter regret on her face.

'You all right?' Janet said.

What do you think? Rachel thought.

'What went on here?'

Rachel told her, fractured sentences, covering her eyes with the heels of her hands on occasion. 'I am in such deep shit,' Rachel said.

'What were you thinking?'

'I was *thinking* that they were both at Ryelands, I was *thinking* they both had the same social worker. All I wanted was for Rosie to tell me if I was on the right track.'

'Did she?'

Rachel groaned. 'No. But she was mad as a bat. I was going to get her sectioned. She wasn't fit to be left on her own. Then she did the high-dive routine.'

'Let's get you to hospital, have that seen to.' Janet meant the cut on her arm.

'No,' Rachel said, 'it's fine.'

'Are your jabs up to date?'

'Yeah.'

Janet fetched her first-aid kit and began to dress the wound. The cut, just like Lisa, and for a crazy moment Rachel wondered if Rosie had killed Lisa. As soon as she looked closer at that scenario, it fell apart: Rosie was ill, paranoid, she could barely function. Rachel couldn't see her travelling a couple of miles to Lisa's, killing her and running away. She was a thousand times more likely to hurt herself rather than another person. Or to be hurt. And now both those things had happened.

'Oh, Christ!'

Gill was across the other side of the square, bearing down on Rachel like a drone. She stopped close by and Janet stepped aside.

'Do you go looking for trouble, or does it just find you?' Gill snapped.

Rachel didn't think she expected an answer.

'The rape case?' Gill said.

Who'd told her? Rachel looked up, startled. Gill had done her homework fast. 'Rosie Vaughan, seventeen, attacked here – well, her flat, up there,' Rachel said. All the lights were on now. People rubber-necking. Regular circus. 'Back in 2008. Downstairs neighbour called us after hearing screams. She'd been half-killed, beaten to a pulp, raped at knifepoint. Not sure of the sequence. She spoke a little at first, gibberish some of it, but that's how we knew about the knife. We got her to St Mary's, did a rape exam. He used a condom, but there were traces.' Hard to batter someone so comprehensively and not leave some traces behind. 'Then she closed down, refused to make a statement, wouldn't cooperate. We built a DNA profile of the suspect, no match – left on file. The neighbour opposite, on her landing, was considered but didn't fit the DNA. Strong suspicion she knew her attacker and so wouldn't dob him in.'

Gill rubbed her hands together briskly against the cold.

'She was at Ryelands, too,' Rachel said, studying her feet. Waiting for the lash to fall.

'And you ran this by me, when?' Gill clapped her hands. 'Oops, sorry. Never. That right?'

'Yes, boss,' Rachel said. She'd lose her job, be in uniform on the beat for the rest of her career.

'I am your SIO. What do those letters stand for?'

'Senior investigating officer.'

They were erecting screens around Rosie's body. There would have to be an inquiry, a full IPCC investigation, a sudden death, even with Rachel's account to go on; a post-mortem would be required to confirm cause of death, an inquest held to establish the material facts. A forum for the family to get their questions answered. What family? The mother who'd ruined her? Who'd mourn for her? The dozy lads she got high with at the canal?

'Senior investigating officer,' Gill went on. 'That means I run the team. Yes?' Her fury was barely contained.

'Yes, boss.'

'This is my syndicate, you are my DC.'

Were. She'd soon be using the past tense.

'The safety of my officers is my primary concern. You are my responsibility. I do not expect my DCs to start freelancing on the side. No forethought, no strategy, no backup. No fucking sense.'

Rachel couldn't work out whether the correct response was *Yes, boss*, or *No, boss*, so she made do with, 'Boss.' She was shivering, cold in her bones.

The air felt icy with each breath. She had flown downstairs, leaping three or four steps at a time on to the landings, heart smacking like a jackhammer, mind chanting *No no no no no! Oh, Rosie, you daft mare.*

Rosie had landed spreadeagled, the glaring light reflecting the pool of blood around her head. Her glasses beside her, the gauzy dress riffling in the faint breeze. Rachel reached her, felt for her pulse as she keyed in her mobile. *Ascertain signs of life.* None there.

No one about. It was dreamlike. The harsh lighting, the frosted air and no one appeared. Falling bodies made a noise, there would have been a thump, a sickening moist sound from the impact. But they were all alone, no bystanders drawn to gawp and chunter, just Rachel and the dead girl. For a laughable moment Rachel wondered if she really might be dreaming and she'd wake up at home or in Nick's bed and the fist in the pit of her stomach would disappear, the anxiety melt away.

'Rachel?'

Rachel looked from the screens and back to Gill,

whose breath streamed out of her nostrils white: dragon's smoke. 'Complaints will want to see you soon as. Don't come in until you're ready. They can wait, if needs be. Something like this – you're going to feel crap.'

You're not exactly helping.

Gill gave another puff of breath. 'Forty-eight hours and you've totalled one of our cars, apparently launched your own private investigation, presented us with a jumper to explain . . .' Meaning Rosie '. . . and brought the IPCC rummaging through my knicker drawer. Far too much attention.'

Rachel wanted to weep, her eyes ached, but she sniffed hard, rubbed at her face. Wouldn't give her the satisfaction.

'Occupational health – there if you need them.' Gill held up her hands, as if she was shoving Rachel away, disowning her, turned on her heels and walked back the way she'd come.

Janet invited her for a drink.

'Haven't you a home to go to?' Rachel said.

'They'll survive,' Janet said.

She took her to a pub, an old-fashioned place with a real fire and lots of little rooms. No bells or whistles.

'Wine, lager, vodka . . . ?'

'Wine. Red, please.' Then she felt a wave of sadness. Why was Janet being so nice to her? She'd really, really messed up. Rachel's throat closed. She tried to swallow.

Janet noticed. Eagle eyes. 'Hey, go sit down.'

'She was only nineteen,' Rachel said, when Janet set their drinks on the table. 'I thought I could talk her into—'

'Did you push her off?'

'No.'

'Threaten her?'

'No – I tried to get her out of there, get her sectioned.'

'So, it's not your fault.'

Rachel still felt lousy. 'But if I'd—'

Janet gave a snort. 'That way lies madness.'

Rachel took a mouthful of wine. She wanted a fag, but she'd have to go and stand in the cold and she couldn't face that yet. 'Here,' she said, 'if you want Gill to reassign me . . .'

'Don't be daft. She came down hard on you because she cares about her team. You put yourself at risk, that's what's freaking her out – not what happened to Rosie. No one could have foreseen that. She jumped – she wasn't pushed.'

'But—'

'Look, you're a liability. You're disorganized, you don't think things through, you don't know when to keep your gob shut, you're tactless, and you're not much of a team player. You can be rude and patronizing and arrogant . . .'

Rachel blinked. 'Don't hold back,' she managed.

'. . . and you're judgemental. But Gill thinks you've got potential. And in among the Evel Knievel stunt, the unauthorized visits and the slagging off of our victims' relatives, I can see that she might just be on to something. So, I'll put up with you as long as she does.'

All of five minutes then. Rachel wondered if she should justify her downer on Denise, but that would mean talking about her own mother swanning off without a backward glance, leaving three kids with a drunken excuse for a man. And Rachel didn't want pity or understanding or shrinks or questions. Besides, Janet was a mother herself, so she could get all defensive or righteous or, even worse, go all gooey and brain-dead, the way Alison did when children came into the conversation.

'You rate Gill, don't you?' Rachel said.

'She's the best,' Janet replied.

'But you're mates, too. Did you train together?'

Janet paused a moment. 'No. Met not long after.' Rachel expected more, but Janet didn't elaborate. They talked about the murder instead.

'Look – Martin Dalbeattie . . .' Rachel said.

Janet shook her head, 'God. You're like a terrier!'

'In a good way?'

Janet raised her eyebrows, 'Depends if you've found a rat or you're savaging next door's guinea pig.'

28

On the drive home, Gill tried to shake off the anger zapping about inside. What a cock-up! The girl playing Nancy fucking Drew and landing them with another dead body. Not that her syndicate would take it. Division would investigate and conclude no foul play, unless someone had a brainstorm and fancied Rachel for it.

She needed to decompress before she got home. The bloody gall of it! They're all working their arses off and Miss Marple's sneaking around on her own shiny new line of inquiry without having the decency to inform her colleagues. *You wanna be in my gang, you stay loyal.* That's what it was like: being stabbed in the back. And Gill had history in that department.

When she caught Dave cheating, she'd been wounded, deep inside. As though the whole marriage had been a sham. Work was her salvation. Work and Sammy. But it became apparent that she'd have to resign; her role in the crime faculty took her away from home, all over the country as a matter of course. And she could be away for long periods, assisting regional forces with particularly taxing murders. It was high-profile work, demanding, painstaking, exhilarating. She loved it. The sense of being that good, of being in an élite unit of detectives with skill and experience so highly regarded. But without Dave, all the parenting, all the school stuff and the family arrangements, all the daily chores would fall on her shoulders. And much as she loved her job, she loved her boy and she needed to be there for him.

The day she handed in her resignation had been the low point. Her boss had expressed great disappointment, promising her that if she ever had the desire to return there'd be an open door for her. Her colleagues took her out for a boozy lunch and she got a taxi back to the digs where they were staying.

That afternoon she had walked to the promenade in nearby Cleethorpes, the wind brisk, smelling of brine and seaweed and candy floss. She'd carried on walking past the pier and on to the wide sands, a handful of figures scattered here and there. She had taken off her socks and shoes and stood at the water's edge. The North Sea was cold, numbing her feet and stinging her ankles. Gulls wheeled above, their harsh cries competing with the thundering waves.

Gill retreated up the beach, to the top of one of the groynes, the lines of rocks that divided the sands and protected against coastal erosion. She sat there till it grew dark. Mourning. For her marriage, for her job. Salt in her hair and on her face.

Then, stiff and cold and thirsty, she went back to pack. Ready for the morning train home. To pick up the pieces, determined not to let that cheating bastard ruin her life.

But the worst moment? Oh, God, worse even than finding them in bed – it still made her feel ill. Three weeks after she had walked in on Dave and his bimbo, Gill and he sat down to talk. She was expecting him to beg forgiveness, plead for a second chance, him thinking that she'd be keen to save the marriage. He had another think coming. Gill had been to a solicitor to obtain advice on her legal rights and how to proceed if she wanted to keep the marital home and ditch Dave, as well as information on his obligations where Sammy's maintenance was concerned. She'd told Sammy his dad was on a training course. They'd not seen each other since she'd finished in Grimsby and come back to Shaw. Unless he'd heard it on the grapevine, he wouldn't know she'd resigned from the faculty. Dave had been staying somewhere else; at his mother's, she assumed. Unless the uniform had taken him in. She couldn't see that working for them. A roll in the hay with one of the lower orders was a whole different prospect from sharing a laundry basket, a microwave and a cheap double bed. Hell, the girl probably still lived at home. Her parents not best pleased with her seeing a man over twenty years older. A forty-eight-year-old. A *married* forty-eight-year-old with a teenage son.

Dave arrived on time, she heard his car on the gravel, steeled herself. He came in, shucked off his coat and pulled up a chair. He still had it, that presence, that magnetism, even in this toilet of a situation. Not just his physique – tall, broad, handsome, piercing blue eyes – but there in the way he carried himself and something indefinable. Pheromones? Gill could not believe her response. She still fancied him, was still drawn to him. Her Judas body betraying her too.

They had been so good together. Bright, energetic, ambitious. Matching each other stride for stride. The sex had been phenomenal. State of permanent arousal, and there like a promise, like a drug, at the end of each exhausting day's work. There too in the morning. Times they met for lunch, took a room, frenetic, greedy.

He didn't say anything now. Sat four-square, arms on the table, hands folded. Wary, perhaps? Something of the big cat in him, waiting. Muscles tensed. She had loved the size of him, the power in his back, in his arms, the way they fit together making love.

'I want a separation,' she said, her voice sounding loud in the kitchen. 'Move your stuff out by the end of the month.' She couldn't help trembling, but fought to keep her voice steady.

Dave nodded once. No quarrel, no question, no pleading. No 'sorry' either. No regret. 'I've moved in with Emma,' he said.

Gill blinked. 'Really? You didn't hang about!' Thinking: do you love me? Did you ever? When did you stop? You cold-hearted prick.

'She's . . . we're . . .' He gave a sort of a gasp.

'What?' Spit it out.

229

'We're having a baby,' he said.

Gill's heart thumped, she felt adrenalin spike through her, scalding. God, the gift that just keeps on giving! It hurt, deep hurt. She screwed up her mouth, biting her cheek; to no avail, tears, treacherous tears, stood in her eyes. 'Get out,' she managed.

'Gill . . .'

'Fuck off!' Enraged.

'The house,' he said. 'We'll have to sort out the house.'

'No.' Her face was wet and she was shaking with fury. 'No way, matey. I'll see you in a fucking hostel first.' The unholy family: Dickhead, Pendlebury and the spawn of Satan.

'Gill, this is completely—'

'Get out,' she screamed, standing and kicking at her chair. 'Get out.'

He shook his head, gave a little snort and grabbed his coat.

When she had cried herself out, she went upstairs and selected his ceremonial uniform. She unpicked the hem of the trousers and fetched a king prawn from the freezer, put it in the hem and re-stitched it neatly. Moved the suit, along with his other clothes, into the wardrobe in the spare room. She felt a tiny bit better then, a very, very tiny bit. Hard to see without a microscope.

29

It was too late to ring Nick. Rachel longed to talk to him, explain something of the freakshowfucking nightmare day. She had caught him briefly the evening before. Told him about her car chase, one in the bag. As a defence barrister, Nick hadn't done more than his opening speech at the Old Bailey and had to wait, garnering ammunition, while the prosecution case was presented. He was confident, that was part of who he was: confident and assured. He'd gone to an independent school before doing his law degree. Rachel hadn't even gone to university, but she'd done well at sixth form – well enough. By then already set on the police, she got work at a young offender's institution and took various courses: first aid, computer training, kickboxing. She learned to drive and volunteered as a special constable.

Nick never seemed particularly curious about her past and didn't talk much about his own. It was the present and future that excited him. The same for

Rachel. On the few occasions when he did ask, Rachel had dismissed her earlier years as boring: *boring house, boring family, dull, middle of the road, thought I'd suffocate . . .*

In the time since she joined the police, Rachel had reinvented herself. Learning new habits, new lifestyle. She chose clothes and accessories carefully, quality items that would last and most importantly of all would lend substance to the impression that she wanted to create: smart, stylish, contemporary. When she got her flat she didn't bring anything from home – not that there was much to bring. If it had been down to Rachel, she'd have set the family home alight and razed it to the ground, but Dom still lived there, and their dad – when he could remember what his address was. In her own place everything was new, clean. She liked it simple, unfussy. It suited her new streamlined life. No baggage, no history, no ghosts weighing her down.

She kept in touch with Dom back then, but on her own terms. She didn't invite him to hers but met him in town. She hoped he'd get out too, soon. He was bright, clever, a daft streak in him that needed channelling. Rachel had worried that he couldn't seem to settle on any one thing. He'd messed about at school, but talked about learning a trade, carpentry or brick-laying, then next month it was catering or Internet start-ups. All ideas and no action. Rachel tried to point this out, but he got the hump. Thought she was getting at him.

Alison was out working by then and doing her diploma in social work, so Rachel was the one minding

Dom. For a while she thought he might try the police, or the fire service. Once she'd left home, she felt her influence weakening. But he was a grown-up, he had to make his own way, sort himself out. Trouble was, he liked to be liked, was easily swayed. 'They're twats,' Rachel remembered yelling at him one time when he'd been excluded from school for disruptive behaviour, along with his so-called mates. 'They'll drag you down with 'em. You'll end up like Dad – or worse. That what you want?'

Now and again he tried to defend himself: 'There's no decent jobs, I've no bits of paper like you have. You expect me to work forty hours a week shovelling chips for five quid an hour? You don't get it.'

'I do,' Rachel had said. 'It's down to you, pal. You find your own chances. No one'll do it for you. You make your own luck.'

And he had. Bad luck. All that potential, all the energy and cheek and charm, lost because of some crackpot caper, some get-rich-quick scheme. Armed robbery. Four years. The shock when she heard, a shower of ice-cold water, then the sadness. Dom gone bad, after everything she had tried. But the overwhelming emotion was anger, spitting tacks just thinking about it. His whole life wrecked, all because he hadn't the sense to say no, to walk away, let some other loser make up the numbers. She couldn't forgive him. He'd chosen that path, he could walk it without her.

How could she ever have told Nick the half of it and kept his interest, his respect? Alky dad, benefit drinker,

Mam ran off and left the kids – chavs the lot of them, brother serving time. Welcome to the Baileys. Nick's smile fading, eyes growing cold with distaste, seeing her as some trashy slag from a council estate, ideas above her station. Fridge full of sterilized milk and pies and chips. Tat on the walls, Jeremy Kyle on the box. Common as muck. Thick as pigshit.

He would never know. That Rachel was gone now. The new Rachel made sure she'd never see the light of day again.

Gill had a face that'd turn milk.

'She's ignoring me,' Rachel leaned over and whispered to Janet. 'She's got it in for me.'

Rachel looked exhausted, bags like thumbprints under her eyes. Janet thought she'd probably taken the suicide harder than she'd ever let on. She had brushed aside any attempt Janet made to ask her how she felt, shaking her head emphatically when Janet suggested she take some time off. Seemed to get no succour from the expressions of sympathy and nods of understanding that the lads had greeted her with as they each arrived for work.

Janet gave it a little while and then went in to talk to Gill. 'You got a moment?'

'Depends.'

'About Rachel?'

'Did you know she was moonlighting?'

'No, she'd hardly tell me,' Janet said.

'Did she talk to you about this rape case?' Gill said.

'Yes. I told her there's nothing in it.'

'And she ignored you?' said Gill.

'So it seems. Look, she was using her initiative. OK, she was wide of the mark – but you can't blame her for the suicide.'

'I don't, I wouldn't. You know how I work.' Gill raised her arms. 'But I can't have anyone breaking ranks. This is my call, Janet.'

'I know that.'

'What's she doing now?'

'Writing up her report for the IPCC,' said Janet.

'So, what changed your tune?'

'Last night – she's trying hard not to let it show, but it's bound to hit her hard. She's going to have to live with that. And if she has the potential you've talked about – and we saw some of that with the shopping,' Janet pointed out, 'then I think she deserves a bit more of a chance. We're not exactly overflowing with brilliant young female detectives,' she added.

'Present company excepted.'

'I said young.'

Gill sighed and shook her head. There wasn't anything else Janet could think of to say, so she went back to her desk.

There was a message on her phone, from her mum: *Thanks for presents going for lunch later u all well? xxx*

Janet's mum had ended up with smash-and-grab presents: bunch of flowers and an M&S voucher. Not good enough really, but it was that or nothing. Her mother had always been there for her, never making a song-and-dance out of it, but happy to babysit, to take the kids on the occasions when Ade and Janet's work schedules clashed. To offer unlimited support after Joshua died.

She had been poleaxed at Janet's sharp swerve in direction at A-levels. Before then Janet had been following firmly in her footsteps, heading for a lifelong career in teaching. Either English or History. Janet had secretly fancied primary, but her mum said there was too little recognition in the field, 'Just look at how few men there are – that says it all.' A feminist streak her mum had, underneath it all.

So when Janet suddenly switched to wanting a career in the police, donning a uniform and working with the riff-raff and the chancers, her mother was at a loss. 'But why?' she kept saying. 'Please, just tell me why?'

Janet couldn't admit that it was Veronica's murder that had prompted her interest, or that one of the things that helped her recover from the breakdown was a determination to try to put things right now she knew about it – that would have been too weird. So she talked of the plus side: the decent pay and stability, the pension, the fact that it would be interesting and varied.

'And dangerous,' her mum said. 'Look at Yvonne Fletcher.'

Policewoman shot in front of the Libyan embassy in London. 'One person,' said Janet.

'What if that's you?'

'They'll teach us to look after ourselves.' Janet liked that idea: of having the guts and the technique to overpower some thug, of being able to break up a fight, make an arrest.

'Perhaps it's just a phase,' she overheard her father say after one such discussion. 'She'll come round.'

'I hope so,' said her mother, 'see sense.'

But she never did.

Rachel looked to Janet, guarded, expecting the worst. Janet flicked her eyes to the corridor, picked up her handbag. Rachel followed her.

They passed Kevin at his desk, sprawled in his chair, hands clasped at the back of his head. 'Who's been a naughty girl, then?' he gloated.

Janet turned as Rachel opened her mouth to protest and flashed her a warning glance. *Don't!* 'He likes the attention,' Janet said as they went through the door into the corridor. 'Don't encourage him.'

In the Ladies, Rachel leaned against the sink. 'Well?'

Janet said, 'I put in a word. She's hacked off. It's the thought of you going behind her back. She understands about the rest, about Rosie. Look, you don't have to see them today, you know, if you're not in a fit state.'

'I'm OK. The IPCC, what could they do me for? I didn't break any procedure.'

Putting a brave face on. 'Didn't exactly follow it either,' Janet said. 'Gill's her own woman, but she expects things to be done properly.'

'So she can sack me anyway?'

'She can do what she likes – shunt you sideways, team you with Kevin for the rest of your natural life.'

'Cow!'

'What's the worst that you can tell the IPCC?' Janet said.

Rachel pulled a face. 'I wasn't wearing my body armour, no personal safety equipment. Barged in, wouldn't take no for an answer. Maybe I was a bit full-on. She was psychotic, seeing things. But I'd no idea she was going to jump.' Rachel looked down at the floor, her shoulders slumped.

'It's a big shock, something like that. If you bottle it—'

'I'm fine. I didn't know what was going on in her head.'

Nor me with yours. 'No, and you tried to get her help, from what you said last night. Just be straight with them,' Janet said. 'They'll be fine. They know what it's like, how it feels to be caught up in this sort of thing.'

'And Godzilla?'

'Grovel.'

30

Gill had watched Janet's interview with Sean Broughton the previous evening and shared the sense that the lad had given them everything he had to give. The gathering anticipation of earlier days was likely to sour into anticlimax at this juncture, so she needed to pull the team together again and agree a new strategy to motivate them to go forward with renewed energy.

She made a quick head count, all present except for Andy, now coming through the door with coffee in hand. He passed Gill her cup.

'Sean's story,' Gill began, 'version three, director's cut. Have we got anything?'

'Motive,' Lee said.

'Yes, jealousy. The mystery shagger and the possible Dear John call.'

'Opportunity.'

'Kevin!' Gill congratulated him. 'And that's our lot. Nothing to put a knife in his sweaty little paws or blood on his trainers.'

Kevin's scanning of CCTV from the cameras on Oldham Road for a sighting of Sean, potentially in the act of disposing of bloodstained clothes or a weapon, had proved fruitless.

'We charge him with theft and possession of controlled drugs, release him on police bail?' She saw nods of agreement. 'Which leaves us where?'

'Looking for lover boy?' Pete suggested.

Gill held out her hand, encouraging him to continue.

'Savvy enough to wear a condom, but until we get the next DNA profile back we don't know if he's got any previous.' The second tranche of DNA profiling – the material recovered from the duvet and bed sheet, skin cells and pubic hair – was still being processed.

'There is an outside chance it's random,' Janet put in. 'The door wouldn't lock properly, so anyone could have gained entry.'

Several people groaned. Not being able to link the killer and his victim was the biggest factor in unsolved murders.

'Let's keep that for afters,' Gill said, 'because it is only an outside chance. To a stranger, the door would have looked locked, no reason to think he could get in. Relatively little disturbance at the scene too, which suggests the struggle was limited. So we widen our frame of reference: Lisa's pals, her druggie mates, friends of Sean's . . .'

Mitch nodded, he had already talked to some of her network, but now he'd develop that with a focus particularly on uncovering any other relationship Lisa was involved in.

'How did her bit on the side get there?' Gill said. 'Car, bike, on foot? Back to the cameras.'

'We don't know what we're looking for,' Kevin protested.

Gill spoke swiftly, 'We're looking for a person slash vehicle seen both going towards Garrigan Street and away from Garrigan Street in our time frame.'

'That could take days,' Kevin groaned.

'Somewhere else to be?' she said.

'No, but—'

'You did very well with the cabbie.' Dropping him a morsel of praise.

'What if it's someone off the estate?' he went on. 'They'd never go round by Oldham Road, wouldn't pass those cameras. What if there's—'

'Kevin.' She silenced him. He gave a mutinous look and began to scribble in his daybook. Possibly a death threat, she thought, or a choice four-letter word.

Rachel said, 'What about the search for the knife?'

'Where do you suggest we start?'

'Say half a mile's radius of the flat: drains, canal, skips.'

Costing the earth and maybe one or two small planets. 'I don't do scattergun,' Gill said, 'waste of resources.'

Rachel sighed and folded her arms, looked to Janet for support. Janet kept her head down, making notes. Not joining in. Good. Janet's turnaround, her championing of the girl that morning had been one for the books. But Janet hadn't lost her sense, she knew which battles were worth fighting, which points worth scoring.

'Lisa put Sean off, so presumably she knew she'd be occupied with lover boy – but she hadn't known that when she left the flat, or she'd have told Sean half three then. So how did they get in contact?'

'Not a phone call,' Pete said. 'There were only three calls that day.'

'The text, then, the unknown number?' Gill said. 'That's most likely, but we can't access it.' She began to draw the briefing to a close. 'Still, we know a great deal more than we did on Monday,' she reminded them. 'Timeline's shaping up, we've eliminated a key suspect. For now.' Allowing that, if they recovered other evidence, they might yet re-examine Sean Broughton. 'I've a press conference later and we'll be asking the public for help. That's likely to keep the phones hot. Devil's in the detail,' she told them. 'Now, I hope you haven't forgotten it's our Christmas do tonight, and I want to see you all there enjoying yourselves.' A chorus of whistles and calls went up. 'You can still remember how to do that, can't you? Good. Until then, take it steady; get it right, lads, yeah?'

'Boss,' the chorus went round. Not fired up as such, but dogged. Dogged would do fine.

While the custody sergeant and Janet went to charge Sean, Gill contacted the FLO and asked him to inform

Denise Finn that Sean was being released. Charged with theft and possession.

'She'll love that,' he said.

'No solid evidence,' Gill said. 'He's looking much less likely.'

'Still a chance?'

'Not enough to mention. Don't get her hopes up. Unless something new and very serious comes to light, Sean Broughton is no longer in the running.'

Christopher Danes was back on to her in ten minutes, while she was going over the draft of the press release. 'She wants a word,' he said. 'I told her you might be tied up,' giving Gill a get-out clause.

But she was a big girl. 'Put her on.'

'How can you let him out?' Denise demanded. 'You know what he's like, what he's done. He's guilty as sin.'

'We *don't* know that,' Gill said. 'I can only charge someone if I have the evidence to do so.'

'He battered her, he's a fucking druggie, what about that?' Denise said.

'That's not proof. Every single officer working on this inquiry is putting one hundred per cent into their work. It might take us weeks, months even, but we will look for the evidence that proves who is responsible for Lisa's death.'

'He's a liar, you know. You can't trust a word he said. He's a liar and a thief and a vicious, nasty bastard. And you just let him go!'

Gill saw that Denise was beyond reason or logic, operating only on her belief that Sean was a murderer.

Still, she kept repeating her position. 'We had no grounds to hold him any longer without charging him. He has been charged with theft and possession of illegal drugs, those are the only crimes we have evidence for at present. What happened to Lisa was unforgivable, a terrible crime, and we want to make sure that the right person is caught and punished.'

There was a noise at the other end of the line and Gill couldn't tell if Denise was crying or spluttering or even laughing with derision. Then Christopher came back on, 'Thanks, ma'am.'

'My pleasure,' Gill said drily. Put the phone down and carried on with her work.

Gill had read through her prepared statement enough times to be able to say it from memory at the press conference. It gave a better impression, appeared more genuine than someone with their head buried in a piece of paper. In common with every other officer at her level, she'd been on several media training courses, learning how to project herself (that came naturally), build a media strategy, how to field inappropriate or challenging questions, how to debate with clarity and precision without getting muddled or personal. Keeping on message, conveying crucial points in a concise way.

Having told the assembled press that Sean Broughton, a twenty-two-year-old man, had now been charged with theft and possession of Class A drugs and released, and having repeated the key facts of the crime in an effort to jog memories, ring bells buried deep in people's skulls, when it came to the ending of her speech, she picked up her notes.

'I'd like to read out a statement from Lisa's family,' she said, and paused, waiting a moment for the attention in the room to focus, the noise levels to settle. 'Lisa was a lively girl, a girl with a beautiful voice who loved to sing. A girl who had her whole life ahead of her. She was loved very much and we are desperately sad at this terrible loss. If anyone knows anything that can help the police, please come forward.'

31

The guy from the Police Federation was on the phone; he wanted to offer Rachel support. Wanted her to be aware that if she was still suffering any mental or physical trauma as a result of the incident she could postpone meeting the IPCC. No one would think any the worse of her for it.

'I'm fine,' Rachel said, ignoring the cold cramps in her stomach and the sense of trepidation.

'We can get a federation rep to be there, make sure your interests are protected.'

'No, really, I'm fine,' Rachel said. Didn't they get it? Any delay would make it even worse.

Rachel had already written her account of Rosie's suicide in her duty report. She had kept it pared back, plain and to the point. Leaving out any thoughts or feelings about the incident. Not relevant. Not helpful.

When the IPCC got there it was two blokes who spoke to her; they'd both been serving officers before moving to Complaints, which gave them an insight into the world they were monitoring. One of them was an old bloke with a lot of wild white facial hair but none on the top of his head. He had a gold tooth, which added to the pirate look he had going on. His name was Roger Harris. Roger. Really! Did they call him Jolly Roger? The other was a looker, reminded her of Nick, though his suit wasn't quite up to par. Warm tone to his voice, but he didn't smile a lot. Jonathan Buckingham.

'You understand that you are being interviewed as a witness?' Roger said.

'Yes,' Rachel said.

'And you are happy to talk to us now?'

Delirious. Everyone's concern, the kid-glove treatment, made it harder for her. She didn't need comfort or tea and sympathy, just wanted to get on with it, get it over with. 'Yes, I'm fine.'

'Perhaps you could tell us in your own words . . .' Who else's am I going to use? '. . . what happened.'

'I went to see Rosie Vaughan at Chapman Tower, New Moston, yesterday at half past eight in the evening,' Rachel reeled off the facts. 'I thought she might have some intelligence related to the murder of Lisa Finn. When I gained entry to her flat, Rosie was clearly mentally unsound. She threatened me with a knife in the hallway. I tried to persuade her to leave with me, offered to take her to hospital, but she became highly agitated. She was hallucinating and appeared to be psychotic. I followed her into the living room. She pushed me back into the hall at knifepoint, then ran out on to the balcony and jumped off.' Rosie had been so frightened, riddled with terror. Whatever demons were fucking with her head were far more powerful than the urge for self-preservation. And if I hadn't been there, would the demons have come anyway? Rachel knew such thoughts were pointless, didn't stop them though. 'I immediately went down to see if there was any chance to preserve life, but she was dead.' Limbs twisted, her skull shattered, blood like a halo. 'I summoned an ambulance and reported it to Division.'

Roger did most of the questioning, asking her to recall what Rosie said and exactly where the two of them had been during the exchanges. Jonathan took notes, the video camera blinked away in the corner. There was never a moment's pressure or hostility. Rachel knew they were on her side and the protocol had to be followed in order to protect the reputation of the police.

Rachel's throat hurt. She blinked. She would not fucking cry. There was no reason to cry. She held her eyes closed until she was sure the danger was past. Her voice went shaky, which was stupid, she hadn't done anything wrong. Roger asked if she needed a break or a drink and she snapped at him: 'What for? Let's keep going.'

'When Rosie ran to the balcony,' Roger said, 'what did you do?'

'Ran after her.' Should have caught her, skinny little druggie, should have got there easily, grabbed her, pulled her back.

At the end of the interview, Roger thanked her and

said, 'It must have been a harrowing experience for you, Rachel. Thank you for talking to us so honestly and openly. It can't have been easy.'

She gave a jerky nod, her eyes stinging, anxious to get out of the room. Outside, she lit her cigarette, shivering in the cold, sniffing hard, sodding wind in her eyes. She just wanted the day to be done, but now she had to go and play nice at some poxy works disco or no doubt Godzilla would be on her back for lacking team spirit.

32

When the lab reported back on the second tranche of DNA results from the scene, Gill, on the brink of leaving to get changed for the party, was the first to receive the information. The DNA on the duvet and on the sheet in the bedroom triggered an alert on the database: a man, identity unknown, wanted for questioning in connection with an unsolved rape case in New Moston in 2008. The victim's name was Rosie Vaughan.

At the Christmas bash, shared with Division, there was food and entertainment, a high-end buffet and a comedian. Then a talent show spot, a magician and a singer – a uniform sergeant, a woman Gill knew whose voice could etch glass – then Mitch and Lee. Mitch on sax and Lee on guitar, drums on a backing track run off a laptop. They did ska versions of 'White Christmas' and 'Rocking Around the Christmas Tree' before the disco started. There was also the compulsory raffle for local charities. Rachel won a giant polar bear that she wanted to give back so they could raffle it again next time, until Mitch said his youngest would die for it so she gave it to him. Kevin had brought along an exploding cigarette lighter, which was funny for about half a second, but he kept at it until Gill picked it up and dropped it in his pint.

Gill watched Rachel, joking with the lads; the girl seemed to be coping all right, but underneath . . . ? You needed resilience to do the job. Emotional resilience. Some of the things you saw and heard were truly horrific. Some of the cases you had to deal with were stomach-churning. If you let it get to you, you wouldn't last ten minutes. You had to be able to sleep at night. You had to believe that most people were not like the scum, the bottom feeders that you had to deal with every day. Coppers needed a measure of detachment, a protective, professional shell to keep away the nightmares, the breakdowns, the straitjacket.

Gill knew people coped in different ways; some talked about the strains of work with trusted confidants, others found sport or charity work or creativity was a way of maintaining a healthy outlook. One of her mentors found peace at his allotment, in the rhythm of planting and harvesting, another in his grandchildren. Gill had no idea what support structure Rachel Bailey had. Whether she'd a tight circle of mates to rely on, to go clubbing with and dance it off, or a boyfriend who looked out for her. Whether she still lived at home with her mum on hand to comfort her and help her feel OK.

Whatever, whoever, she'd likely need them in the next few weeks. Because not only would Rachel have to deal with the trauma of witnessing a suicide but she'd also be wrestling with the fact that she had tried and failed to help the girl.

There were a handful of cases that had got to Gill, pierced her defences. One had been Janet's baby. Not a murder at all, but an unexplained natural death. Gill had handled it all with equilibrium over that long, long day. Trying to support the family, to be sensitive even as she knew she was intruding: having to secure items for forensics, and then to persuade the couple to let the infant go. She had held it all together while she was with them, while she completed her records and checked all the exhibits had been logged, even while she attended the post-mortem, the tiny body poignant on thetable.

She had driven home in the early hours and parked on the drive. And then it had hit her. The utter, bloody sadness of it, and she finally let go, weeping and sobbing until she was drained. Exhausted. She had been young herself then, just twenty-six. Younger than Rachel Bailey was now.

There were a few times after that when she found herself haunted by the horrors of a murder, or the suffering of those left behind. Early on, one of her bosses in CID had advised her: *Don't think about the victim's feelings, don't dwell on what it was like for them, or the atmosphere. Concentrate on the facts, the evidence. Stay dispassionate, objective, distanced.* That was the only way to do it without going under. Even the best detectives were only human and at risk; some found themselves on long-term sick, or plagued by PTSD or drinking 40-per-cent-proof for breakfast.

'You are luckier than you'll ever know,' Gill said to Rachel, sitting down beside her.

'How do you make that out?'

'Because the second DNA profile gives us a scene-to-scene link. Unknown offender involved with both Rosie Vaughan and Lisa Finn.'

Rachel stared at her, excitement shining in her eyes. 'A match?'

'Yes, cock. So tomorrow you get off your arse and see where that takes us next.'

Rachel grinned, nodded her agreement. 'They had the same social worker, Martin Dalbeattie,' she said.

Gill barked a laugh. 'They lived in the same house. They probably had the same everything: doctor, dentist, candlestick maker. Janet,' she called her over. 'DNA links Rosie Vaughan and Lisa Finn.'

Janet looked stunned. Gill saw Rachel smirk.

'How many kids at Ryelands?' Gill asked Janet.

'Twenty, bit more,' Janet said.

'Go back tomorrow, the two of you, and see if any of them, past or present, are looking good for this. Not on the database, may have slipped through the net. I'm talking *residents*.' She wagged a finger at Rachel. 'Sexual offences, inappropriate relationships with other kids there . . . If you uncover any candidates, see whether they can be alibied for Monday.'

'Yes, boss,' said Janet.

* * *

Janet had one eye on Rachel, who'd been chugging it down like there was no tomorrow and was back at the bar. Still – get away with it at that age.

'You did good, kid, with Sean.' Gill held out her glass. They clinked. 'Cheers.'

Janet took a swallow. 'Is that vodka?' She looked at Gill's drink. A huge wine goblet, filled with clear liquid. 'Am I going to be sick monitor again?'

'Cheek!' Gill jabbed her in the ribs. 'It's tap water – I'm driving.' She glanced at her watch. 'Early start.'

'They were good, Mitch and Lee,' Janet said.

'Need a drummer. Hey, Andy,' Gill shouted across to him, 'you not fancy drumming with them?'

'No sense of rhythm.'

Not true, from what I recall. Janet shook her head, giggled. Should slow down herself.

'Right, I'm off. Be good,' Gill said.

Janet saluted. Andy moved closer, offered her a drink.

'I'm fine.' She pointed to her glass.

They talked, heads close so they could hear over the music. He persuaded her to dance too. The floor was crowded and people were really letting their hair down now. One guy doing some northern soul moves, a circle of admirers around him, his limbs like rubber. When had she last danced? It felt good, she swung her hips and turned, couldn't keep the grin off her face. Bit of fun.

Another drink and she saw Rachel leaving. Wondered how she'd found the party. Couldn't have been easy in

254

the shadow of what had happened. An inquest into Rosie's death had been opened and adjourned, pending further investigation. When it reopened Rachel would be a key witness, though it could be months till then.

Pete was making a complete tit of himself with a woman from CID. A mix of air-guitar and heavy metal rocking. Janet got a stitch laughing.

Andy was attentive and witty, making her feel . . . real again. She was flushed and warm with the drink and the dancing and his interest when he said, 'Come outside, I want to show you something.'

'I've heard that before, officer,' she joked, trying to make light of the butterflies inside and the depth of his gaze. She let herself be persuaded. Outside through the double doors on to the wide terrace. And it was snowing. Big, fat, soft flakes of snow and a winter's moon, full and bright. The gardens muffled thick and white.

'It's beautiful,' he said, 'you're beautiful.' And his breath was warm on her cheek, his mouth firm on hers. Just a kiss, she promised herself, that's all, just a kiss.

'I'd better go,' she managed when they came up for air. Her heart beating too fast.

He touched her face, she could feel his hunger. She wanted him so much.

'Don't go. Please. Stay with me, Janet.'

She closed her eyes, felt snow, tiny fingerprints of cold on her eyelids, on her cheeks.

'Janet,' he whispered her name again. She knew it was wrong. She had Ade, she had kids, for chrissakes.

She looked at him again, his lips, his eyes. She couldn't speak. This was stupid, dangerous, destructive. She was going home. This minute. Now.

She nodded her head. And she saw him swallow, the movement in his throat.

She texted Ade – easier to lie that way, no chance he'd hear the deceit in her voice. *Staying at Rachel's x.* The kiss seemed to screech hypocrisy and she almost changed her mind until she looked over to Andy at the hotel reception desk, and pressed send before she could back out.

It was so strange, making love with Andy after all the years of only knowing Ade. Strange and exciting. The way he looked at her, drinking her in with his eyes, the tenderness he displayed and then the passion. She was lost for those hours in some parallel universe where she could be impulsive, instinctive, abandoned. As though she had shed her skin and emerged a different being.

The guilt came on waking. As soon as she opened her eyes to the unfamiliar room, Andy beside her, looking younger in his sleep. A shrivelling inside, like a stomach full of burning acid. A weight across her shoulders. What have I done? Knowing it was a dreadful mistake. She was not wild and impetuous, that wasn't the person she was at all. She was careful, sensible, responsible. She was the one who stuck to the rules and made wise decisions and slept easily at night as a result.

Outside, the snow had gone, the magic wonderland

dissolved by heavy rain, clouds still hovering low. Brooding. How could she do this to Ade? The thought of him ever knowing brought her out in a cold sweat.

33

'Keys,' Janet said as they reached the car park.

'How long you going to keep that up?' Rachel said.

'While I live and breathe.' Looking ratty.

Rachel threw them to her.

The day was grotty, wet and gloomy. 'Did I miss any-thing last night? Anyone throw a punch or get their kit off?'

'Don't be ridiculous,' Janet snapped.

'God, who pissed on your chips?' said Rachel.

Janet didn't answer, maybe she'd drunk too much and was fighting a hangover but not wanting to let on.

At the children's home, Janet introduced Rachel to Marlene.

'Oh, yes, you rang about Martin Dalbeattie,' Marlene said. 'Was he any help?'

Janet's smile froze in place and she turned to Rachel. Rachel, not feeling all that good any more, said, 'We've not spoken to him, yet.'

'You've heard about Rosie Vaughan?' Marlene said,

obviously not knowing Rachel had witnessed the whole thing. 'So awful. That poor girl. Everything stacked against her, relentless – we just couldn't get her to access mental health services.'

Janet murmured something back and Rachel studied her shoes. She didn't want to think about Rosie, with her spindly arms and that pathetic ring of junk like a charm bracelet round the sofa. Though every time the cut on her hand throbbed, it all came rushing back at her. Rachel felt the bile of revenge. I didn't do it, she told herself. The bastard who raped and beat her – this is on his head. And before him the mother who abused her, who made her do things that no child should ever suffer. The mother had done her time, punishment served, but Rosie's rapist was still out there. Rachel wanted to get the bastard now more than ever.

Once they were settled in Marlene's office, Janet said, 'We want to find out if any of the boys who've been here since 2008 had a reputation for sexual violence?'

Marlene raised her eyebrows in a question mark.

'We've got some forensic evidence suggesting a possible link between Rosie Vaughan's rape and Lisa Finn's murder.'

'Oh, God.' Marlene closed her eyes for a moment. 'What a waste,' she said, 'both of them. You do everything you possibly can, but . . . they didn't deserve . . . no one deserves—' she broke off, upset and angry. Rachel felt awkward, suddenly too hot in the room.

'You're right,' Janet said. 'But anything you can do to help . . .'

259

'Of course.' Marlene sat up straighter and swivelled round to the computer on a workstation at right angles to her desk. 'Nobody springs to mind, but I'll just have a look.' She keyed some strokes and peered at the monitor.

There was a climbing frame in the garden and Rachel could see a toddler scaling one of the sides, bundled up in a bright red padded all-in-one. She had a sudden rush of fear that the child would fall, felt sweat break across the back of her neck and her mouth fill with saliva. Get a grip.

'Of course, once our kids move out we wouldn't necessarily know what's going on,' Marlene said. 'Some of them move away or lose touch, even though social services have a duty of care to continue assisting the most vulnerable.'

'It wouldn't be anyone with a criminal record,' Janet said. 'Whoever this person is, they're not on the database.'

'I can't see anyone here I'd have any doubts about,' Marlene said, turning back from the computer.

'Would you be happy to send us the names,' Janet said, 'so we can double check?'

'Sure.'

'Did Rosie and Lisa know each other?' Rachel asked.

'Yes. Not friends, though. Rosie was chummy with a girl called Angela – they were the same age, and Lisa was a couple of years younger. In fact, Lisa and Angela had a few scraps.'

'Where's Angela now?' Rachel said. Rosie knew her rapist, Rachel was sure. If Angela was close to Rosie,

260

perhaps she'd have an idea who it might have been.

'I can get her last address for you.'

'Could you send us a list of all the girls who were resident here, same dates, 2008 onwards?' Janet asked.

'And those that are here now?' Marlene said.

'Yes, please: names and dates of birth,' Janet said.

Marlene nodded in agreement.

'Can you think of anyone from outside the home who knew both Lisa and Rosie? Boyfriends, hangers-on, dealers?' Janet said.

'No one I knew about. There are a lot of problems with gangs targeting care homes, grooming girls for sex, but so far we've escaped that.'

'What about the staff?' Rachel said baldly. Out of the corner of her eye, she noticed Janet wince, heard her draw in a short breath of air.

Outrage sparked in Marlene's eyes and her face set like a mask. 'Our staff are all CRB checked and trained to rigorous standards,' she said frostily.

'Martin Dalbeattie was their social worker,' Rachel pointed out, 'both of them.'

Marlene looked as if she'd explode. 'Martin worked with us for almost twenty years. He was an exemplary worker, hugely well respected. You can't barge in here, making libellous and completely groundless allegations on some sort of fishing expedition—'

'I'm sure Rachel didn't mean—' Janet started her peacemaker routine.

But Rachel wasn't going to let it drop. 'If he had an alibi . . .' she said.

'Rachel!' Janet glared at her. 'I do apologize,' she said to Marlene.

'Not on my account,' Rachel said. The kid outside was on top of the climbing frame and bawling.

'Will you just—' Janet shot at her.

'Look, having a fistful of qualifications is no bar to crime. The world's full of nutters who deliberately work in places like this—'

Marlene leapt to her feet. 'We have never, ever,' her eyes glittered, 'had one allegation of sexual impropriety brought against any member of staff. I live in the real world, I know what goes on. Hell, half the kids in here come from that sort of horror show – and we look after them.' Really losing her rag.

Janet spoke quickly, 'We're aware of that and we are not here to ask about staff. I'm sorry. If you could send through those names, we'd appreciate it. You've got my email. We can check if any others have come to harm since leaving care.'

Marlene's eyes were hard, her nostrils flaring. Like a horse with a cob on. Rachel half expected her to whinny and start pawing the ground. 'Certainly,' she said, squeezing out the word like it'd kill her.

'Jesus! What charm school did you go to?' Janet muttered as they reached the car, out of earshot of Marlene, who stood on the front steps, arms folded, lips pursed, obviously intent on seeing them off the premises.

'She shouldn't be so touchy,' Rachel said.

'Rachel, you were suggesting, without any grounds, that her colleague, a man she respects and admires, is a potential rapist and murderer. That's outrageous. You know what it's like when someone accuses a cop of being dirty?'

They got in the car. 'Sometimes they are,' Rachel pointed out.

'Yeah, but we hate it, don't we? The possibility that someone's joined the other side. It's sickening.' Janet started the engine, buckled her seat belt. 'And if someone starts putting it about that a good cop is corrupt, it's a total nightmare. Try and see it from her point of view.'

'Why?'

'Because a bit of bloody empathy' – Janet was riled now – 'will get you a damn sight further than slinging your weight around. We want her cooperation. I know Marlene; she's brilliant at what she does, so your little party piece won't put her off doing the best she can to protect those kids and get justice for them, and she'll come through with the list. But a different face, a different day and we'd be whistling for it. Acting the way you did is like cutting off your nose to spite your face. You need to improve your communication skills.'

Rachel stifled a yawn, stared out of the window and let her drone on for a bit, wondering how she could establish Martin Dalbeattie's whereabouts on the day of Lisa's murder without anyone finding out.

34

'Mum?'

'Sammy?' Expecting him to ask about a sleepover or money to go to the cinema.

'I'm at hospital.'

'What?' Gill's heart bucked in her chest. 'Why?'

'I'm OK – broke my wrist.'

'How? What happened?'

'Argument with a car.'

Her blood ran cold. *I should have been there.* 'Which hospital?'

'The General, A and E.'

'Right, stay there. I'm on my way.'

Gill asked Andy to step up. Hopefully she'd be back in the saddle soon enough.

'Anything I can do?' Janet asked when Gill gave her the news on her way out.

'No, ta.'

Her mind was spinning fantasies as she drove: what if he had internal injuries too? They didn't always present themselves immediately. What car? Some pillock taking the lane too fast, fifty-five in a thirty-mile zone? Had they even stopped? Which hand? If it was his right hand, how would he cope at college? Hit and run? Had anyone else been hurt? Oh, God. He'd have said, wouldn't he? Would he?

The car park was chock-a-block, so she pulled in near the ambulance bay. Where had he been when it happened? He must have already had an X-ray if he knew it was broken. Why hadn't he called her earlier?

She spotted him straight away, on the chairs in the waiting area, talking to another patient or relative, an older bloke.

'Sammy, you OK?'

'Hi, Mum, it's cool.' He looked relieved she was there. One wrist, the left, was in a basic sling, but not cast or bandaged. His fingers were cut and grazed and she saw the denim on both his knees was torn, with traces of blood and dirt there. She sat beside him, touched his right shoulder gently. 'Does it hurt?'

'Yes.' He nodded.

'They should give you something,' she said. Leaving him to suffer!

'Said they will, after I've had the bandage on, then I've to come back to the fracture clinic in a few days for the plaster.'

Gill shook her head. 'Did the car stop? Where were you?'

'This is Matthew,' he said, indicating a man on the other side of him.

What did she care?

'It was his car,' Sammy said.

'Really?' She'd break Matthew's wrists, both of them, then his ankles.

'He brought me here.'

'Oh, how kind,' she sneered.

'Mum,' Sammy said.

'Runs you over but at least he stops, eh?'

'Your son was skateboarding, in the dark,' Matthew said crisply. 'I didn't see him until I was on top of him. It could have been a hell of a lot worse.' He was blazing, but containing it – just. A craggy face, greying hair. Well spoken.

Gill was mortified. She turned to Sammy. 'I have told you—'

'I know,' he said quickly. 'I didn't realize it was so dark. It wasn't when I started.'

'What were you doing on the fucking road,' she hissed. Aware of heads turning, of voyeurism rippling around them.

'It's the best surface,' he said.

'We've a whole driveway, Sammy.'

'It's not as smooth.'

She glared at him and he shut up.

'I do apologize,' Gill said to Matthew.

He gave a stiff nod. 'It's the distal radius, simple fracture, I'd say. I'm a GP,' he added.

'It must have been an awful shock,' Gill said.

'Yes,' he admitted, relaxing a little now as he realized she did understand the situation.

'You—' Gill shook her head at Sammy, lost for words. She could imagine what Chief Super Arsehole Dave would make of it: *Sammy running wild, getting in harm's way, no supervision while Gill was at work.* He's sixteen, she said to herself. He could marry, join the army, live independently . . . so why hasn't he got the sense not to go skateboarding on the road in the bleeding dark? When she thought of what might have happened, her stomach turned over. She felt a rush of love and exasperation in equal measure. She didn't know whether to kiss him or kick him. Did neither.

Dave had left her to it, to all intents and purposes, but never missed a chance to criticize her. She had called his bluff a few months ago, during the school holidays. She'd done her utmost to pull together a hotchpotch of activities, trips, and visits so Sammy wouldn't be left to his own devices too often. Even so, there were days when she had no choice but to leave him home alone. And she trusted him to be OK, but Dave got to hear of it and took her to task. Rang her up and started flinging accusations at her.

'You do it then,' she had said.

'What?'

'You have him. Stick him in with what's-its-face – bunk beds or whatever. Sammy would love that.' Not.

'Don't be ridiculous,' Dave snapped.

'What's ridiculous? If you don't like how I'm coping with him, then pull your bloody finger out for once. He can live with you, come here the odd weekend. You see how easy it is.'

'Gill—'

'No, you don't want that, do you? You just want to stand on the sidelines, taking cheap shots. Well, you can go to hell.'

'Your car?' Gill said to Matthew now.

'Bodywork, headlight.'

'BMW,' Sammy said.

Shit. 'Send me the bill,' Gill said, 'please. Here' – she got out one of her cards – 'the email will reach me, or . . .' She scribbled her address on the back.

He took it. 'I'm just down the road. The barn conversion.'

'That's you? How's it going?'

'Slowly. Camping out, but it'll be fabulous when it's finished.'

'Nice views.'

'Sammy Murray,' a nurse called out. They all got up.

'Thanks,' Gill said to Matthew. 'And I am sorry.'

'Just glad it's only a broken wrist.' He smiled and nodded farewell.

It might only have been a broken wrist, but it made everything – eating, dressing, going to the toilet – a major operation. Sammy had a dicky fit when Gill offered to help him get changed. 'I've seen it all before,' she argued.

'No way!' His face red.

She told him to put something loose-fitting on, trackie bottoms or pyjamas, no zips or buttons.

'What about college?' he said.

'Soon as you can manage it, you're going in. You can't afford to miss stuff now. I'm going to burn that bloody skateboard.'

'Mum!'

'Then you get lights and a helmet and pads, the works.'

'I won't go on the road again.'

'Too right. Ever. Sworn in blood. Skate park or the drive, that's it.'

Janet rang and Gill filled her in. 'Never a dull moment, eh?' Janet said.

'Know what I've got him for Christmas?'

'Go on.'

'Sodding snowboarding session.'

Janet laughed, 'Can you get a refund?'

'Serve him right if I didn't. Good job it was a doctor. He gave him a lift to the hospital.'

Janet sucked in a breath, 'Ooh, I don't know,' she said, mock worried, 'getting into a stranger's car.'

'Shut up!' said Gill.

'You sure you don't want us in tomorrow?' said Janet.

'You hoping for some overtime, bit of spends for Santa?'

'No – I can get my ironing done.'

'I'd rather save the budget for when we really need it,' Gill said. 'There's nothing we have to do at this stage where time is of the essence.'

'OK, see you Monday.'

The whole business had obviously worn Sammy out

269

and he was in bed by ten. Gill tidied up and poured herself a generous glass of wine and then rang Dave.

It was late, which was no bad thing; mess up the whore's beauty sleep or wake the brat. It was Pendlebury answered. Dave was out. Oh, you poor cow, Gill thought, resisting the temptation to ask where, see what lies he'd spun her. 'Just tell him Sammy's broken his wrist, will you?' Gill said matter-of-factly. 'And Dave'll need to help out next week.'

'Oh,' she said, disconcerted, and before she could frame a more comprehensive response, Gill said, 'Bye.'

Gill did wonder about texting Dave, a little interruption to his shagfest, but couldn't be arsed. She set their own phone to take messages, eager to banish Dave for tonight, and curled up on the sofa. You never knew what was round the corner, did you? Why was it so hard to remember that? Given that her job involved the sudden rupture in people's lives, she shouldn't have been surprised at the pitfalls and accidents in her own, but she was. Natural optimist. What was the alternative, some sort of premonition anxiety all the time? Walking along with one eye half-closed, shoulder raised, waiting for the blow to strike?

Who'd be a mother? Default position: guilt, responsibility. The first reaction when Sammy called, as if she was at fault, to blame, could have prevented it. Guilt was useless, Gill knew; certainly free-floating, groundless guilt was, and she didn't dwell on it. Men – Dave, to be specific – it would never occur to him to feel guilty. He'd immediately be apportioning blame, not claiming any. She thought briefly of Denise Finn, losing first her son, then her daughter, to drugs, to violence. Herself a victim of her own mother's inadequacy. A circle going on and on. Now they'd released Sean, who'd represented everything evil that had befallen Lisa. Denise would have no one to rail against, to blame.

Going up to bed, Gill heard a fox barking, the noise high and raw, like a scream. She looked out of her bedroom window, left the lamp off, but still couldn't spot the animal. Over the way, she could make out a light in the velux of the barn. Matthew's house. Thank God it was him Sammy tangled with and not some nutjob boy-racer or a little old lady who'd have had a heart attack. Close escape.

She was asleep in minutes, dreaming of tobogganing and chasing foxes in the snow.

35

Coming home to Ade, Janet felt sure he'd sense that she had lied, someone who knew her so well, for so long, who knew her inside out and had watched her go from a scared schoolgirl to a woman and a mother. How could he not tell? Not smell it on her, hear it in the spaces between her words?

'Good do?' he asked.

'Same as ever,' she replied. 'The buffet was better though, think they got a new caterer in. How's Elise?' Changing the subject. Elise had come down with a bug. Sick daughter, loyal husband – and where'd she been? Tucked up with another man in a smart hotel in town. Jezebel. Ade didn't ask her anything else about the evening and she dared to think she'd got away with it.

She went up to see Elise, who was in bed with the telly on. She looked feverish but if she could cope with the telly she couldn't be too bad. Janet felt Elise's forehead. Hot and dry. 'You had some paracetamol?'

'At four.'

'More soon then. Like a drink?'

Elise shook her head.

'It's good to drink.'

'I had one.' Her eyes were heavy.

'Food?'

'No. Can you top up my phone?' she said.

'What do you do with it all?' Janet said.

'Speak to people, text people – it's a phone, Mum, what do you think I do with it? God.' Dripping with sarcasm. Elise ill was a mixture of martyrdom and bad temper.

'OK,' Janet agreed. 'Poor thing,' she sympathized and Elise assumed an expression of such suffering that Janet had to work very hard not to snigger at her.

'Where were you last night?'

A clutching sensation in her belly. 'Works party, stayed at Rachel's.'

'Who's Rachel?'

'New woman at work.' Janet felt uncomfortable lying. She'd picked Rachel because Ade hadn't met her, didn't know her, unlike Gill. Less chance of him ever catching on. How could she think like this? 'So, half an hour, take the tablets. Early night, eh?'

'Don't forget the phone.'

'I'll do it now.'

Janet tried to imagine how she would feel if Ade cheated on her. But it just didn't seem realistic. Who'd have him? Morose, set in his ways, dull. When had he become that man? Safe, yes, reliable; qualities she had craved, had valued. But how close was safe to dull, reliable to boring?

And she'd be shocked to the core if Ade slept with someone else. He wouldn't do that. He just wouldn't. He loved her, for all his faults. He loved her and the girls. He'd never dream of doing something that might jeopardize all that. And nor would she, in the normal course of things. It made her feel ill. She'd betrayed her own morals, her personal code of conduct. Yes, it was only one night, a single night, and never to be repeated. A lot of people would think she was ridiculous to condemn herself so harshly for one slip. Get over yourself. Chalk it up to experience and move on. But that wasn't how she was wired. And although she kept trying to forget, she could not find a way to forgive herself.

Dalbeattie's number burned a hole in Rachel's notebook all Saturday night. She went to the gym, worked the treadmill, did some weights, swam fifty lengths after. She could still feel the pull in the back of her thighs from chasing Kasim when she hadn't been warmed up. One call. One call and devise a clever way of finding out where he'd been on Monday afternoon. Market research perhaps? Don't be a tit, she told herself, he's off limits.

She'd hoped Nick might be back for the weekend, but when she had sounded him out Friday morning, him in a rush, he said he was staying in London and catching up with some old friends. What friends? Had he known them at school or law school? She wondered briefly if she had anything to worry about but squashed the thought. Nick was into her, no doubts on that score. He made the running when they met and Rachel had been

274

careful to appear interested but relaxed. Played it casual and saw it made him want her more. Want more of her. Each time it was Nick who raised the stakes, calling her to get together again, pushing for a weekend away, persuading her to meet up even when they could only snatch a couple of hours and he had to go out after and entertain clients. So she wasn't going to turn into Little Miss Needy anytime soon. Quickest way to kill the relationship stone dead.

Sunday the boss had given them off. Sunday morning she drove up to Marsden and went for a run up along Stannedge Edge. Then she mugged up her tier three modules. It was a tough qualification to pass and not worth putting in for without plenty of preparation.

Rachel rang Nick. Listened to him talk about his weekend in London and how they should have a weekend there together some time, and then he asked how her new job was going, said she sounded a bit tired.

'Not great,' she said. 'I tried to bring a girl in for sectioning on Thursday and she jumped from the fourth-floor flat. Topped herself.'

Suicide Act 1961 decriminalized the offence of taking one's own life. Still a criminal offence to aid, abet, counsel or procure . . .

'Rachel! Why didn't you tell me?'

'Middle of the night before I got back, and Friday there wasn't a chance.'

'God, how awful. You OK?'

'Yes, just . . . bit shitty. Works do Friday night.' Trying to sound brighter.

'Any funny business with the photocopier?'

'No. Was at this hotel.'

'So you're making friends?'

And enemies. 'Janet's OK, I guess.'

'High praise indeed,' he laughed.

'I have high standards, me.' She smiled.

'Is this the same Janet you described as an uptight WI reject?'

'Modified my opinion a bit.' Suddenly she really missed him, wanted to be having this conversation face to face over a meal in one of the Michelin places in town, or at his flat afterwards. Wanted to be making love, or laughing with him. Not going to bed on her own. 'Do you know what you're doing at Christmas?' she asked, surprising herself because she always let him take the initiative. Maybe his parents would expect him there?

'Ah . . .' he sounded disappointed, 'Monty has invited me to his. Three-line whip.'

Monty, sort of poncey name you'd give a poodle, was Nick's head of chambers. Monty was God in pinstripes. Rachel waited a beat, just in case the invitation extended to her. Imagined four-poster beds and vast rooms with huge fires, sweeping staircases, people with frightful accents and fabulous wealth.

'Shooting and fishing,' Nick added. 'You'll see your folks?' Was he worried about her being lonely?

'Yeah, probably. Same old.' She'd put in an appearance at Alison's on Christmas day. Watch the kids get fractious with all the excitement and sugar, have turkey and the works, keep her glass well topped up and slope off soon as she could.

By four o'clock Sunday afternoon she couldn't sit still. She prepared her spiel: . . . *a survey of local transport, it'll only take two minutes, we sample a day of the week, ask you to tell us the time and distance of any journeys you made and the method of transport used. If I can ask you about Monday . . .*

If he refused to tell her, she'd have to find another way to dig. Of course, he might just lie: *No, never went out of the house all day* and there'd be no way, posing as a market researcher, to verify it.

She had a beer and some cheese and crackers, said her spiel again then punched in his number before she changed her mind.

'Hello?' Woman's voice, middle-aged.

'Could I speak to Mr Dalbeattie, please?'

'Sorry, he's not here.'

Oh my God, he's done a runner! Her pulse increased. 'Can I try later?'

'No, he won't be back till Wednesday. I can take a message.'

Back from where? 'I did try Monday,' she blagged.

'Sorry, I must have missed you,' the woman said.

I, not we. 'He was away then? Anywhere nice?' Rachel gritted her teeth, wondering if such nosiness from a caller who hadn't even identified herself would spook the woman.

'The Algarve, two weeks' golf. All right for some. Do you want to leave a message?'

'Just doing a telephone survey on local transport, that's all. Thanks for your time.'

Mission accomplished. But that left Rachel strangely deflated without anyone in her sights for the Lisa Finn killing or the rape of Rosie Vaughan.

Sammy usually rode his bicycle to school. Not possible now. Gill started work too early to be able to give him a lift.

He said it didn't hurt so much, but she could imagine he'd be knocked and jostled in the course of the day and wondered if she should keep him home. She couldn't take a day off now though, that'd be impossible.

'We've got PE in the afternoon, I can't do that,' Sammy said. 'So I could come home at lunch.'

'Good idea. I'll get your dad to take you and fetch you home. You'll be all right till I get back after that. Order a takeaway if you get hungry.'

'OK.'

Dave had already spoken to Sammy about his accident earlier that day and Gill had warned him then that he would need to help out, not knowing if Pendlebury had passed on that bit of the message. Now Gill rang again and explained what Sammy needed.

'Maybe he should just take the day,' Dave said.

'His exams start in January,' she said, 'he can't afford to miss anything.'

He sighed. 'OK, what time's lunch?'

'They break at twelve twenty,' she said. Couldn't resist adding, 'You do remember where the school is?'

He hung up on her. The phone rang again almost immediately.

'Now what?' she snapped.

'Gill?' Not Dave. Fuck.

'Hello?'

'It's Matthew, Matthew Parkinson.'

'Oh, hello. Sorry, thought it was someone else.'

'How's Sammy?'

'He's fine, really. Probably be fit for school tomorrow.'

'Good. I . . . erm . . . got a quote from the garage for the car.'

'That was quick!'

'Called on my way home yesterday – bloke's a marvel, workaholic.'

'And . . . ?' Gill steeled herself.

'Seven five nine,' he said.

Ouch! 'Fine.'

'There's no hurry.'

'No, no. I'll drop you a cheque in. If you're there now . . .' Gill did not want to put it off and forget it and then find herself even more embarrassed.

It was a twenty-minute walk along the dirt track to the farm and Matthew's barn. The bad weather had left the lane churned up with black mud from the surrounding peat, scattered with pockets of water. Gill had her wellies on. She should get out more, walk more, she never seemed to have a moment to do so. Certainly not when she was heading a major inquiry. She could hear the whine of a power tool growing louder as she got closer to the dwellings. Sheep were grazing in one of the farm meadows and the farmer had left a bale of hay there for them.

The lane divided in two and she took the fork to the barn. Matthew's car was parked outside the building. She felt nauseous when she saw the damage, the crumpled metal and shattered headlamp. It was a miracle that Sammy had survived with only a fractured wrist.

The outside of the barn looked finished, large windows and door, slate roof, the stone walls repointed. He must be raking it in. The door was ajar and the drone of the power tool came from inside. She waited for the sound to stop, then called out, 'Hello?'

Matthew came out, looking dishevelled and dusty. Pulling a dust-mask from his nose. 'Hi, come in. Come in.'

Gill looked down at her wellies.

'Don't worry, the floors are covered.' There were dustsheets underfoot.

Inside, a wide central hall led through to doors at the back and a flagged patio overlooking the moor and the reservoir beyond. Either side of the hallway freshly plastered walls divided off the rooms.

'It's lovely,' she said.

'Will be,' he said. 'Let me give you the tour.'

He walked her through, discussing the choices he'd made for the heating system (wood burning stoves and back boilers), how he'd found a drystone waller to repair some of the boundary at the rear, and showed her the job he was currently occupied with: sanding reclaimed timber for surfaces in the kitchen. His enthusiasm reminded Gill of her own when she and Dave were planning their home. She took her wellies off to go up to one of the mezzanine rooms; the new wooden staircases glowed clean, the colour of honey. 'This will be a twin room,' he said. 'I've a daughter, first year at uni, so she can visit – and friends, of course. The other side is bigger and the bathroom's in between.'

He offered her tea: a microwave and a calor gas stove served as a makeshift kitchen.

'No, I'm fine, thanks. I'd better be getting back, let you get on with your sanding,' Gill said. 'Here,' she passed him the cheque.

'Thanks for this,' he said.

She nodded. He walked her to the door. She pulled her boots on. As she stepped out, he spoke in a rush, 'I wondered if you'd like to go out for a meal sometime?'

Oh. My. God! Gill coughed. A date! He was asking her on a date! 'I'm pretty busy at the moment . . .' she began.

'When it's quieter?'

Is it ever? 'Yes, yes, that'd be lovely, thank you.'

'Good,' he smiled.

Gill felt a fresh spring in her step and had a daft grin on her face as she went back up the lane, deliberately walking in all the puddles.

36

'Madam.' Monday morning and Gill stood at her office door, her dark eyes sparkling, but not with humour.

'Boss?' Rachel said.

With a twitch of her head, Gill indicated that Rachel should join her. Had the IPCC been on? Was there some problem about Rosie's death? Apart from the fact it had happened? Had Gill found out that she had called Dalbeattie?

'You know what an order is, do you?'

She wasn't a happy bunny. Rachel's stomach tightened.

'Because from where I'm standing it's hard to tell. Marlene Potter?'

Fuck.

'Now, I don't videotape our conversations, but I could swear I told you to ask Ryelands about residents, looked-after kids, any scrotes or scallies among them with form for sexual violence or knife crime. I'm not imagining that, am I?'

'No, boss.'

'You heard it too?'

'Yes, boss.'

'Then where in buggeration do you get off making totally unfounded allegations about staff?'

'Boss.'

'Tunnel vision, Rachel. You go around like that in this job, banging on about your pet theory and not looking at the wider picture, you'll either walk into a wall or off a sodding cliff. Marlene wants to make an official complaint.'

Oh fuck-a-duck with knobs on.

'I have asked her to reconsider. One professional,' she weighted the word, sticking her neb forward, implying that Rachel was a far cry from belonging to that club, 'to another. Told her you'd witnessed the suicide, messed your head up, robbing you of sense and manners.'

'Thanks, boss.'

Gill snorted. 'Don't thank me yet. You got right up her nose, girl, and she doesn't rattle easily. She'll be back to us tomorrow. I'll ask her to wait in line.'

Rachel frowned.

'Me, Janet . . .'

'What about Janet?' Rachel said.

'She'd like to live long enough to collect her pension, see her daughters grown up.'

The car chase. But she's over that, Rachel thought, she stood up for me on Friday. 'But she—'

Gill glared. She jabbed a finger in her direction. 'Out. Now. Go.'

Bet she's going through the change, evil-tempered witch.

'Maybe I made a mistake,' Gill said to Janet.

'What are you going to do?'

'I can ship her back to Sutton.'

'Is that fair?' Janet said.

'Not five minutes ago you wanted her head on a platter. You begged me to get shot. Why are you batting for her now?'

'Look at her, Gill; we were like that once, remember?' Janet had joined the force not long after Gill. Still a man's world back then, the training course at Bramshill an ordeal of sweaty men oozing testosterone, a mine-field of sexist innuendo and harassment. Andy a higher life form among the Neanderthals. Janet felt a flare of heat in her cheeks. Bloody Andy. She avoided Gill's eyes, not wanting her friend to read anything there that shouldn't be. The hardest thing wasn't going to be keeping it from Ade (he probably wouldn't notice if she brought the Chippendales home for a group shag) but keeping it from Gill. Who would come down on them both like a ton of bricks, if she ever found out. Gill knew only too well what it was like to be cuckolded. She'd hate Janet for this. 'We had it so hard, we fought every step of the way, we even made mistakes.'

'I was never like that,' Gill said disparagingly, arms crossed.

'No, you sprang fully formed, tits, teeth and political savvy, detective chief inspector.'

'She's a mad bitch, she's not house-trained. She's out of control,' said Gill.

'She's scared witless. You know that feeling, the sickness at the pit of your stomach. She reminds me of you.'

'That's ridiculous! Totally ridiculous!' Gill flung her hands up.

'Easy on the outrage. What's the quote – the lady doth protest too much?' said Janet.

'We've the crass comment to the mother, now a complaint from a senior social worker—'

'Hang on, the mother didn't make a complaint. Rachel was trying to find her some support, just put her foot in it.'

'She's impetuous and she's a crap communicator. One more incident and I'll have to put her on efficiency proceedings.'

That morning Janet and Rachel divided up the names that Marlene sent through, cross-referencing them against the various databases. Janet took the boys and ran them through HOLMES, where all major incidents were catalogued. Rachel used the intelligence database to input the names of the girls who may have been logged as victims.

Janet's neck was aching, her eyes feeling the strain. Perhaps she needed new glasses? The rest of the team were out throwing the net wider, digging deeper into Lisa Finn's recent life. It was like panning for gold, Janet thought, sifting through the muck and mire for long enough until you caught sight of something that gleamed. A crumb, a grain to make it all worthwhile. At least it meant she wasn't faced with Andy. A dream turned nightmare.

'Lunch?' Janet looked over to Rachel, who was sucking on her pen as she studied her screen.

'Can do,' she said, indifferently.

'You don't usually eat?' Janet teased.

'Course I eat. You sure you want to be seen eating with me?' She flicked her eyes towards Gill's office. Like it was the playground and friendships were always being tested, little cliques formed and broken.

'I think I can cope,' Janet said.

They went into the Old Grapes, the pub opposite that did bar food on a lunchtime. Janet chose hotpot and red cabbage, just the thing for a winter's day. Rachel picked a spicy chicken dish. As they sat down, Rachel cast a glance at Janet, looking wary.

'What?'

'Well, I thought you might have something to say.'

'About?' said Janet.

'Me. A talking to, a lecture.'

She was paranoid. 'Lunch, Rachel, that's all it is: lunch. Did they not do lunch in Sex Crimes?'

'Worked through usually, butties on the job.'

'And breakfast? Coffee and a cigarette?'

Rachel stared at her.

'Sorry,' Janet sat back, 'it's my mother act, that's all.' Obviously not appreciated.

The food arrived and they ate, Janet trying to make small talk. 'Where you from then?'

'Middleton. You?'

'Chadderton, never left. My kids went to the same primary school as I did.'

'That might be another place to try,' Rachel said, 'the school Lisa and Rosie went to, when they were in care.' Back to the case, and suddenly Rachel was engaged again. Much more comfortable than with the personal stuff.

'That'd be North Manchester High. Big school,' Janet said.

'But the teachers'd know if anyone had been in that sort of serious bother.'

'Yes. Suggest it to Gill.'

'You suggest it. If it comes from me, she'll sack it.' Rachel scooped another forkful of chicken, ate it.

'No. She's not daft – quite the opposite – and she's not petty.'

'Try standing where I am.'

'Rachel, she has valid concerns about your conduct. You'll end up on an action plan if you don't watch your step. Look, if you want to stay in the syndicate—'

'I do. More than anything.' She met Janet's eyes and all the guile, all the front peeled away. Janet saw how worried Rachel was at finding her future in the balance.

'Well, think before you act and think before you react. You could go a long way under Gill Murray.'

'You haven't.'

Janet nearly choked on her hotpot. 'You're wrong,' she said. 'I don't want promotion because I don't want to be stuck sorting out budgets and managing people. I do want to be working major incidents and I do want to be catching killers and I am. I want to be one of the best, and this syndicate is.'

'I know,' Rachel said, pushing her empty plate to one side. 'I knew there'd be a lecture.' There was a glint of humour in her eye and Janet laughed. 'I need a fag,' Rachel got to her feet.

'See you back there.'

By mid-afternoon they hadn't found any of the ex-Ryelands residents as a complainant in a rape or assault case. Nor flagged up any ex-resident charged with such an offence in the same period.

'You'd think, with this shower, there'd be one or two caught waving their willies about or jumping the local totty,' Rachel complained.

'They're not all bad 'uns,' Janet chided her. 'Some of them are orphans, or their parents get ill. Kids end up in care for all sorts of reasons.'

'Yeah, but most of them are pretty fucked up.'

'Keen on generalizations, aren't you?' Janet said.

'They're generally true. Have you asked about school?'

'Not yet. She's been out. There are these girls that Marlene's put on the email who are still at Ryelands. She says they knew Lisa, time coincided. Could be useful to talk to them.'

'Different ages.'

'Yes, but sometimes the young ones know more about what's going on than anyone else. Mine certainly does,' Janet said. 'I'll go myself.'

'Why?' said Rachel.

'It's called tact and diplomacy.'

Rachel shrugged. ''Kay. I could see Angela Hambley.'

'Rosie's friend?'

'If I'm allowed?' Rachel said.

'Be my guest.'

'She's in Cheetham Hill.'

'Wear your body armour, then.'

Rachel laughed, 'Yes, Mam.' Cheetham was one of the rougher parts of town, dirt poor, mixed ethnicity, still dominated by gang crime and the associated fallout.

37

'I'm sorry,' Janet said as soon as Marlene opened the door.

Marlene held a hand up to stop her. 'No problem. There's always one, isn't there? Come in. I've told Amy and Samantha that you're coming and that it's in connection with Lisa's murder. Do you want me to sit in?'

'Entirely up to you,' Janet said.

'I'll leave you to it, then. I'm drowning in paperwork, third-quarter accounts.'

Sooner you than me.

Janet spoke to the girls individually in a 'quiet room' at the back of the house. It looked out on to lawns and another play area, as well as a fenced-off vegetable plot.

Amy was a lumpen girl, who chewed gum and answered Janet's questions in an adenoidal whine. Her eyes watered and she seemed to be upset about Lisa, though she had very little to say. Lisa was OK, according to Amy, but she didn't really bother with the younger kids. She got into fights sometimes, Amy remembered the fights, but they were with different people, no one in particular. She remembered Sean too, and a faint blush coloured her pasty cheeks when she said his name. Had she had a crush on him? Amy hadn't ever seen anyone else show interest in Lisa, or cause her bother. Janet asked her if any of the boys were known to hassle girls or act out of order.

'Like rape 'n' that?' she said simply.

Out of the mouths of babes. 'Yeah,' Janet said.

Amy shook her head.

Samantha, tall and dark-haired, wearing tons of make-up and the latest trendy clothes looked like a wannabe model. She was fifteen and remembered Lisa well. They had even shared a bedroom for a couple of years when Samantha first moved in.

Her answers echoed Amy's, though she chattered more and kept interjecting to say how awful it was and ask questions about the murder and the investigation that Janet couldn't answer.

'We're going to the funeral,' Samantha said. 'You know when it is?'

Janet shook her head. 'No date yet.'

'Be a school day, though, innit?' Hopefully.

Sweet Jesus, Janet thought, some girl's dead and all it means is an excuse for a day off school.

Janet had been to so many funerals for murder victims. The worst, without doubt, were when a young person had died. Parents, friends and family crazed with grief or frozen with shock. Kids nowadays were more often included in the ritual. Or the school would hold a special assembly, plant a tree, initiate an award in the young person's name. There'd been nothing like that for Veronica. Janet and the rest of her schoolmates not even aware the girl had died.

Parents burying a child. So very wrong. Joshua's funeral had been intensely sad. Janet and Ade had got through it by clinging to each other. She had felt brittle and weak, as though she was made of thin glass, ready to shatter, but she had also felt a great depth of emotion behind the glass. Love and pity and sadness and anger that heightened everything: the colours of the flowers, jasmine and hyacinth and tiny narcissi, the breath of wind on her face and the smell of earth and fresh-mown grass. As though her senses were over-compensating for Joshua's lack of them. Her life swelling, too bold, too bright in the shadow of his silence, his absence.

As she was leaving Ryelands, she got a call from Rachel. No hellos or intros, just, 'I'm at Angela Hambley's, there's something you need to see.'

The term mouthy could have been invented for Angela, who on seeing Rachel at the door immediately gave a theatrical sigh. ''Aven't you got nothing better to do?'

'Than what? What do you think I'm doing?'

'Wasting time, innit. Wanting to know who robbed the offie, did I see anything. Well, I didn't.'

'I'm not here about that,' Rachel said. She'd noted the off-licence opposite, the windows covered in sheets of plywood.

'Well, what then? I have got a life to lead, you know.'

292

Angela had a sharp little face, pointed nose, streaked hair pulled back in a ponytail, a Langley facelift. A stud in one nostril. And skin burnt orange, the colour of wood-stain. Rachel could smell the yeasty fake-tan smell on her.

'Can I come in?'

Another big sigh. 'Can I stop you?' She stood aside, forcing Rachel to squeeze past. 'On the left.'

It was a bedsit, reasonably tidy, woodchip paper, flat-pack furniture, central heating. A double bed under the bay window, sofa parallel to the hall, table and chairs at the other end. Telly bracketed to the wall. Proper curtains. Rachel had seen all sorts used to cover the windows as she drove up the street: striped sheets, beach towels, one place had a patchwork of cardboard. Angela wasn't doing so bad. A small kitchenette, fridge and microwave, sink. A noticeboard with photos on over the sofa, too far away to make out.

'I want to ask you about Rosie Vaughan,' Rachel said.

''Aven't seen her in ages,' Angela said.

'How long ago?'

She twitched her shoulders. 'Couple of years, maybe more.'

'Were you still in touch in 2008?'

'No. You talking about when she was raped? I was asked about all that back then by one of your lot. Said I never seen her much after I left Ryelands, innit.'

'I thought you were mates?' Rachel said.

'For a bit.' She was defensive. Why? Because she'd

jacked Rosie in, then felt bad when Rosie's life went off track? Let her mate down? 'You have to make do, somewhere like that,' Angela added.

'Did Rosie have a bloke, a boyfriend?'

Angela's eyes went still, guarded. 'No,' she said, and Rachel didn't believe her.

'You know she's dead?'

'What?' That stopped her in her tracks, some emotion rippling across her face. Fear? Disgust?

'Thursday. She killed herself.'

'Fuck,' said Angela. She rubbed at her arms, they were bare, the room was warm.

Rachel couldn't see any needle marks, no sign in either the girl's appearance or the state of the flat that she was a hardened drug user. Maybe she was the one that got away.

'She slit her wrists?' Angela said.

'Why'd you think that?'

'She cut herself,' she said flatly.

Rachel nodded. Her throat felt dry. 'She jumped from her balcony.'

'Oh, God,' Angela said. 'Did she leave a note?' A ring of something in her voice and her eyes. Alarm? Anxiety?

'I can't tell you that,' Rachel said, so she'd think there was one. Hoping it might be a lever to prise whatever Angela was hiding out of her.

'So what you here for? Like I said, I 'aven't seen her for years.'

'You both left Ryelands in 2008,' Rachel said. 'See each other at all after that?'

'A bit. We'd not much in common – she was a bit stressed, innit? Probably only seen her two or three times in all. Can't help you.' She made to move, but Rachel wasn't done. 'What about Lisa Finn?'

'You what?'

'Lisa Finn?'

'She were murdered,' Angela said. 'I know that much. All over the telly. Is that what this is about? Is that why you're here?'

'You were at Ryelands with Lisa too.'

'So?' She frowned. 'What you getting at?'

'Two of you didn't get on so well, from what I hear.'

'She was a right pain, always looking for a scrap. I wasn't frightened of her, not going to let her muck us about.'

Rachel said, 'Lisa have a fella?'

'Yes, Sean. They arrested him. Aren't you supposed to know that?' She pulled her lips in a sneer.

Rachel ignored the jibe. 'Was there anyone else that had a relationship with Lisa?'

'No, she was a junkie,' Angela said.

'That make a difference?'

'Skanky, aren't they? Dirty. Get AIDS.'

Rachel was getting nowhere fast. On the surface, Angela knew nothing, couldn't help, so why was she so tense, why the glimpses of fear, of being found out? Rachel tried another tack: 'Did Rosie have any enemies? Was there anyone who wanted to hurt her?' The assault had been vicious, uncontrolled.

'No, she was all right really.' Angela grimaced. 'Just a

bit mental, bit of a nutter. Couldn't help it.' Another quick shrug.

On the way out, Rachel paused by the sofa, to see the photographs on the display-board. Centre place was one of Angela with a birthday cake, candles, *16* written in icing. The photograph had been torn in half so only two people were in it: Angela and a man, blond hair, the look of a tennis player. James Raleigh. Looking younger, but the same guy. Rachel's scalp tightened. What the hell was he doing at Ryelands? At Angela's sixteenth birthday party?

That's when she called Janet.

38

They were standing in the hallway at Angela's. Janet looked at the photograph. Rachel pointed to the man: 'James Raleigh,' she said. 'Lisa's support worker in the community. When I spoke to him, he never let on he had ever been near Ryelands.'

Janet frowned. 'Hang on.' She checked her book and called Marlene, introduced herself and asked Marlene if James Raleigh had ever been a member of staff.

'No.'

'In 2007?'

Marlene hesitated. 'I was on maternity leave some of the time, but I'm pretty sure we didn't have any change in the staffing.'

'Do you know him?' Janet said.

'A little. Lisa was on his caseload. He's fairly new in the job, North Manchester Area.'

'Marlene, is there any other reason he might have been at Ryelands if he wasn't on staff?'

'Well . . . on a placement, possibly? Hang on.'

Janet watched Rachel pace the hall. A few seconds later Marlene came back to the phone. 'Yes, he was in the final year of his social work degree then. On placement for six weeks, I was still off.'

'Thanks,' Janet said, 'that explains it.' She looked at Rachel. 'A placement.'

'Doesn't explain why he pretended he were never there?'

'Did you ask that specifically?'

Rachel twitched with irritation. 'No, but he kept saying things like "Ryelands will be able to tell you more than me", and "I've only known Lisa since she left". He deliberately gave the impression that he was completely separate.'

'Well, he is – job's different.'

The door opened and Angela came out into the hall. 'I'm not staying there all bloody day,' she complained. 'What's going on? I want my photo back. You can't just take it.'

'Come in,' Janet said to Rachel. They went to the kitchen area, Angela sat at the table, Janet too. Rachel stood. 'Angela,' Janet said, 'we want to ask you about this picture.'

Angela's face tightened. 'What about it?'

'This man here, who is it?'

Angela blinked once. Janet saw the muscles by her ear move as she swallowed. 'James,' she said. 'He were a student.'

'You still know him?'

'No.' She tapped her fingers over her phone. 'What you asking about him for?'

Janet didn't answer. 'Who was in this part of the photograph?'

'Can't remember.' A red spot flared on each of her cheeks, beneath the orange tan.

'Why did you cut it off?'

'Spilt summat, some tea or something, innit. It's my photo, up to us what I do with it. Can do what I like.'

'Of course you can,' Janet said. 'You know where he is nowadays – James?'

'Not a fucking clue,' she said. Her hand closed over her phone.

Liar.

Janet got out her own phone, set the photograph on the table. 'I'm just going to take a picture of it.'

'Why?' The girl's voice was high with anxiety. 'Can you do that? Isn't that against my privacy, like an invasion of my privacy?'

'We could get a warrant,' Rachel threatened her, 'take all your gear?'

'What for? You can't do that, you mad bitch. I 'aven't done anything, innit. I never seen Lisa Finn since I left Ryelands.'

'Was it Lisa you cut off the photograph?' Rachel said.

The girl sat, suddenly mute, looking as if she'd burst, lips tight, cheeks puffed out. Giving furious little shakes of her head, ponytail bouncing.

'It was Rosie, wasn't it?' Janet said. 'She's not in the picture. You were mates then.'

'No, you're wrong,' she said quickly. But Janet was sure she'd guessed correctly.

'Who then?'

'Marlene.'

The girl was lying; Marlene had been on maternity leave.

'Why cut Marlene off?'

'I told you, I spilt something on it.'

'Or maybe you just wanted the two of you, together,' Rachel said, 'all lovey-dovey.'

'Don't know what you're fucking talking about,' she snarled.

Janet captured the photograph, making sure the date and time stamp showed correctly. 'What happened between you and Rosie?' Janet asked. 'Best mates, weren't you?'

'Nothing. She was mental. I told her, innit.' She jerked her head at Rachel. 'Rosie was freaky, I couldn't be doing with it. I've got to go to work,' she said, scraping back her chair.

'Where d'you work?' Janet said.

'What's it to you?' Janet didn't speak and finally Angela added, 'Tesco's, if you must know.'

Janet wanted to congratulate her; jobs were scarce for young people, bound to be harder for someone like Angela whose education had likely been disrupted. 'Can I take your number please?' Janet said. 'We might want to talk to you again.'

Angela froze, then gave a little snort. She wasn't happy about it, but she gave Janet her number.

'She says she's not seen Raleigh,' Janet said, out on the pavement. 'Do you believe her?'

Rachel pulled a face.

'Me neither. We hang on, let's see if the neighbours know any different.'

They waited down the street until Angela emerged, wearing a bright red coat, crossed the road and disappeared from view.

They returned to the entrance and rang the bell for the other flats in Angela's house. Got one reply. A man who had a room upstairs at the back. His English was fractured, but he understood their questions. And when Janet showed him the photograph of Angela and James Raleigh and asked if he had seen the man at the house, he nodded enthusiastically. 'Yes, many times, boyfriend.'

It was just what they wanted to hear.

'Don't get on your hobby horse again,' Janet warned Rachel once they were on their way back. 'It's a coincidence, he did a placement there.'

'She was bricking it, especially about the photo. Three years later, she's still got it on the wall, he's showing up at her flat all the time – she's probably shagging him.'

'We don't know that.'

'Ten quid, twenty.'

'I'm not betting on it,' Janet said.

'Honestly, Janet – why did Raleigh not mention that he'd met Lisa before she became his client?'

'There might be a simple reason: she absconded during his time there, or was ill, or whatever.'

'For the whole six weeks—'

'Don't just leap at the first fence, Rachel. Think about it. You're looking to prove something that might not be there. You're starting with a narrative and straight away you're off looking for evidence. We do it the other way around: we look for evidence and then we build the narrative.'

'We need to check him out,' Rachel insisted.

She wasn't listening. 'First Dalbeattie, now Raleigh—'

'Dalbeattie's got an alibi. Golf on the Algarve.'

Janet stilled. Unbelievable. 'I did not hear that, did I? I did not just hear you say that.'

'Whatever!' Rachel folded her arms. 'Take a left here.'

'Why?'

'Neighbourhood office, get his car reg.'

'We don't even—'

'It's five minutes,' Rachel said.

Janet did as she asked. 'How do you know which is his?' she asked as they drew up. Half a dozen cars in the car park behind the security fencing.

'Because when I left him last time, there was only one car out front. There – the blue Nissan Micra.' Rachel wrote the registration down.

'OK, imagine you're on to something. Talk me through it, because I'm really not seeing it.'

'Right. Raleigh does his placement and meets them all

– Lisa, Rosie, her pal Angela. The following year, he rapes Rosie, beats her up.'

'Why?'

'I don't know. Because he's a scuzzy bastard. Then he rapes and kills Lisa.'

'Again, why?'

'Still a scuzzy bastard.'

'Two years between the attacks.'

'OK. But maybe there were others; you know how few women report rape to us.'

'Very different attacks too: one woman is beaten, the other is stabbed – just once.'

'But listen, we've got a DNA match for someone in both attacks. And now we've linked Raleigh to both women. And Angela Hambley is lying through her teeth.'

Janet sighed. It was tangled, chaotic, unclear.

'We ask him for a DNA sample,' Rachel said.

'Gill won't do that, not on such a shaky basis. We can't just go asking people for DNA samples at random.'

'It's not random,' Rachel insisted. 'He's a link.'

Janet gave a shrug.

'So what, we do nothing? Let the bastard waltz around and get away with it?'

'The only chance we have is to look at him more carefully first; tactfully, subtly. Was he in the area, can we find his car? Groundwork. *If*,' and she stressed the word, 'Gill's OK with it.'

'If she's not?'

'Forget it.'

Rachel shook her head, hit the heel of her hand on the dashboard.

Janet decided it would be wiser to ignore her little tantrum. And they drove on in silence.

39

Back at the station, Andy met her in the corridor. 'Janet, can I just check something with you?' Sounding as he usually did, but she could see from the tension in his jawline and his knuckles whitening round the file that he held there was a subtext.

'Sure.' She went with him into the meeting room.

He closed the door.

'It was a mistake,' Janet said, wanting to get in first. 'I'm sorry.'

He didn't say anything for a moment. Did he agree? Then he nodded slowly.

'Ade, the kids. What were we thinking of?' She gave half a laugh. Didn't feel at all amused. 'Just put it behind us, yes?'

'Is that what you want?' he asked.

Didn't he? 'Yes,' she said firmly. Because she couldn't do this, feel like this. The guilt was horrible.

He waited, moved as if he'd speak, then didn't.

The door flew open and Janet jumped.

'Not interrupting, am I?' said Kevin in his leery way.

'No,' said Janet.

'Fuck off, Kevin,' said Andy, throwaway, but Janet saw a murderous glint in his eyes.

'Right, Sarge,' Janet said for extra cover. It'd be a total nightmare if Kevin suspected something. 'I'll pass it on to the CPS case officer, soon as.'

'Appreciated,' said Andy. Then he turned to Kevin: 'Aren't you meant to be scanning CCTV?'

Janet escaped, left them to it. A shaky feeling inside, not unlike in the aftermath of Rachel's car stunt.

'You tell her.'

'We'll tell her together.' Janet knocked on Gill's door and Gill waggled a hand: come in.

Rachel followed in Janet's shadow, knowing she was out of favour and not wanting to sabotage the mission.

Janet cleared her throat. 'We've been to see Angela Hambley, an old friend of Rosie Vaughan, less than friendly with Lisa Finn back in the day. Angela got very arsey when Rachel started asking questions.'

'As you might.' Gill's eyes gleamed brightly.

'Small detail, and it could well be nothing,' Janet said diplomatically, 'but James Raleigh, Lisa's personal advisor . . .'

Gill nodded.

'. . . was in a photograph, on the wall, looking very cosy. He'd done a placement at Ryelands when all three girls were there. Angela claimed to have no idea whether he was still knocking around, even though his photograph's on her wall and she's cut off the other people in it. Most likely her mate Rosie.'

'Raleigh never let on to me though,' Rachel said, impatient at how slow Janet was to tell the tale. 'He talked as if he had only met Lisa once she was living on her own when he got given her case. Acted like he'd never set foot inside Ryelands.'

Gill waited.

'So,' Janet said, 'maybe we could ask him about that?'

'You saying he could be a person of interest?'

'Well, he's interested me,' Rachel put in.

'Why does that not surprise me?' Gill said nastily. 'Which makes you the last person to go back and talk to him.'

'Oh, boss,' Rachel complained, damned if she'd keep quiet.

Gill stared at her. Then came to a decision. 'Smacks of desperation,' she said. 'No grounds there, not unless you give me some more.'

'What if we can find him in the vicinity of the scene?' Janet said.

Gill raised an eyebrow.

'We could ANPR his car,' Rachel said.

A moment while Her Maj made up her mind. 'No sign – you park it,' Gill said crisply. Bit unreasonable, Rachel thought, but they'd have to take whatever crumbs they could. 'Do it,' Gill said. 'In fact, Rachel – you do it. And that man is off limits unless you can you bring me his car in Collyhurst in our time frame.'

'Yes, boss,' they answered in unison.

*   *   *

Rachel ran the registration through the PNC first and got confirmation that James Raleigh was the registered keeper. An address in Royton. She thought about the argument Lisa had had in the taxi, telling someone to get out of her life, stop telling her what to do – Raleigh? But that didn't fit with the data from telecoms: no call logged then between Raleigh and Lisa.

Rachel set up the data for the ANPR, automatic number-plate recognition system. Developed to combat terrorism, it had become an effective tool for tracing vehicles in many other crimes and was far more efficient than trawling through CCTV if a car reg was known.

Her thoughts wandered as she waited for the software to do its thing, finding all the locations that the number plate was 'pinged' on Monday afternoon. Kasim had been up in the magistrates' court on Wednesday and remanded on bail. He indicated he'd be pleading not guilty to the charges and so, if he kept that up, the case would go to trial in the crown court and Rachel would likely be called to give evidence against him. She was pretty sure all her paperwork was up to scratch on that. Nick would be opening for the defence at the Old Bailey tomorrow, or Wednesday, if there were delays.

Her stomach was growling; she thought briefly of burger and chips or pie and peas, but didn't want to take a break. She wanted to prove she was right and give Gill something to stick in her pipe. Rachel scoured the results on the screen. Her pulse accelerated. She had Raleigh on Oldham Road at 1.55 and 2.34. Perfect timing.

'Got you, you prick!' she said aloud, and went to tell Janet.

'He works in the area, keep that in mind,' Janet said. 'He could have been visiting a client.'

'Yeah – Lisa.'

'Another client.'

'Who lives on the same estate.'

'Yes. That's his job, neighbourhood social worker. Half of Collyhurst is probably on his books. We treat him as a witness, all nice and friendly, we don't ruffle his feathers, we don't tip him off.'

'How can we ask him his whereabouts on Monday without tipping him off?'

'We have ways,' said Janet, a glint in her eye. 'But we need to see what Gill thinks.'

'Got him coming and going, boss.' Rachel was champing at the bit, 'Not so desperate now, eh?'

'Oy! Don't you get cocky.'

'No, boss.'

'So what do you want to do next?'

'Arrest him,' Rachel said immediately. 'Failing that, cut his balls off.'

'Question him as a witness, see if he's got a reason-able explanation,' Janet said.

'Is the right answer.' Gill pointed to Janet with both her index fingers. Rachel wondered if she did her nails every night; the polish was never chipped.

'If we arrest too soon, we put him on guard, he clams up, won't cooperate, even goes no comment. Plus the small matter of not having strong grounds,' Gill said. 'But if we talk to him as witness first, there's a chance we'll get information we can use in a subsequent interview under caution. Yeah?'

Rachel nodded her agreement. It did make sense, even if it was frustrating.

She rang and asked James Raleigh if he could call into the police station: they had a few more questions about Lisa and hoped he could help. He made excuses and Rachel pressed him, 'Perhaps in the morning?' Keeping her voice sweet. He dithered a bit, but finally settled on an appointment in between two client visits.

On the way home, Gill thought about Rachel, about what Janet had said: *She reminds me of you.* But Gill knew she had never had that reckless impetuosity. Like a puppy after a ball – any ball would do. And if that couldn't be reined in, Rachel wouldn't be able to progress, she'd quickly be regarded as a loose cannon, not fit for promotion. Gill's options in dealing with the problem were limited: she could do nothing, bide her time and see if the detective had the smarts to learn from her mistakes and seriously tackle those areas needing improvement; put her on an action plan and if necessary institute efficiency proceedings; she could cut her loose and shuffle her back to Sutton; or she could play bad cop, keep Rachel on a short lead, punish her with the most tedious of tasks. But she hadn't recruited the girl to see her prospects narrowed, her potential squashed. Gill wasn't that sort of leader, or manager. She wanted to see Rachel fly.

Sammy was on the sofa. He'd found a way to operate his console with only one set of working fingers.

Gill watched him manipulate a footballer into a scoring position. The soundtrack commentary set her teeth on edge. 'You eaten?'

'Yes.'

'Your dad make you something?'

He didn't answer.

'Sammy?'

He let his head fall back against the top of the sofa cushion. 'Emma,' he said.

Gill tensed. 'Emma fed you. Where?'

'At their place.'

'Who took you to college?'

'Mum,' he complained.

'Who picked you up at lunch?'

'Emma.'

'And this morning?'

'Emma. Dad was busy.'

Busy? Fuck that! One day, two car rides and he sent his slaggy whore to be chauffeur. And cook! Gill was tempted to ask Sammy what he'd been fed, but she wouldn't lower herself.

She went into the kitchen and shut the door. When Dave answered she piled straight in: 'Couldn't you have bloody done it yourself? He's your son.'

'You're being petty.'

'I don't want that cow near him.'

'Gill! Have you listened to yourself?'

'No. Zip it, fuckwit. If I ask you to do something for Sammy, I'm asking you. You do precious bloody little as it is.'

'Gill, you need to grow up and move on.'

'Oh, yeah?' Her blood boiling, that red mist behind her eyes. 'Like you have? Who is it you've moved on to now? Saturday night? Bigger tits, has she? Fresher uniform? Emma not twigged yet? Slow on the uptake, eh?'

'Took you long enough.' Hit her like a slap. Bastard.

'I knew,' she said. 'I knew back when Sammy was in nursery and you were so pally with Sally the sergeant. But I thought Sammy was more important than hanging your dick out to dry. You were the one who fucked this family up, Dave, and there is no way that your tart is going to play stepmother to my son. He needs a father, not a stepmother!' She ended the call, her whole body shaking, cursing under her breath. How dare he! How dare he still make her feel this way. How long would it take before she could think of him without feeling the spite in her mouth when she said his name, the hurt when she thought of him and Emma in their cramped little house with their snotty little kid.

She flung open the fridge door and got out a bottle of gin, there since the summer. No tonic, but Sammy's lemonade would do. She mixed the drink and added ice and a chunk of lemon. Stuck an Amy Winehouse CD in

312

the player and turned the volume up. She made herself a stir-fry, prawns and veg, oyster sauce and noodles, slugging the gin as she cooked and doing the odd dance step to the music. She had double her chocolate ration to follow. Fuck it.

She thought about Matthew. Nice bloke on first acquaintance, nice place, good taste, not afraid to roll up his sleeves and get stuck in, money to splash about. Good job, people person like herself. She had been flattered by his interest – delighted, if she was honest – to be seen as a woman and not a boss or a mother or a pal. As a woman, a potential lover, mate, partner. So long since she had been that. But how could she even entertain him when she was still so . . . She struggled to explain it to herself. So . . . What? Hurt? Damaged? Distrustful? All three.

He was only talking about a meal, though, when she had time. Could be weeks away, months. But I'd be leading him on, she thought sadly, because I'm not ready. Because I'm scared of someone hurting me like that all over again.

40

Rachel was desperate to interview Raleigh, but Gill was unsure about it. The girl had too much invested in it, seemed convinced that Raleigh was responsible for the rape of Rosie Vaughan as well as the murder of Lisa Finn. Conviction could hamper her performance in interview, prevent her really listening. How capable was she of being objective? The track record so far told against her. But should Gill give her a chance to make amends, up her game? She discussed it with Andy over a quick breakfast in the canteen: 'Do you think she could rise to the challenge?'

'I don't know,' he said. 'I've not had much time with her. If she doesn't, we could be in a right mess.'

He sounded flat, not like Andy. OK, he usually kept things to himself, never one to prattle on, but he generally had more of a spark. Gill hadn't heard of any problems on the domestic front. His work had been exemplary. Was he just tired, some minor health problem? She'd keep an eye on him; if he didn't buck up, she'd have a quiet word.

'I could use it as part of her training development plan. She wants to go for tier three. Make sure she does a full prep with Janet.'

He pulled a face.

'You're not sure?'

'Like you say, this one's got personal for her. Is it the best place for her to start?'

'I'll ask her. Treat her like a grown-up, see how she responds.'

Rachel had a sulky look on her face until she grasped what Gill was actually saying. 'And you treat it like a witness interview, all smiles and sympathy. Can you do that?'

'I can, yes.' Rachel nodded her head.

'No pressure, no innuendo, no bullying, no snidey little comments.'

'I know.' Rachel was almost running on the spot, so eager to get at it.

'You'll plan and prep with Janet, and I'll be watching you in interview. This will count towards your application for the tier three course. So, you will be grace incarnate. I want that man to come away feeling smug and safe and valued.'

'Yes, boss.'

'You understand why?'

'Of course,' she said impatiently.

Gill turned her hand round in a circle. 'Enlighten me.'

'Because we want him to open up, we want him to

315

talk, then when he gives us a shedload of lies, we've got him by the balls.'

'And if we jumped the gun – slagged him off, shouting, screaming, making threats?'

'He wouldn't tell us anything.'

'Right.' Gill stepped back to let her leave. Pointed two fingers in a V-shape at her own eyes and then back towards Rachel. I'll be watching you.

'Janet,' Andy came to her desk, 'Lee says Ade's downstairs, he wants to see you.'

Her stomach dropped. Ade never came to work. He knew! He'd found out. How? She looked at Andy, saw he was worried too, his face pale, eyes alert.

'Shit. Do you know . . . ?' she said.

Andy shook his head quickly.

'Right.' She got up, fluttering in her belly, her chest tight. Self-consciously she smoothed back her hair. Would he make a scene? It wasn't Ade's way in the general run of things, but then this wasn't a normal occurrence. Maybe Ade, being cheated on, would turn into some raving loony, go berserk and shout the house down. Give Andy a bloody nose.

Janet saw Gill peer across from her office, antennae twitching. Sharp as a tack. Janet forced a smile Andy's way for Gill's benefit.

She went downstairs, trying to relax her face muscles, bracing herself.

Ade was sitting in the foyer. She saw him before he noticed her. He didn't look particularly agitated.

316

He was tapping on his phone – surfing the news pages, Janet saw as she reached him.

'What?' she said.

'We've had a phone call,' he said.

'Yes?' Who? Some tittle-tattler? Who knew? No one. Had someone seen them leaving the works do together?

'Mr Fairley, he wants to see us with Taisie after school. Today, if possible.'

Oh, thank fuck for that! She felt weak at the knees. 'You could have rung me,' Janet said, cross now that she had been panicked, going on the offensive.

'I was passing, thought we could sort it out now.'

'Well, I can't go,' Janet said.

Ade gave a snidey little laugh. 'You never can.'

Had he come to pick a fight? Janet took a breath. 'Slight exaggeration, but this week, no way. I assume this is about the sugar-plum business?'

Ade shrugged. 'Wouldn't say. Didn't want to discuss it over the phone, said it wasn't appropriate.'

Pompous dick. Mr Fairley would get on a whole lot better if he hadn't been so up himself. 'Shit,' Janet said under her breath. 'I hoped we'd killed it before he found out. Unless it's something else? You'll have to do it without me.'

'Same as bloody usual,' he snapped. And went. Leaving Janet wondering what on earth that was all about.

Rachel had done the plan and prep with Janet and that had gone well. If Her Maj was letting her have a crack

317

at Raleigh, Rachel assumed that Marlene had not followed through and lodged an official complaint.

When Raleigh arrived and she went down to reception to meet him, Rachel felt a surge of animosity hot in her belly. Something she must hide well if she was to do this right. He was taller than she remembered and broad-shouldered. He wore navy chinos, a white shirt and a navy wool sweater. She could smell aftershave. Shiny and squeaky clean. She put on a big smile, shook his hand, thanked him for coming in, made an inane comment about the weather.

'You released Sean,' he said. 'How come?'

'I'm sorry, I can't discuss that with you,' she said as she took him through to the interview room. He looked puzzled when he saw the set-up, the tape recorder, the video camera in the corner, Janet with her notepad.

'Sorry if it looks a bit official,' Rachel said, 'but we record all witness interviews like this now. And there are a number of things I need to make you aware of – protocol.'

He shrugged, gave a smile. 'OK.'

She went through them with him: the fact he was not a suspect (you so are, mate!) was free to leave and so on, free to consult with a solicitor.

Her instinct was to lean forward, arms braced on her knees to question him, but she remembered what Janet had told her about posture and settled back. *Act as if you're a market researcher* (Rachel had grinned at that, though she hid it quickly) *really interested in getting the answers, but not at all bothered what they are. Neutral.*

Consciously Rachel relaxed her hands, balled like fists, and her feet. 'Thanks very much for coming in, we do appreciate it. Please can you tell me first how you know Lisa Finn.'

'I was her personal advisor, since she left Ryelands.'

'What did that involve?'

He exhaled. 'Whatever she needed, really – help with claiming benefits, managing her finances, career guidance, liaison with medical services. The aim is to make sure the young person makes a smooth transition from being looked after to being fully independent.'

Rachel nodded a couple of times as he spoke, to show she was paying attention. 'How often did you meet with Lisa?'

'Weekly at first, then just once a month.'

'The last time we spoke you told me you hadn't seen Lisa since November the twenty-fifth?'

'That's right.'

'How was she then?'

'Not too bad. I was a bit worried about her boyfriend, Sean – he was an obstacle to her addressing her drug dependency. That wasn't anything new, though. We were aiming to get Lisa into rehab, but we weren't making much progress. The family – her mother, Denise – wanted that to happen, but Sean was a complicating factor.' He smiled ruefully. His teeth were even, startlingly white; bleached, Rachel imagined. Vain git.

'And on November twenty-fifth,' Rachel repeated the date, 'did she mention any trouble, any threats of violence, harassment, arguments, anything of that nature?'

'No, nothing. She had divulged in the past that she and Sean had a somewhat chaotic relationship, arguments would lead to violence, domestic abuse,' he added, 'but in November she didn't mention anything about that.'

'And you didn't see Lisa after November twenty-fifth?'

'No.' He shuffled slightly, crossed his ankles.

'Did you hear from her after that?'

'No.'

'Thank you.' Rachel surprised herself with how genuine she sounded. Now she had to be careful. She and Janet had discussed the wording for this next question; it was vital that it didn't make him defensive, set off any alarm bells. 'We are building up a picture of Lisa's movements last Monday and collating details on any callers to Fairland Avenue and even people passing through the estate. Were you in the neighbourhood at any time on Monday?' She tried to keep her expression bland, as though she expected him to answer in the negative.

'No, no.' He waved away the suggestion. 'Office all morning, then case conference at the town hall in the afternoon.'

Got you! Rachel's pulse accelerated. 'The office is in Newton Heath and then you were at Manchester Town Hall?'

'Yes.' He looked at his watch, uncrossed his ankles

and put his hands on his knees, signalling he thought they were nearly through and he was ready to leave.

'I think that's everything.' Rachel gave him a smile. 'Is there anything you'd like to add your statement?'

'No, that's fine.'

'Can I just ask you to wait here a moment?'

'Yes.' The slightest touch of uncertainty in his reply.

'Thank you. Interview concluded at twelve twenty p.m.'

Rachel forced herself to move slowly until she got outside, Janet behind her. 'Yes!' Rachel said under her breath, fists raised in victory. 'We've got him!'

'It's a beginning,' Janet agreed.

'It's an arrest, that's what it is.' Rachel could feel the excitement thrumming in her veins. She was going to get the bastard, oh, yes!

Rachel went to see Gill, breathless when she got there, dying for a fag, too.

Gill turned away from the screen showing the video feed to the interview room and surveyed Rachel. Her face remained impassive for a moment and Rachel felt a wobble of doubt, then Gill grinned. 'Nick him!' she ordered.

Rachel couldn't get there soon enough. Raleigh got to his feet as she came into the interview room. She dove straight in: 'James Raleigh, I am arresting you on suspicion of the murder of Lisa Finn. You do not have to say anything, but it may harm your defence . . .'

321

The smile died on his lips. A glare of outrage replacing it, disbelief glittering in his eyes.

'. . . if you do not mention, when questioned, something which you later rely on in court. Anything you do say may be given in evidence against you.'

'This is some sort of joke,' he blurted out.

'Can you put your hands out.' Rachel got out her cuffs, not yielding to the impulse to slam the cuffs on, pinching his wrists as she clamped them shut. 'You will accompany me to the custody sergeant, who will explain your rights, then ask you to surrender your possessions. You will have the right to a solicitor and we can provide one for you if required. We will be making a search of your premises, so if you have the keys that will save the risk of any damage on entry.'

'You can't do this,' he insisted.

'Watch me,' Rachel told him.

'I didn't kill Lisa,' he said. 'There must be some mistake. I want to speak to your superior officer,' he stumbled over the words.

'Senior,' Rachel corrected him. 'I'll pass that request on. Don't hold your breath.'

He huffed and puffed all the way to the custody suite. Rachel booked him in and waited, savouring the sight as the custody sergeant went through all the rigmarole, asking Raleigh to empty his pockets, phone, car keys, house keys, wallet and then getting him to sign a property slip for them. He had two phones, Rachel felt a nudge of excitement at that – she knew one would likely be kept for his dirty little assignations.

322

He was fingerprinted and the sergeant said they would now take a DNA swab.

'No way,' Raleigh said. 'I don't give my permission.'

'We don't need your permission,' Rachel said. 'You don't cooperate, we can hold you down and rip hairs off your head. Need the say-so from a superintendent. Your call, pal. I'd rather we did it the hard way.'

'This is not fair,' he argued, but submitted to the swab being taken. He'd gone ashen by the time they took him to get changed. His clothes would be kept as potential evidence and he'd be given a disposable jumpsuit to wear. He still kept muttering denials and protesting that it was a farce, a mistake, crazy.

Now, Rachel thought, wired with energy, I really do need a fag.

41

Things moved quickly after that. His phones were given to the telecoms officer for an analysis of all the data stored on them. Gill dispatched a team to search his house for the murder weapon, bloodstained clothing, any property belonging to the victim. And for seizure of his computer. A search was made of his car. Fingerprint analysis revealed Raleigh's prints on the door jamb to Lisa's bedroom and bathroom, though the partial print on Lisa's gold cross did not match Raleigh.

The prepaid phone immediately yielded useful intelligence. Raleigh had the numbers of both Angela and Lisa Finn in his contacts list. His stored text messages showed several sent to both girls, among them one that made the hairs on the back of Janet's neck prickle: Raleigh had sent a text to Lisa at half past twelve on the morning of her death. *C u @ 2 babe x* Babe! Oh, the bastard.

'Janet,' Gill said, 'take someone and talk to Angela, will you? See what she can tell us.'

Janet scanned the office. They were all out, bar Andy. Who looked over and smiled.

Her heart sank. 'Yes, boss.'

'Ade – what did he . . .' Andy asked as they drove to Cheetham Hill, the shops along the main drag awash with Christmas decorations, sledges and inflatable Santas.

'Nothing. It's fine. Kids' stuff.'

'Right.' Then he turned to work: 'What's she like – Angela?' He obviously wasn't any more keen than she was to dwell on recent events.

'Gobby,' Janet said, 'prickly, but she did talk to us, even if half of it was lies. And she's holding down a job, so she has got something going on upstairs.'

'We appeal to her intelligence?' Andy said.

'I'm not sure I'd go that far,' Janet said drily.

She appreciated the fact that he was keeping things on a professional footing. But found it hard to act naturally in his presence, especially when they were alone like this. Her own voice sounded brittle in her ears, her smile false. God, did she regret what had happened. Too much drink coming on top of another miserable spell with Ade, which left her feeling unloved, middle-aged and in a rut. Not at work, but every other way. Andy seemed as anxious as she was to minimize the opportunity for any more lapses of judgement. That was good, wasn't it? So why was there a part of her still fantasizing about the guy? Why did part of her wonder if she'd made the wrong choice way back, sticking with

Ade, dependable Ade the boy next door, instead of upsetting the applecart when she'd met Andy at training. Taking the leap, choosing the unknown. But then she'd never have had Joshua, Elise, Taisie. Everything would have been different. Oh, God, why couldn't she just get over it? Put it behind her, like she was pretending to do on the surface?

The rain had stopped, Janet thought, or maybe it was only suspended as grey mist. The dog-end of the year. Grim. All well and good if you were huddled round the fire toasting marshmallows, but there wasn't much of that in the Scott household these days. Oh God. She'd have to pull herself together, make more of an effort, for the girls at least. It was a difficult age. Both of them yearning to be grown up, not wanting to do anything, have anything that smacked of being a little kid, though they were still kids all the same.

Finding them on her doorstep, Angela gave a groan and rolled her eyes at them. 'This is harassment, innit.' One hand on her hip. She flounced back into the house and they followed her into her room.

'Sergeant Andy Roper' – he showed his warrant card – 'you already know DC Scott.'

'We've arrested James Raleigh,' Janet said.

The girl's jaw dropped. 'What? What the fuck are you talking about? What for?'

'On suspicion of the murder of Lisa Finn.'

'No,' Angela said, her eyes filling, her hand going to her mouth.

'Hey, come and sit down,' Janet said. Before you fall.

For once Angela didn't have a comeback, too shocked for that. She lowered herself on to the settee. Janet sat beside her, Andy fetched one of the kitchen chairs for himself. He flipped open his daybook, noted the time and looked over at Janet.

'No way,' Angela said quietly, her chin jutted out, but Janet could see the quiver around her mouth. She was struggling.

'We know you're having a relationship with James,' Janet said.

Angela moved as if to deny it, but Janet's expression stopped her. She saw they knew. 'He can't have done it,' she said. 'He was with me, innit.'

Oh God. 'When?' Janet said.

'Monday.'

'What time?'

Angela hesitated. 'All day.' Tears in her voice.

Janet said, 'We have proof that isn't the case, Angela. And it would be extremely foolish of you to perjure yourself out of some sense of loyalty.'

Silent tears rolled from Angela's eyes, she wiped them away.

'Let's start again,' Janet said. 'You and James have a sexual relationship.'

'Yes,' she said.

'How long for?'

'Year and a half.'

'How did you meet?'

'At Ryelands.'

'And Rosie Vaughan. Did James go out with her?'

'He broke it off,' she said, 'when we got together.'

'You told me earlier that you'd only seen Rosie twice after leaving Ryelands. Is that why? Because of James?'

'He liked me and she could never have coped with it, him being my boyfriend instead of hers. She was bothering him, anyway. Obsessive, innit. Wouldn't leave him alone, threatening to get him into trouble if he left her. Best to have a clean break all round.'

The threats were of interest. Was that what had led to the beating and the rape? Rosie, cut off from Angela, suspecting he was shagging around and trying to pull weight? 'And Lisa Finn – was she another of his girlfriends?'

'No way,' Angela insisted. 'Never. There was just me.' Janet absorbed that. 'He wouldn't do that to me. Go with some dirty junkie. He was a social worker, he had to see Lisa for his job, that's all.' Trying to convince herself. 'He loves me. He wouldn't do that.'

Janet felt a wash of guilt, she loved Ade and look at what she'd done.

'When did you last see James?'

Angela wavered. Still wanting to protect him, to protect some shred of the fantasy she'd been living. But, Janet guessed, not knowing what answer might best help him. 'Thursday,' she finally said.

'This last Thursday? What time?'

'About six.'

'When did he leave?'

'Seven-ish,' she said, defensively.

'That evening?'

Angela gave a nod. Wham-bam-thank-you-ma'am. Janet bet he never stayed the night, never took her anywhere. Using her like a prostitute, not even having to pay. 'Did James say anything about Lisa's murder?'

'Said they'd got Sean for it. It had been on the news.'

'Anything else?' Janet said.

'No. Only that it was an awful thing, one of his clients, innit.'

'Did you know before – that Lisa was one of his clients?'

'No. Confidential all that,' she reeled off.

'And how did James seem when he told you her boyfriend had been arrested?'

'I don't know . . . pleased, like they'd got someone for it. Just normal.'

'Did he ever speak to you at all about the assault on Rosie Vaughan?'

'No, I was the one told him, 'cos the police had been round. He didn't even know it had happened.' Her voice shook. 'He hadn't seen her for ages, see, 'cos he was going with me.' Another tear tracked down her face.

She wasn't stupid, Janet thought. The sheer effort, the energy it must have taken to build and sustain the wall of ignorance she'd built. To keep him unsullied in her mind. To shout down the whispers of suspicion about Rosie, about Lisa, about all the other girls that he popped in to see when the whim took him. To believe she was the only one, special, different.

'I'd like to take your phone,' Janet said. 'We are

329

having to examine all communications made to and from James as part of our investigation.'

'He's innocent, he didn't do nothing,' Angela said again.

Janet got out an evidence bag and held it open. 'Can you please place your phone in the bag?' She wrote out a receipt and passed it back to Angela. 'Has James ever been violent to you?'

'No,' she said.

'Has he ever raped you?'

'No, fuck off, he'd never do anything like that!' She was angry, her face darkening.

'Has he ever threatened you with a knife?'

'No. He's not like that,' she said. 'You'll see. He wouldn't hurt a fly.'

42

The meeting room was buzzing, people chipping in, speculating about the arrest. Gill could see Rachel thriving on the attention, the closest she had come yet to acting like a team player. Sing when you're winning.

Denise Finn had been dumbfounded on hearing of the arrest of another suspect. 'What twenty-eight-year-old? Who is it?' she asked. And, 'Not Sean?' she said more than once, as though she might have got the wrong end of the stick.

'Good news and bad news,' Gill began. 'Good news: we have a text from Raleigh to our victim arranging to visit her at two p.m. on the thirteenth. We have his car in the right place at the right time. We know he has lied to us on several counts. Bad news: we found nothing at his place of residence apart from the right make of condoms, no knife, no bloody togs. High-tech crime unit – still have to get back to us. Andy and Janet – Angela?'

Andy and Janet looked at each other, some weird,

polite dance going on as to who should talk. 'Somebody,' Gill prompted impatiently.

'Grooming,' Janet said, 'apparently for his sole use. Met the three girls at Ryelands, started shagging Rosie, then Angela. Tells Angela he's broken off with Rosie and she must do the same. Divide and rule. Told Angela she was the one and only. Probable he was still visiting Rosie. At some point he starts seeing Lisa, too. The texts say it all. Same style for both Angela and Lisa. His MO seems to be: send them a text, turn up, get his end away and leave. Angela swore blind he never laid into her. One thing she did say might be of interest: Rosie had threatened to report Raleigh, get him into trouble if he didn't treat her right. Perhaps she tried that once too often?'

Rachel tightened her mouth. Gill saw she was disturbed by the likely truth of what Janet suggested.

'I've told forensic submissions that we want to run Raleigh's DNA against our profiles immediately, if not sooner. Other thoughts?' Gill said.

'If he did kill Lisa,' said Mitch, 'why has he kept his sent messages? Why not cover his tracks?'

'Because he's an arrogant wanker,' Rachel said, earning herself a round of applause.

'You may be right,' Gill said, 'but it's a good question. Lee?' He usually had something useful to say on the murkier aspects of human behaviour.

'People keep trophies, that's a similar risk. Others keep things like the murder weapon because they aren't sure how to dispose of them.'

'So, he couldn't work out how to delete his texts?' Kevin sneered.

'Or he chose not to,' Lee said. 'Rachel might be right, he's a narcissist, the only world view he accepts is his own, high functioning, copes with social interaction well, but has a total lack of empathy and an inflated sense of self-importance. Any challenge to him, how he sees things, is completely disregarded. He is never wrong.'

'Like the boss,' Janet joked.

Gill took a bow.

'More bad news,' Pete said. 'The business about going on to a case conference at the town hall checks out. He arrived at ten to three, no mention of blood-stained clothing. I think somebody would have said.'

'It might not have been visible,' Rachel said.

'Right, these guys need to plan and prep,' Gill said. 'Solicitor?'

'With him now,' said Andy.

'Who is it?' Gill asked.

'Meacham,' Andy said.

She nodded. Could be worse.

'Is that good?' Rachel asked.

'Course it's not good,' said Kevin. 'It's a solicitor, yeah?'

'She won't dick you about,' Gill said, ignoring Kevin. 'She'll play it straight. The rest of you, you know what you're doing? The slightest shred of something relevant and I want it pronto. Get going.'

* * *

333

Janet was helping Rachel rehearse the major steps of the interview when Gill stuck her head round the door. 'Got you a present,' Gill said, eyes bright. 'Raleigh's DNA – it's a match in both scenes.' Rachel gave a gasp, shot a look at Janet, *I told you so*. Janet felt her own skin tingle in turn.

'But listen' – Gill held up her finger – 'from the outset you explain we want to discuss two separate incidents with him, then you divide the interview up. Understand?'

'Yes,' said Rachel.

'Start with Lisa, take that as far as you can, and then tell him you want to talk about another matter. Keep them completely distinct,' Gill said. 'Have you eaten?' She jerked her head. 'I'm going down.'

'We should,' Janet said to Rachel.

'I can't,' Rachel said.

'Running on empty, not wise,' Janet said.

'I'll live,' Rachel said.

'I'll bring you a bun,' Janet promised, and went with Gill.

'She did good,' Gill said to Janet as they set their trays down. 'Reckon she can sustain it?'

'I'm not sure. I hope so. D'you think I need some eject button – you know, agree a phrase to say if she's veering off course?'

'Might undermine her?' Gill cut into her baked potato, scooped up a forkful, chewed and swallowed.

'Yes,' said Janet. 'I could always suggest a break

if necessary.' She had some soup. 'How's Sammy?'

Gill exhaled dramatically. 'Sammy's OK, it's his bloody father that's the problem.' She stabbed her fork into the potato.

'What now?' Janet said.

'I asked him to do the school run—'

'College,' Janet corrected her, knowing Sammy complained if Gill called it school, him being in sixth form and all.

'—college run,' Gill accepted. 'And he only sends his floozie! Typical.' She ate some more.

'Well, it's a lot to ask, Gill,' Janet teased her. 'A return journey, no less.'

'And she fed him. Bitch.' Gill sat forward, leaned in towards Janet. 'I got asked out,' she announced.

'What! Who?'

'The bloke who knocked Sammy down.'

'Bit of an extreme way to get an introduction. What's he like?'

'Very nice,' Gill beamed.

'You said yes?'

'I said maybe some other time. I can't imagine it, can you? Starting on all that again. After all those years with buggerlugs . . . going with someone new . . . don't know if I can.'

Janet squirmed inside, prayed it wouldn't show on her face. She wanted to change the subject, but that would look weird. 'Course you can,' she said. *I did*, she thought. It would be good for Gill, she'd had a hard few years. Janet knew she found it lonely. It was time she found somebody who really appreciated her. 'Give us the low-down then?' Janet said.

'He's called Matthew. He's a GP. Separated, I think, grown-up daughter anyway. You know where the farm is, the one you see from ours? Well, he's doing up the barn.' She cleared her plate, set down her knife and fork and slapped the table. 'Still, no chance at the moment, too much on. Andy,' she said abruptly, 'anything wrong that you've heard of?'

Janet nearly choked. She forced the mouthful of soup down. 'No, why?'

Gill shrugged. 'Seems a bit off.'

Oh, hell. 'Maybe he's sickening for something,' Janet said. 'I'd not noticed, seems fine to me.'

Gill stared at her, a tad too long, and Janet's stomach turned over, her nerves jangled. 'What?' she said.

'Rachel,' Gill said, with a bob of her head, 'I think she's gonna work out fine.'

'Yeah.' Janet breathed again. 'You know how to pick 'em.'

'So I'll not send her back?'

'Not on my account.' Janet smiled and struggled to drink a little more of her soup.

'Can I take you back to the statement you made earlier today when you denied being in the Collyhurst area at all on Monday the thirteenth,' Rachel began. 'That is what you said?'

'Because it's true,' he said coldly. Janet made notes, his answers would be on video and tape as well, but the paper gave her a chance to make observations too, flag up anything they might want to revisit.

'You are the registered keeper of a Nissan Micra . . .' Rachel quoted the registration number.

'That's right.'

'And you are the sole driver?'

'Yes.'

Rachel set a document down on the table. 'I am now showing the suspect exhibit number BD4. This is a map drawn up using data from our automatic number-plate recognition system. The crosses here show places where your vehicle was captured on Monday' – Rachel pointed to the document – 'the times are printed alongside each location.'

He became very still.

Janet hoped Rachel would wait, use the silence to exert pressure and force a response. But Rachel went on: 'Explain that to me?'

'I may have been mistaken.' Raleigh looked at his solicitor, who wasn't giving anything away.

'Are you now saying you were in Collyhurst?'

'Apparently,' he said crisply.

'Yes or no is fine,' Rachel said. A little jibe that she didn't need to make, that Janet wouldn't have bothered with because it slightly weakened her position, indicated that he was getting to her.

'Yes, then,' he said.

'What were you doing in Collyhurst?' Rachel asked him.

'I can't remember,' he said.

Good, starting to fudge, knowing they were getting dangerously close.

'Visiting a client, perhaps?'

'No, I don't think so.'

'Visiting Lisa Finn at Fairland Avenue. Am I correct?'

He swallowed.

Rachel placed a second document down on the table. 'I am now showing the suspect exhibit number TC2. This is a transcript of the text sent from your phone to Lisa Finn's phone that morning. Please will you read it out to me,' Rachel said.

A look of hatred flashed over his face and Janet tensed. It was not unknown for suspects to lash out during an interview. And who knew how Rachel would deal with physical violence. If her chase after the taxi driver was any guide, she'd probably break the guy's nose, which would not play well with CPS. But then Janet saw Raleigh close his eyes, calming himself before reading the message, his tone wooden. '"See you at two babe."'

'And the last letter?' Rachel said.

'An x.'

'A kiss,' Rachel said.

'Yes,' he replied, between his teeth.

'I'll ask you again: did you visit Lisa Finn at Fairland Avenue that afternoon as arranged?'

He didn't speak. His eyes were hard, full of loathing. Keep it steady, Janet willed Rachel.

'No,' he said quietly.

'No?' Rachel repeated. 'Would you like to reconsider

that answer?' He stared at her hard, defiant, then Janet saw his gaze falter. He was weakening, she was sure. As the evidence built, he was being forced into a dead end with no way out.

'Can you explain to me how your DNA ended up in Lisa's bedroom?'

Raleigh flinched, eyes blinking shut. Then he gave a shallow laugh. 'All right . . .' He raised his hands briefly, let them drop. 'I was there. We had sex. That's all. And she was perfectly fine when I left.'

That's all? Just abusing my position of trust, fucking the clients. Janet noted his admission.

'You had sex with Lisa on the Monday afternoon?'

'I just told you that.' Arsey again.

'What time did you arrive and leave?'

'I got there about two and left around half past two, to go to the town hall.'

'While you were at the flat, please describe to me which rooms you went in,' Rachel said.

'The bedroom and bathroom.'

'Nowhere else?'

'No.'

He wasn't scared, Janet thought. He was angry that he had been caught out, but he didn't appear to be frightened of what else they might have on him. Was that because he had no more to reveal, or because his personality type made him overly arrogant?

'On Monday, did Lisa resist you? Try to stop you?'

'No, she wanted me there. She likes me,' he said.

'Lisa was expecting to have sex with you?'

'That's why I was there.' Sneering, puffed up with his own inflated self-worth.

'This had happened before?'

'Yes.'

'How many times?' Rachel said.

'Eight, maybe ten.'

'When did you first have sex with Lisa?'

'I can't remember.' Something else he didn't want to admit to? Why?

'But you had been seeing her for sex on a regular basis for some months?'

'She was seventeen,' he said, as if that made it all right.

'And she was your client,' Rachel said.

Tricky ground, Janet thought, ethics. Best left to the lawyers. Morally repugnant, but Rachel's job was to tease out the facts and figures, and only that.

Raleigh didn't even have the grace to look ashamed. Said nothing.

'When you left, where was Lisa?'

'In bed.'

'What was she wearing?'

'A robe thing.'

'While you were there, did Lisa go into the living room or kitchen?'

'No.'

'Lisa was found dead shortly after your visit. What can you tell me about that?'

'Nothing. I told you: we had sex, I left and she was fine.'

'Did Lisa take drugs in your presence?'

'No, I think she had some before I arrived.'

'What made you think that?' Rachel said.

'She was high, uninhibited.' He gave a slight smile, made Janet want to vomit.

'Did you attack Lisa Finn?'

'No. I've told you I didn't. Why would I?'

'Perhaps she argued with you, got aggressive – she had a history of such behaviour,' Rachel said.

'No, we were fine. We went to bed, then I left.'

'What did you do with the condom?'

He moved his head back in surprise. 'I flushed it down the toilet.'

Rachel put a photo on the table. 'I am now showing the suspect exhibit number TP3. This is an item of jewellery that belonged to Lisa. Do you recognize it?'

'Yes.'

'Was she wearing it on Monday?'

'Yes, I think so.'

'Did you take it off her?'

'No.' He frowned, apparently not understanding why he was being asked about the cross and chain.

'Did Sean Broughton know you and Lisa were having a sexual relationship?'

'No, nobody knew.'

'Why was that?'

He stared at Rachel, his eyes flat. 'Because I'd lose my job.'

'Lisa lost her life,' Rachel retorted.

Nooo, thought Janet.

The solicitor complained as Raleigh said hotly, 'That has nothing to do with me.'

Rachel sat back. 'Let's go over everything you've told me in greater detail.'

He sighed bitterly and moved in his chair.

'Starting with when you first met Lisa.'

Another hour and Janet could see that he was finding it hard to maintain the veneer of civility, but even so his account had remained unwavering. Rachel finally declared they would take a break and Pete stopped the recording. Rachel went outside to smoke and Janet joined her there.

'OK?' Janet asked.

'Slimy bastard,' Rachel said.

'Yes, you need to be careful with that, letting it show.'

Rachel rolled her eyes.

'You were fine ninety per cent of the time, really. It's not easy.'

'You think he's lying? About the murder?'

'I'm not sure,' Janet said. 'I think he is telling the truth about the sex being consensual: the text messages, what we know about Angela, all makes that plausible.' She shuddered. 'I'm freezing. I'll go up.'

'I don't think he's got a clue, that we're after him for Rosie too,' Rachel said, blowing out smoke. 'D'you want coffee fetching?'

The first time Rachel had offered to get her anything. 'Thanks. Need something to keep me awake.'

'Boring you, am I?'

'Never that,' Janet smiled, and hurried in as another gust of icy wind blew round the corner.

43

As far as the high-tech crime unit could see, James Raleigh had been circumspect in his use of the computer for his sexual activities. No email traffic with the women he manipulated, no Facebook friends or chat-room sites. Nothing with other men that implicated him in any wider abuse.

Gill summarized for the team: 'He's been careful to target women who were over sixteen and so avoid prosecution for statutory rape if found out. Of course his behaviour is totally unprofessional and we'll see him struck off for what he's disclosed so far. We've nothing on him for the murder. He's put his hands up to consensual sex with Lisa and that's our lot. We ask him about Rosie Vaughan next. Now, riddle me this – Lisa's cross and chain: DNA traces from skin cells on the chain tells us it's a woman. No hits, no previous record.'

'Her mother,' Rachel said. The girl had a real downer on Denise Finn.

'Her mother gave her the necklace,' Janet pointed

out, 'she would have handled it. That could easily account for it.'

'Back in April – that's eight months ago,' Rachel said.

'Dating DNA is a minefield,' Gill reminded them. 'It can last months, years even, and there's no reliable way to pinpoint when it was left there. Thankfully, that didn't occur to James Raleigh or he could have blown you off by saying he shagged Lisa weeks ago and the mucky mare hadn't washed the sheets since.'

'Probably hadn't,' Rachel said.

'What about Angela?' said Andy. 'She's besotted with Raleigh. If she caught wind he was two-timing her with Lisa—'

'The pair have a history of animosity, fights at Ryelands,' Mitch agreed.

'Angela was slagging Lisa off when we were there,' said Janet.

It was worth following up. 'Mitch and Kevin, can you go fingerprint Angela and get a DNA sample. If necessary, we ask Denise after that. But I don't see any reason to go disturbing her at this time of night.'

'So, how you fixed, lads?' Gill looked from Rachel to Janet. 'Round two?'

'Yes, boss,' said Rachel.

'Think on,' Gill said to her. 'He's getting tired, but so are you. Collected, clear, impersonal – yes?'

'Yes,' Rachel said impatiently. Gill raised an eyebrow. 'Ma'am,' Rachel added.

That attitude showing again. Gill wasn't going to pull her up now; she'd been very pleased with Rachel's

345

conduct in the first suspect interview and hoped she would maintain it in the second one.

'I told you earlier that there were two matters I wished to discuss with you,' Rachel said. 'I now want to ask you about your relationship with Rosie Vaughan.'

His face set, frozen like a rabbit in headlights, except Rachel couldn't see any fear in his eyes. She wanted to see it there, she wanted him to be petrified, chattering with panic, the way Rosie had been.

'What about it?' he said.

'You had a sexual relationship with Rosie Vaughan?'

'Long time back, yes.'

'When was that?'

'Two or three years ago.'

'How did you meet her?'

'I can't remember.'

'Perhaps I can help you there,' Rachel said. 'You worked on a placement in Ryelands in the spring of 2007, April and May. Rosie was resident there. You began the relationship then.'

'OK,' he was dismissive.

'Is that correct?' Rachel said.

'Yes.'

'Rosie moved out of care in February 2008, into a flat in New Moston. You continued to see her, to have sex with her?'

'For a bit.'

'Could you be more specific, Mr Raleigh?'

'No, I can't remember.'

'So the relationship might have lasted until 2009 or even into this year?'

'No not that long, it was over by the Easter, I'm sure.'

'Easter 2008?' she checked.

'Yes,' he said.

'On June twentieth 2008, Rosie Vaughan was the victim of a serious sexual assault, rape, carried out at her home address. Can you tell me where you were on that date?'

'How the hell should I know? It's two and a half years ago.'

'Was your relationship with Rosie Vaughan consensual?'

'Yes.'

'Like your relationship with Lisa Finn?'

'Yes.'

'And Angela Hambley.'

He closed down, his face impassive.

'Or is that not consensual?' Rachel said.

'No, it is.' He stretched his neck, discomfited.

'We have forensic evidence that places you at the scene when Rosie Vaughan was attacked and beaten, when she was raped at knifepoint. Forensic evidence that you carried out that assault.' Suck on that and swallow.

He shook his head, said vehemently, 'No, no way.'

'Rosie didn't like the idea of sharing you, of you leaving her. She had threatened you in the past, that if you messed her about she would report you. Did she threaten you on that date?'

'No, I don't know what you're on about.'

'Did you rape and beat her to keep her quiet?'

'I wasn't there,' he said.

'The science suggests otherwise.'

He stroked at his head, the blond hair still shining, thick and healthy. 'I wasn't there,' he said again. He kept it up like a parrot. Rachel was pissed off with him. She knew he had done this. There had been something satisfying about seeing him in his police-issue jumpsuit, stripped of his status symbols: no neat wool sweater, no fancy watch, no trendy shoes. Something sad too, when the DNA was confirmed, in the knowledge that she had been right about Rosie: she had known her rapist. This was the man who had brutally battered Rosie, robbing her of her hope and sanity, setting the seal on her descent into a twilight world of drugs and paranoia. Rachel had to trap him, but they had no other evidence to confront him with. All she could do was try and wear him down.

'Rosie Vaughan had bruising to the face, her arms, back, legs, vagina and throat. She soiled herself in the course of the beating. She never recovered psychologically. On Thursday she took her own life.'

'Very sad,' he said blandly. 'But as I keep saying, I had nothing to do with any assault. I wasn't there.'

Rachel felt a tremor of rage grip her, she thought of Rosie's eyes, livid with panic, the unsteady way she had walked along the canal, the shape of her when she hit the ground. 'I don't believe you,' Rachel said, fighting to sound strong and in control.

'That's your problem,' he said.

Tosser, with his smart little comments. Heat flared through her, her guts tightened. She'd slit his throat, cut his cock off first. She stood suddenly, he jerked back in reaction. 'Interview terminated.' She rattled off the time, and quit the room. Halfway down the corridor she stopped, hit at the wall with her fists – fucking fucking bastard. Choking with rage.

Janet came and stood close by. 'You did your best.'

'It's not good enough,' Rachel rounded on her. 'He'll walk. He'll walk, Janet. He did it, he did Rosie, whatever else. Maybe not Lisa, but Rosie.'

Gill sent them home. 'Too late to go back for more,' she said.

'Tomorrow?' Rachel asked. Was this it? Would she get another chance?

'I'm not sure we'll get further. Let's sleep on it. You did all right, kid.'

Rachel shook her head, rejecting the praise, eyes aching. No. She did crap. He was gonna get away with it and there was nothing she could do.

44

'How was Mr Fairley?' Janet asked Ade.

'He wants to put her on a behaviour plan. She'll be monitored for a month and she's barred from the Christmas trip.'

'That's a bit steep,' Janet said.

'He wants to make an example of her, apparently.'

'And you let him? Didn't you object? She's eleven years old, Ade, she didn't think about—'

'If you wanted to express an opinion, you should have been there.'

'Didn't you stick up for her? What about the others? She didn't dream this up on her own,' she said.

'She won't say who they are,' he said.

'God. How's she taking it?'

Ade shrugged. 'Hard to tell.'

'I'll have a word.'

'Wait,' Ade said, 'there's something else.'

Janet felt dizzy. He did know. That explained the peculiar visit at work. 'I'm tired,' she tried, 'just want to get to bed.'

'Janet, we need to talk about this now.'

Her throat closed. Sweat on her scalp. Her chest hurt. 'What?' she managed. She wanted to freeze things, rewind, change everything. She wanted to disappear.

'Sit down, for chrissakes,' he said.

She did as he said. She couldn't look at him.

'It's Elise,' he said. 'She's seeing this lad.'

Elise? Elise! Oh God. Janet began to laugh.

'What's so funny?' he said. 'She's thirteen.'

'Well, who is he? How serious is it?'

'I don't know, some boy at school. He's in Year 11.' Like it was the mark of Satan. 'You're her mother, you need to talk to her, make sure she's not doing anything stupid.'

'We're talking about Elise here. When have you ever known her to act stupid? She's got common sense stamped through her like Blackpool rock.'

'If she got into trouble . . .'

'She knows all about safe sex. And she's only thirteen. I don't think it's anything to worry about. It's normal. We should be pleased. Anyone who can cope with Elise and her high standards has my vote. She's a great kid.'

'Sure about that, are you? It's not as if you see much of her,' he said.

'That's not fair,' Janet said.

'No, it isn't. Not on any of us.'

'If you want to have another row about my work patterns, I'll try to fit you in next month. Meanwhile, I'm going to see my daughters, and then I'm going to bed.'

Janet fetched Taisie's phone. Upstairs, Taisie was in bed but awake. Janet sat down on the bed. 'Here—' She handed the phone to her.

'You said a week.' Taisie glowered suspiciously.

'Well, it will be a week, tomorrow. Dad told me about Mr Fairley. Seems a bit tight.'

'He is proper tight. Candice Waller swore at him and she's still going on the Christmas trip.'

'I'm sorry,' Janet sympathized. 'I don't think there's anything I can do. Maybe those friends of yours who were in on the joke should not go on the trip either. Show some solidarity.'

Taisie shook her head. 'They wouldn't do that.'

'No, thought not. Hey, think next time.' Janet tapped her own temple.

'Can I go to Phoebe's for a sleepover on Saturday?'

'Is it a party? Aargh! I've got déjà vu.' Janet clutched her head.

Taisie laughed. 'Just a sleepover.'

'Give me their number first.'

'OK.'

'I love you.' Janet kissed her.

'Yuck,' said Taisie, force of habit.

Elise was on MSN. Janet didn't make any attempt to snoop at the conversation. 'So, what's his name?' she said.

Elise flushed, put her hand to her head and groaned. 'Connor,' she said.

352

'Dad says he's in Year 11.'

'So?'

'Nothing,' Janet said, 'just interested. I don't need to do any safe sex—'

'Mum!' Elise recoiled, interrupting her. 'No! We don't even, we're not—' She pulled a face.

'Good, fine, sorry! Thought I'd better check.'

'I'm thirteen,' Elise said. 'I'm under age. You should know that.'

Janet kept a straight face. 'That's right,' she said. 'OK. Bed now. It's late.'

Janet lay in bed, her thoughts slowing, relaxing towards sleep. They were all right, her girls, they were fine. Ade kept on raising the issue of her work, implying she was a bad mother, neglectful, absent, but it really wasn't like that. Sure, there were times in the early stages of each murder investigation when she put in long hours and saw little of them, but it wasn't always like that. They're fine, she reassured herself again, everything's going to be fine.

And she'd make sure it stayed that way. She'd forget about Andy; she had to. It would get easier with time: the awkwardness, the fear of someone finding out. New Year soon. A fresh start. Everything's gonna be fine, she thought again. And then she slept.

Rachel shouldn't have answered the phone. It was ringing as she walked in the flat, she had expected it to be Nick – who else, this time of night? It would be a relief to talk to someone, even about inconsequential things, to take her mind off James Raleigh and her sense of defeat, of inadequacy. Distract her from the fact that Rosie's funeral was at half past eight in the morning.

It was Alison. 'Where've you been?' she said. 'I've been trying for hours.'

'Work,' Rachel snapped. 'Where d'you think?'

'Till this hour?' sounding as if she didn't believe her.

'Yes, interviewing a murder suspect,' Rachel said.

'Really! God, did he confess? Was it that lass in the papers – Lisa?'

'Yes, it was. No, he didn't.'

'Wow.'

There was a pause. 'So, anything else?' Rachel said. 'You rang me, remember.'

'I'm going to see Dom on Friday,' Alison said quickly. 'You could come.'

Not this again. Rachel felt a wave of displeasure, anger. 'How many times do I have to tell you . . .'

'It's Christmas,' Alison went on. 'Can't you think about him for once?'

'Try not to, does my head in. I'm not going, Alison. I don't want to.'

'You can be really hard-faced sometimes, you know that? What if it was me?'

'Don't be thick.'

'Prisoners with family support . . .' Alison started her touchy-feely spiel.

'No,' Rachel said.

Every time Alison brought it up, it felt like ripping a scab off a wound, opening it up again. When all

Rachel wanted to do was bury it. The deeper the better.

'He always asks after you, you know.' Emotional blackmail now.

Rachel had a flashback. Dom in the under-thirteens. Man of the match. Slathered in mud and running across to her. Rachel, frozen stiff on the edge of the pitch. Their dad had promised to come, but they all knew he'd get waylaid in the bookies or the boozer. Alison at work, her Saturday job. So Rachel turned out. Bored senseless until Dom had the ball, scored not once but three times.

He had run over to her, happy as a pig in muck and just as filthy, arms raised and yelling, 'Who are you, who are you.' Some chant from the terraces. 'Did you see?' he demanded, eyes sparkling, stupid grin on his face. 'Did you see?'

'Wicked!' she'd agreed. Laughing as he did a back-flip, his football boots sending up clods of earth from the field.

It'd broken her heart when they came to arrest him. When he was charged with armed robbery.

Rachel closed her eyes. 'No,' she said to Alison.

'But Rachel if you'd only just—' Alison tried to prolong the conversation. Rachel hung up. *Armed robbery: a robbery where the defendant or co-defendant was armed with a firearm.*

She opened a bottle of wine and closed the curtains. Sat there drinking and channel-hopping until the bottle was empty, the central heating had gone off, the cold was stealing into the room and she'd a halfway decent chance of getting a couple of hours' kip.

On the drive home, Gill ran through arrangements for the following morning. Sammy needed to go into the fracture clinic and she was torn – she could take him herself but she needed to be with the team, not desert them when the case was feeling blocked. Or she could ask Dave – *tell* Dave – but then he might delegate the task to the whore. The whore would have to take the brat with her, too. And who knows how long they'd be there. Could be hours, long enough to go insane and start eating the other patients; certainly long enough to show Pendlebury the downside of stepmummyhood. In fact, she mused, maybe that was the solution: kill her with kindness.

By the time Gill had picked Sammy up from the friend he'd gone home with, making fulsome apologies for the lateness of the hour, she had decided to send Dave on hospital duty and see what materialized.

He wasn't best pleased when she told him: 'But it's slap bang in the middle of the day!'

'You can tell the time, very good!'

'Can't he get a taxi or something?'

'You'd let him go on his own?' she tried to shame him.

'It's not as if it's an operation or anything,' he said.

'I'll cancel it, shall I? Risk him having a wonky wrist for the rest of his life.'

'Don't be an idiot,' Dave said. 'Tell him I'll pick him up at break.'

Or your driver will? Gill thought of Pendlebury as a chauffeur girl. She was so young, could have been Sammy's sister, Dave's daughter. Gill wondered if anyone seeing Dave with the spawn-child assumed Dave was the granddad. Cherish that thought.

'This murder you're on,' he said, 'all very smash-and-grab.' Implying that arresting then releasing two suspects in quick succession was chaotic in some way. 'Lost your touch?'

Shows how much you understand. Gill hated it when he talked about her work, especially as she knew in her bones she was the better copper. Dave at chief superintendent grade was out of his depth, wearing armbands in a tidal wave.

'Just remind me, Dave – how many murders you been SIO on? Three, wasn't it, last count. Stick to what you know – then again, your division,' she countered, 'reported crime up two per cent, rest of us still on a decrease. There's always early retirement, Dave.' She hung up, then wondered if he knew when break-time was.

Sammy said goodnight. She pointed to her cheek, demanding a kiss.

'How's it feel now?' she asked him.

'Just a bit achy,' he said. 'What are we doing at Christmas?'

Not snowboarding, pal. 'Grandma's,' she said, 'I told you.'

'Forgot.'

'Why?'

'Emma was asking.'

Was she now? Planning to poach him? 'OK,' she said brightly. 'Well, that's what we're doing. And you can have your mates round one day in the holidays – be a break from all that revision you'll be doing.'

Shouldn't it be getting easier, Gill thought, the whole post marriage stuff? When she heard of people splitting up amicably, it was beyond her grasp. She couldn't ever see a time when she and Sammy would play happy blended families, popping round to Dave's for a jolly Christmas dinner or to celebrate New Year. Auld Lang Syne. Gill would sooner feed the tart mistletoe stuffed in her turkey and stick holly in Dave's Y-fronts.

Dave's little dig about the inquiry needled at her even as she tried to distract herself watching the rolling news programme. She thought her way through the evidence they'd now assembled, the timeline that had tightened, the forensics that gave weight to witness and suspect accounts. Preparation for the morning to come when she'd walk it through with the team and recalibrate the direction of the inquiry.

James Raleigh would walk. It would rankle with Rachel, but Gill hoped the girl would heed her advice, have the emotional maturity to accept the situation.

When she finally got to bed, the wind kept her awake, buffeting the house, sending something, a plant pot perhaps, rattling round the garden, then chucking hail like shotgun pellets against the window.

It was easy to feel self-doubt in the dark, in the wee, small hours. She hadn't lost her touch though; that was just Dave being a dickhead. She'd show him; she'd show them all. It might take weeks or months, years even, but they would find Lisa's killer and make it stick.

45

Rosie's funeral was at Blackley crem. A public health funeral, which meant the state was picking up the bill. Rachel arrived late and the only people there were the three lads she'd seen at the canal. At least they'd come, even though they hadn't a decent suit between them. In the daylight they had that pinched, spotty, malnourished look of kids half-feral, poor complexions courtesy of crap food and drug abuse.

They regarded her warily as she took a seat in the chapel, wondering maybe if she'd bust them. Not appropriate, in the circumstances.

The coffin, plain and unadorned, was at the front of the chapel. There was a small bunch of dark red roses in cellophane on top. The sort that have no scent. Rachel imagined the three lads clubbing together, or maybe nicking a tenner from one of their mums' purses to get the bouquet. The generous wreath she clutched felt ostentatious now, as if she'd set out to outdo them, which was the last thing on her mind.

The minister was saying something about Rosie having a brief life but now being at peace. He didn't make reference to her troubles or the manner of her death. Another person arrived, so Rachel wasn't the last. Marlene. She sat with Rachel, which was a bit full on. Christ, there were enough empty seats.

Rachel kept her jaw clamped tight as the man asked them to remain silent for a moment and think about Rosie. What a sodding waste, was all Rachel thought. Steeling herself against those images that wouldn't go away, highly coloured almost Day-Glo in her mind. The scale of scars etched on Rosie's forearm, her eyes darting to the corners of the room, the still, silent figure on the ground, her gauzy dress fluttering, and the first sight she'd ever had of Rosie, curled and motionless in the bedroom, slippery with blood.

Then it was done. The minister explained that Rosie's ashes would be put in the garden of remembrance and he thanked them for coming.

The boys got up and ambled out, self-conscious and awkward.

'Is there any news?' Marlene said to Rachel.

Rachel shook her head. Only bad. The fuckwit who raped her is Teflon-coated, nothing sticks. And we're getting nowhere fast with Lisa Finn.

Rachel and Marlene placed their flowers on the coffin.

Outside the day was bleak, wintry, the trees bare of leaves, stirred in the wind, the sky grubby.

'You were there when she died?' Marlene said.

Rachel hunched up her shoulders, trying to get warm. 'Yes,' she said. Not that it's any of your business.

'Your boss told me. I'm sorry, that must have been awful.'

Rachel nodded briskly. There was something in her eye, a speck of dust or something. Thickness in her throat. She blinked and sniffed. The three lads had reached the gates, matchstick men.

'She tried before,' Marlene said, 'when she was with us.'

Rachel looked at her, then away to the graves among the grass. 'You're saying it's not my fault?' She sounded bolshie, hadn't meant to.

'How can it be your fault?' Marlene said. 'Of course it's not your fault.'

'Right,' Rachel sighed. 'I've got to go.'

'Take care,' Marlene said.

'Yeah. Bye.' Rachel walked swiftly to her car.

Whose fault was it then? Rosie's mother, who'd destroyed her childhood and set the seal on her future? The doctors and social workers, who didn't care for her enough? Raleigh, who had broken her body and with that her mind as well? But none of them were there that night, were they? Only Rachel. And if Rachel hadn't gone first to the canal, then again to the flat, if she hadn't pressed Rosie to talk about the rape, hadn't pushed her for a name, if Rachel had let her be . . . then would she still be alive? Either off her face on drugs or slicing at her skin, building fires under the bridge, sleeping on the sofa in her charmed circle?

362

Rachel left, ignoring the speed limit, passing a cortège on its way in. The coffin surrounded by huge floral arrangements spelling out Mum and Nana. Some old woman then. A stream of vehicles following. Rachel didn't look at the occupants, she'd had enough misery for one morning. She'd be a whole lot better once she was back at work and busy.

First thing Wednesday, Gill passed on the information about James Raleigh sleeping with his clients and other young and vulnerable women to the Director of Social Services for the city. She explained the police were not preferring charges, there was not enough evidence to do so, but Raleigh would remain a person of interest.

'That's his CRB status in shreds,' she told the team. 'He should be hearing later this morning that he is suspended, pending a disciplinary hearing, and he'll have trouble getting a job washing cars when they are finished with him.'

Rachel still exuded resentment; Gill needed to talk to her about that. Not good for the work atmosphere, or the girl's occupational health.

Gill had done a storyboard combining their timetable and the evidence to date. Stick figures with initials for the protagonists. She passed copies around to the team. A larger version was clipped to the flipchart.

'Anyone ever tell you you had an artistic side?' Janet said as she picked hers up.

Gill glanced at her.

'They were lying,' Janet said.

'Who's the Yankee?' said Kevin.

Gill peered over her glasses.

'Here', he pointed to a stick man, US on its triangular torso.

Cretin! Give me strength.

'Unknown suspect,' Lee laughed.

Gill clapped her hands to interrupt the mutterings about drawing and graffiti and Minnie the Minx. 'Are you sitting comfortably? Monday, thirteenth of December, half ten in the morning and Lisa Finn gets the bus to town. Sean Broughton goes to the Jobcentre. In town, Lisa shoplifts clothing and accessories. At twelve thirty she gets a text from her personal advisor James Raleigh saying he'll be visiting at two that afternoon,' Gill pointed to the picture on the flipchart. 'Lisa calls a cab. She's picked up at five past one. She trades the stolen goods for heroin. In the taxi she receives two calls, one from Sean, one from Denise. She lies to Sean, saying she won't be home until half past three that afternoon. He's itching for a fix, but she puts him off. There may have been words exchanged – though he denies that. Lisa tells her mother she's too busy to talk. At quarter past one Lisa arrives home. She may have taken heroin at this point.' Gill indicated the next drawing: 'Two o'clock and James Raleigh shows up, shags Lisa in the bedroom, depositing skin cells on both the duvet and the sheet, and leaving a pubic hair on the sheet. He uses and disposes of a condom. Traces of lubricant from that are recovered with a vaginal swab. His fingerprints are lifted from the bedroom door jamb and the basin in the bathroom, but not found in the living room or kitchen. Raleigh leaves at half two. Allegedly, Lisa is in bed at this point, wearing her dressing gown and the cross and chain. Now' – Gill tapped the drawing of the unknown suspect – 'between half two and half three when Sean Broughton returns our unknown suspect' – Gill pointed to Kevin – 'pitches up. There is no sign of forced entry but—'

'Door latch is faulty,' Pete chipped in, 'anyone could just waltz in.'

'Lisa is killed in the living room. There is little sign of a struggle. Suggesting . . . ?'

'She didn't know she was in danger,' said Rachel.

'It wasn't a prolonged attack,' added Lee.

'Yes. Forensics tell us Lisa was stabbed in the chest once and whoever held the knife moved back into the kitchen, leaving drops of blood on the floor. The cross and chain was torn from Lisa's neck and found in the kitchen by Sean Broughton, who stole it. We are awaiting DNA results for Angela Hambley, who had possible motive, but until those results are in I want to be discreet. Dig around, see what we can find on Angela. Need a swab and prints from Denise, too. We know she handled the jewellery in the past. Contact the rest of Raleigh's phone contacts – have we any other members of his harem to consider? Talk to Sean again. What was Lisa doing in the days before her death, who was she—'

'Doing,' Mitch interrupted.

'Ha, ha! Seeing,' Gill said, 'in the weeks before her

murder. Who visited the flat? Who knew the door was broken?'

'She didn't let them in,' Rachel said suddenly. 'She'd have got dressed, least put her kecks on.'

A flash of insight again, the sort of contribution that made Gill's pulse beat faster.

'Unless it was a punter and she was on the game,' Kevin said.

'Nothing to support that,' Andy said.

'So we are likely looking for someone who'd been to the flat before. Talk to Benny Broughton too, see if he's heard anything.'

Once Gill had established that everyone was on track with their reports and their tasks for the day, she asked Rachel to stay behind.

'You can't make it personal,' Gill said. 'You need to come to terms with it, or it'll eat you up.'

'I'm all right,' Rachel said crossly.

'No, you're not, you're steaming because that twat is going home any minute, because we can't touch him for the rape.'

'He did it,' Rachel said. 'I know he did it.'

'You're probably right. Hand on heart, I'd find him guilty – but we are not the jury. All we can do is find evidence and build a case. There isn't a case to answer here; the victim's dead, she never pressed charges or gave us a statement, the DNA wouldn't stand scrutiny, he can claim he left it there on another occasion, his expert would argue the same. No witnesses, nada. You need to let it go.'

Rachel blinked, set her jaw, resistant.

'We still have a case to investigate – Lisa Finn. I want you putting everything into that.'

'And just forget about Rosie?' Rachel said.

'Forgetting's not easy. But pack it up and stick it on a shelf somewhere, otherwise it's a distraction. It will compromise your effectiveness in my syndicate. And it'll make you bloody miserable. See a counsellor, if you have to . . .'

Rachel snorted at that.

'. . . take up yoga, sky diving – whatever floats your boat. But you stop lugging this around like some rock tied to your leg. Got it?'

'Yes, boss.'

'Now, go with Janet, get a swab and fingerprints from Denise – nicely!'

46

A second man has been questioned and released by police investigating the murder of seventeen-year-old Lisa Finn. The twenty-eight-year-old— Rachel wished they'd change the radio station. They'd stopped off to grab lunch, Janet had gone to drop something at the dry cleaners, and Rachel was buying sandwiches when she heard someone say her name. 'Rachel? Rachel Bailey?' A woman in the queue behind her. 'I knew it were you. Bloody hell. How long is it?'

Not long enough. Shit. Beverley Buckshotter. Neighbour. They were the ones got the table-football set.

'How's your Dom doing? How long's he got left?'

Beverley. One of Dom's conquests, for all of five minutes.

'Good, yeah,' Rachel blagged, 'a while longer, yet.' One eye on the window, purse at the ready, praying that Janet wouldn't be back just yet.

'You're still in the police?' Beverley prattled on. 'You did all right for yourself. I see your Alison now and again. Lovely girl, isn't she?'

Rachel peered over the counter. What was the shop girl doing, for fuck's sake, milling the flour and slaughtering the pig?

'Lovely family,' Beverley said. Rachel smiled weakly, trusting she meant Alison's lot. Their own family would never have been dubbed lovely, not even by the most charitable of observers.

Rachel stood on tiptoe; she was putting the bacon on now. Come on, come on, move it!

'I'm still on Langley, got twins now.'

'Really?'

'Lads. Drive me round the fucking bend,' Beverley confided, patting Rachel's arm. Rachel resisted the urge to pat her back, good and hard, send her flying.

'It's not worth working, you know,' Beverley added.

Always was a lazy cow. Janet was there now, crossing the road. Fuck!

'Cost of childminding – it's a joke. You got any?'

'No,' Rachel said. The girl was cutting the sandwiches, slowly, making a ceremony of it, like the Chinese people in the park with their slow-motion exercises. Sliding them into the bag now. Shift yer arse.

'We had a right laugh, didn't we, down the rec?' Beverley hooted.

Freezing cold, sharing cheap wine and cheaper fags. Miserable.

Janet came in the door.

'Drinks?' the girl said.

No, ta.' Rachel thrust a tenner at her, took the sand-wiches. Bit her tongue while the girl got change.

'See you then,' Beverley said. 'Give Dom my love, yeah?'

Rachel intercepted Janet: 'Hi.' Kept walking so Janet had to follow.

'Friend?' Janet must have caught Beverley's last bit.

'Lunatic,' Rachel said out the side of her mouth. 'Nutter thinks she knows me. Never seen her before in my life. Fruitloop.' And she kept walking, not giving Janet a chance to see she'd not got any coffees.

Denise did look ten years older, Rachel thought. She peered at them, the alcohol fumes coming off her strong enough to set light to. If she fires up a fag, she'll go up like a bonfire.

'Hello, Denise,' Janet said, 'may we come in?'

Rachel had a flashback to the evening they delivered the death message, only nine days ago, how she had really not taken to Janet. Snotty cow. She'd had her wrong. First impressions perhaps not Rachel's strongest suit.

'Christopher rang, said you let the other bloke go, too,' Denise said. She walked with exaggerated care down the hallway, hands raised slightly in case she needed to brace herself, a gait that Rachel recalled from her youth. Her dad, taking a beat too long to do any-thing, the stage immediately before he lost all control and turned into a witless human wrecking ball.

'That's right,' Janet said, behind Rachel. Rachel

370

turned and made a face to Janet, tongue jutting, eyeballs swivelling. She's bladdered. Janet caught on, nodded.

'Who was he?' Denise said, the words slurred.

'We can't tell you that. Would you like a coffee?' Janet offered.

'Trying to sober me up?' Denise said. 'Go on then.' She sat down heavily in her usual place on the sofa. Rachel thought she could smell vomit underlying the cigarette fug and the stink of booze.

Janet went into the kitchen. Rachel had the bag with her, the fingerprint and DNA kit. She set it on the floor by her feet. Looked again at the photographs of Lisa and Nathan. They hadn't bothered with school photos in the Bailey family. Always a struggle to get payment and the slip signed in time. 'Who needs a photo?' he'd say. 'Got your ugly mugs to look at whenever I feel like it.'

One year the kids had got a photo done for his birthday. That must have been Alison's idea. Gone to the studios in town after school. Alison would have been thirteen or so, Rachel and Dom still in primary. The photographer had sat them sideways in a row, in height order. Alison had gone in the following week to collect it and bought a frame off the market to fit. He'd been pleased as punch, stuck it on the wall above the fireplace. A few months later the glass got cracked when Dom was mucking about with a bouncy ball. No one ever fixed it.

'She was a right handful,' Denise said out of the blue.

'Really?' Rachel wasn't sure what else to say. Let her

ramble on until Janet came back with the coffee. What excuses did her own mother make for running off? Couldn't manage the three of them – they were better off with their dad. Yeah, right.

'Wouldn't listen, wouldn't ever listen.' Denise shook her head and the skin on her neck trembled like an old woman's. 'You shouldn't have let him go,' she said to Rachel.

'Sean?'

'Yes, Sean. Who else? Whether he held the knife or not, she'd still be alive if it wasn't for him.'

Rachel didn't follow the logic. If he hadn't held the knife, then how was it his fault? Didn't stack up. Unless Denise thought he'd hired a hitman. But it didn't matter; the woman was talking to herself. Rachel just happened to be in the room. Denise lifted her glass, took a drink. Brownish liquid. Sherry? Rum? There were bottles of both on the side table.

'But she wouldn't have it. Shacked up with a druggie. He were using her, that's all it was. When I think of her,' Denise began to gasp, 'dying like that, when I think of her—' Denise waved her glass, her eyes watery, her face flooded with colour.

Don't then. 'Maybe it's best if you—'

'Like a little tart, half-naked, like some prossie.'

Rachel felt something grab her spine. Her blood beat in her ears. How did she know? She swallowed. The crime-scene photos, the one where the duvet had been removed. Lisa with her Chinese dressing gown rucked up beneath her, baring all. *Like a little tart.* No one had told Denise any of the graphic details. How could she know? Unless . . . Rachel felt it all slot together like a pool player clearing the table, dropping one ball after another: the DNA on the cross and chain was Denise's – not from months ago but last week when she tore it off her daughter; the phone call in the taxi when Kasim overheard Lisa telling someone to get off her back, stop telling her what to do: it had been her mother she was yelling at.

'The things she'd say,' Denise cried.

Rachel got carefully to her feet, anxious not to break the spell. She needed her to keep talking while she was still addled with drink and uninhibited. She crouched down closer to Denise. 'She pushed you too far,' Rachel said, her heart in her throat.

Denise took another drink, some of it dribbled down the side of her mouth. Then Rachel's words seemed to reach her. Rachel saw Denise begin to recoil, retreat.

'We tested the cross and chain,' Rachel said quietly. 'That's why we're here, to take your fingerprints. We know, Denise.' Rachel felt too warm, dizzy, the swirl of excitement making her nauseous.

She heard movement from over her shoulder, Janet returning. Rachel held her arm out behind her back, palm showing: *Stop*. Didn't risk looking away from Denise. The movement sent a sharp pain from the wound on her hand. A picture in her head of the cut on Lisa's arm; the cut Denise had inflicted.

'What did she say?' Rachel held her breath.

'Terrible things,' Denise said, staring ahead, seeing

nothing but perhaps her child, the slut, the junkie, her impossible daughter. 'Evil things, evil things about Nathan, about me,' she gulped. 'She wouldn't stop.'

Janet moved. Rachel knew she was about to interrupt, to talk about cautions and procedure. Rachel couldn't let her. 'I know,' Rachel whispered. 'Terrible things. She shouldn't have done that.' She could feel the tick of blood in her temples, hear the click of saliva in Denise's mouth. 'Where's the knife, Denise?'

Slowly, Denise turned her head. Her eyes were heavy and dull, a frown marked her brow.

Rachel's heart beat too fast. 'We need to sort this out now.' She tried to sound calm, like Janet would: 'Where's the knife?' Rachel heard the intake of breath as Janet prepared to speak. Hand still behind her, Rachel splayed her fingers, moved her hand down in a patting motion: *Quiet!* She waited, every muscle taut, not daring to move, to speak, willing Denise to answer.

'Under the sink,' Denise said simply. 'Behind the bin bags.'

Rachel's stomach clenched and there was a whining in her ears. She looked at Janet then inclined her head a fraction: *Go look.*

Janet turned, still holding the coffee. Rachel listened to her footsteps recede. Denise had her eyes closed, brow still furrowed. Her glass with a little drink left in it, pressed to her chest. There was the rustle and clatter of Janet moving things about, then a pause. Footsteps. Janet came back in, her face stark. She gave a nod.

For the second time that week, Rachel Bailey arrested

someone for the murder of Lisa Finn. This time it was her mother. This time they had the murder weapon.

'She just confessed?' Gill had them all in the meeting room.

'Not straight out,' Rachel said. 'She was raving, you know, going on about Sean then Lisa. Then she said this stuff about how she died like a tart, half naked. We never told her that.'

'Right,' Gill agreed.

'Then when I told her we were testing the chain, it was as though she knew the game was up. She was saying how Lisa had slagged her off and said stuff about Nathan. That's when I asked her where the knife was.'

'You jammy sod,' Gill said.

'She doesn't even like you,' said Janet.

'She was that drunk, she could barely work out who I was,' Rachel said.

'None of it's under caution,' Andy pointed out.

'No,' Rachel said, 'but it's on record in my daybook and it's on the custody record and she signed both those and that's after caution. With the knife, the phone call, the fingerprint on the cross – even if she goes not guilty, we'll have her.'

'Got to wait till she's sober,' Gill said. 'Then, Janet, you interview her.'

What the fuck! 'Why can't I?' Rachel said. 'I got the confession.'

'Janet's doing it,' Gill said.

'But I want—'

Gill glared. 'Shut it, Sherlock.'

'It was me she told,' Rachel said. This is way out of order.

'Listen, I don't have to explain my decision to you. But, for the record, Janet is my best interviewer, she has years of experience and this will be an interview requiring a high degree of sensitivity, empathy and neutrality. Qualities you're well short of. This woman killed her daughter. How can you possibly imagine what that's like?'

Everyone listening. Rachel felt her cheeks burn. Bitch. 'And Janet can? Why's that then, she kill someone an' all, did she?'

Janet rolled her eyes and Lee put his hand to his head. Rachel felt embattled, knew she was making things worse.

'No, but she has life experience and skills, the ability to communicate with Denise as though she is a human being deserving of humane treatment, whatever she has done.'

'I did that with Raleigh,' Rachel objected.

'Barely,' Gill spat the word. 'You are the wrong person for Denise Finn. Grow up. This is not a debate.'

Smarting, Rachel forced herself to sit there while the discussion continued.

'We have traces of blood on the knife, matching Lisa,' Gill said.

'What did Christopher say?' Andy asked.

'Gobsmacked,' Gill said. 'She'd not let anything slip

to him, just kept on about how difficult Lisa was, how Sean had ruined her.'

'She'd have let him take the fall,' said Pete, 'if we'd charged him.'

'Could be,' Gill replied. 'Shifting the blame: "If he hadn't been feeding her the drugs, I wouldn't have got into a barney with her." Justification. Was the row about drugs?' Gill asked Rachel.

'She didn't say, just that Lisa said evil things about her and Nathan.'

'Who was also on drugs before he killed himself,' Mitch said.

'Families, eh? Who'd have 'em? Right, we're aiming for five p.m. for interview, and I'm not issuing a press release as yet, so no blabbing about it to all and sundry. Get cracking.'

'Grab a bite?' Janet asked Rachel as she stood up.

Rachel hesitated.

'Don't sulk,' Janet chided her. 'It'll give you frown lines.'

'Like I care.'

'Grapes in ten?'

They were doing Christmas dinner on offer. Two for nine ninety-nine.

'It's what we do as a team that counts,' Janet said, 'we're not in competition.'

'Yes, I know,' Rachel said. 'It's just . . . I got nowhere with Raleigh.'

'Not true; you established his involvement with

the victim and eliminated him from the inquiry.'

'But Rosie—'

'I know,' Janet said. 'We don't always win, Rachel.'

It's just not fair. 'And she's so bossy,' Rachel added, 'she really gets on my tits.'

'She's the boss, it's her job to be bossy,' Janet said.

'Nothing ever gets to you, does it?' Rachel said. 'All water off a duck's back. How do you do that?'

'Underneath I'm paddling like buggery. Besides – our little car crash? I lost it then, you forgotten already?'

Rachel let her have it. She looked across for the waitress, starving now. Thought of Denise, carrying the knife home on the bus, sitting in and waiting for the police to come knocking. 'Why do you think she did it?'

Janet shrugged. 'Don't know, but I'm aiming to find out.'

47

'You understand the allegation against you?' Janet began, having done all the preliminaries for the video recording.

'Yes,' Denise said. Her fingers were knotted. She was shivering occasionally, though the room was an even temperature.

'Will you tell me what happened?' Janet asked. Leaving the territory wide open for her.

Denise took a breath and released it. She held her head in her hands. Janet guessed that the enormity of the story, the task of telling it, defeated her. She didn't know where to start.

'You rang Lisa on Monday the thirteenth, at lunchtime,' Janet prompted.

'Yes,' Denise said with a sigh. 'I wanted to ask her if she'd done anything about getting into rehab, but she bit my head off.'

Janet imagined it: Lisa in the cab, almost home, craving a fix, having scored the drugs she needed, and expecting a visit from James Raleigh. She lied to Sean, needing to keep the coast clear, and next thing her mother's on the phone. 'What did she say?'

'She went off on one, didn't want me telling her what to do, sick of me interfering. I wasn't interfering.' She raised her eyes to meet Janet's. 'I wanted to help her. I wanted her to get help.'

Janet nodded slowly, giving her the space to continue.

'She said she didn't want to see me any more, that was it, she didn't want me in her life.' Denise closed her eyes briefly. 'I was in a state, really upset. She's all I have—' She broke off. 'I tried to put it . . . to forget . . . in my head . . . thinking of Nathan . . . I'd done . . . and she . . .' Denise was almost incoherent until she said, 'She was always pushing me away. I wasn't going to sit back and let her ruin her life. Find her dead from an overdose, or sent to prison. She was all I had left—' She broke off again, coughed and cleared her throat. 'I couldn't settle. I had a drink, a couple, but it didn't touch me. In the end I went round there.'

How? On foot? On the bus? In a taxi? Janet knew her questions would wait. The fine-grain detail would come later. For now, Denise needed to tell her story without interruption or qualification. Janet trusted Rachel would be making notes of any gaps in the narrative or any inconsistencies. There would be plenty of time to return to them later.

Denise was picking at her nails, her face drawn with misery and fatigue. 'She was off her head,' she said, 'swanning around with just this scrap of a negligee thing on. She wouldn't listen. Soon as she saw me, she's effing and blinding, telling me I'm crap this and crap that.' Her face crumpled, and Janet saw tears in her eyes. 'I did love her,' she said, appealing to Janet. 'I always loved her, even when . . .' Unable to continue, she stopped, covering her eyes with her hand.

'You all right to carry on?' Janet said softly.

Denise sniffed, reached for a tissue from the box on the low table and wiped at her face. 'So, she was shouting and screaming because I told her to sort herself out, that Sean was a loser, that he was dragging her down with him. And her brother—' Again she halted, as if a switch had been thrown, cutting the supply of words. Her hand to her mouth, a fist stopping her lips.

'Take your time,' Janet said. She could feel Denise's anxiety, taut as cheese-wire in the atmosphere. She could hear the sound of the machines, the tape recorder, the camcorder, the high-pitched hum of the central heating, the breathing of the people in the room. Her mouth was dry.

When Denise began speaking again, it was almost a whisper: 'I said, look at Nathan, look at what the drugs did to him,' she gulped. 'She said, she screamed at me, "It wasn't the drugs, it was you, you're the reason he fucking killed himself. It's your fault he was a junkie, 'cos you never gave a shit for him or for me."' Denise was weeping as she spoke, her words choppy, her breathing laboured and uneven, her chest rising and falling as if she was having an asthma attack. 'She

381

grabbed at her chain and said, "You can have this, I don't want anything from you," and she yanked it off and threw it at me. It landed in the kitchen and I went to pick it up. I was going to go then. She was off her head. When she got like that there was no dealing with her.' Denise gave a shuddering breath, 'But then she said, "Why do you think Nathan strung himself up outside your house? Because he wanted you to know it was your fault." '

Oh, God. Janet could imagine how that would have cut Denise to the core.

Denise glanced at Janet. Her lips were chapped, Janet could see a tiny thread of red blood in one of the cracks. 'I just wanted to shut her up,' Denise said, 'stop her saying those lies, those evil things.' Denise fell quiet, only the rattle of her breath accompanying the play of her emotions.

Janet heard Rachel clear her throat.

'The knife,' Denise said, 'the knife.' She swallowed, hit at her temples with the heels of her hands, a swift and violent gesture that made Janet flinch, though she restricted her reaction to a blink. 'The knife was on the sink. I just wanted to stop her saying those things. I never—' she broke off, distressed.

'Yes,' Janet said. She had pain in her stomach now, deep and twisting.

Denise was sweating around her hairline, little beads of liquid visible. 'I can't—' she said.

'Have a drink of water,' Janet suggested. It was vital not to break the interview now, so close to a full

382

confession. Denise didn't want to tell her what she had done, did not want to admit the awful truth of it. Janet could tell she was finding the pressure of the situation intolerable, but it was her job to keep her here, keep her talking, build her story to its climax.

Denise lifted the cup, her hands shaking so badly that drops of water spilled over the side and dripped on to her overalls. She sipped some water and put the cup back down.

'OK,' said Janet, meaning, *Carry on, keep going*.

'She was still shouting, screaming, "Why did you ever even have me? Just dumped me, first chance you got. You either fucking me over or . . ." she said it . . . I couldn't . . . she said it.' Denise shook her head slowly, bowed forwards, her hands over her nose.

Said what?

'I don't know how she knew. How did she know? She was a new baby. I never told anyone. She couldn't remember, not that young.' She sounded bewildered.

Janet was confused. 'What did Lisa say?' She kept her voice soft.

' "Smothering me." She was only a baby, how did she know? No one knew. "Smothering me", she said that, straight out.' She stared at Janet, and her brow creased, eyes questioning, avid with pain.

Janet felt pressure squeezing in her chest, felt her skin tighten and chill. 'That's why you put Lisa into care, back then?' she said.

There was a beat or two, Janet counted the thump of her own heart. 'I thought I might do it again,' Denise

383

said in a whisper. 'I was so tired and Lisa was a terrible baby.' Denise raised her hand as if to cup it over her own face. 'I didn't want to hurt her. I couldn't trust . . . She were better off in care.'

Janet understood. She had put Lisa in care to protect her from harm, from Denise herself. Who had tried to smother her once already.

Silence hung in the room, Janet waited, resisting the images that danced just out of sight, ghosts and grief. Concentrating only on the here and now, the woman in front of her, her face ruined by drink and tragedy.

Finally Denise stirred. 'When she said that, and the knife, I had the knife, and she came at me, she's shouting, "Do it, go on, do it. You killed him, you gonna kill me as well now? Go on then, you shitbag, you bitch!" On and on, and I wanted her to stop. And I—' Tears rolled down her cheeks, dripped from her nose.

Janet sat without moving, waiting for the final act.

'She just kept coming and I pushed the knife and she fell.' Denise closed her eyes. When she opened them she stared unseeing at the floor. 'She didn't move or anything. I went home,' she added.

'Thank you,' Janet said. They had the confession. 'We're going to have a break now. And then I'd like to talk to you again and your solicitor will probably want to talk to you some more before that. OK?'

As Janet emerged, her head spinning, shaky, acid burning behind her breastbone, she found Gill in the corridor. Gill didn't say anything, but signalled understanding in the look she gave her. Janet needed fresh air, she needed to be outside, away from the building, from the violence of Denise's life, from the pity and revulsion she felt.

'Janet,' Rachel called, her voice bright, animated.

'Leave her,' Gill said. 'Just leave her be.' A serious undertone that must have got through because Rachel didn't come swinging out after her.

Janet walked round the block, only dimly aware of the traffic and the fierce easterly wind coming down off the Pennines, and let the memories flood back.

That moment never left her: calling his name, amused that, after his usual fussy night, he was now so soundly asleep. Joshua. Putting out her hand, cupping his cheek. Lukewarm. His lips, the faintest kiss of blue feathering the pink. And her heart climbing in her throat, a wave of terror rippling up her spine, clawing at the back of her skull, robbing her of breath, turning her bowels to water.

'Joshua—' Shaking his shoulder.

Then screaming for Ade. Screaming as she lifted him up. *Baby baby please wake up please wake up Mummy's here wake up wake up Joshua.*

They wanted to take him, but it was too soon, she wasn't ready. How could she ever be ready? With his soft blond hair and his tiny teeth, his eyes the same colour as hers. My babe. My boy. She could not relinquish him.

The other police officer, Gill, kept coming in, with tea, with offers of help. What help? Anyone she could ring?

The thought broke Janet's heart afresh: her mum, her dad, her mates. All the people who loved Joshua. Who didn't yet know . . .

Ade lay at the other side of the bed, the baby between them. He was caressing Joshua's back, the tears dry on his face. He spoke occasionally, sounds more than words, groans of sorrow.

Gill came in again. They had to take Joshua's feeding things from the kitchen, his bedding, to try and help them understand why he had died. Though usually there was no explanation. 'We have to try our best,' she said.

Did Janet cry? Hard to remember now.

Afterwards there were tears. A vale of tears, but then the shock and grief seemed too deep, any sobs buried under the weight of them, deep in the core of her.

They wanted to take him. Her arms pulled him close. Another night. Another day. A few more hours.

She would die herself, she would lie down and die. Or go mad. Already she could feel a tsunami of guilt and blame swelling. Ready to smash her sanity, the ability to function. Send her howling in the wilderness, pursued by demons.

They said that she and Ade should choose some clothes for him, change him. One last time. They needed to take his clothes. The clothes he was wearing. She cried then. Yes. She remembers that. Hot tears dripping on to the babygros and little outfits as they tried to choose.

When they took him it was as if they had torn her

skin away, her skin and the soul of her. Leaving her raw and damaged.

Ade had held her all night long. The doctor had given them both something to take. But Janet had not wanted to sleep. Because sleep felt like an abandonment, a travesty. And if she slept she might forget. And wake up to fresh horror. And she feared her dreams.

They couldn't account for his death. Janet and Ade had done everything right, kept the room at a reasonable temperature, not too hot, not too much bedding, baby on his back, though he was old enough to roll over by then, mattress passed all the required safety tests. Joshua had no infection, no hidden heart problems, no problems of any sort. He was a healthy baby. He was dead.

You can't hurry grief. Janet learned that in the years afterwards. Grief took its own sweet time, broke all the rules, there was no template. People talked of stages and milestones, but they were just clumsy labels that dissolved as the white-water roared around her. There was no map taking you from A to B, it was a whirlpool and you went round and round, got lost for ever. The bereavement counsellor gave them one piece of advice that made some sense: *Whatever you feel, it's all right for you to feel that. There is no right and wrong.*

Oh, and she felt so many things, in amongst those heavy numb days. Anger hot enough to melt iron, jealousy, fury. For weeks she could not see a child, a parent, without an urge to hide or hurt them. Repugnance, at herself, at her weakness. Guilt.

The damp spot at the back of his neck, the way he threw back his head when he chortled. He would never grow another tooth, learn a new word, or wear school uniform, play an instrument or marry or mess up and get hooked on drugs or fail his exams or have children of his own, apply for a job, learn to swim, watch the sunrise, emigrate and leave her missing him. He'd never say mama again.

Denise had stood over her child's cot and tried to smother her. Janet had stood over her own child's cot and tried to bring him back to life. And now she had to go in there and do her job, indifferent to any such irony and with all the empathy she could muster.

48

The final interview was a three-hour marathon with Janet teasing out every tiny little detail from Denise. All the stuff about how she'd got the bus down there and back, how she'd wrapped the knife in a tea towel and put it in a carrier bag to take home. How there had been a bit of blood on her coat sleeve so she had put it in the wash and it had come out fine. How she had known the door wouldn't be locked, had just gone in and found Lisa in the living room. How Lisa's robe had come apart when they were arguing and Denise had told her to cover herself up and Lisa had screamed at her to get out, to fuck off, she never wanted to see her again. How easily the knife slipped in. She only meant to frighten her into silence. How Lisa fell and Denise still held the knife. How Lisa had hit the edge of the coffee table, breaking one of the legs. Denise made no apology for blaming Sean for her daughter's death. And even in the light of her own confession, seemed still to hold him accountable.

* * *

Rachel had gone with Janet to lay the charges. They'd done it! They'd got the bitch. Her first murder case solved. She felt like going dancing and getting hammered. Even the spurt of frustration and anger she felt every time she thought of James Raleigh and what he'd done to Rosie Vaughan didn't diminish the sense of victory in the Lisa Finn case. When they left the custody suite and got back to the office, there was a round of applause. Her Maj was grinning like a Cheshire cat. 'Command are most impressed, as they should be.' Andy popped a bottle of fizz, only enough for a thimbleful each, and then it was back to work.

Gill called Rachel into her office, stood arms folded, peering over her specs. 'There's always a process of adjustment when someone joins a syndicate,' she began, 'not officially a probation period, but a chance to test the waters, get to know each other . . .'

Like dogs sniffing bums.

'. . . not exactly been a smooth ride, Rachel, has it?'

Her stomach dropped. She was going to kick her out. Oh, God.

'More of a bull in a china shop. So, if you've any second thoughts . . .'

'None,' Rachel said quickly. Don't do this to me.

'Want to think about it?'

'No.' This is all I want to do, please, please!

Gill studied her for a moment. Rachel's mouth was

390

dry, her stomach knotted up. If you dump me, I will rip your fucking throat out.

Gill gave a curt nod. 'Right, then. Make yourself useful.'

'Yes, boss.' Legs like water.

Outside, in the dark, she turned her back to the driving sleet and lit up, closed her eyes, let the relief crawl through her. She was in. Everything was going to be all right.

Rachel leaned across her desk to Janet. 'Want to celebrate – us and the lads?'

'No, ta. Could do with a night in, what's left of it.'

She did look wiped out, Rachel thought. Am I missing something? That business of wanting to be alone – what was that about? 'Where'd you go off to? Earlier?'

'Anyone ever told you you're a nosy cow?' Janet said.

'Blame the job,' Rachel said, still wanting a proper answer. 'Well?'

Janet tutted and looked up from her files. 'Nowhere. Just needed some air, recharge.' She smiled, blue eyes, clear and frank.

Rachel didn't believe a word of it; there was something else going on, but obviously Janet wasn't going to let her in on it.

'Do you think she'll get off on manslaughter?' Rachel asked.

'Could go either way,' Janet said. 'Depends if the defence can whip up enough sympathy for her. Less than a year since Nathan's death, she's still half-mad with grief. The provocation might well be grounds for a partial defence.'

Manslaughter on grounds of diminished responsibility, the act carried out while the balance of her mind was disturbed. Rachel shook her head. 'I'd give her life, no parole. I said, didn't I – wasn't fit to be a mother. If people like that keep having kids—'

'People like that?' Janet raised an eyebrow. 'What would you suggest, Rachel? Mass sterilization, camps, euthanasia?'

'Don't be soft.'

'I am going home.' Janet got to her feet. 'Domestic duties to perform. If you fancy coming, it's chicken korma tonight at ours. Meet the kids?'

'No, you're all right,' Rachel said. 'I'll make a start on this.'

Janet smiled. 'They don't bite,' she said.

'No, they might drool though, or get snot all over me,' Rachel said.

'More likely to use up your phone credit and nick your lipstick.'

'Some other time – century.'

'Night, then. Don't work too late.'

'No, Mum.'

'And Rachel . . . ?' Rachel looked up, Janet by the door. 'Don't forget to power down the computers and turn the lights off.'

Rachel nodded.

'And drive carefully,' Janet said.

Rachel flicked a V-sign.

'And wash your cups up,' Janet yelled from out in the corridor.

Rachel grinned, turned the page and began her report.

ACKNOWLEDGEMENTS

Many thanks to Sally Wainwright, Diane Taylor and Red Productions for a great show whose wonderful characters were a joy to write about. Thanks also to Diane for generous help and advice about police work – any mistakes are mine; to Sarah Adams and Rachel Rayner at Transworld for the opportunity to write the novel and to my agent Sara Menguc for all her support and hard work.